QUIET TIME

Stephanie Kane

COLD HARD PRESS

Denver, Colorado

PRAISE FOR *QUIET TIME*

"Stephanie Kane does it again. Quiet Time keeps your mind thinking and your heart racing – What a great read!"

– Rikki Klieman, Court TV

"Life's greatest dramas play out in family life. And never have those passions more relentlessly imprinted on generation after generation than when they enfold in a vacuum of secrecy.... The end is riveting and a surprise—but that's what Kane is all about."

– The Denver Post

"An atmospheric gothic-like work of suspense that imbues the reader with the feeling that something is going to happen very soon. Stephanie Kane is a terrific storyteller who knows how to grab the attention of the audience and keeps it."

– The Midwest Book Review

"Kane's work is just as good as the trial mysteries written by Steve Martini."

– The Drood Review of Mystery

"Kane weaves an intricate story. Her prose is refreshing and light."

– I Love A Mystery

"Will hold you in suspense to the very last page."

—Rikki Kleiman, *Court TV*

Also by Stephanie Kane

Blind Spot
Seeds of Doubt
Extreme Indifference
A Perfect Eye

QUIET TIME

First published in 2001 by Bantam Books

Cold Hard Press
Denver, Co

ISBN Print: 978-1-7336715-2-1
ISBN Digital: 978-1-7336715-3-8

Library of Congress Number: 2019916991

PRINTED IN THE UNITED STATES OF AMERICA

Book interior design by Susan Brooks
Cover design by Marcel Venter

For John

In memory of Beverly Lewis

I gratefully acknowledge the wisdom and support of my editor, Kate Miciak; my agent, Angela Rinaldi and Leslie Hoffman, Rick Boychuck, Alan Shafer, Uma Shafer, Bob and Jane Stein, Patrick Kelly, David Tenner, and Jerry Gross. Most of all, I thank my husband John L. Kane, Jr.

She saw it from the corner of her eye, a glimmer so faint it might have been a trick of shadow. And then she was hit.

She was turning toward him when the steel claw struck her square across the bridge of her nose, rending skin and shattering bone. Shock, disbelief—could this be happening to her? *She kept turning even as her chin flew back and the gashes in her nose welled dark with blood. The rake slipped from her fingers and skittered across the floor. Her throat closed. She could not scream.*

He swung a second time and the blunt end caught her temple, slamming her into the red tool chest and scattering nuts and bolts across the cement. As she raised a hand to shield her eyes, the third blow splintered two knuckles and crushed the second joint of her ring finger, dissolving her watch in a web of cracks. Cradling her battered head, she slid to her knees, then fell face-first onto the floor. She tried to crawl but her fingers lost their grip on the cool cement and the weapon plunged into the back of her skull.

With that blow her universe imploded. She had no thoughts, none at all. No pain. Pain belongs to survivors. Her last sight that brilliant Saturday in May was motes of dust playing tag in the band of light six inches from her nose, where the garage door stopped short of the concrete.

Her killer gazed at her a long moment, then turned and left through the utility room door.

Chapter One

Sunlight poured onto Sari Siegel's face in the airless porch of their second-story apartment jutting out over Broadway. As she burrowed into her pillow Tim's arm tightened about her waist and he drew her close, clasping her small round buttocks and draping his thigh across her hip. The sweat from the copper hair on his chest tickled, and he moved his hand to her glossy hair, sweeping it aside to nuzzle her neck.

She squinted at the alarm clock on the dresser across the narrow room. At a quarter to eight she could already hear Saturday-morning traffic in the street below, and the air was so arid her nostrils twitched. Her gaze wandered to the faded poster of the dove on the cracked wall above the dresser. END MASS MURDER IN VIETNAM. A relic from junior high school days, but it reminded her of home. Beneath it the lab manual for her biology class lay facedown beside a marbled composition book whose binding had not yet been cracked.

She looked at Tim's arm, which had crept back to her waist. The silky hair was so red it glinted, but the T-shirts he'd worn framing houses over spring break had left his biceps and shoulders paper-white next to hers. His long limbs and fiery hair were an odd match for her petite build and olive complexion, but they fit together perfectly in bed. Breathing his familiar scent, she molded herself to his groin. When his fingertips began stroking her breast she blinked once and then her eyes fell shut. He knew what she liked, she never had to say.... As he entered her, a single thought shimmered in her head: One week from today she would be Mrs. Timothy Scott.

The phone rang twenty minutes later while Tim was in the shower and she was frying his eggs over easy—the way he liked them. After a brief conversation, she hung up and reached for the plastic pitcher in the cupboard over the sink. Pipes groaned on the other side of the wall as the toilet in the next apartment flushed, and she heard Tim yelp at the surge of hot water. When the shower stopped she twisted the faucet and began mixing his orange juice.

As soon as school let out two weeks before they'd moved into the walk-up flat in this rambling house at Locust and Broadway, halfway down the hill leading from the University to downtown Stanley. Although Broadway technically divided the campus from the residential part of town, the University's tree-lined paths, sandstone buildings and tiled roofs blended into the surrounding neighborhoods abutting the foothills.

Because of its size and location, 655 Locust could have housed one of the smaller departments of the liberal arts college or a professor with a large brood of children. Over the years, additions had been slapped on every which way and the interior divided into oddly configured units for students and the marginally employed, leaving them a kitchen just large enough to turn around in and a converted porch for a bedroom that was so cold in the winter, ice formed on the inside of the windows and froze them shut. But Sari fell in love with the apartment the moment they saw it. The sunshine in the alcove stained her supermarket coleuses magenta and chartreuse, and living on the Hill meant they were no longer just students.

"It must be eighty degrees already."

She turned to see Tim in the doorway in his denim cutoffs, sweat dotting the reddish stubble above his lip. He'd been trying to grow a mustache since school let out but his sideburns were more successful; the auburn growth reached from his temples to the milky knob of his jaw.

The skin below was so tender, she would bury her nose in it while they were making love, feel it throb...

"And a hundred in here," she replied.

"At least." He grinned, knowing exactly what she was thinking.

"When do you have to be at the rec center?" she asked. Tim played for the Wings, in an amateur hockey league, and coached kids on the weekends.

"I'm leaving as soon as I eat. Peewees are at ten and I'm working on a new set of drills for the Juniors." Handing him his juice and eggs, she followed him to the front room, where he settled on the daybed with the plate balanced on his knees. "What are you going to do?"

From the window she gazed at the turquoise pool at the College Townhouses next door, glittering in the morning sun. Last spring's residents had left after finals and the summer students wouldn't arrive for days, and if she sneaked in early enough, she could paddle a few laps and no one would notice. But it hardly seemed right to luxuriate in a pool while Tim sweltered at a hockey practice.

"Get a head start on my reading," she replied, leaning over to wipe a spot of yolk from his lip. He pulled her to his lap, and it turned into a long kiss. "Want me to bring you a sandwich before the one o'clock practice?"

"Nope, it'll be too hot to eat." He gulped the rest of his juice, handed her his plate, and reluctantly rose.

"Your mother called while you were in the shower."

He stopped with his hand on the doorknob.

"What'd she say?"

"Nothing. Just to tell Laura the transmission's still out on the Dodge and she'll have to find some other way to get back from Gillman." Tim's sister had dropped out of the University in her junior year but was still living in Stanley, twenty-five miles north of Widmark, the state capital, which was another ten miles from the suburb of Gillman where Tim's parents resided. "She couldn't reach her on the phone and thought maybe we'd see her before she left."

"The Dodge?"

"Your dad was going to have the brakes changed on Laura's car and let her borrow the Dodge for the week."

"Anything else?" Hope lay beneath the casual words.

"You mean about the wedding?" She turned toward the kitchen. "No."

"Did you ask if she was going to come?"

"Of course not." She felt him watching as she sponged egg off the chipped stoneware. "The only reason we're having a minister is because of her."

"Are you kidding? To a Catholic, the Unitarian Church might as well be City Hall. You must've talked about more than the transmission."

"They had inside chores and yard work to do before it got too hot, and then your dad was going to a seminar." Catching a glimpse of Tim's face as she reached for the dish towel, Sari cast for details to make her conversation with his mother sound longer. "Some self-improvement guru. She was in a hurry to hang up."

"At least she called." *She's trying,* he meant, *why can't you?*

"Tim, we have to—"

"Later, honey, I need to warm up." Wrapping his arms around her waist, he stooped to kiss the part in her hair and was gone.

Sari smeared suntan lotion on her cheeks, secured her shoulder-length black waves with a barrette, slipped on her sandals and left the apartment. Telling herself to forget Peggy's abruptness and Tim's disappointment, she cut across the campus to the Bryant Library lawn to read up on the birth of the solar system. Lying on her stomach, she reached into her backpack for a yellow highlighter and began skimming the introduction to her biology text.

Her pen whipped across millennia, from the mass of energy and matter that erupted and collided to form stars to the medieval notion of spontaneous generation. Could they really have believed maggots originated from meat, and mice from sweat-soaked shirts and wheat? She flipped two pages ahead. Once their parents saw how much she and Tim loved each other, how *right* they were, they'd come around... Missing links, heredity versus environment. She was marrying Tim, not his family; what did religion or the rest matter? She would adapt, they would *evolve*, and in the sands of time, who cared whether his parents liked her. With that, she was finally able to focus on her text and it wasn't until her shoulders began smarting beneath their tan that she went inside, found an empty carrel on the third floor, and reimmersed herself in the molecular soup.

The next time Sari looked up it was a quarter past twelve. As she hurried from the library the heat radiated from the pavement, and by the time she mounted the steps to their apartment her tank top was plastered to her back. Knowing she would be late, she jumped in and out of the shower and changed into Tim's faded Gillman High T-shirt before starting down the Hill to the rec center. Despite the fresh clothes, her shirt was clinging by the time she reached her destination.

The hockey rink was in the municipal recreation center on Birch Street. Its cinder-block walls and metal roof also housed a swimming pool, weight room and gymnastics area, all of which were empty when Sari arrived. Hurrying through the lobby, she was greeted by a blast of cold air as she stepped through the glass door to the deserted rink. The clock behind the scoreboard said one, and she made her way through the stands to the exit onto the outdoor basketball court, the damp cloth between her shoulders pressing her forward like an icy hand. Blinking in the sudden brightness, she spotted Tim at the far end of the court. Like a beacon his red hair drew her forward.

Off-season Tim's teams stayed in shape by playing roller hockey with wheeled skates on asphalt and a ball instead of a puck, and now a dozen junior high school boys stood watching him circle the court cradling the ball against the blade of his stick. The only sounds were the *tap-tap* of plastic against wood and the dull rumble of wheels on pavement as he threaded his way through a slalom course of orange cones. Eyes straight ahead he skated faster and faster from one goal to the other, manipulating ball and stick so smoothly they might have been a third appendage. As he came to a stop at the end where she was standing, he saw Sari for the first time. The smile that began at his lips and suffused his features in a flush of unexpected joy was private, meant only for her. As she stood watching him she remembered the first time she saw that smile.

Adapting to college was more than simply culture shock: stepping off the plane in Widmark last August, Sari had been literally stunned. It was her first time away from home, in a place that had meant no more to her than a pink square on the map to the left of the Mississippi. She arrived the day before orientation, so eager to put two thousand miles between her and her parents that it wouldn't have mattered where the plane landed. The moment she inhaled arid heat and began squinting in the brutal sun she knew she'd made a mistake. But she'd insisted she knew what she was doing. Now she had to tough it out.

When the airport shuttle dropped the new arrivals at Chase Hall, the kids tossing Frisbees on the lawn were pale-eyed and golden, with legs as sturdy as tree trunks and the self-assurance that comes from being raised in places where every high school had a football field and swimming pool. Sari felt insubstantial and dark and for the first time, her intellect seemed a disadvantage. As she unpacked her trunk and hung an Indian-print bedspread on the wall to make her room seem cozier, she resisted the impulse to call home.

By the third week she'd landed on her feet, at least so far as academics were concerned. Her social life was another matter. There were two classes of girls at Chase: prom queens from out of state who brought flasks of low-calorie salad dressing to the dining hall and paired off with boys whose shorts had loops for pitons and rock hammers, and girls from Fort Jackson or Mesquite Springs whose mothers sent them Care packages of lemon bars and fudge. Moon-faced Ronnie across the hall was technically neither; from California, which might have made her a bona fide outsider if not for her membership in the Sierra Club and hundred-dollar Vibram-soled hiking boots, she was the closest Sari had to a friend.

That morning the Student Union had been a madhouse. It was the deadline for dropping and adding courses, and traffic between the cafeteria and bookstore made conversation impossible. Ronnie wanted a doughnut to fortify her for her eleven o'clock class, which was starting in ten minutes, but a flash of color caught Sari's eye. A half dozen canvases were displayed on the cinder-block walls outside the grill.

"Come on," Ronnie insisted, tugging at her. The door swung open, expelling a band of boys in Hawks jerseys who smelled of cinnamon buns and fried meat. "I'm going to be late for French."

"I just want to look..." In the wake of the jocks Sari was able to move closer. The paintings were a mixed bag—a monochromatic landscape that seemed to be pottery jugs but was the San Juan Basin, a too-pink watercolor of the foothills, and a raunchy cartoon inspired by R. Crumb. But one work stood out: an extraordinarily lifelike acrylic of a youth peering into a glass sphere. The banner over the exhibit read *Outstanding Freshmen.*

"If that's the best the Fine Arts Department has to offer," Ronnie sneered, "civilization's in a heap of trouble." Following Sari's gaze, she added, "Bring on the Ouija board..."

"There's someone inside trying to climb out."

The silky hair and translucent skin of the portrait's subject drew her but Sari was transfixed by the figure in the globe. Pressed cheek and flattened palms said urgency, and now she recognized him as a miniature version of the boy holding the glass. Isolation and claustrophobia, her parents' old apartment on Willow Street... *How could the artist know?* She glanced over her shoulder, but the only one looking was a tall boy with red hair and a backpack standing behind them.

"Gross!" Ronnie said.

"No, it's perfect," she insisted. "Look at his expression, how desperate—"

"Sari, that painting is shit. It's just another self-absorbed dweeb staring up his own ass." Loud enough for the guy behind them to hear, and Sari flinched. "I'm getting something to eat before I starve."

As Ronnie trundled off to the cafeteria, the boy turned to Sari. His features were delicate, but his pale skin and dark eyes made his hair flame. "Were you kidding about it being good?" he asked.

"No, I really like it."

"But the perspective's off, the face inside the ball is flat." The careless way he dropped his pack suddenly made her realize she knew nothing about art, and up close the copper in his hair gleamed. "And you can tell he had a problem with the hands. The brushwork—"

"Can't you see what he was trying to do? The whole *point* is the distortions." He'd captured her father's rigidity and her mother's explosions, life in a shrinking bubble. "When he looks at himself he isn't sure what he sees, or maybe he thinks they don't see the real him. Either way, he has to break free."

"Do you think he will?" She couldn't tell whether he was making fun of her. "It sounds like you know him…" Sari was jostled from behind and he reached out. His hand was rough and cool and his T-shirt smelled medicinal, a blend of scents she couldn't recognize. Self-conscious, she drew back.

"I don't know anyone, I just got here."

"New York?" He pronounced it the right way, not "Noo *Yawk*" like the kids at the dorm.

"Brooklyn. And I like his technique."

The boy smiled and everything stopped. Like a curtain lifting, it revealed him with a suddenness and intimacy that was almost physical, and she was no longer aware of the crush of students streaming from the cafeteria, the pocked linoleum or the greasy odor of burgers and fries.

Then the bell at Chapel Hall clanged the start of the next class and Ronnie was bearing down on them with a half-eaten bear claw.

"Come on, we're going to be late." She poked Sari with her free hand. "Don't you have Latin American lit?"

As they rushed off, she thought she saw him wave.

Two Fridays later, Sari awoke to the foothills draped in white and an eerie silence in the dorm. The only warning had been a windstorm the night before and the odor of manure in the air, but for her dorm mates that was enough. At breakfast she learned they had exchanged Frisbees for goose-down parkas and skis and taken to the hills; with eight inches of powder at Dakota Ridge, the ski season was off to an early start and not even Ronnie could be found. Dreading the weekend, she thumbed through the *Campus Daily* with more interest than usual. When she came upon the ad for skating lessons at a studio down the Hill she stopped.

Free Trial—*No equipment or experience needed!* She'd always wanted to learn how to skate, and the picture of the girl in a flared skirt pirouetting in ankle-high white boots erased any doubt.

On Saturday morning she trudged through spitting sleet to the rec center. The table in the overheated lobby was unmanned but held a clipboard and pen. When no one appeared, she wrote her name and address on the sheet. Had they started without her? She glanced around the lobby for a clock but saw none. To her left was a swinging door with an arrow that led to the locker rooms, to her right a tall glass portal with black lettering that read Rink. Without another thought, she pushed through it and entered the rink.

The sudden cold made her catch her breath. The rink was surrounded by wooden boards three feet high and metal bleachers. In the center of the ice stood a dozen dwarves in black and silver jerseys. Their shoulder pads made them almost as wide as they were tall, and their heads were encased in helmets and face masks. Towering over them in full regalia was a man who was obviously their instructor. As Sari watched, he pushed off with one leg and began circling the rink counterclockwise in effortless loops. Halfway through the second circuit he swiveled his hips and continued skating backward without missing a beat.

The clock behind the scoreboard read three minutes to ten and she looked over her shoulder toward the lobby. The freezing cold had traveled all the way up her nose, and the fluid grace of the man on the ice brought back a childhood of skinned knees from roller skates. If she left now, no one would know... But the thought of trudging back up the Hill in the sleet to an empty dorm stopped her. The ad said ten, she was in the right place, and how difficult could it be? All she needed was to find out where to get the skates. The instructor had glided to a stop in the middle of the rink; the boys were gathering around him.

"Mister!" she called out. But the tall figure made no response. Hugging her arms to her chest and wishing she'd brought gloves, Sari walked through the stands to the boards. "Hey, Mister!"

As he glanced in her direction and then turned back to his boys, she felt her cheeks burn. It wasn't as if she was interrupting, they were just standing there and all she wanted to know was where to get the damn skates. *Forget it, just leave*...Before she knew it she was on the ice.

A whistle shrilled and the boys began lining up at one end of the rink. Focusing on the man, she took another step forward. Now he turned.

"Lady, you can't—"

Sari tried to stop but her left foot skidded sideways. She threw out her opposite hand but over corrected and pitched to the right. Her heels flew out from under her; she landed on her tail bone with a hard thud.

"What do you think you're doing?" He was kneeling over her, the words angry puffs of white from the grids in the mask inches from her face. In the background she heard giggles. Go *now*, before you make a complete ass—"You don't belong on the ice!"

Her butt hurt like hell, the frost on the seat of her pants was melting into a cold wet stain and suddenly she was furious.

"I have every right to be here. The ad said ten o'clock, and I was trying—"

"Ten o'clock?"

He reached to help her up, but she shook off his glove. "The free lesson." She got to her feet, only to slip again. "If you'd had the courtesy to answer, I wouldn't be on your precious—"

"Lesson?" He looked over his shoulder at the boys, who were waiting for her next pratfall. "This rink is reserved for hockey practice."

Determined to keep her balance this time, she rose to her feet and reached in her hip pocket for the clipping from the *Daily*. Shredded and damp, proof she was entitled to be there. Throwing back her shoulders, she handed it to him. He stripped off his gloves, unbuckled his chin strap, and removed his helmet. Red hair tumbled out.

God, no. Not the guy from the Student Union.

His dark eyes scanned the newsprint. He'd never recognize her, they'd spoken only a moment. That nonsense about connecting with his smile? Hormones, Ronnie said... The seat of her pants was soaked and she'd never felt like such a fool. But the ad had said *ten o'clock*, she was sure of it.

His eyes touched hers and in them Sari saw laughter. Snatching back the clipping, she looked at it for the first time since Friday.

Sunday. The paper said *Sunday.*

A dozen chins were tipped up expectantly and he turned to a boy at his right. "Can you beat that?" he said, shaking his head in disbelief. "They messed up the time! It said right there the skating lesson is at ten." The dancing eyes met hers. "If I were you, I'd complain to the *Campus Daily.*"

She was speechless.

"Okay, guys." He blew his whistle. "Thirty seconds to line up for wind sprints!"

Leaving his helmet and gloves on the ice, he took her arm and guided her to the ring side. Through the cold she inhaled clean perspiration and finally identified that mystery scent. Ben Gay and adhesive tape. Depositing her on dry ground, he leaned closer. "About that free lesson, Brooklyn. Hang around and I'll be glad to give it to you when practice is over. .."

From the highest stand, Sari watched him disappear at the end of the practice in the direction of the locker room. She slowly walked back to the lobby and read every announcement on the bulletin board, then bought a juice from the dilapidated cooler in the corner. As she stooped to pop off the cap, she heard a coin jangle in the slot above her head.

"So you really liked that boy with the globe?" he asked.

"You were pretty rough on the guy who painted it," she replied.

"I lost you at the fountain. Your friend was too quick."

Ronnie was right, he had been hitting on her. All he'd seen in that portrait were its flaws…She zipped up her jacket and started to rise.

"That painting was mine," he said.

Was that the moment she'd fallen in love? Then or soon after, because now, just eight months later, she could scarcely remember a world without Tim at its core…

"That's my son," a voice behind her said now. "He never loses control, does he?"

Turning to the bleachers, Sari was jerked back to the present. How long had Tim's father been there watching?

"Mr. Scott!" Fighting the paralysis his presence always evoked, wondering why Tim's mother hadn't warned her he was coming. "What are you doing here?"

Warren fingered the arsenal of mechanical pencils lining the breast of his long-sleeved shirt, then reached in the hip pocket of his navy blue trousers for a hanky. Immaculate as always, from his slicked-back hair to the oxfords on his feet. Tightly laced and spit-shined.

"I thought I'd surprise Tim."

While the rest of his players skated around the orange cones dribbling balls with their sticks under the brutal sun, Tim had moved to the goalie at the other end of the court. As Sari watched, he squeezed the boy's shoulder reassuringly and then skated three yards back. Had his mother known Warren was coming?

"Peggy called this morning," she said to fill the awkward silence. Forty-five minutes from Gillman to Stanley, and that's if you were speeding. Maybe she hadn't known… "I guess she forgot to tell me."

"I decided at the last minute," he replied.

"How was the seminar?" At his blank look, Sari regretted having asked. Now she would never think of the name of his self-improvement guru. Winning friends and influencing people. "You know," she continued, "the one on…"

"Dale Carnegie." He shrugged. "It was postponed."

Tall and lanky like Tim and with thinning hair, Warren Scott had his son's dark eyes and refined features, coarsened only slightly by age. It was his Vitalis and Old Spice cologne that personified him, in the same way the rubber band around Sari's father's wallet stood for Max Siegel. But any resemblance between the two men ended there. Unlike Max, a printer by trade who always paid cash and affected helplessness with regard to anything outside the sphere of type and ink, Tim's father was an accountant who prided himself on taking advantage of the "float" and approached predicaments with a unflustered competence Sari found irritating. What was it he always said? *Let's work the problem.*

Warren's plaid flannel shirt was too heavy for the weather, and the band of the T peeking out from under the collar was soaked with sweat.

But he seemed oblivious to his own discomfort. Her eyes traveled to the swelling on the left side of his forehead, an angry lump the size and color of a small plum.

"What happened to you?" She reached out, hesitating as he flinched. "That looks like it hurts."

"It's nothing." He continued watching Tim, who was slowly lobbing balls at the goalie's face mask. Each throw came a little faster but the boy was no longer flinching. "I was cleaning the closets this morning and a lawn chair fell on me."

"Would you like some ice? I can get it from—"

"No, I'm fine." As he refolded his hanky and leaned forward to return it to his pocket, she drew back from his cologne. The clove masked something sour.

"Aren't you dying in that shirt?" she asked. "I showered right before I left and I'm already soaked…"

But Warren's attention seemed riveted on the court, where Tim was lining up the boys for scrimmage. "Remember, guys," she heard him call out. "Rule number one: don't let anyone run your goalie. Protect your man at all costs!"

"That's my son." Warren said again, his eyes glued to Tim. "No one ever has to tell him the score."

With a toot of the whistle the scrimmage began, and they watched in silence until the practice was over. Warren smiled only when Tim came to the bleachers, hair dripping and jersey drenched.

"What're you doing here, Dad?"

"I wanted to see where the two of you are living. After that, I'm going to find a place for the rehearsal dinner."

Sari ignored Tim's look. "Rehearsal dinner?" she asked.

"Peggy didn't tell you?" Warren's unblinking gaze impaled her, then he turned to his son. "Hit the shower, Tim, so we can get going."

What other surprises were in store? As Tim headed for the locker room, she tried to smooth it over. "We didn't know you wanted to give us a dinner."

"Peggy and I discussed it this morning."

"You don't have to—"

"It's the least we can do." Without another word, he rose and walked into the rec center.

Now she'd really done it, insulted the entire Scott family and the horse they rode in on. But if they were planning a dinner Peggy must have decided to attend the wedding. Maybe Tim was right, they were finally coming around.

After the last player left, the three of them got into Warren's Oldsmobile for the drive up the Hill. As Sari climbed into the backseat, she drew her feet in and heard a snap. Her heel burned and she looked down in dismay. She'd stepped on something wedged under the seat and broken it clean in half. Reaching down, she pulled out what was left of a laminated yardstick emblazoned *McBride*. The biggest hardware store in Stanley, maybe the entire state.

"Oh, my God! I'm so sorry…"

The gash in her heel was bleeding profusely, dripping from her sandal onto the carpet under the backseat and compounding her humiliation. Batting a thousand. Peggy's phone call, being caught off guard about the rehearsal dinner, bleeding all over Warren's car…She pressed her thumb to the cut to stem the flow.

"I'll get you another," she said.

"It's nothing," Warren replied.

"But I broke your yardstick. I'll—"

"No."

From his tight smile in the rearview mirror she could see he was upset. Over the mess she was making in his car, or the loss of his measuring tool?

"At least let me pay—"

"They just started giving them away as a spring promotion."

Tim winked sympathetically and Sari settled back in the seat with her palm to her heel, mortified at her clumsiness. When they turned off Broadway at Locust and pulled into a space halfway down the block, she jumped out first.

"Are you sure you want to come up? We're still fixing the apartment."

She turned to Tim for help, but he looked away. "We were planning to have you and Peggy over for dinner after the wedding...."

Switching off the motor in reply, Warren pocketed his keys and they cut across the gravel and dandelions in the backyard to the stone steps leading to the side entrance. As Tim unlocked their door at the second floor landing, she tried to remember whether she'd made the bed and if there was iced tea in the refrigerator. She knew they had instant.

Tim went to the alcove off the bedroom to stuff his hockey gear in the hamper; she dashed in the bedroom and pulled up the spread.

"Iced tea?" she called from the doorway.

"That would be nice," Warren replied, and she busied herself making a fresh pitcher. After serving it to him in a tall glass she went to the kitchen for a Band-Aid and soapy water to clean the Olds. As she returned to the living room with her pan and sponge, she saw Warren had abandoned his tea and was staring in the mirror opposite the front door. Probing his forehead with his fingers, reaching in his hip pocket for his comb—she was about to offer him a cold cloth, but something in the way he slicked back his hair silenced her.

"Where are you going with that?" he asked.

"To clean your backseat."

"I told you, it's fine!"

"But—"

Tim came in and began describing the sudden death play the Wings had won in their league championship in April, and she smiled at him with relief. But as Warren settled back on the daybed and Tim switched to the courses he was planning to take in the fall, she realized there was something off about the conversation. Tim never chattered; with Warren it was strictly Q & A. Why hadn't Peggy said anything about Warren coming?

"So I qualified for advanced placement in calculus," Tim was saying, "and got the highest grade in the class in chem. Sari's cramming two semesters of biology into the summer session. But she'll ace them, like she always does..." She glanced uneasily at Warren, who was slumped forward on the daybed with his head in his hands, massaging his temples with his thumbs. Tim was loading up on science to please his father, but his real love was art. That was one of the conflicts between them: Warren wanted him to be an engineer. "She has a three-hour lab five days a—"

Warren abruptly stood. "I have a lot to do this afternoon, Tim." As he pushed back his hair with the heel of his palm, Sari registered his fatigue. The heat must be getting to him after all.

As if reading her mind, Tim said, "Feeling okay, Dad?"

"I'm fine, son, just a little tired. I'd better hit the road."

"How's your foot?" Tim asked when the door closed behind him.

"Fine." It was throbbing, the bandage already soaked through. "I can't believe I was so clumsy."

"You heard him, he's probably got half a dozen more at home." Tim was frowning, his thoughts clearly elsewhere. "But something must be wrong. I've never seen him act like that."

"He said he was tired…"

Tim shook his head. "He didn't interrupt me once. Hell, I don't think he heard a word I said. And wasn't he supposed to be at a seminar?"

"I'm just glad he came." She poured the untouched tea down the drain.

"But why bother?" His fingers grazed the silver goalie that crowned the Wings' trophy. His father hadn't even noticed it. "It's not like he wanted to see the place, he never even looked."

"I'm surprised he stayed as long as he did, the way he was dressed."

"And what was the idea, coming here before the wedding? You know what Mom said…"

"Maybe she's had a change of heart." Sari came up behind him and wrapped her arms around his hips. "Isn't that what you were telling me this morning?"

He turned and hugged her. "Yeah, maybe it'll be okay after all."

Chapter Two

His first Saturday off in weeks and Ray Burt had to spend it with his wife shopping. They made the whole circuit, exhausting local establishments before winding their way through the suburban malls that hitched Widmark to Gillman and its other satellite communities like a pack of mutts on a leash. They'd just returned from Rainbow Plaza, a daisy chain of retail stores in a complex with all the charm of an airplane hangar, when Marion remembered one more item on her list.

"Jesus, can't we give it a rest?" He'd slipped off his Sears, Roebuck dress boots and was lounging in the family room with the curtains drawn, switching the remote from tennis to golf. "It's over ninety degrees already."

"It's not like we do this every weekend, Ray."

"You're damn right. If I'd known we was gonna spend the day traipsing to hell and gone, I'd of volunteered for an extra shift. At least I'd get overtime."

"Oh, quit complaining, you're becoming an awful pill." She bent over his easy chair and planted a kiss on his sweating pate. "Want some lemonade?"

"If it means I can sit another five minutes before we go back to

Bataan. These dogs are pooped, honey." He pointed at his feet, his brown eyes gazing up mournfully at her.

"It might help if you put on those tennies I bought and a pair of shorts."

"Not on your life. I don't know which is worse, the thought of wearing my skivvies in public or going back to that goddamned mall."

"If it's such a big deal, I'll go myself. Give me the keys to the Chrysler, Ray."

"The only one who gets behind the wheel of that New Yorker is yours truly." He reached for his boots and lumbered to his feet. Wincing and pretending to stumble, he gave in. "Come on, Missus..."

Ray had always wanted a Chrysler, and when the '68 New Yorkers rolled off the assembly line twelve years earlier he knew that was the car for him. The Department's dull but reliable Chevys and Plymouths made him yearn for power under the hood. The following season Chrysler screwed up the body, transformed that sleek charger into a frumpy nag, and he kicked himself for not having taken out a loan to buy the older model. That was when he began studying the classifieds, praying for the second chance he finally received when the county coroner over in Mesquite Springs died and his widow had put the New Yorker on blocks. Word got to Ray, and he made her an offer that very day. Marion ragged about playing second fiddle to a V-8, but Ray was in heaven. His father never even owned a car.

Out again in the blistering sun, the New Yorker's burgundy metallic finish sparkled and her air-conditioning hummed like a champ. While Marion picked out a birthday card for her niece at Walgreen's, Ray filled the tank with premium and checked the oil, then ran a stubby finger across her hood. Although no one but him could tell she needed it, he'd wax her bright and early tomorrow morning while Marion was at church. If the Lord was half as wise as she claimed, he'd understand. Not that Ray believed in an afterlife; sixty-five years in the here and now would be more than enough for him so long as he was able to spend it on the job.

When they'd tromped through every fabric and notions store between Gillman and the state line, Marion suddenly decided it was more efficient to visit apparel shops. After all, it wasn't as if she actually *bought* anything... Stationing himself in a folding chair a discreet distance from the dressing room at the fourth Fashion Bar that day, he thought of his recliner and sighed. Scratch the Giants game. If he was lucky he might catch the last couple of innings, though if he mentioned it his wife would be sure to come up with that many more errands.

Then she started in with sporting goods, and Ray was tempted to make a smart remark. But he bit his tongue. Marion's capacity for shopping, even on weekends, was not unlimited, and as the bounce in her step flattened he detected early signs of boredom. He followed her docilely into Bigg's, but when he saw her head for the rods and lures, he'd had just about enough.

"Since when do you care about fishing tackle?" he demanded.

"It's for you, when we go up to the cabin in Torrance."

"I have no intention of wasting my time throwing a hook in the water and waiting for some poor sucker to nibble. I do that for a living every day of the week."

"You know what the doctor said..."

"I'll live a lot longer if you let me go home and park my ragged butt in the La-Z-Boy. This is supposed to be my day off, for Chrissakes, not a marathon!"

"I'm not leaving till we buy a tackle box, and that's all there is to it. If you don't want to pick it out yourself, you can stand in the corner and glower."

He watched with resignation as Marion headed down the aisle toward a display of fly rods. Based on his wife's inherent indifference to athletic equipment, he'd give her three minutes and no longer. A pup tent was pitched in one corner with a camp stove and lanterns, and against the wall stood a glass display case with an assortment of hunting knives. He walked over. A boy of ten or twelve was gazing hungrily at a red-handled ax. Ray smiled. Must be getting ready to go camping with his dad.

He glanced over his shoulder for Marion. There she was, precisely on schedule, heading his way with a dark green tackle box. She waved and pointed in the direction of the checkout stand. No use telling her he'd never use it, not if he wanted to be home in time to catch the Giants or grab a decent nap…

Marion stood in line behind a petite blonde in her early thirties whose hair rippled halfway down the back of her turtleneck sweater. Must be roasting on a day like this, Ray thought. A black and red checked hunting shirt was under her arm, from its bulkiness an extra large. Husband must be a big guy. When the woman turned he saw she was wearing dark glasses. It was hot and bright outside, but in a store? Must've had a good time last night, he thought wryly.

"Joey?" The blonde craned her neck, searching the aisles. "Come on, we're going now!"

As Ray turned to look, the boy from the camping display approached but kept his distance, avoiding his mother as the line inched forward. When he was just within reach, she jerked his arm.

"We've got to hurry, he's waiting in the car. You know how he gets…"

The boy stared at the wheel of Swiss Army knives beside the register and gave no sign of having heard. Her turn was next. She peered at the cardboard tag on the shirt, holding the cardboard to the light to read the price. Ray watched sympathetically. They printed them so small these days, but anything would be hard to see with those shades on… Finally she removed her glasses and he gave a silent whistle. Look at that shiner.

Saturday morning in Gillman. No wonder she was walking around half blind and all covered up; her old man must've wiped the floor with her last night. As the salesclerk rang up the shirt and she fumbled in her purse for her wallet, he saw the kid was still looking at the knives and pretending not to know his mother. Without thinking, he stepped closer to Marion and squeezed her arm.

She glanced up in bewildered amusement. "What's that for, you old goat?"

Ray peered over his wife's shoulder and found the boy by the door, staring out at the parking lot. He followed his gaze to a Ford pickup idling in the loading zone and tried to catch a glimpse of the figure behind the wheel. As the woman paid for the shirt, snatched the boy by the arm and hurried to the truck, Ray tightened his grip. Maybe he doesn't know how she got it, he thought, maybe she lies and says she fell. If she had too much to drink Friday night, he might even believe it…

Nah.

A kid that age always knows the truth about his parents. Ray knew about his old man. Always.

When the call came three hours later Ray was dozing on the recliner in his backyard, half listening to the Giants on his transistor radio while a fly cleaned its leg on the rim of his lemonade glass. Before Marion ran out of things for him to do he'd mowed the lawn, trimmed the edges around the sidewalk and scrubbed the barbecue for the bratwurst they'd be grilling that evening. Now he reluctantly opened his eyes as she called through the kitchen window.

"It's Dispatch!"

" 'Kay."

"I hope this'll be quick."

"That makes two of us." He waddled into the house. Marion was shucking early corn in the sink and he gestured for her to turn off the water. "Burt here."

"Lieutenant, it's Dispatch."

"Yeah, so?"

"We need you at a crime scene: 4990 South Cleveland. Off Grand Avenue—"

"I know where it is." Bunch of boy scouts playing with matches. "Who's at the scene?"

"Two uniforms. Meat wagon's on the way."

"Messy?"

"Don't know yet. Call came ten minutes ago."

"How many?"

"Don't know that either."

"Yeah, okay." He rubbed his eyes. "Lew Devine on duty? I don't want any of them Academy punks messing up the scene."

"I'll check." The line went silent as Marion watched from the sink, knowing dinner would be late. His first weekend in—When the officer returned, Ray had already guessed the answer. "Sergeant Devine is off today, sir."

"Well, roust him, he's probably at that stable out in Hays. You didn't think twice about calling me, did you?"

"Will do."

"Have Lew meet me there. And radio the uniforms. Tell 'em to keep all them looky-loos and kids with bikes away from the house. Neighborhood like that, there's bound to be folks tramping all over, poking their noses where they don't belong."

He hung up the phone and glared at his watch. Seventeen minutes past five. Perfect end to a lousy day.

Chapter Three

By the time Sari and Tim returned from picking up his wedding suit at a mall north of Widmark, their flat was as stifling as the car and they could hear the phone as they walked up the stairs. Dropping the plastic garment bag on the daybed, he caught it on the fifth ring.

"Hello?"

"Son, you need to come home right away." Tim's face froze. "There's been an accident."

"What's wrong?"

"Can you call Laura?"

"Did something happen to Mom?"

"Just bring your sister as fast as you can."

Tim's mouth went dry and his father hung up before he could ask another question. He turned to Sari, who was already at his side. "Something's happened, I think Mom's been hurt."

"Is she okay?"

"I don't know." He slumped on the daybed and squeezed his eyes shut. "He just said to get Laura and come home."

"Do you want me to call her?"

"No, I'd better do it." He dialed Laura but her line was busy, and when he tried it again it rang over and over with no answer.

"Maybe you should call back. Maybe it was a car accident and she's in a hospital." He didn't want the answer, but finally he picked up the phone and dialed his parents' number.

"Tim, is that you?" The voice was unfamiliar. "This is Louella Harvey, from next door."

"What's going on?"

"We've been trying to reach Laura but we can't get through."

"Is Mom okay?"

"Didn't your father tell you? They found her in the garage "

He dropped the phone and sank to the floor with his knees to his chin.

"Tim?" Sari whispered. "What's wrong?"

He gripped his elbows because it felt like his chest was about to explode.

"What?" She knelt at his side. "Tell me!"

"She's dead. My mom's dead."

—

When the call came Laura Scott was dressing for work. "We have to go to Gillman." Tim sounded out of it and Laura wondered if he'd had a quarrel with Sari. Fastening a jet earring with one hand, she hunted for her lipstick. "I'm coming to pick you up."

"I'm about to leave for—"

"Something happened to Mom."

"I was there this morning and everything was fine. Is Dad—"

"We're swinging by in ten minutes." Behind the words Laura sensed panic, and she forgot about the lipstick. "Can you be ready?"

"What happened?"

"Mom's dead." His voice broke. "Where the hell have you been? They've been trying to reach you for the past half hour!"

Laura hung up and walked into the bathroom. Standing over the sink, she unclasped her earrings. She began running a comb through her cropped chestnut hair, then bent over the toilet and vomited.

—

They set off for Gillman in Sari and Tim's Mustang, with Tim at the wheel and Laura staring dry-eyed out the rear passenger window. Sari sat beside him, holding his hand as she watched the Turnpike hurl past. She tried not to think about Peggy's abruptness that morning, or Laura's perfunctory greeting. If Peggy's death was anything but an accident, someone would have said so. She'd been in such a hurry that morning…

As they turned onto the highway just north of Widmark, she glanced at Tim. He looked numb. Digging her nails into the edge of the black vinyl seat, Sari tried not to think about the Mustang dragging them back to Gillman.

She remembered how excited Tim had been when they found the ad in the paper four weeks earlier. Warren recommended an automatic transmission because it left no room for human error, but Tim leaped when he saw the four-speed stick shift and the wild pony charging across the grille. This is it, he cried, *freedom!* They'd bought the car with her savings from cashiering at the campus co-op and his from framing houses, and registered it in Sari's name the same day they found the apartment on Locust. What's mine is yours, Tim said, but they both knew the Mustang was hers in name only. And now it was carrying them back to Gillman. Meeting Laura's eyes briefly in the rearview mirror, Sari wished she wasn't the only stranger. An accident, she thought. No matter how much Peggy hated her, she couldn't have been so opposed to her son's marriage that she'd kill herself.

She glanced once more at Laura, stony-eyed in the back seat. When Tim said he had an older sister, Sari had been envious. A sister was an ally, and if you were anything alike it was proof you weren't a changeling left on the wrong doorstep. My mother will adore you, he'd said, she'll teach you to sew. Nothing about Laura, just that she'd dropped out of school and was living with a pot-smoking creep Peggy couldn't stand.

What does your mother look like? she'd asked. Like me, was the only description Tim gave, and Sari went nuts trying to fill in the blanks. When can I meet her? Plenty of time later, he said, for now I want you all to myself... Think of something else. Anything. That first date with Tim.

Chico's, the Mexican restaurant down the Hill. Tim forgot his wallet, had only eighty cents in his pocket, and until the place closed they feasted on flour tortillas dipped in the salsa that sat on the table with the pepper and salt. Giggling at the sour-faced waitress, his fingers touching hers where no one else could see. After two weeks, classes were an unbearable distraction from their time together. She ran to meet him at his physics lab and he camped on the floor outside her Italian class at Chapel Hall. Weekend hikes, the dollar movies on campus. Tim left love notes in her textbooks, illustrated in ink and colored pen. Silken gloxinias and glorious birds that soared perilously close to the sun.

They studied at a table tucked away on the third floor of Bryant or curled up on the floor of the lounge at the Student Union. When Tim picked her up from class and whisked her away in the middle of a conversation with a classmate about Friday's Italian quiz, she shrugged apologetically and basked in the glow of belonging. Her mother asked if she'd made friends yet; she told her she hadn't had time. What about Ronnie? Helen Siegel persisted. We have nothing in common, Sari explained.

They had their life together all planned: after graduation a one-room cabin up in Garnet Hill, where Tim would paint and she would grow snapdragons and poppies. He had his heart set on a goat, and so long as it didn't eat the flowers, she didn't care. The walls would be paneled in beetle-kill pine and the beams exposed over a sleeping loft that would extend halfway across the floor. At least three children, and everyone would sleep in the loft, where it would be cozy and warm. Closed doors meant secrets, there would be none of those. ...

—

When the Mustang finally turned onto Grand Avenue, traffic slowed almost to a standstill. It was six o'clock but Sari could smell the asphalt as they inched forward in the oppressive heat, and when they made the right onto South Cleveland everything came to a halt.

Neighbors in sunglasses and Bermuda shorts clustered on lawns, staring at the two-story brick-and-frame house with butternut trim. The curb in front of the Scotts' residence was empty but police cars and Hallett County Sheriff vans lined the remainder of the block, and a metallic maroon Chrysler had pulled into the driveway next door. Tim tried to park in front but a sheriff's deputy waved him on. He pulled in anyway and the officer strode to the driver's side, his face dark with anger.

"What's the matter with you people, can't you see there's been a tragedy here?"

When Tim leaned out the window and said, "We're family," the cop directed them to the Harveys' driveway and they edged in past the Chrysler. As they came to a stop and exited the car, a walkie-talkie scratched the air, but the flashing lights on the ambulance backed up to the Scotts' garage were extinguished. When Sari saw paramedics smoking in the driveway, she knew they were too late. Everything that mattered had already happened.

Tim's father stood in the center of the lawn, gazing across the street at nothing in particular. A man half as wide as he was short and wearing a silver and turquoise bolo tie stood on the grass behind him. As Sari watched, he removed his tan stockman's Stetson and mopped his brow with a rumpled handkerchief. His flat heart-shaped face revealed nothing, but his brown western-style sport coat strained as he spoke in the ear of a younger man in Tony Lama boots, tight Levis, and a black ball cap with a SWAT logo. The second man nodded once and scribbled in a pocket-sized notebook.

Tim left her on the steps and approached his father with hands outstretched.

"What happened?" she read from his gesture. She was too far away to hear, but something in his father's response made Tim hesitate.

As Warren glanced over his shoulder at the men behind them and stepped closer, Tim reached again to embrace him. Warren stopped short, then bridged the gap in one long stride. Looping his arm around Tim's shoulder he leaned forward until their faces were inches apart. Tim stiffened, and Sari saw his fists clench. Chin tilted at precisely the same angle as his son's, Warren murmured something and waited for Tim's curt nod. They parted like filings flung from opposite poles of a magnet.

Chapter Four

The first thing Ray Burt noticed when he pulled into the neighbor's driveway was that the Scotts' home was completely exposed. Nothing but a postage stamp of a lawn between the front door and sidewalk, no trees, bushes or fence, not even a railing around the stoop. As he removed his Stetson and mopped his head with his hanky, he saw the two-car attached garage was also unsheltered, but a wooden gate on the far side led to a backyard surrounded by a six-foot grape-stake fence.

He glanced behind him at chest-high shrubbery in the neighbor's yard, then across the street. A Dutch elm planted too close to the foundation shaded the front of the ranch-style home directly opposite the Scotts'. A thick growth of junipers concealed the basement windows of the house next door and a late-model camper was parked in the driveway. As he wondered what would attract an intruder to 4990 South Cleveland when juicier plums were ripe for the plucking, one of the uniforms approached.

"What've we got?" Ray asked.

"One victim, sir, in the garage. Looks like she surprised an intruder."

"Sergeant Devine here yet?"

"Dispatch just located him."

"You first on the scene?"

"Yes, sir. My partner and I caught the call twenty minutes ago."

They crossed the driveway to the Scotts' yard. The barricades weren't up yet but the neighbors were keeping their distance. A bunch of them huddled across the street, curious but quiet, almost respectful, as if they were afraid whatever the Scotts had was contagious. Ray had seen it hundreds of times. Witnesses to history. Then there were neighborhood kids pulling wheelies on the asphalt until one of the uniforms finally told them to stay the hell out of the way.

"Who reported it?" he asked.

"Her husband."

Ray glanced over his shoulder at the only man near the house who was not in uniform. He looked as though he were waiting for someone to tell him what to do.

"He the one who found her?"

"Yes, sir."

"Who was she?"

"He says she's his wife."

"What's his name?"

"Warren Scott."

He left the patrolman and walked over. "Mr. Scott? I'm Lieutenant Burt of the Hallett County Sheriff's Department. You found your wife, is that correct?"

"Yes." Warren's voice was flat.

"Must've been a terrible shock."

"It was."

Ray noticed he was wearing a flannel shirt with a white T underneath, and polished black oxfords. Odd choice for a Saturday in late spring. The paleness of his skin was broken only by a nasty bruise above his left temple.

"I'm sorry about your loss."

Warren said nothing, just kept staring at the house directly across the street as if all the answers lay behind its half-drawn drapes. An ambulance pulled up with lights flashing but the siren off, and one of the officers directed it to back into the driveway. Ray instructed the uniform not to let any paramedics into the garage until after the coroner arrived and Forensics was finished, then knelt for a closer look at the door. It was closed except for a three-inch gap where it should have met the pavement. As he rose, he noticed the gate to the backyard was ajar. He returned to the lawn.

"Is there someone you need to call?"

"My son Tim's on his way down from Stanley with his sister."

"Anyone close who could help when they get here?"

"Louella Harvey next door. I went over when I found her. She's a nurse but she said it was too late, there was nothing we could do..."

The mobile crime unit was pulling up, but Ray kept his eyes on Warren. "I have a few questions. You don't mind, do you?"

"No."

Ray left him and gave an order to one of the uniforms. He waited until he saw him return with a gray-haired woman, then grasped Warren gently by the elbow. "Let's go inside, it'll be cooler." As they entered the house, Warren drew a handkerchief from his hip pocket and dabbed at his forehead.

The front door opened into a foyer, with a formal living room to the right and a dining room to the left. A staircase leading to the second floor faced the entrance and the kitchen was at the end of the short hallway that ran along the steps. A row of religious paintings hung straight in their frames and an unnatural stillness prevailed despite the muffled voices in the kitchen. Glancing up the stairs, Ray noticed a small radio and a desk lamp balanced between spokes of the railing.

Two men in sport shirts and polyester slacks entered behind them, one toting a square black suitcase. "Where do you want us to start, Lieutenant?"

Ray poked his head in the dining room, where the only signs of disorder were the doors of a china cabinet standing open and drawers pulled halfway out the buffet. "Garage. After that do the rest of the house, starting with the ground floor. When Devine gets here he'll be in charge of collecting evidence. Any questions, ask him. I'll be with Mr.

Scott." He turned to the officer at the threshold to the kitchen. "Keep everyone but the coroner out and send Devine to me when he comes."

Stepping into the living room, Ray was immediately struck by its prim decor. Parlor would more accurately describe it, he thought, which was strange because houses in this neighborhood had no pretensions to such formality. But the room was small and fancy, very neat, with a plush carpet and white couch and matching love seat with plastic covers on the arms. For special visitors. He sat carefully on the edge of the couch and gestured for Scott to join him. "Tell me what you know."

"I don't know anything, Lieutenant."

Swallowing his impatience, Ray summoned a sympathetic smile. "When did you find your wife?"

"When I returned from Stanley, I parked on the street and came in the front door. I called her name but there was no answer." Spoken in a monotone, maybe shock. "I walked back through the kitchen to the utility room. The door to the garage was open and she was lying on the floor. I went next door for Mrs. Harvey."

"Why did you look in the garage?"

"I—that was the only place she could be." As Warren shifted on the love seat, Ray tried to decipher the expression in his close-set eyes. These first moments were crucial. "I went up to her and touched her arm."

"What'd you do next?"

"Went to the kitchen to wash my hands."

You could hardly blame a guy for wanting to was his hands after touching a stiff, but this was his wife they were talking about. "Why'd you do that?"

"To get the blood off them. There was blood all over her."

"When you touched your wife—By the way, what's her name?"

"Peggy." As Warren Scott crossed his legs but kept his hands folded, Ray was reminded of a schoolboy who knows the only thing that counts is what's visible above the desk. "Margaret Kathleen, but we called her Peggy."

"You don't mind if I call her that too, do you?" Warren shook his head. "When you touched Peggy, was there any sign of life?"

"I knew she was dead."

"How'd you know that?"

"I tried to move her arm, and it was stiff."

Ray glanced up to see Lew Devine in the doorway. In his polo shirt and Levis he looked like he'd just dismounted from a horse, which he had. Dispatch reached him at the stable in Hays where he kept a bay gelding, but Lew always carried his badge and gun, and now the 9mm Walther PPK automatic rode in a holster at the small of his back and his tin was clipped to his black leather belt.

"This is Detective Sergeant Devine." Lew nodded at Warren. "Mind if we step outside a moment and talk?"

On the front stoop, Ray positioned himself to keep an eye on Warren through the open door. "Coroner here yet, Lew?"

"In the garage."

"What's he say?"

"Looks like she got hit in the face with a shotgun. Brains all over the place. Blood on the garage door high as the ceiling."

Warren hadn't budged from the love seat, and if he was trying to listen it wasn't obvious. "First guy on the scene said it looked like a burglary," Ray replied.

"There's loot from the house strewn around, but how many burglars you know carry a shotgun?"

Ray sighed, but it did nothing to dispel his queasiness. Once again his gut was on target. "I hate these domestic things."

"How do you make him?"

"Too soon to tell, Lew. He's either in shock or the coldest fish I've met, and there's that shiner on his forehead. I want him to take us on a walk-through."

They returned to the living room where Warren was sitting precisely where they'd left him, ankles crossed and hands in his lap as if he were waiting for the teacher to call his name. Those oxfords gleamed. Devine followed him and Ray across the foyer to the ransacked dining room as Ray took the lead.

"I can tell Peggy was a good housekeeper," he began. In response to

Warren's blank look he added, "Everything in its place, right?"

"Yes."

"So tell us what's out of place, Mr. Scott. Mind if I call you Warren?"

He shrugged and walked to the buffet. "They must have been looking for silverware."

"Don't touch, Forensics is dusting for prints. Your kids live at home?"

"They're up in Stanley. Tim's at the University and Laura works in a restaurant." Warren turned from the sideboard to the undisturbed crystal in the shelves above.

"Just tell us what's missing or out of place." Warren nodded and absently reached for his forehead. "That's quite a bump," Ray added. "Maybe we should have one of the paramedics look at it."

He dropped his hand. "It's nothing."

"How'd you get it?"

"I don't remember."

Devine shot Ray a look which he pretended not to see. "Today?"

"Yes."

"Before you went to Stanley?"

"Must have."

"Maybe we should have someone take a look. Skin's broken and you don't want an infection…"

"I'm sure it'll be fine."

Nothing obvious was missing from the dining room and they moved to the kitchen. A small hallway just past the refrigerator led to a powder room with rose-sprigged wallpaper and the utility room, which housed a washer and dryer and the portal to a dog run. Through the doorway to the garage Ray saw the coroner and one of his assistants kneeling over something on the floor. He returned to the kitchen, where cabinets stood open and a technician was already daubing counters with black powder.

"Sorry about the mess, Warren, but it can't be helped. Those cabinets usually open?"

"No." Warren knelt to peer under the sink. "Looks like the ice crusher's missing." Devine raised an eyebrow and made a note in his book, then followed them to the family room. "Turntable to the stereo's gone," Warren continued. "I think they took the television too."

"What kind of set did you have?"

"A Zenith color."

"Anything else?" A rack on the wall held several rifles polished to a high gloss. "That a Remington?"

"Yes."

"It's a real beauty." Once again Ray avoided eye contact with Devine. "And look at that Winchester. Those the only guns in the house?"

"There are more rifles and pistols in a cabinet in the basement."

"Any shotguns?"

"A couple I use for duck hunting."

"Those down in the basement too?"

"They should be."

They left the family room to the print technicians and returned to the foyer. Mounting the steps, Ray saw the linen closet at the head of the stairs was open and the shelf at eye level held an assortment of prescription pills, including pain relievers. The contents appeared untouched and he turned his attention to the rest of the second floor. Aside from an alcove off the master bedroom that housed a dressmaker's form wearing an ice-blue satin gown with beading basted around the collar and shelves stacked with patterns and bolts of cloth, every room on this floor was ransacked. Drawers were pulled halfway out in the daughter's bedroom, three dollar bills sat on the nightstand beside her bed, her dresser was pushed over, and a television antenna lay on the floor. Warren said a black-and-white TV and a digital alarm clock were missing.

The master bedroom was frilly and indulgent, with gathered curtains of eyelet lace and a white ruffled flounce on the vanity, the sort of room Ray imagined might belong to the daughter of a wealthy man. Crystal perfume bottles with atomizers were neatly arrayed, and an antique brush and comb set with silver handles lay undisturbed beside a cluster of pill bottles, but dresser drawers sat upright on the plush carpet. A gold wristwatch lay on top of one drawer and a pair of binoculars was in plain sight in the walk-in closet. Warren was unable to confirm whether any of his wife's jewelry had been taken, though a clock radio was apparently gone.

The tour ended at the son's room in the basement, a cluttered space where skis and a bicycle leaned against one wall and another was covered with pen-and-ink drawings. Propped between the bed and a sheet of plywood mounted on cinder blocks that served as a desk was a four-by-six-foot portrait of a teenage boy gazing in a glass sphere. Ray slid out the canvas and examined it. Although the youth's reflection was distorted, it was amazingly lifelike, and now he saw there was another figure inside the globe.

"Is your son the artist?"

"Tim painted that at school."

"It's almost like a photograph." But there was something disturbing about the subject matter; it was as if the second boy were trapped and trying to climb out. "That's incredible, for his age…"

From Warren's shrug it was impossible to tell whether he was modest or merely indifferent to his son's achievements. "He's won a few prizes at art shows."

Above them hung a handmade display case with dozens of ribbons and medals pinned to the blue velvet lining. Ray turned to the shelf of trophies. "He win those too?"

"Hockey."

"Quite the athlete." Ray folded his arms and leaned against the doorjamb. "How come you went to Stanley today?"

"Tim coaches on Saturdays, and I wanted to watch his practice. Then I had lunch and looked at restaurants for the rehearsal dinner."

"Rehearsal dinner?"

"Tim's getting married next weekend."

Ray glanced past Warren's shoulder at Devine, who stood at the far wall scribbling in his notebook, a slight frown on his hawkish face. "What restaurants did you check out?"

"The Lamplighter and Foothills Inn."

"Any others?"

"Not that I recall."

"What time did you get to Stanley?"

"A little after noon."

"What'd you do before that?"

"Chores, then I dropped my wife's Cadillac at a service station for an oil change." Ray glanced at Warren's shoes. Oxfords for chores? Warren turned to Devine and added, "Gillman Sinclair. They'll tell you it was about nine o'clock." He couldn't have been wearing them; Top-Siders would have been more like it. "How'd you get home?"

"My daughter Laura gave me a lift."

"So Laura was here this morning too?"

Warren blinked and Ray pasted a mental star beside the question. "She followed me to the station so I could drop off the Cadillac, then brought me back and left." "Change clothes before you left for Stanley?"

Was that surprise in the narrowing of his flat eyes? "No."

"Remember anything else you did this morning?"

"Not really." He shrugged again. "Just a regular Saturday."

The rest of the basement was storage for camping equipment, skis, and boots. When Ray rattled the handle of a metal gun cabinet, Warren withdrew a ring of keys from his pocket.

"Those your shotguns?"

"Yes."

"When's the last time you fired one?"

"December, I'd guess. I haven't been duck hunting since then."

"I noticed you have a dog run. Where are your dogs?"

"My last one was a Labrador." A spasm crossed Warren's face, so elusive Ray almost missed it. The first time he'd registered any real emotion. "I had to put her down two months ago."

They went back upstairs, where technicians had left surfaces smeared with soot and another team was photographing the rooms. Ray felt a pang of sympathy for Peggy Scott. She wouldn't have liked this at all.

By the time they emerged into the heat and clamor of the front yard, the ambulance attendants were standing around feeling important but waiting to be told what to do. A woman across the street pointed until Devine shot her a look, and she turned away.

"We'll need a formal statement, Warren, just a little detail on what you've already told us. Will you be around?"

"I have no plans."

"Good." As Ray and Devine stood off to one side talking, a green Mustang pulled into the driveway next door and discharged the two Scott children and a young woman with black hair.

Chapter Five

Stripped of its status as a home, 4990 South Cleveland was now a set inhabited by actors. Wandering unchallenged with Tim from room to room, Sari struggled to remember the house he'd brought her to eight months before. In the hands of strangers it was somehow less forbidding.

Back then the rooms had seemed larger, with unwritten rules posted at every door. Foyer for greeting visitors and hanging coats; living room for important guests. Rifles hung from a rack in the family room where trophy antlers commemorated Tim's first hunt, and the kitchen was straight out of *Better Homes and Gardens,* with a place for every appliance and Formica counters that gleamed even in the midst of preparing dinner. Sari couldn't help thinking Peggy would have been horrified at her parents' apartment on Willow Street; the kitchen was so small her mother papered the walls in two patterns to enlarge it, and the refrigerator stood guard at the end of a hallway. Under Peggy's watch it would be unthinkable to spread homework over the dining room table or drop a newspaper on the floor. When Tim showed her the upstairs, all doors had been closed.

Now plainclothes and uniformed officers swarmed the first floor, flashing pictures and peering at surfaces for prints. The kitchen, the nerve center of Peggy's universe, looked like the before shot in a Spic and Span commercial, with the cop at the threshold to the utility room a grim reminder of what lay beyond. Then Louella Harvey descended.

"Don't you kids go in the garage, it's an awful mess and they won't let us clean." She clutched Tim's arm. "There's blood everywhere, and of course your mother's still—" Her lips compressed in mid-sentence and she turned back toward the kitchen.

The stumpy man with the bolo tie came in and introduced himself as Lieutenant Burt. His expressionless eyes blinked from Tim to Sari, and then back.

"You Tim?"

"Yeah."

He looked at Sari. "You a friend of the family?"

"Sari's my fiancee," Tim replied. "We're getting married next week."

Burt's face twitched. "Come with me." His stubby forefinger stabbed at Tim.

—

"I need you to help me, son," Ray Burt said.

When there was no response, he led Tim to the door between the utility room and the garage and gave him a gentle push. "Take a deep breath and tell me what you see." The garage was a nightmare, nothing Tim could conjure in a waking moment. Lights were mounted in two corners so photographers could capture every angle, and he tried to orient himself but the flashing bulbs robbed even the familiar of comfort. His old Schwinn stood against one wall and the Styrofoam picnic cooler waited where it always did, in front of the spare tires for the Dodge. A plastic garbage can sat in the center of the floor where the Olds was normally parked.

A flash illuminated the garage door and dark streaks suddenly appeared on the upper panels, with splatters near the ceiling. Eyes straight ahead, soon it will be over, look anywhere but down…But Burt pushed him two steps forward and he finally looked.

She was crumpled facedown between his grandfather's red tool chest and the garage door, with her arms cradling her head and a gardening rake just beyond the reach of her outstretched fingers. Slender and still, she looked like a girl sleeping in a slick of blood on that cold cement floor. Maybe she was asleep, like when he was small.... A seductively sweet odor filled his nostrils, the wine-tart scent of crabapples rotting in the grass, and he quickly turned his head. But the lieutenant's presence at his shoulder was relentless.

A band of light illuminated the floor where the garage door stopped short of the concrete. A safety zone, like the lines in a coloring book. Just stay within the lines.... But Tim blinked, and when his eyes focused they were on his mother's feet, clad in white sneakers like a child. Her long pale legs in their gardening shorts were freckled with blood, and from the waist up she was drenched in it, her bare shoulders stained with rust and her hair matted and black. His stomach began to heave, and he turned and stumbled past Burt to the sanity of the utility room.

—

When Tim returned to the dining room he seized Sari's hand and pulled her from the chair. From the doorway Burt said, "I know this is rough, Tim, but I need you to stay close. Understand?"

Ignoring him, Tim pushed his way through the kitchen to the family room and out the sliding doors to the patio, but the detective grabbed Sari's arm.

"Not so fast, miss. I need a word with you."

"I don't know anything."

"Did you see Warren Scott today?" His eyes were small and muddy, too brown to be green. As she stared into them he released her.

"He came to the rec center to watch a practice."

"What time did he arrive?"

"I—don't know." She looked out the patio door at Tim, who was kneeling beside a yellow rosebush that was just coming into bloom. As she watched he leaned forward and buried his face in a blossom. "He was already there when I came."

"Did you know he was coming?"

She shook her head. "Peggy called, but—"

Burt's hand froze on its way to the inside pocket of his jacket. "You spoke to Peggy Scott this morning?"

"She wanted us to get a message to Laura, Tim's sister." In response to his unasked question she added, "Laura was coming home to drop off her car, but Peggy was worried she'd have no way to get back to Stanley. There was some mixup about the Dodge."

Burt exhaled, and Sari felt her own tension drain. His disappointment was an odd relief. "Did you give Laura the message?"

"No, we didn't see her."

Reaching in his jacket again, he removed a ball-point pen and spiral pad. "What did Scott say when you saw him?"

"Nothing, just hello and stuff like that."

"Did you ask him what he was doing there?"

He'd planned to attend a Dale Carnegie seminar.

"I—" She'd asked about that seminar and Warren had said it was postponed. "He came to Stanley to find a place for the rehearsal dinner. We didn't know they—" Hearing herself babble, she abruptly stopped. Warren acted like the seminar was no big deal when she'd asked; what was stopping her from mentioning it now? Burt's pen was poised over his pad.

"Didn't know what?" he prompted. "What didn't you know?"

"That they were giving us a rehearsal dinner. Look, I don't know anything!" She turned to the door. Tim was still bent over the rosebush, gulping the fragrance as if he were trying to drown in it. Like that golden retriever she'd seen on a hike in the foothills, rolling in the sun-blackened carcass of a magpie. The tips of its wings still cobalt, iridescent in the fading light… *What had they done to him in that garage?*

"What time did Tim go to the rec center this morning?"

"Before nine." She took a deep breath. This was almost over, there was nothing to tell. "He had a ten o'clock practice, but he wanted to warm up first."

"Was he there the entire morning?" Burt insisted.

Now they were on safe ground, and Sari seized the initiative.

"Of course he was! What are you trying to say?"

"Now, just hold your horses. No one's saying nothing..."

Before he could regain his balance, she ran out the door. Two men in uniforms knelt on the grass, gliding their hands in circular motions as if they were blind.

"What are you doing?" she asked.

"Looking for shotgun wadding. We think she was shot in the face."

Sari and Tim got down on their knees and, grateful for the mindless activity, crawled around the yard with them until the sun finally set.

—

As the officers packed up their equipment, Tim returned to the house and Sari went to a pay phone at the gas station two blocks away. She told him she wanted to stretch her legs, be by herself a few minutes, and that much was true. But what she really needed was to hear her mother's voice.

Hurrying down Grand Avenue she remembered her last conversation with her parents, two weeks earlier, when she and Tim announced the wedding date. Her father had hit the roof. Marriage will be a disaster! he roared before threatening to cut off financial support and then making her promise not to drop out of school. She'd put it to them as nonchalantly as possible, you can come to the wedding or not, makes no difference to us, but her mother saw right through it. How could you think I wouldn't be there? Helen cried, and Sari bit back the response. *Because you never are.*

It was past eight o'clock local time, which meant her father would be asleep in Brooklyn and her mother settling down to read. Helen answered on the first ring.

"Sari? Is everything all right?"

"Tim's mother is dead."

"What?"

"They think it was a burglar."

"My God, I can't believe it! Are you all right?"

"Yes, but I don't know about Tim. Can you come?"

"Of course." Sari knew from the rustling that Helen was reaching for her Kents. But it didn't matter; if her mother was coming, everything would be all right… "I'll be there as soon as I can."

"Don't wake Dad, okay?"

—

Helen Siegel hung up the phone and looked at Max lying on his side and snoring softly. What good would it do to rouse him? But this was about Sari, and he'd never forgive her if she didn't. She leaned over and grasped his shoulder.

"Max? Wake up, that was Sari."

"Sari?" His eyes jerked open. "What's wrong?"

"She's all right, she's fine. Something happened to Tim's family."

He sat up. "Is he okay?"

"Not Tim, his mother. Peggy."

"You talked to her over Christmas, didn't you?" The words were thick on his tongue, and he switched on his lamp. "What's the matter, is she sick?"

"There's been some kind of accident. She's dead."

"We should never have let her go out there, Helen."

"Since when have we ever *let* Sari do anything?" She struck a match with trembling fingers and drew smoke deep into her lungs. "She's always done exactly as she pleased."

He closed his eyes. "Maybe she'll come home now, maybe she'll—"

"I told her I'd be there as soon as I can."

"They can't possibly think they're getting married!"

"If you think this will have any effect on their plans, you don't know Sari. She'll go through with the wedding no matter what." She stubbed out her cigarette. "Don't you remember when she threatened to secede from the family?"

"That was a long time ago."

"Not so long, she was thirteen."

How well Helen recalled the manifesto her daughter posted on the bathroom mirror at Willow Street, neatly printed on lined notebook paper without a cross-out or spelling error—how many attempts must she have made, to get it so right? Having calculated how many square feet her bed and dresser occupied, she proposed to pay her share of the rent from baby-sitting income and reimburse them for food on a weekly, daily, or hourly basis. Water and electricity could be handled with a flat fee per use or separately metered. She hadn't had a cavity in over four years, and if Christian Scientists could do without doctors, so could she…

He grunted and switched off his light. "We'll see about it in the morning."

"Sari's not coming back, Max."

But he was already feigning sleep.

Belting her dressing gown, Helen decided to make herself a cup of instant coffee. The caffeine didn't matter; she'd never rest tonight. Things were happening much too quickly. Just six months since they even knew there was a Tim Scott, and since when had the prickly creature who wouldn't let Helen hold her hand crossing the street ever asked *her* for help?

As she padded downstairs to the kitchen she strained to hear the tenants in the garden apartment. They'd bought the brownstone three years earlier, when Max sold a half-interest in the printing plant and she'd pressed him to move because the apartment was claustrophobic. But she'd been immediately overwhelmed by the space. When she suggested advertising for a nice young couple to occupy the ground floor after Sari left for college, Max said they could carry the mortgage without collecting rent. What he didn't realize was how Helen yearned for the indecipherable sounds that carried through the locked door and up the stairwell, so different from the war of words during Sari's youth and the prolonged silences that punctuated her days after her daughter left.

Setting the kettle to boil Helen told herself not to worry, that Sari and her father were cut from the same cloth. With Sari it was always an announcement and never a discussion. When Max called her incorrigible in the third grade she ran straight to the dictionary to look it up, and was proud once she knew what it meant. The emancipation proclamation on the bathroom mirror was neither her first nor last.

Taped to the refrigerator where they could not be overlooked, her missives concluded, "I would appreciate a prompt reply to this, or at least an acknowledgment of receipt. I believe you know where I can be reached…" And when she was angry or hurt, she'd retreat into that articulate precision of hers as if she were a miniature lawyer and everything could be reduced to a rational argument. *We never talk,* she wailed, but Helen never knew what to say to her. When she left for college Max didn't want to let her go because anything could happen two thousand miles away. But Sari said it was Stanley or nowhere, and he was not about to let the light of his life renounce higher education.

As she sipped her coffee and listened to the house settle for the night, Helen remembered when Sari brought Tim home with her over Christmas. She'd called the day finals were over to say she was coming east with someone she'd met at school. The two of them drove all the way from Stanley to Brooklyn, thirty hours nonstop in an old car Tim borrowed from a friend. When Max took the subway to the Lower East Side the next morning for the bagels and smoked fish his daughter loved, she lit into them as if she'd been starved. On Christmas Day Tim asked if he could call home to wish his parents a happy holiday, and when he was finished he handed Helen the phone and said his mother wanted to speak with her.

"Mrs. Siegel?" A cool, tentative voice crossed the wire. "This is Peggy Scott."

"Tim's a wonderful boy, we're enjoying our visit with him so much…"

"How does it feel to have a new son?"

Helen sank into her chair. "What?"

"Didn't you know they intend to get married?"

"But they just met, they're much too young!"

"I agree."

"They haven't said a word about marriage." Helen tried to regain her balance. "You know how kids are."

"Tim doesn't have to say anything. I know my son, and this is very important to him."

"Maybe they'll change their minds."

"Nothing will change Tim's mind. And I don't want to lose him." The words came in a rush, and Helen tasted Peggy's fear. "We're such different families, we're not like you people at all—"

You people?

"I understand, Mrs. Scott." The reassuring laugh stuck in Helen's throat. "But you know how impulsive eighteen-year-olds can be. Let's wait and see what happens."

That was the only time she spoke to Peggy Scott. She never told Max what Peggy said or discussed the matter with Sari or Tim because she assumed, as with most of the boys Sari brought home over the years, that Tim was a passing fancy she'd outgrow in a few months. But this time was different. If Helen wanted to protect her daughter, it would be up to her to bring her back.

She rinsed her cup and set it on the drainboard. It was almost midnight and the television in the garden apartment was off. Max could dream all he wanted about Sari coming back to the fold, but Helen had no illusions. Whatever disaster awaited her daughter, she had no doubt Sari would fly into it headfirst, like a moth to a flame.

Chapter Six

Curled up on the strange mattress beside Tim, Sari stared at the window above the desk in his basement room. It opened onto the lawn between the stoop and garage, but from this angle it was a black pit. Like the hole in which they'd fallen. None of this was happening, they'd wake up tomorrow in Stanley and shake it off as a dream...

The departure of outsiders from the house on South Cleveland had left a sullen void. One by one the Scotts settled around the dining room table, maintaining a silent vigil unbroken by food or drink. There were a dozen questions Sari wanted to ask, but even Tim looked away when she tried to catch his eye. And there they sat, each wrapped in his own misery, until the room became so dark their features were no longer distinguishable. Wordlessly they went their separate ways.

As her eyes adjusted to the blackness, Sari focused on the ceiling where Tim had long ago painted a galaxy of phosphorescent stars. The water heater outside the door rumbled and subsided and kicked to life again as she searched in vain for a familiar constellation. Upstairs the phone rang once, and after that the house was still. She reached for Tim but his fingers were as lifeless as twigs. She slung her leg across his thigh and from his long sigh knew he was awake.

"Tim?"

He lay on his back, his only motion an occasional blink as he gazed at the ceiling, but as she continued to hold his hand his fingers flexed and his skin began to lose its chill. She closed her eyes and pictured their apartment on Locust, tried to remember whether she'd watered the coleuses before she left for the library that morning. Was Peggy simply in a hurry to prune her roses, or was there another reason for her clipped tone when she'd called? She probably hadn't been oveijoyed when Sari answered the phone; she seldom called the apartment at all. Did she really have a message for Laura? Or did she say that only when Sari answered?

Directly above and to their left was the garage where Peggy had died. The very walls seemed to throb with her presence. What if she could sense Sari there tonight, in Tim's bed? And what had he seen when the stubby detective led him away? From Tim's face she knew it must have been awful, but when she asked him he wouldn't say.

Think about something else, anything else.

She rolled closer to Tim. Gathering his jersey about her waist, she remembered the only time she'd been in the garage, when Tim was looking for a bicycle pump after dinner in early spring. She smelled the dank cement floor, saw the fiberboard on the wall where families of wrenches and screwdrivers hung in rows according to size. Was that where Peggy—

The stillness was broken by Tim. A sharp gasp from a nightmare, a shuddering moan... He rolled to face her and she reached for him.

"Tim?"

Breaths hitching now, fast and warm on her shoulder. But he seemed not to recognize her, and as he rose on one elbow his body clenched like a massive fist.

"Tim?"

Unrecognizable, a trapped animal gaping in rage and disbelief... She drew back and his face seemed to melt like tallow.

"—should never have—"

He began to sob, and she wrapped her arms around him and pulled him to her breast.

"Shh, shh…"

As tears bled through her jersey, she adjusted her breathing to the beat of Tim's heart. Gradually it slowed; his sobs became pants, the pants sighs. The sighs lengthened, and she closed her eyes and lay still until one seemed to issue from his very depths. When she was certain he was asleep she left his bed and sat at his desk.

What would happen to them?

The casement window was open to the night air, and the sprinkler sputtering on across the street carried her back to that October evening when Tim first brought her home. Lawns were shaggy and fatigued, and asters were gathering their strength for a last surge of color before dying down. As she mounted the steps outside this window, she'd felt an anticipation so acute it made her throat sore. He'd told her so little about his mother. Vivacious redhead, homemaker type—what did that really mean?

When Peggy met them at the door her smile said she, too, had been waiting. She was tall and slim, with pale eyes and Tim's hair, her fine skin beginning to show the effects of sun in the way fair people do. But there was a tentativeness to her greeting, and when she extended her hand it was a sparrow landing an instant before flying off. Her smiles and frowns were truncated, as if she'd been warned that emotions cause wrinkles, her enthusiasm already fading as she accepted Sari's bouquet of mums and daisies with an oddly formal grace. Was this the woman Tim described as cheerful and witty, sure to adore her?

As Peggy turned to hang their jackets, Tim snatched a kiss and Sari racked her brain for scraps of information. Tim said his mother had gone to work as a bookkeeper at a manufacturing firm a year earlier, when Warren left his job at Reynolds Industrial to start a consulting business. With Tim facing college and Laura having two years to go, her income had been a necessity. … .

Following Tim's mother down the hall, she focused on the swirling white blossoms on her teal rayon dress. It had a white collar and cuffs and was nipped at the waist by a narrow belt. The fabric was far too luxurious for such a prim pattern, the fit so flawless she knew Peggy had sewn it herself. When Tim had told her his mother made her own clothes, she'd gone to So-Fro Fabrics to see about classes with the hope of impressing her. But now the A-line pattern from Simplicity and polished cotton in a pastel print waiting in the trunk of Tim's borrowed car seemed childish, lacking in confidence.... As Tim's sister met them at the door to the kitchen, Sari set all thoughts of sewing aside.

At twenty Laura was leggy like her mother and thinboned. She wore no makeup and the mole at the corner of her right eye was the only blemish on her perfectly oval face. Cropped chestnut hair made her look untethered, as if she'd dropped from the sky, and her black turtleneck played waifishness against sophistication. She peered at Sari with an inexplicable intensity before her eyes cut away. Like Peggy's, they were the palest of grays. If she exchanged a single word with Sari that night, Sari couldn't remember it the next day.

Warren was the most difficult to read. He acknowledged Sari with a watchful superiority, an expression that implied she was not quite what she seemed, and subtly controlled all interactions. A glance at his wife sent Peggy to the refrigerator for his aperitif; she carried his wineglass to the sink when he was through. He seemed most attuned to Laura, who nodded understandingly when he complained the mild weather was keeping the elk at lower elevations, where too many amateurs were hunting. The only person who didn't defer to him was Tim; the distance between father and son made Sari wonder whether she was the source of tension.

"Chin up," Tim whispered, "you're doing fine..."

But it only got worse. Unbeknownst to Sari, Tim had taken his mother aside and told her Sari was a vegetarian. The first inkling of disaster was when she offered to help Peggy set the table.

"I apologize for the fried chicken, Sari, but it's Tim's favorite and I always fix it when he comes home. He says I'm the only one who makes it the way he likes." With a nervous smile, Peggy reached into the refrigerator for a butcher-wrapped package. "Tim says you're studying Italian, so Laura ran to the store for prosciutto. You do eat melon and prosciutto, don't you, dear?"

"I love it, Mrs. Scott."

"Good. We'll have it as an appetizer."

Hottentot or Rastafarian, anything would have been preferable to a Jewish vegetarian at 4990 South Cleveland that night. Having renounced meat in high school simply to drive her mother crazy, Sari would have eaten pork chops if they were offered, but her reassurance ignited something quite different in Peggy. She'd thought prosciutto was a kind of cheese, like provolone, and Sari didn't have the heart to warn her it was ham, but she must have realized her mistake because the appetizer platter appeared with cantaloupe and cubes of cheddar. Then she darted about the kitchen, whipping up meatless dishes. It was the last thing Sari expected; her mother would have made a good-natured crack about not running a restaurant and passed the guest a basket of bread.

Dinner began with Warren asking Tim about his classes. Without waiting for a response, he launched into a monologue on the conspiracy among *The New York Times, The Washington Post,* and East Coast forces that controlled the country's wealth. Firms like Goldman Sachs and Lehman Brothers. Each time he directed a rhetorical question at Sari, she opened her mouth to reply and he continued as if she weren't there. Her own father had used the dinner table to drill her and her brother on spelling and state capitals, but he *cared* about the answers...

"—only ones worse are the Texans," Warren was saying. "They're grabbing every piece of prime real estate in the mountains." He gestured at Sari with his fork. "You know what they're going to do? Fly their relatives up by the thousands until we're another Fort Worth." Sari nodded and Laura passed him the mashed potatoes. "Of course," he continued, "with all the bleeding-heart liberals and Bambi-loving backpackers at the University these days, what difference does it make?" Peggy presented him with the platter of fried chicken, and he described in excruciating detail how to dress a deer.

With each bowl of hastily prepared vegetables trundled out for Sari's benefit Peggy was more animated but remote, and Sari knew it would be an insult to take a piece of chicken. Warren going on and on about cash management and a study that proved only fifteen percent of financial success was due to technical knowledge and the rest attributable to "human engineering," Tim giving her knee a sympathetic squeeze under the table... It was exhausting to sit there and nod, but when she realized no one had the slightest interest in what she thought, she began to think she might get through this. Warren was planning to take a leadership course to double his earning power, and his voice softened only when he asked Laura to pass the peas... Then the boom dropped.

"Tim tells me your father has a small company back in New York."

Sari nodded, but this time he was expecting more.

"He's a printer," she added. Nothing fancy, Max would have said, it pays the bills.

"And he owns a brownstone in Brooklyn." Warren paused just long enough to add emphasis to his next words. "Business must be in your blood."

The only sound was the clank of the serving spoon against the bowl of potatoes as Peggy reached to clear it. Sari knew she was being baited, but she couldn't sit there and pretend not to understand.

"I've never known anyone who works as hard—" she began.

"What could be more American than having your own business?" Tim interrupted. Warren's fork stopped in midair, a finger to the wind. Should he let this treason pass? "Isn't that what you just did?" Tim continued.

"Nobody's really in business for himself anymore," Warren relented. "Big Brother's the silent partner. Peggy, where's that dessert?"

Tim's mother had made a Harvey Wallbanger cake from orange juice and banana-flavored liqueur, and she recited every ingredient breathlessly, as if in a race to get it all out. When they rose from the table, Peggy refused Sari's offer to help with the dishes. She could do them faster herself... The message was clear: Sari was as alien to them as they were to her.

Afterward she sat with Peggy on the couch in the den, poring over photo albums. The first documented the early years of Peggy's marriage to Warren, and Sari was surprised to see that although Tim's mother wore a veil and long white gown, the wedding party consisted of only a handful of people. Warren was stiff in an ill-fitting tuxedo but his bride glowed. What came next was the shock. An exhausted-looking Peggy stood on the stoop of a bungalow with two infants in her arms. From their lace caps Sari could tell they were girls. She glanced at Peggy and saw her staring at the photograph before quickly turning the page. Did Laura have a twin?

Every family event from then on was documented, from a wide-eyed Peggy caught unaware feeding infant girls at two weeks, one in her arms and the other beside her in a carrier with a bottle to her mouth, to year after year of homemade birthday cakes. Peggy turned the pages faster and faster, as if she couldn't wait to get through the album. She seemed to assume Sari knew who the other child was, and it was only when photos of Tim began to appear that she relaxed. The last picture of the girls showed them in a meadow of daffodils at age five, wearing frilly bonnets and matching Easter dresses. With a sigh of relief, Peggy started to close the book but a frayed sheet slipped to the floor. When Sari stooped to retrieve it three innocent faces met her eyes.

Even in a sketch these babies were enthralling. A light hand had been used with the pencil, short curls were captured with fine scribbles, and delicate shading evoked plump cheeks and limbs. The girls, perhaps three years of age, faced each other while looking protectively at the boy centered in the lower half of the page. The twins' features were the same but their personalities distinct, as if the artist had no difficulty penetrating tender flesh to identity, and the boy, two years younger, gazed up at them with the unbridled adoration Sari knew so well. The portrait was unsigned.

"This is fabulous!" Sari exclaimed impulsively.

Peggy took the drawing and silently tucked it in the binding.

"Who did it?"

"I did," Peggy replied.

She turned to the next album. Another sheet was wedged between pages of photos of Tim with Warren on a camping trip unfurling lines of wriggling trout, and Warren in a chef's hat grilling steaks. Peggy passed the drawing to Sari.

These children were in ink. Befitting their age, the lines were bolder, more impressionistic. Grinning sassily, Laura sprawled in Warren's lap with his arm at her waist, while her more proper sister, with feet crossed to display lace-edged anklets and gleaming Mary Janes, perched at the other end of the sofa. Tim sat securely in the second girl's lap, a chubby hand resting lightly on her clasped fingers.

"They're marvelous!" Sari cried. Peggy's eyes welled, and Sari's curiosity was swept away by compassion. How she must have loved them… "Are there more?"

"No." Peggy closed the album and replaced it on the shelf. Indifferent to praise, accepting that her gifts didn't matter. But if Sari couldn't ask what happened to her other child, she was unwilling to let Peggy's remarkable talent go.

"You're so artistic, why did you stop?"

"There was no time." She sounded old. "With children, everything changes…" Then Tim came in and the conversation was over.

"Why didn't you tell me Laura had a twin?" Sari asked on the way home.

Tim shrugged. "She died when she was six."

Maybe that explained Peggy's remoteness, the joyless way she tended to her family's needs. "What was her name?"

"Allison."

Sari waited for him to say more, but Tim was staring ahead at the road.

"What happened to her?" she asked.

"Something wrong with her heart."

"How awful! Was it sudden?"

"I really don't remember."

What right did she have to pry the lid off the Scotts' pain? No wonder they were so private.

"Laura likes you," Tim said, reading her mind. "It just takes time."

But Laura was in her own world and the Scotts' rejection seemed insurmountable. Sitting at Tim's desk now, eight months later, Sari felt the pain of that dinner as acutely as if it were yesterday.

Thank God it wasn't suicide. They'd never accept me then, she thought, and was promptly ashamed. What could be worse than being killed in your own garage by an intruder? Trying not to imagine Peggy's last moments on the other side of the wall, she cradled her head in her arms and fell asleep.

—

When the stillness was broken by the crunch of gravel in the driveway just before dawn, Sari's eyes flew open. At first she couldn't remember where she was. Looking up she saw a shadow creeping across the lawn... Front steps creaking, a jangle and metallic scrape—she flew to the bed and cried in Tim's ear, "Someone's in the house!"

He came instantly awake, pulled on his shorts, strode to the gun cabinet outside the door and reached for a rifle. Hesitating, he chose a shotgun instead. His eyes as impenetrable as beach glass, he loaded it, slipped off the safety, and started upstairs with Sari clinging to his waistband. At the first floor landing by the entrance to the kitchen they heard a step groan, and Tim peered around the bend. Fear and rage condensing in his naked back, he raised the shotgun and pointed it at the shadow slinking up the stairs.

"Stop!"

There was a sharp intake of breath; the figure froze.

"What are you doing in my house?" he shouted with his finger tensing on the trigger. "I'll blow your fucking head off, you son of a bitch!"

"Tim?" The voice was high-pitched with fear. "It's me! Laura!"

The upstairs light flashed on to reveal a crouched form hugging the banister. Glancing at Tim, Sari saw he and Laura wore identical expressions of shock. Pupils wide and staring, almost black. Riveted on each other.

The door at the head of the stairs swung open and Warren came out, dressed in the clothes he'd worn that afternoon.

"Put down that gun, Tim." He sounded annoyed. "You're scaring everyone."

As Laura slowly rose in sweater and jeans, the scent of smoke wafted down to Sari. More acrid than cigarettes, a stale odor her musky perfume could not conceal. Her eyes met Sari's. Defiance. Sari wondered whether she'd been with the guy she saw Laura with last winter. At the Laundromat, before finals ... But this time she sensed fear.

"I'm sorry," Laura said, "I didn't want to wake anyone."

"Where have you been?" Tim demanded. Shotgun lowered to his side, lips taut, dark eyes unreadable...Laura flinched at the accusatory tone but continued up the stairs.

"You really wouldn't want to know."

They all returned to bed, and Sari didn't sleep until the sky in the basement window lightened to a watery pink.

Chapter Seven

It was Simon Evans's policy not to see clients at home. This was as much in deference to his wife Edith as it was a prudent precaution in view of the nature of his clients' problems. A physically imposing man with fading hair and the face of a fatigued basset hound, he had spent twenty-five years defending criminals of every stripe that Sunday morning when Warren Scott came to see him.

Simon had cut his teeth on street crime, but his real prominence came from representing Black Panthers in the sixties and Tito Garcia and the Cry for Justice. There was no client he couldn't afford to refuse, and though he still represented some without a fee or at a significantly reduced rate, their cause had to be correspondingly compelling. The distance to Chauvenet Park from the coal mining town in Cornwall where he was born could be measured in more than miles, as he reminded himself every time he drove his vintage Jaguar up his tree-lined driveway.

Scott had phoned the night before and would have come then if Simon let him, but the only reason he agreed to see him at all was that he'd been referred by Hal Williams, a fellow member of the choir at Wesley United Methodist Church. Simon called Hal just before midnight on Saturday to find out how well he knew Warren Scott.

"Always nice to hear from you, Simon, even at this hour." Sensing restraint in his friend's voice, Simon inwardly sighed. If not for Hal, he would have sent Scott elsewhere when he called. "I met Warren at the Rotary Club."

"How well do you know him?"

"Well enough to refer him to the best criminal defense lawyer in this state."

"How *long* have you known him?" he persisted.

"Years, but to tell you the truth I really don't know much about him. We've gone hunting together a number of times and he's a good shot, the meticulous sort. Very patient with his son. He called me a couple of hours ago and said he needed the name of a good criminal lawyer, fast. Didn't say what his problem was, and I didn't ask." Williams hesitated. "If I had to guess, I'd say it's something to do with his taxes. He's not too fond of our government."

"I don't handle crime anymore, Hal, you know that. Not even protesters."

"But I hoped you'd make an exception for him. He sounded a bit desperate, like someone too numbed to cope…"

Scott showed up the next morning promptly at nine. Any questions Simon had about what sort of trouble his visitor was in were dispelled by the Sunday *Post,* which reported that a woman in Gillman by the name of Peggy Scott had been killed in her home by an intruder, precise cause of death to be determined. In cardigan and leather slippers, Simon had just finished his coffee and newspapers when the bell rang. Before he could rise, Edith answered and he heard them talking in the front hallway. When she led Scott to his den and left, discreetly closing the door behind her, Simon deposited the paper in the stack at his feet and slowly rose from his chair. Waving his visitor to the couch, he immediately began the process of sizing him up the same way he did potential jurors, equal parts calculation and intuition.

"Mr. Scott? Have a seat and tell me what brings you here."

Scott was in his mid to late forties and as intense and yet cold a fellow as Simon ever met. He'd long since stopped speculating about whether his clients did the things with which they were charged, and he didn't care. His job was to defend, not judge, and it only got in the way if a fellow spilled his guts before Simon showed him the police reports. There were two reasons for this. First, if he confessed Simon couldn't call him as a witness later, not if he knew he was going to lie on the stand. Criminal defense lawyers learn the cardinal rule early: If anyone ends up going to jail, let it be the client and not you. Second, and more important, Simon couldn't persuade a jury of his client's innocence if he knew the contrary was true. But Warren Scott was not about to pose either dilemma.

"My wife was killed yesterday."

"Have you been charged?"

"No, but I've been questioned. They always charge the husband, don't they?"

Damn, he was cold.

"Were there any witnesses to her death?"

"No."

He noted Scott didn't say "Not that I'm aware." At least the chap was honest.

"Where was she killed?"

"In our garage. She was hit in the head."

Easy, now…

But Simon had snatched many a victory from the jaws of defeat. Deciding to use Scott's gaffe to determine how quick on the uptake his guest was, he wrinkled his brow in confusion.

"Surely the autopsy hasn't been performed?"

"No." Warren's eyes searched Simon's, and he gave a small nod. "Of course not. We don't know how she died yet." Simon leaned forward in his seat. Time to stop shillyshallying. "Do you have an alibi?"

"I was with my son in Stanley."

"Then why are you concerned?"

"Wouldn't you be?"

"Perhaps, but I'm not in your situation. Did you and your wife get on well?"

"As well as you can after twenty-four years." As Scott's lips twisted into a smile that under other circumstances might have been pleasant, Simon decided he'd heard enough.

"Mr. Scott, if you are to be charged with anything it will be first degree murder. The death penalty is, regrettably, alive and well in our fair state. My fee is fifty thousand dollars, cash, for pretrial services. If the case goes the distance you will pay me another fifty thousand. In advance and nonrefundable."

Scott didn't question the amount. Insurance funds, no doubt. All he asked was, "How soon do you need it?"

When Simon ushered him out the front door, Edith came down the hall and joined him. Together they watched Scott climb into his Olds. As he drove off, Simon closed the door and turned to her.

"What did you think of him?" she asked.

"Distant. Unemotional. Not a touch of remorse or regret, and if that means he's either innocent or a sociopath, I'm neither God nor a psychiatrist. He was like anyone else in his position would be, concerned about saving his ass. We got along fine."

"Are you going to represent him?"

"If he can come up with the fee." Her lips tightened and he patted her hand. "If I had to like my clients in order to represent them, my dear, I wouldn't have lasted six months in this business. You know that."

"Well, it's fortunate you don't need to like him, Simon, because that man murdered his wife." She turned and walked into the kitchen. "I'm certain of it."

Simon heaved a sigh of resignation. Edith's instincts about people were infallible.

—

Ray learned the D.A. had assigned the case to Taylor Philips when Philips called him at home Sunday morning and summoned him for a personal report. Ray refused to come to the phone. Marion had to take the message.

"Who does he think he is, the Attorney General of the United States? It's Sunday morning!"

"He was very polite."

"You think everyone's polite, Marion, that's one of your problems." Ray bit his tongue. He had no business flaring up at his wife like that. In a softer tone he continued. "If the world was anything like you imagine it, I'd be out of a job."

"You're making this worse than it is, Ray. Quit complaining and get dressed."

"What's the matter with what I'm wearing? He calls me on a Sunday, he gets what he asked for. No more, no less."

But he slipped on his bolo tie and polyester sport coat. A good cop was always on the job; he didn't need his wife to remind him of that.

As he drove to Ponderosa Hills, Ray wondered how an assistant district attorney five years out of law school could afford a quarter-of-a-million-dollar house. Could he be on the take? Then he remembered Philips married into it; his debutante wife was the daughter of a senior partner at one of the fancy downtown firms. Word was Philips was just serving time in the D.A.'s office, cutting his teeth in the courtroom before joining her daddy's shop. Couple years there, then maybe a run for Congress. Sky's the limit after that. Of course he was the D.A.'s fair-haired boy; it never hurt to have supporters with connections and cash when November rolled around.

Coasting up the circular drive, he noted with satisfaction that his New Yorker was far better maintained than the dusty black Porsche parked at Philips's door. Ray's own father had spent a lifetime working for the railroad, more often drunk than sober, but that didn't—He hid his surprise when Philips himself answered the door. What, the maid's day off?

"Glad you could make it, Lieutenant. I couldn't wait until Monday to be briefed, and it's so much more effective face-to-face." Philips smiled affably, but Ray caught the glance at the Rolex on his tanned wrist. Gift from the wife? "Can I get you something to drink, an iced tea?"

A beer would've been more like it. It was another scorcher.

They walked through a marble hallway past a curved staircase with an Oriental runner, into a spacious living room with a wall of glass overlooking a thirty-foot pool. A matched set of rug rats splashed at the shallow end as a looker in a two-piece bathing suit floated on a rubber raft. Must be Missus Moneybags. Philips led him to an overstuffed chair facing away from the window and settled on the opposite couch. A gilded mirror hung directly behind Ray's head.

"So what kind of a case do we have, Lieutenant, any suspects yet?"

"It's a little soon, Mr. Philips."

"That's crap and you know it. If we don't have a suspect in the first twenty-four hours, the chance of an arrest decreases fifty percent. If we don't have one in three days, we can kiss a successful prosecution good-bye." Philips smiled tightly and Ray considered suggesting an enema. "—want an arrest and I want it fast."

Fifty percent, Ray's sweet ass. What operational manual did he pull that mumbo-jumbo from? Philips glanced up and to the left, and Ray resisted the impulse to look behind him.

"That's an interesting statistic, Mr. Philips, but I can't produce a suspect out of thin air." As the assistant D.A. rearranged his face into a smile that said I'm a team player and I know you are too, Ray wished Lew Devine were there to cover his tail. But Philips backpedaled an inch.

"What do you have so far?"

"A forty-three-year-old woman with no apparent enemies was killed in her garage late yesterday morning or early afternoon. Loot from the house was strewn where she was hit. It looks, at least on the surface, like she surprised a burglar in the middle of the job."

"On the *surface?*" The D.A.'s voice cracked with dismay.

So he'd thought it would be a slam-dunk, maybe even the case he'd retire on... Ray knew hot-dog D.A.'s were more dangerous than bad cops. The balance of power had shifted, and he ran with it.

"There's some awfully strange things about the setup. First off, it's the wrong kind of neighborhood. Burglars target expensive homes, they don't waste time on places like 4990 South Cleveland." He avoided looking at the china figurines on the marble mantel. The furniture in this room alone cost more than either Burt or Scott would earn in a lifetime, but why remind Philips of that? "Neighborhood's one step up from starter homes. Families who live there can't be making more than thirty grand a year, thirty-five tops, and that's with Mom and Pop both working."

"So he was desperate, maybe a junkie..."

Ray shook his head. "Most he'd get would be a color TV, some silverware if he was lucky. Only thing he could count on would be Scott's gun collection which, by the way, was untouched. And he owns expensive guns. None of that Japanese junk. A gold watch and some other stuff was left behind too." As Philips's eyes darted past Ray's shoulder again, Ray wondered what the hell he was checking out. The swimming pool? "Burglars are lazy cowards, but they're not stupid. They do as little work as they have to, and they never mine dry holes."

"What else?"

"Forty-nine ninety South Cleveland's on the corner of a high-traffic intersection. Grand Avenue, especially on a weekend, is one of the busiest streets in the west end of the county. That house is completely exposed, no foliage or landscaping, and there's no way out the back either, because there's no alley and the yard butts right up to the neighbors at 4985 South Knox. There's a fence, but have you ever tried scaling grape-stake? And the timing's all wrong."

"What do you mean?" Philips had tented his fingers under his chin in an effort to look engaged, but he was having a difficult time concealing his frustration. Ray's spirits soared.

"A Saturday morning in May, in a neighborhood like that? C'mon. Everybody and his sister's gonna be outside. On weekends folks can't afford to do anything else. They'll be washing their cars, mowing the lawn, hanging laundry, standing around shooting the breeze. No burglar casing a joint is gonna pick a place where he'd have to trip over people on his way in and out."

"So who do you think did it?"

"Maybe the husband, maybe not. Depends on alibi and motive. Neither of which we've had a chance to look at yet." Ray paused. He had to give the poor slob some hope. "The coroner hasn't even said how she was killed or when, but we have a pretty good lead on the time…"

Philips lunged like a dog at a scrap of steak. "And?"

"Peggy Scott was wearing a watch on her right wrist. The crystal smashed when she lifted her arm to protect herself and the hands stopped at ten-oh-two. We don't know yet whether the blow caused the watch to stop or blood seeped into the mechanism after she was killed. For all we know, it could've been running slow or even stopped beforehand. So we're having it analyzed."

"Where was the husband?" Philips' eyes had shifted again, and Ray itched to look.

"We don't know."

"Well, lean on him, then. Lean on him hard." As Philips stood he squared his shoulders, and Ray noticed for the first time that he was two inches shorter in his loafers than the wing tips he wore at the office. Did Eliot Ness need lifts? "I want a confession!"

"One that'll stick?" Unable to resist any longer, Ray turned and caught Philips gazing in the mirror behind Ray's head. The bastard was all face, no talent, and vain to boot, and he couldn't wait to tell Lew… He ducked his chin before Philips caught him looking, and the D.A.'s eyes jumped to the swimming pool.

"Do you think I want to make a fool out of myself with a case that gets thrown out?"

Fool of himself?

Philips's three-year-old dachshund probably beat him at poker. He needed Ray more than Ray needed him, and they both knew it. Worse, Philips knew that Ray knew, but it was time to cut the crap. If Ray didn't solve this case Philips would shove it up his ass.

"Look, Mr. Philips, Warren Scott isn't some street punk who can't keep his mouth shut. He's probably talking to a lawyer right now. They'll give us one formal interview and then tell us to suck eggs. I can't waste our only chance before we even know for sure what time his old lady got whacked, much less *how.* "

"I thought she was shot in the face…"

"That was an assumption the first officer on the scene made based on the damage to her head. The coroner's doing the autopsy today, and we need to analyze the blood spatters. Whoever did it took the weapon with him."

Chapter Eight

When Sari awoke Sunday morning Tim was gone. Still wearing her clothes from the day before, she went upstairs, feeling like a thief as she crept past the icons in the front hall. At the entrance to the dining room she stopped. The window was open and the drapes fluttered softly. Summer drifted in through the screen and across the street a lawn mower droned, but the Scott house was as antiseptic and self-contained as a vault. Outside she could breathe…

"Going somewhere?"

She turned and saw Tim's father. How long had he been watching her?

"I was looking for Tim."

"I'm afraid it's just you and me."

As Warren took a step closer his smile broadened, and Sari realized he was enjoying her discomfort. His neatly combed hair and the tan strip of adhesive on his forehead made her shorts and Tim's Gillman High T-shirt feel even more rumpled. The hallway was suddenly stifling.

"Where did everyone go?" she asked.

"Laura and Tim went to the Sinclair to pick up Peggy's car. They didn't want to wake you."

"When will they be back?"

"I've wanted an opportunity to chat."

What did they need to chat about?

The door was directly behind her, but it might as well have been bolted and chained. Straightening, she stepped past Tim's father to the kitchen. He followed two steps behind her. At least she'd have room to turn...

Laura must have risen early because the counters were scrubbed and the linoleum waxed, ridding them of the scuff marks and fingerprint soot that branded the house an official crime scene. As Sari drew a glass from the cupboard above the stove and filled it with water from the tap, she turned and saw Warren leaning against the breakfast table with his arms crossed. Five minutes, that's what it would take for Tim to get back. Her eye fell on the stainless steel coffeepot on the counter, and the words were out of her mouth before she could stop them.

"Would you like a cup of coffee?"

"That would be nice."

Now she was in for it. Her mother wasn't fit to speak to until her third cup, but why hadn't she paid more attention on any of the thousands of occasions when she'd waited for Helen to jump-start her day?

As she carefully removed the lid from the pot, she felt Warren's eyes between her shoulder blades. He could hardly expect her to carry on an intelligent conversation while she was busy fixing coffee, could he? In the reflection in the shiny metal surface she caught his movement. He'd left the table and was at the counter by the refrigerator. If Peggy had a jar of instant, she could just add water. Or maybe they were out of coffee altogether...

"Second shelf," he said, "on the right." Was that amusement in his voice?

Reaching up, Sari was greeted by the familiar blue Maxwell House can. Thank God it was a brand she recognized. She turned on the hot water full blast and filled the pot to the brim before covering it, trying to picture what her mother would do next.

How long could it take to pick up a car?

"Aren't you going to put the grounds in the basket?" he asked.

Suddenly nothing was more important than proving to Warren Scott she could make a goddamn cup of coffee.

"It holds them better when they're wet, that's what my mother says." As if her mother were an idiot. "We do things differently back east."

"So I've heard."

Pulling the stem and basket from the pot, Sari dug in the aromatic grains for the white plastic scoop. Grounds go *in* the basket, that much she knew. "This whole thing must be awful for you," she said to distract him.

"Some things happen for the best."

With her back to him, she turned the can and peered at the directions. One scoop for every two cups, but how much water did the pot hold? Six scoops should be enough. "We have to make the best of it, you mean."

"Exactly. That's why we need to talk."

Had she missed something? As she tried to remember the last thing Tim's father said, she knocked the scoop against the side of the pot: ground coffee scattered all over the spotless linoleum. Hands shaking, Sari wet a sponge and bent to wipe the floor. Warren was too quiet. *Where was he standing?*

"You know," he continued from the counter by the stove, "I came by your apartment before I went to the rec center yesterday morning."

It must have been while she was at the library.

"When was that?" She took her time wiping the linoleum.

"Oh, around twelve-thirty. I knocked," he said, "but there was no answer. I waited a few minutes, then left. I guess you were in the shower."

She turned and found herself face-to-face with him.

"I thought you went to McBride's."

"You were mistaken." His smile thinned. "Didn't you tell me you took a shower right before you came to the rec center? Maybe you didn't hear because the water was running." It could have happened that way, she thought as she clamped the lid on the pot. She'd come home from the library late, jumped in the shower and left immediately afterward. Maybe he knocked and she didn't hear... She stared at the glass knob, willing amber liquid to spurt in the bubble.

"You did say you showered, didn't you, Sari?" She turned. Warren's breath was warm on her face, and she wanted to run from the kitchen, down the hallway, out the door... Tearing her eyes from his, she stared once again at the pot. *Where the hell was Tim?*

"Good," Warren said as if she'd answered. "We needed to get that straight."

"Well, look who finally woke up!" Tim said. Turning as one, they saw him with Laura in the doorway. Laura looked tired but scrubbed, and there was no sign of the cowering creature who'd slunk up the stairs the night before. Right behind them stood their aunt Kay. As Tim glanced from Sari to Warren his relief was replaced by uncertainty. "The Cadillac's in the driveway, Dad."

Now that it no longer mattered, the coffee was percolating furiously and Sari began searching the cupboards for mugs. She had to get Tim alone, to tell him what his father said. Was that what they were arguing about on the lawn yesterday?

Kay Butler marched into the kitchen with a cardboard bakery box in one hand and an enormous straw purse in the other. She was Peggy's oldest sister and Tim's favorite relative, and Sari was so relieved to see her she could have kissed her. They'd met twice, first at a hockey game where Kay showed up to cheer Tim on, and then at a party she gave that spring to celebrate her son's birthday.

Kay's broad shoulders and regal posture, glossy brown hair, keen eyes and freckled skin exuded a competence and vitality that stood in stark contrast to her younger sister's pale fragility. But the plain truth was it was impossible to imagine Kay at a loss. Whether running the personnel department at the company where she worked or shepherding her own children through the daily crises of their lives, she was the type who always knew what to say and do. Despite the nine-year difference in their ages the sisters lived within minutes of each other, and Tim had told Sari they'd never spent a birthday or holiday apart.

Now Kay dropped the box of pastries on the kitchen table and held out her arms to Tim. As he clung to her, Laura hung back, but Sari saw her meet her aunt's gaze with the same defiance she'd shown the night before. Kay nodded stiffly but her lower lip trembled. Releasing Tim, she marched to the cupboard on the right side of the sink for cups and set them on the table. Then she began to pour coffee, sniffing curiously at the black brew but making no comment. When they were all seated she addressed Warren for the first time.

"I know how difficult this must be for you."

"Thanks." There was an ironic edge to his tone, and Sari tried to remember why he hadn't attended the party for Kay's son. Had Peggy said he was working? "It's nice to know you and Bud are there if we need you."

"Speaking of help, Liddie and Myra are making arrangements for the funeral because it's too much for Mother to handle. She's gone to pieces."

"I appreciate your sisters' offer, but I can handle it myself."

Kay glanced at Sari and set down her cup.

"We'll bring her home to Walker County, of course."

"Aren't there enough Dannhauers buried at St. Augustine's?" Warren replied.

Kay's jaw tightened. "Mother will want—"

"Maybe that's why Peggy left."

Laura pushed back her chair and carried her cup to the sink. She dumped the remains of her coffee down the drain and turned on the water full blast.

Kay raised her voice to be heard. "Peggy would have wanted—"

"I think I knew my wife better than you did."

The color leached from Kay's face, setting off her freckles like spatters of rust-colored paint. Rising unsteadily, she turned to Tim. "I'm here whenever you need me, dear. Anytime, day or night." Retrieving her purse, she kissed his cheek. "Call me as soon as you get back to Stanley, hear?" Before anyone could say another word, she looked at Sari. "Walk me to the car," she said in her best take-charge voice.

She followed Tim's aunt down the front hall. Kay was moving so quickly they were almost trotting as they reached her station wagon.

"What did he want from you?" Kay demanded.

"Who?"

"Warren. When I walked in, you were white as a sheet."

"Nothing. He just… I'm not really sure what he wanted."

Kay nodded once.

"I may not have been able to protect Peggy while she was alive, but I'll be damned if—" She caught herself. "You take care of Tim," she said as she slid behind the wheel of the Chevrolet. She turned the key in the ignition, the color now high on her cheeks. "He's going to need you more than ever."

"I don't think it's really hit him yet."

Kay looked straight at her then, and Sari saw the tears in her eyes sprang from anger rather than pain. "Pray it never does."

"What should I—" she began, but Kay's automatic windows were already rolling shut and the car was gliding from the curb.

—

"Why do you think Kay wants you to call her?" Sari asked Tim later that afternoon.

"She likes you, she told me." Traffic on the highway heading north was light, but Tim kept his eyes on the asphalt. They were on their way back to Stanley. He'd wanted to spend another night in Gillman but the walls were pressing in on Sari, every word not spoken rang in her ears. The undercurrents in the Scott family were too swift and deep to fathom, and she couldn't bear the thought of Tim, too, becoming a stranger.

"She thinks you know something," Sari replied.

He dropped his right hand to her knee. "And your mother says *you're* the one with the imagination…"

"Maybe we should postpone the wedding."

His hand jerked. "Not get married?"

"That's not what I said. But maybe now's not the time."

"My mother was attacked by a burglar in her garage, Sari, that's what happened. Nothing my crazy aunt says means a goddamned thing!

I don't want you talking to her."

"But she's your—"

"Did you see the way she lit into Dad? He needs us now." Downtown Widmark sailed past, a skyline so compact it could fit in the palm of her hand. They passed under a viaduct leading to the old meat and vegetable markets. This area was a slum, too impoverished to interest even the most resolute of Warren's do-gooders. I can leave this alone, Sari thought, stop before I go too far... But there were supposed to be no secrets.

"Speaking of your father," she said, "I had the strangest conversation with him today."

"When?"

"While you were gone."

Tim's hands tightened on the wheel, and Sari looked away. On the bluff to the west perched an old Italian neighborhood that was rapidly turning Hispanic. She had the strangest urge to laugh. *Pagliacci's*, she thought as an unlit neon clown beckoned from the roof of a restaurant. Maybe Peggy asked the wrong guy for prosciutto...

"About what?" Tim pressed.

"He says he came to our apartment first and not McBride's, but I cut my heel on that yardstick in his car." Warren could have been right about the shower, it would only make it worse to raise that now. "Don't you remember?"

"That yardstick must have been in his car for weeks."

"He said they just started giving them out."

"Are you calling my dad a liar?"

"Of course not!" But wasn't she? "I'm just trying to figure out—"

"Do you have to analyze everything to death?"

"Okay, forget it." The Mustang slowed and Sari realized they'd been passing every car on the road. She reached for Tim's hand, but it was still clenched on the wheel. "I'm already an outsider, Tim, I don't want to make things worse. Not now."

"That's exactly why we should get married." He switched to the left lane without signaling, and a horn bleated as the car behind them swerved. "Christmastime with your folks was the best I ever had. Do you know what it's like to walk into a stranger's home and be welcomed with open arms, to be asked questions and know someone *cares* about the answers? I can talk to your dad, Sari, he listens to what I say. And your mom treated me like her own son..."

They had driven to New York nonstop, with Tim at the wheel through a blizzard in the high plains, sleet in Indiana and Illinois, more snow in Pennsylvania, and on the final leg the staggering beauty of the Delaware Water Gap at dawn, cliffs jutting from the mist like a primeval fortress. A hundred miles from home, Sari called her parents to tell them where they were. She got into an argument with her mother over something so inconsequential she couldn't even remember, a product of Helen's hypersensitivity or her own fatigue, and begged Tim to turn around and drive back. But they pressed on and emerged on the other side of the Lincoln Tunnel at midnight, two days before Christmas. At the first stoplight outside the tunnel boys wielding squeegees assaulted their windshield, banging on the hood and demanding dollar bills. When a transvestite in a towering wig at Times Square asked Tim if he wanted a date, he hung on to the steering wheel for dear life.

As they crossed the Brooklyn Bridge to the narrow tree-lined streets of her childhood, Sari felt the elation and apprehension that always accompanied trips home. Helen opened the door, gazed at her with longing and disappointment before swooping down to envelop her in a fierce embrace, and turned to Tim. After a brief hug, he trundled upstairs to a guest room on the third floor. There he slept for most of the following day while she and her mother had their usual spats, escalating to shouting and door slamming on Sari's part, angry tears and vows to leave at once.

Tim was an ideal houseguest, grateful for whatever Helen served and quick to help with the dishes. But Sari knew even then that her mother was uncomfortable around him. Helen was used to looking in someone's eyes and being able to tell how he felt, and she couldn't do that with Tim. Her father took him on a tour of Brooklyn Heights and the Lower East Side, in his element recounting the history of each neighborhood. But if Sari was fooled at all it wasn't for long. In one of Max's letters to her that spring he referred to Tim twice, misspelling his name first as "Tom" and later as "Tin." These might have been easy slips if her father hadn't spent his life in the printing trade, setting type from the time he could read. And with Helen, things were never what they seemed....

"Of course they love you," Sari reassured him. Tim liked her mother, and when she'd told him Helen was flying out later in the week, he'd seemed relieved. "But they're complicated people, they have problems like any other family."

"I thought you were on my side."

"That's not—"

"What happened to my mother has nothing to do with us." She stared out the window, at a loss for words. "It's an easy call, Sari, you're either with me or you're not."

"What was it like, growing up?" she finally replied.

"You know, you saw…"

Tim didn't like to talk about his family. Naturally she'd been curious, especially about Allison, but after that first dinner in Gillman he'd deflected her questions. What's important is the future, he said, the family *we* create.

"I mean when you were little."

"Mom stayed home and baked, and my sisters were always the best-dressed girls because she sewed their clothes." So there *were* some things he remembered. Tim's lids drooped and she realized with a pang how exhausted he must be. "Just like the Cleavers, except maybe quiet time…"

"Quiet time?"

"After Allison died Mom would go to her room to rest, and we had to go to ours and close the door. She made us whisper and we couldn't play games or go outside till quiet time was over. And Dad made me skate."

"How could he *make* you skate?"

"From the time I was five, he'd pile me in the car and drop me at the neighborhood rink every morning before school."

"What about Laura?"

"He never made Laura do anything she didn't want to do." Tim's laugh was so unlike the carefree sound that came from deep inside his chest. This one was tight, guarded. Would she ever hear the other again? "As soon as I was old enough I had to compete. By my senior year at Gillman High the sight of a rink made me sick."

"But you were captain of the team, they won the state—"

"—championship, but that was in spite of me, not because of me. My timing was off, I was tensing up, but Dad didn't care. After all, a win's a win." Tim sounded more resigned than bitter, and she wondered how Peggy felt about forcing her son to pursue a sport he hated. "That's why I didn't go out for the college team. It wasn't until I started coaching and joined the Wings that I could enjoy hockey again."

"Tell me more about quiet time," she pressed. "It sounds a little weird."

"I went looking for my mother once, I couldn't have been older than five. The shades in her room were drawn and it was so dark I could barely see. She was lying on the bed with a cloth over her eyes, and I said, 'Mom?' but she didn't answer and it scared me so much I ran back to my room and never looked for her again. I never told anyone."

"Where was Laura?"

Tim massaged his lids. "Her own room, I guess. It was a big house." He shrugged, but the gesture seemed as artificial as his laugh. "After quiet time was over, Mom would come out and we'd help her fix dinner, but we still couldn't make any noise."

"Where was your father?"

"Sometimes home, sometimes—"

"Was she depressed because of Allison?"

He shrugged. "There were long periods when she wasn't even around."

"Where was she?"

"Dad said she was visiting her mother." He frowned, as if the memory were painful. "But it wasn't always that way. Other times she took us to the reservoir and we'd march up and down the path, gathering stones and tossing them in, and she bought ice cream to keep us going. Same way at the mall; she made Laura try on everything, and if she liked the way a dress looked on her she had the clerk bring it in every color until finally she got tired of it, pulled out her checkbook and bought them all. And on to the next..."

"I thought your mother made Laura's clothes."

"Look, I'm not saying it makes sense. Maybe Mom was bored. But she was in such a good mood those days, she'd cook dishes that needed lots of chopping and stirring, and we could rattle pots and pans to our hearts' content. She laughed and joked with Dad and it was a hell of a lot better than quiet time."

"Did you ever wonder what was wrong?"

"She was just moody."

"But she was so artistic. I saw the drawings of you and your sisters..."

"Can't we talk about something else?" Tim was slowing for the speed trap at Garfield, and she searched for a safe way to keep the topic alive.

"It's hard to believe Laura had a twin."

"When they were infants, they looked so much alike Mom used colored barrettes so strangers wouldn't confuse them. But she and Dad could always tell them apart. They wore the same outfits and had their hair cut the same way, but Allison was Mom's favorite."

"How could you tell?"

"They were always together."

"What about Laura?"

He shrugged. "Different personality, I guess. She went places with Dad."

As they approached the scenic overlook just east of Stanley with its dramatic view of the foothills, Sari's thoughts returned to Saturday.

"I was surprised to see your dad at the rec center."

"Yeah."

"After we got to the house, I saw you talking to him on the lawn."

"I'm not getting into that." He reached for the radio and twisted the dial until rock music blared. "We're almost home. Can't we leave it behind for one night?"

"But—"

At the plea in Tim's eyes, Sari stopped. A kaleidoscope of impressions swirled, words and images that shifted too swiftly to register. But now was the time for loyalty. That was what Tim needed, not doubts. So they made love that night in the apartment on Locust and spoke no more of the wedding or his mother's murder.

Chapter Nine

It never hurt to return after the husbands left for work, Lew Devine reminded himself. He'd canvassed the Scotts' neighborhood on Sunday and now the real work would begin. Few cops had the stamina or skill to interview the ladies, but Lew knew women were no different from horses. The trick was letting them come to you, because once they thought *they* were in control they'd give you anything you wanted.

Lew was well aware of his physical appeal. His black hair was flecked with silver, not salt-and-pepper but enough to show he'd been around, and his high forehead suggested a sensitivity that was an intriguing contrast to his rangy build and rugged features. He'd been lonely since his wife Cindy moved out six months before, some crap about needing to communicate, if that wasn't the dumbest thing he'd ever heard. If she wanted to communicate, leaving was a great way to start. And she'd constantly ragged him about his friendship with Ray, called him a throwback. To what? Lew wanted to know. That always stopped her short.

Despite their twenty-year age difference, both partners had come to police work through the military. Ray liked to say his academy was Korea; for Lew, it was Vietnam. They enjoyed beer and baseball, John Wayne and Glen Campbell, and had no use for football, golf, or sports bars. And they made a helluva team on the job. Ray loved footwork but distrusted technology, so-called profiling and trace analysis, the cornerstones of modern criminology. He instinctively focused on the human side of a case and his greatest asset was his ability to gain the confidence of strangers. Like the softer sex, he wanted to know why.

Lew handled the physical evidence because he had better rapport with the police technicians than Ray did. Which meant he had at least some rapport, a level of civility Ray found difficult when dealing with any of the modern breed of cop. His only other friends were a group of flatfoots just this side of retirement who Ray trotted out at his annual dog and pony show for the Gillman Rotary Club, where he pretended to tout the gadgets overgrown boys found so engaging. Much as Ray enjoyed the attention, Lew was the one in whom he confided how out of his depth he really felt.

When they teamed up Ray assigned Lew the peripheral witnesses, often women. Though Lew jokingly complained he never got to interview anyone important, they both knew he could get things out of a woman Ray never knew were there. But the real difference between them was Lew was going somewhere on the force and Ray had topped out at lieutenant. His clashes with the brass in the D.A.'s office had earned him a reputation of being impossible to work with, and although Lew warned him patience was wearing thin Ray seemed incapable of reversing his course.

Lew parked at the end of the Scotts' block and made quick notes of his conversation with the owner of Gillman Sinclair, who'd been servicing Peggy's Caddy since Warren bought it used a couple of months earlier. The convertible was in mint condition and had been brought in that Saturday for a lube job and oil change. Not having done the work himself, all the owner could say was Scott's son and daughter retrieved the car Sunday morning. Jotting a reminder to return when the mechanic who serviced the Caddy was back on duty, Lew flipped through the last five pages of his notebook.

He'd run into nothing but blank walls on Sunday, but he just wasn't buying that nobody saw or heard a thing because housewives were always minding each other's business. As he reviewed his notes he put faces to names with the help of certain characteristics recorded in a private shorthand that was no one's business but his own. Then he perched his SWAT cap on his head, clipped his handcuffs to his belt and fastened his holster, and five minutes later was seated on the patio in the backyard of 4985 South Cleveland with a tall glass of iced coffee the only thing between him and the woman of the house.

The Picuccis had lived across the street from the Scotts for four years. Gene Picucci told Devine on Sunday he'd never seen an emotional outburst from Scott, whom he described as an avid hunter with a big collection of guns. When Picucci knocked on Scott's door late Saturday to offer condolences Scott acted like nothing was wrong, but then again, maybe he was in shock. He'd said Peggy was friendly but didn't come on too strong. A lady.

"Mrs. Picucci—"

"Angela."

"Angela. When I talked to you and your husband yesterday, I forgot to ask a couple of questions. Do you mind if we go back to where you were Saturday morning?"

She crossed her legs. Not long, but nice. A matter of decoding signals, Lew reminded himself, and not moving so fast they got spooked.

"Sergeant Devine—"

"Lew."

"Lew." Those big brown eyes zeroed in on his handcuffs and traveled up his tanned biceps. Polo shirts were made for weight lifters, and Lew gripped his glass so his forearm tensed as she laid her hand palm down on the table and leaned forward. "I turned the sprinkler on around eight and put in a load of laundry, then I did the breakfast dishes and went back outside to move the hose. Gene was running errands."

"Did you see anyone enter or leave the Scotts' house?"

"Just Warren in his wife's Cadillac with his daughter following in her Barracuda."

"What time was that?"

"Around nine, maybe a little later. Then I went back inside."

"What'd you do after that?"

She thought. "Hung up the clothes."

"In the backyard?"

"Yes. I turned off the sprinkler and planted zinnias by the front door. I gardened for at least an hour."

Lew believed her. The Picuccis' flower beds were weeded and the grass freshly mowed. "What time do you think you started?"

"Oh, a little before ten." She uncrossed her legs and extended the left so her toes were almost touching his cowboy boots. The nails were painted crimson. He sipped his coffee and smiled.

"Did you see or hear anything unusual?"

"No, just that woman standing at the Scotts' front door." *Bingo.*

"What woman?"

"Didn't I tell you yesterday? You asked if I saw anything strange, and she looked perfectly ordinary, so I wasn't thinking about her. I hope I haven't done anything wrong…"

Lew bit his tongue and broadened his smile. "Of course not, Angela, you've been very helpful. What did she look like?"

"Oh, mid-forties. She was wearing peach-colored shorts with a belt and a matching sleeveless blouse and she had something tucked under her arm. It could've been a purse, but I don't think so."

"What was she doing?"

"Ringing the bell. And I saw her look at her watch, like she was in a hurry."

"Anyone answer the door?"

"When I went back inside she was still waiting."

"Any strange cars on the block Saturday?"

"Not really. A blue pickup with wood panels was parked down the street for a while, and there may have been a man in the front seat. It was there early, when I turned on the sprinkler. A pretty color blue."

"Was it there later, when the woman came to the door?"

"I didn't notice."

"When you say wood panels, do you mean on the side of the truck?"

"No, it was more like slats coming up from the bed, along the sides."

Lew jotted a note. "How far up?"

"Oh, about eight feet."

"From the ground?"

"The back of the truck."

Right. Capping his pen, he switched gears.

"How well did you know the Scotts?"

"Like Gene said yesterday, we knew him better than her. At least we saw him more often."

"What about Mrs. Scott?"

"We hardly ever spoke. If I didn't know she worked I'd have thought she was an invalid. But some people are that way. Not friendly." As she drained her glass her velvet eyes caressed Lew's, and he knew he could have her eating right out of his hand. Gene wouldn't be back at least until lunch, and . . . "—think I need protection, Detective?"

Lew hesitated, marveling at the power of unspoken communication. Then he considered what he'd already learned and how many other doors he needed to knock on that morning. Not much there, he reluctantly decided, but the woman in peach-colored shorts. And potential trouble. Nice legs ain't worth it. He thanked Angela Picucci and made his getaway before he changed his mind.

His next stop was the Coopers at 4985 South Knox, the house directly behind 4990 South Cleveland. They'd been neighbors since the Scotts moved in a few years back but didn't socialize. The wife was home all day Saturday, watered the backyard around ten and hung three loads of wash before noon. During that time she heard a loud noise from the Scotts' house, as if something fell.

Unsuccessful at pinpointing the time of the crash, Lew declined an offer of tea. The interview and those that followed yielded nothing new but confirmed his impression that the Scotts' neighbors were good folks, observant and honest. If strangers invaded the sanctity of 4990 South Cleveland that Saturday, they would have known. As he drove up the block a final time, he scanned for signs of construction but saw none. What else would a pickup truck be doing in this neighborhood?

Glancing at his watch he considered returning to the Picuccis', but it was uncomfortably close to the husband's lunch hour. As he headed back to the office, he was cheered by the thought that maybe the autopsy results were in.

—

When Devine returned, Ray had just finished the coroner's report and was reviewing photos of the crime scene. Now that they finally had a time and cause of death to work with, Philips had been calling every five minutes to ask when they planned to haul Scott in for questioning.

Handing Lew the blow-up of Peggy's watch, Ray pulled out his pocket knife to mine the grooves under his nails. "I took it to Friedrick's to see if he could tell whether it stopped running from the blow to her wrist."

"That hole in the wall at the Gillman Mall?" Lew replied. "Why didn't you send the watch to Kevin Day at the SBI?"

"So I could get back a useless bunch of crap? At least Fritz Smelnic gives a straight answer." Gouging the bed of his thumbnail, Ray winced. "The State Bureau of Investigation's nothing but a bunch of high-priced shirts trying to make us locals look like morons. If ifs and buts was candy and nuts, we'd all have a Merry Christmas."

"You're a dinosaur, Ray, a friggin' dinosaur. This is just the kind of thing that landed you in trouble before."

"Smelnic knows a helluva lot more about watches than any of those bums at the SBI."

"How many times has *Friedrick* testified in court? When Philips finds out, you'd better duck." Lew tossed the photo onto the desk. "What's the morgue say?"

"Peggy died before noon. Numerous blows to the head with a blunt instrument."

"There was nothing like that at the scene, just a broken piece of plywood."

"She was hit with a hammer on the left side of her forehead below the hairline. There's a one-and-a-half inch dent in her skull, discoloration and a contusion in the shape of a circle." He folded his knife and handed Lew another blow-up. "See?"

"They say what kind of hammer it was?"

"Christ, Lew, a hammer's a hammer." He planted his elbows on his desk. "The day the SBI can identify the one that killed Peggy Scott, I might start taking them seriously."

"What about her other injuries?"

"Repeated blows with the weapon. The guy kept swinging even as she was going down. With each hit the blood splattered behind his back onto the walls and garage door."

"What cut her face?"

"The lacerations on the bridge of her nose came from the claw end of the hammer."

Lew grimaced. "Nasty."

"Yeah." Ray slid the photos back in the folder and slumped in his chair. "He may have whacked her with the board, too. We didn't spot it while she was in the garage because her hair was soaked with blood, but they picked a sliver of laminated plywood off her scalp at the morgue. I asked the SBI if the pieces matched." He laughed mirthlessly. "Ten bucks says we'll never get a straight yes or no. You get lucky today?"

"Woman came to the Scotts' door around ten that morning."

"Yeah?" Ray sat up straight. "Who?"

"Don't know, the lady across the street just remembered. Along with a wood-paneled pickup truck parked down the block, no year or make. But it was a *pretty* shade of blue." Lew rolled his eyes. "She said the side panels were eight feet high."

"From the bed of the truck?" Lew nodded and Ray sighed. Women were notoriously unreliable when it came to heights and distances. He remembered one who swore the man who'd assaulted her was seven feet tall, and the fun the perp's lawyer had with that. "Get a decent description of the woman at the door?"

"Middle-aged broad in peach-colored shorts. Ten to one it was the postman."

"I doubt it. When it comes to other broads, they're usually right on the money. You better go back and find out if anyone else noticed her. It bothers me no one saw anything strange."

"I know." Lew reached for his notebook. "Want me to look into that truck?"

"What would a burglar have done, park his pickup half a block away and carry TV sets down the street in broad daylight? Gimme a break. And you know how many wood-paneled pickups there must be in Gillman, let alone the Widmark metro area? I don't care how pretty the color was."

"Yeah, without a plate it's damn near impossible. How 'bout putting heat on the kids? Didn't Warren say he went to Stanley to surprise his son?"

"There's nothing worse than sending a boy to clean up after a man." Ray's voice was grim.

"Ain't it a little soon to be deciding whose dirty work it was?"

"Whoever did this must've been covered with blood. And I mean drenched in it, Lew. The splatters show where he was standing." Ray got to his feet and positioned his chair where Peggy had stood, then raised a stumpy arm above his head. "He came up behind her from the left and swung with his right hand. There's no blood on the floor to the left of her body, and the rest of the place was soaked. No footprints, just smears, but his shoes had to have been soaked. So how come no one saw him leave?"

"Seems pretty obvious to me…"

Ray sank in his chair. "I don't care what Philips says, it's too soon to haul Scott in."

"Those kids up at the University are into all kinds of shit, and not just grass. Maybe the daughter kept something stashed in Gillman." Lew shook his head. "And what about the son?"

"Almost lost his lunch when I took him into the garage."

"Little rough on him, weren't you, Ray?"

"Nah, you're never too young to face the facts." He was silent so long Lew wondered if he was asleep, but when he opened his eyes they were chips of glass. "Leave Scott's son to me. How'd you like to interview his daughter?"

Chapter Ten

Helen Siegel walked off the plane Tuesday morning clutching her United ticket and wearing a smile as unnatural to her as mascara. It was her first trip west. Sari and Tim met her at the gate, and driving down the turnpike she kept her eyes on the side of the road as if she dreaded the sight of the foothills ahead. When blacktop bisected rolling pasture at the outskirts of Garfield, she finally spoke.

"I didn't know sheep got that big, Tim."

"Those are calves, Mrs. Siegel."

Suddenly Sari longed for Brooklyn's gray skies, its broken sidewalks, and garbage trucks whining before dawn. She smiled brightly at her mother.

"I thought they were sheep the first time I saw them, too."

Helen's eyes flashed, and Sari braced for the explosion that meant her mother felt she was being patronized. But this time more was at stake; Helen simply nodded and patted Sari's hand. Sari squeezed back and began chattering about her biology class, wishing they were already at the hotel.

At the outskirts of Stanley they passed a drainage pond high with spring runoff. A breeze combed the surface, and as a gust swept it smooth. Sari thought of the winter her father took her and her brother Sam up the Hudson with family friends. One of the couples had a cabin in Sloatsburg near a mill pond, and after a morning of hiking the adults went inside for coffee while the older children headed for the pond with ice skates. She was the only girl, at six too young to be anything but a nuisance to the boys but too old to sit with adults by the fire. And wherever Sam was, Sari wanted to be.

They were two years apart but Helen claimed Sam never let Sari out of his sight from the day she was born. Sari remembered it differently, especially once her mother went back to work and the two of them squabbled every day in that empty apartment after school. Which comic books to spend their allowance on, who got the last glass of juice, why Annie Oakley guns didn't make her a desperado. But Sam was her idol and usually didn't mind her tagging along.

That day was an exception. Perhaps it was the older boys her brother wanted to impress, or maybe he wanted to roughhouse just once without watching a little girl out of the corner of his eye, but he told her to go back to the cabin. "You don't have skates," he said. "Neither do you," she replied, but he was already running to join the others in the center of the pond. When he saw her still watching, he turned back and chased her almost to the spillway. *Stay with the grown-ups,* he warned.

The afternoon was clear and crisp, deceptively cold beneath the brilliant sky. As the wind began to pick up, Sari waited until she saw Sam disappear in the knot of boys chasing a wooden puck, then turned toward the bank. The stand of willows was bowed with ice and the eroded shore exposed brawny roots. She would watch from the shelter of the branches, where no one could see. With Sam a blur of blue rushing to keep up with the bigger boys, she turned for a last look.

Just short of the bank, where the ice was fragile and the current swift, Sari's toe broke through the surface. Snowsuit soaked, mitten lost grabbing at a shelf that splintered in her fingers, a malign force seizing her by the ankles and dragging her under. Too fast to scream, so cold it burned. She bobbed once and tried to cry out but frigid water slapped the breath from her. Going down for the second time, she caught hold of a root and screamed.

The next thing she knew, she was naked under a blanket in her father's lap, shivering before a blasting fire. Concerned faces bending over her and whispering frostbite, gentle fingers stroking her, learning much later one of the boys heard her cry and the oldest pulled her out. Her clothes were ruined and they never found her boots, but watching her underpants dry scratchy and stiff on the grate, all Sari could think was she wanted her mother. Then they bundled her in her father's sweater for the long drive home.

At the apartment, Helen took one look and screamed. Yanking the socks off Sari's hands, she glared at the white splotches on her knuckles. She slapped them. Hard. *Don't ever do that again!* And then it was Max's turn to bear Helen's rage. Even then Sari sensed they were not the family her mother planned to have, she was not the daughter Helen wanted. If her mother finally took her in her arms and comforted her as she later claimed, there was no memory of it. But now Sari needed her and she had come. Reaching for her mother's hand, she felt a rush of gratitude.

—

"You're so thin, dear," Helen was saying. "Take half this sandwich. It's too much for me."

Tim had dropped them off at the Hancock House, and they'd picked up something for her mother at the coffee shop because Helen never ate on planes. Now she was removing the cellophane from the tunafish and laying it out on the low table in her room.

"I'm not hungry, Mom."

Helen eyed the waffle-cut slices of dill suspiciously. "Not even the pickle?"

"No, thanks."

"Well, at least keep me company." Sari sank into the opposite chair. "Is it the weather?" Despite the air-conditioning Helen fanned herself with her ticket folder, and Bellodgia wafted across the table. "It's so dry, I don't know how you stand it. The minute I stepped off tbe plane my face shriveled like a prune."

If Widmark were Hawaii, she would complain about the humidity.

But the sheer familiarity of her mother's scent was so comforting Sari wanted to avoid a fight at any cost.

"The sky's always blue," she replied, "and the snow melts quickly from the sun." God, she sounded like the weather woman on Channel 4.

Helen slid the sandwich two inches closer to Sari. "You never liked snow when you were growing up." *And you never said no to a pickle*, Sari read, *even a dill.* Maybe her mother wasn't crazy about her marrying at eighteen, but she had nothing against Tim, and surely she could see his pain. She took a deep breath and resolved to proceed at Helen's pace.

"I'm not saying I like it now, Mom, it just melts fast."

"Don't you miss the ocean? You always said you wanted to live on an island." Dipping into her purse for Kents, Helen probed for an opening while the tuna sat like a line in the sand. "You read *Mutiny on the Bounty* and that book about the man who lost his way to the South Pole a dozen times. Nancy Drew was too tame—"

"Mom, I'm worried about Tim. He's locking it all inside, he doesn't want to talk—"

"Maybe it's best that you leave him alone."

"What?"

"Darling, what are you doing in this place?" Helen lit her cigarette and waved it at the window. "It's not like New York, there are no opportunities—"

"Since when did we go to the opera or plays?" This was going all wrong. "There are plenty of opportunities here."

"Speaking of which, I almost forgot to tell you." Setting her cigarette in the plastic ashtray, Helen rummaged again in her purse. "I ran into Andy Cohen last week on Montague Street. He's home from Yale for the summer, and when he asked about you I gave him your number. I know I have his somewhere—"

"What do you think you're doing?"

"What's wrong with keeping in touch with old friends? As I recall, he was pretty special. For two years all we heard was Andy this, Andy that…"

"That's the past." Sari walked to the closet and ran her fingers over the nubby silk of her mother's sand-colored slacks. She'd been with Helen the day she bought them at Macy's, had cajoled her into the extravagant purchase, and they celebrated by having shrimp cocktails and Nesselrode pie for lunch before taking the subway back to Brooklyn. Queens for the day, Helen had joked... Why were those occasions so rare Sari could even remember what they ate? "I'm not like you, Mom."

"Darling, stay here tonight." Helen was fiddling with the ashtray, avoiding her daughter's eyes. "There are two beds and Tim won't have to come back. He looks exhausted."

"Exhausted? He's *paralyzed*—"

"You don't know the first thing about his family. They're nothing like us."

So she'd come to pry her away from Tim, drag her back to Brooklyn like a child. Resentment rose in Sari's throat. What right did Helen have to pretend their family was a model of togetherness?

"I'll tell you what I do know," she replied. "When the Scotts eat dinner, nobody walks on eggs or raises his voice." *They sit there like zombies, listening to Warren rant about Texans and Jews...* Anger spilled over, the need to wound drowning common sense. "Warren asks Tim about school instead of drilling him in spelling and math, and Peggy doesn't stand at the stove glowering because she can't bear to watch her children get ulcers."

"You don't even know what happened to that poor woman." Fingers trembling, Helen tried to light another cigarette. "For all you know—"

"I know everything about them that matters. Peggy sews her own clothes, she even knows how to bake a pie." *And Peggy would have served a dozen vegetarian dishes if she hadn't run out of ingredients, and Warren wanted me to say I was in the shower when he knocked on the door...* "They're a real family, Mom, they—"

"Pies? Do you think that's what marriage is?"

"I asked you to come because I need your help!"

"You can't go through with this wedding." Helen snapped her purse shut. Subject closed. "It wouldn't be fair to Tim's family."

"We both know this has nothing to do with Tim or the Scotts," Sari said, trembling with the effort to regain control. "Just because you were disappointed—"

Helen stopped shifting in her chair. "What are you talking about?"

"Your marriages." There. Out in the open, too late to turn back. "Both of them."

"I was too young, and so are you."

"You think you're saving me from being hurt." Marriage on the rebound, a family Helen didn't want. How different it was with her and Tim! "But I'm an adult now."

"You're only eighteen!"

"Like you were." Face-to-face now, steeling herself against Bellodgia and the tears in her mother's eyes. "I'm going to marry Tim Scott, and you can't stop me."

"Am I supposed to pretend that's not a mistake?" Helen reached for her daughter but she was already out the door.

—

Fleeing the Hancock House, Sari let the wind dry her cheeks. She'd been crazy to think her mother would support her, should have realized the only reason she came was to bring her home. And what a loveless place that was! She'd never felt her parents belonged together. Their marriage didn't make sense, but it wasn't until she was nine that she understood why.

It was nighttime on Willow Street. Her ninth birthday, a grown-up occasion. Her father had taken Saturday off from the plant to escort six little girls to the movies, cake and ice cream afterward, capped by a sleepover with Sari's best friend Karen. The first time she'd been allowed to have a guest overnight.

They'd stayed up late watching Charlie Chan on TV and then a sappy romance. Lights out, calls for buttered toast and drinks of water, Helen indulging them, whispers and giggles, finally falling asleep to the hum of the refrigerator in the hall. It must have been past midnight when Sari woke to sounds on the other side of the wall.

She'd heard it before, the creaks and sighs, headboard rapping against plaster, her mother crying out softly, then stillness and her father's snores. Something comforting in that late-night intimacy. Unsure what it was, listening but not wanting to hear. Sam's room was at the other end of the hall, and when she asked he sniggered and said next time wake him up. That's how she knew it was private. But tonight was different.

It started as usual. The polite protest of the bed in response to a sudden shift in weight, her father murmuring, her mother's little laugh. Sari's eyes flew open, but she settled back as she recognized the sounds. Remembering Karen, she peeked at the rollaway cot to make sure her friend had not heard. The rise and fall of the blanket reassured her, and Sari burrowed into her pillow.

At the squeak from the drawer in her parents' night-stand, she opened her eyes again. Didn't they know she could hear? Maybe they would stop... A blessed lull and a silence that lasted a beat too long. The refrigerator whirred at the end of the hall, a soothing sound that said it would be all right. Then her mother's low *don't*. Mortified, she looked at Karen again. Awful enough if she heard the other, so much worse to be wakened by a quarrel. But Karen sighed in her sleep and rolled onto her side.

"Don't touch me." The contempt sharper than the words, traveling through the wall like a slap. Why was she pushing him away?

"—like him?" her father demanded. Feet landed heavy on the floor and the mattress squealed as he rose. "Tired of trying to live up to—" He thumped off to the bathroom, leaving Sari locked in her misery, no longer caring what Karen heard. Anger for her father and *at* him, for not being enough. Covering her face with the pillow, torn between wanting to disappear and die...Who were they fighting about?

But she knew.

The first clue to the existence of the man in the photograph had come at her aunt's house in New Jersey the previous Thanksgiving. Sari had been setting the table while her father and uncle watched football in the basement with the boys. Lace cloth, gleaming silver with a swirled crest, cut-glass goblets for the children's grape juice. One napkin short, she went into the kitchen. Her mother and aunt were standing with their backs to the door, and her aunt leaned forward to open the oven. As she began basting the turkey with a rubber-bulbed wand the skin crackled and spit, scenting the air with garlic and thyme.

"—anniversary coming up," her aunt said. Rising, she squeezed her sister's shoulder. "I know you miss him…" Helen nodded and her shoulders hitched.

"Bad time of the year," she murmured in response, and Sari backed out before they saw her.

Who could they be talking about? Her parents' anniversary had been months earlier, in September. She tried to think of anyone else who married or died at the right time but drew a blank. Over dinner her mother smiled too much and drank an extra glass of wine. On Monday after school while Sam was off with friends and her mother still at work, Sari searched her drawers. Nothing in her jewelry box or in the silk pouch where she kept the jade necklace Max had given her two birthdays ago. In a small lacquered box, where she kept clippings of baby hair and doll-sized pink and blue identification bracelets, Sari found the photograph.

He was loose-limbed and fair-haired and wore a sloppy grin. His army cap was tilted to the side, but the uniform was pressed and snappy and his right arm engulfed her mother. Helen was beautiful, so beautiful Sari almost didn't recognize her; the only pictures she'd seen were with her and Sam, as if her mother had no life before them. But that was a lie, because here she was young and glowing, her hair glossy and waved and her enormous eyes filled with wonder. *Does anyone have the right to be so happy?* those eyes asked.

Returning the photo to the box, Sari tucked it in the back of the drawer with her mother's scarves. All night she thought about it. The photo had no caption or date, just the serrated edges that showed it was part of a roll, and she tried to imagine other scenes. A boyfriend, she thought, my mother had a boyfriend. If they'd really been in love they would have married, so obviously nothing came of it… But the glow of her mother's smile burned, and Sari felt somehow cheated. Why didn't she smile like that for them? Finally she confronted Helen.

The picture was taken on his last leave, before he was killed in Belgium. She'd been very young, eighteen, far too young to marry. And they *had* been married. Sari was being silly, blowing it all out of proportion... Of course she loved Max. It was a long time ago and there was nothing more to say. Not even his name. But are you happy, Sari wanted to ask, do you really love us? Subject closed. When she told Sam he shrugged and said what did it matter, she'd married their dad and belonged to them. The next time Sari looked for the lacquered box, it was gone.

As the toilet flushed and she heard her father's weight drop onto the bed, Sari squeezed her eyes shut. Their marriage was a lie; her mother settled for him because her real love had died. It was another family she'd planned, another daughter she wanted, and Helen's rage and resentment had at last made sense...

Stopping now at the Student Union at the center of the campus to catch her breath, Sari soaked her feet in the fountain and tried to pretend she was no different from the other students. As she listened to their chatter about classes, the remorse that had been nibbling since she left the Hancock House threatened to swallow her whole. Her mother had flown all this way and they'd botched it, another failure in a lifetime of missed connections. Why hadn't she made it clear how much she needed Helen's support? She owed her mother another chance.

And it wasn't just about Tim that she wanted advice. She needed to talk to someone about the day of the murder. Warren coming to Stanley made no sense; when they showed him the apartment he hadn't budged from the couch. And that strange conversation the next morning, when he said he knocked on the door while she was in the shower... Fishing in her pocket for change, Sari went to the pay phone outside the cafeteria.

"Mom? I'm sorry—"

"Did you change your mind? We can order room service."

"It's about that day. When Peggy was killed." She plunged ahead. "There are things I've told no one."

"What could you possibly know about it?"

"The way Tim's father was dressed, how he sat on our couch."

When no interruption came, Sari grew more confident. Her mother was listening, she was taking this seriously. "And he must've gone to the hardware store before the rec center, but he said—"

"That has nothing to do with what happened."

"But Peggy didn't tell me he was coming, and she—"

"You know nothing, Sari."

She clutched the receiver. "I know what I *saw.*"

"Sometimes what you see and what are real are two different things." Helen paused and Sari braced herself for what was coming next. "I'm not saying you're making things up, but it's easy to exaggerate when you're emotionally involved."

"I'm not exaggerating, Mom, believe me—"

"And what if you aren't, but you're just plain wrong? Do you know what that would do to Tim?" If you really love him, put him first. "The police officers are professionals, dear. This may not be New York, but they know what they're doing. If Warren did that awful thing they'll find out without any help from you." The last phrase was punctuated by the striking of a match. "Stay here tonight. We can find an old movie to watch, like we used to…"

Charlie Chan and a sappy romance.

"I can't, Mom."

She hung up and dug in her pockets for another quarter. If her father was surprised to receive a collect call at the printing plant, he hid it.

"How's the weather out there, Sari? Keeping busy with your classes, did your mother land all right?"

"Dad, I need to talk. There are things I know—"

"Sari, look. The sooner you put this whole chapter behind you, the better." She closed her eyes. "I know you're having second thoughts about marrying Tim, don't tell me I'm wrong. It may have seemed the thing to do before but now your brain's saying something else. It's a good brain, you should use it."

"This time I need a different kind of advice." There were loud voices in the background, and Sari waited while Max put his hand over the receiver and shouted, *Hold the wire, I'm on the phone!* Communicating with her father was like dropping endless quarters in a slot machine, but no cherries appeared. "What would you do if you knew something about a crime, Dad, but telling it might hurt someone you love? Would you pretend it never happened?"

When Max finally responded, his voice was weary.

"I've got nothing against the University, Sari, but with your grades you can still enroll in a college back east. If you change your mind in a couple years and want to go back, what have you lost?"

"I expected this from Mom, but not from you! You taught me never to lie."

"Sari, Sari. You need distance from Tim, the Scotts. It's time to get your life back on track. *You can be anything you—*"

"What I want is to be married to Tim Scott. Are you saying to forget what I saw?"

His answer was barely audible: "Yes. Don't get involved."

Chapter Eleven

In a tired shopping strip on the north edge of Stanley sat Peach's Restaurant & Grill. The sign showed a buxom lass in a whalebone corset, lifting her petticoats to display a garter, but at mid-afternoon on Tuesday the place was empty and dark, and as Lew Devine peered through the glass he saw chairs stacked on tables and the bar draped with a sheet.

Walking around to the For Rent sign on the padlocked rear entrance, he jotted the phone number and called from the booth across the street.

"Peach's, Vera speaking."

"I'm looking for Laura Scott. Does she work there?"

"We're temporarily closed."

"Does Laura work there?"

"Who *is* this?"

He injected a smile into his voice. "A friend."

"Cut the shit, mister."

"Could you tell me how to reach her?"

"Not till I know what you're after. With all that girl's been through…
What do you people want, blood?" The phone banged in his ear.

Lew found Laura's address in his notebook and drove to the run-down duplex on Acacia, where a chain-link fence enclosed crabgrass and packed dirt and a tangle of purple and white petunias struggled under bottle caps and cigarette butts in a clay pot on the stoop. He didn't need to be a genius to know announcing he was a cop would ensure the door being slammed in his face. Leaving his SWAT cap and gun in the car, he rapped lightly, then louder when there was no response. A dog whined somewhere out back, and he was about to leave when the door swung open on a chain.

"Yeah?"

A bare-chested man in his late twenties peered through the dimness with bleary eyes, body odor pungent.

"Is Laura home?"

"What you want her for, man?" His breath stank of more than last night's beer, and Lew retracted his head. But an odd defiance shone in his eyes as he sized Lew up.

"I need to speak with her. Is she home?"

"Home?" The doper gave a mocking laugh. Lew wondered what he was crashing from. "Yeah, she's home. Back in Gillman with Daddy, at least during the day. She works nights, as if you didn't know."

"Where?" Lew asked, wondering who the guy thought he was.

"Catch her at Jug's if you don't already know what she looks like." His bleary gaze swept Lew's upper torso, and the tautness of the officer's physique seemed to enrage him. "You think I don't know who you are? You have one hell of a nerve—"

Lew took another step back. The last thing he wanted to have to do was take a defensive swing at a jealous lover, even as pathetic a specimen as this. He raised his hands in a conciliatory gesture. "Look, I've never met her. I swear."

The freak's eyes narrowed in confusion, and then he spotted the badge holder on Lew's belt. "Who the hell are you anyway, the heat?" But his voice had lost steam. Laura was two-timing the guy, and he didn't even know who his rival was. Watching him process this latest humiliation, Lew saw the anger again begin to build. Must be meth, Lew thought. Coke was a little rich for this freak's blood.

"Thanks for your trouble. Sorry to have disturbed you..."

The door jerked shut and swung open off the chain, and Lew got his first good look. The creep's matted hair was shoulder-length and you could count every rib. Blue jeans flared at the bottom, so greasy they were almost black, toenails curved like talons. As Laura's boyfriend crossed the threshold, Lew saw a length of steel chain looped in his fist. "I asked what you want!"

"Hey, man, no harm meant, I just need to talk to Laura." Lew took another step backward, keeping his eyes on the freak's hands. "I'm leaving now."

"Don't let me catch you around here again, creep." He reared back his head and a wad of phlegm hit the toe of Lew's ostrich-skin boot. Driving off, Lew saw him watching from behind the grimy curtain.

He stopped at a gas station to find the address for Jug's and drove east to the Diagonal. The roadhouse sprang up on the shoulder without warning, its windowless facade anything but inviting. Turning onto cracked asphalt, Lew circled to the dirt lot in the rear and parked beside a late-model Lincoln. When he knocked at the door a pudgy man in his fifties answered.

"Are you Jug?"

The man squinted, then guffawed. "What are you, pulling my leg?"

"You the owner?"

"You're not a Stanley cop." He looked past Lew at his car. "What are you, State?"

"Hallett County Sheriff's Department." Lew flashed his badge and the man waved him in. Pouring two mugs of coffee from an industrial-sized urn in the kitchen, he walked Lew to the bar.

"We open in an hour, so make it quick."

"Laura Scott work for you?"

"What's the problem?"

"Is she a barmaid?"

"You kidding? What a waste that would be."

Lew peered from the Harley hubcaps and chains on the walls to the wooden platform at the other end. "Does she dance?"

The owner laughed once more and selected a toothpick from a shot glass on the counter. "Laura's one of my most popular girls. She's choice."

"How long's she been working here?"

"A few months. She has quite a clientele." The toothpick rolled. "But she's a nice girl, know what I'm saying?"

"You mean she doesn't turn tricks on the premises?"

He spat the toothpick onto the floor. "Look, mister, we run a clean place. Sure we have rough customers and yeah, they like tits. But my girls are strictly topless, they keep their pants on. What they do when they leave ain't none of my business."

"Where'd she work before?"

"A tavern. When they shut down, she started dancing." He leered through stained teeth. "The tips are better."

"Why'd the tavern close?"

"License violations. They were selling beer to underage kids. Half the joints on the Hill do it, too." He reached for another toothpick. "But that's Stanley for you. Bunch of lousy hypocrites."

"Is Laura working tonight?"

"I don't want you bothering her. She's got enough trouble, living with that speed freak."

"I'll wait till she gets off. What time does the show start?"

"Around ten. She does three sets, takes a break, and goes back on at eleven. Fridays and Saturdays she does a late set."

Driving back to town Lew tried to remember what Laura Scott looked like. He'd caught just a glimpse of her Saturday while Ray was getting names. A mouse with gray eyes and light brown hair. He'd see just how choice she was soon enough.

—

Nightfall had transformed Jug's from a drab roadhouse to an island of neon and heat. At nine o'clock the music throbbed with a violent pulse audible in the lot packed with motorcycles and pickup trucks. The only women in the bar were a tough-looking mama with a scar under her eye taking orders from the booths and a young girl onstage who was so thin she looked plucked. Her hennaed hair was her only remarkable feature, and it spilled down her back in waves, the strobe creating the illusion of lushness and movement, but when she finally peeled off her top there was nothing to see.

The bikers ignored her and when she left the stage no one cared.

Nursing a Coors, Lew stayed as far out of the way as he could. He'd had a burger and fries at McDonald's before checking out the Lamplighter and the Foothills Inn. The manager at one place remembered a phone call about a rehearsal dinner, the other didn't; neither recalled a personal visit from Warren on Saturday. Now he was in no mood for games. Jostled once, he gritted his teeth and apologized, and after that was left alone. Biker bars disgusted him; at Lenny Jester's, at least the girls washed.

When the music started up and Laura came out, there were a couple of whistles and then the place got quiet. Even the bartender turned toward the platform. The music stopped.

Laura waited until all eyes were on her, then began a slow dance to her own beat. Her crimson hot-pants and snug sweater were more revealing than nakedness and every move was in response to an invisible lover who could have been any man in the room. When the music began, she threw herself into it, every beat a thrust, every pause an exquisite reprieve. She finally peeled off her top to reveal taut white breasts with dark nipples and the crowd went wild, banging glasses and beer mugs onto tables and the bar in a thunderous cacophony. She stood for a moment with her shoulders thrown back, cropped hair copper under the strobe, then quickly left the stage. The music stopped, the bar lights came back on, and everyone ordered another round.

Lew left his mug on the counter and went to the parking lot to cool off. He couldn't believe the girl on the stage was the same one he'd seen Saturday. No wonder that pathetic speed freak was jealous.... Two greasers in black leather pants came out behind him, looked him over and headed for the rear of the building. Lew faced the other way, at the trucks speeding by on the Diagonal, and briefly regretted leaving his gun in his car. When he finally looked to the far end of the lot he saw a small figure climb into the driver's side of a beat-up Barracuda. He walked over.

She had on a brown corduroy jacket over her sweater and a pair of faded jeans. Was she ashamed of the outfit she'd been wearing? Her head rested on her arms, which were folded across the steering wheel, and now he could see the red highlights in her hair. Softly he tapped on the half-open window.

"Laura?"

She rolled up the window and pushed down the button. He tapped again. She stared straight ahead and tooted the horn, a short angry blast. As he jumped back, she honked once more. When he didn't leave she finally rolled down the window.

"Get out or I'll call the bouncers! Whatever's left of you will be dog meat."

"I'm a cop, Laura, I'm not here to hurt you." He flashed his badge.

She ignored it.

"I need to ask some questions about Saturday," he continued.

"What are you doing, spying on me?"

"I didn't know where else to find you. I went to Peach's but the place was closed, and your friend at the duplex on Acacia said you worked here. That's it, I swear."

She looked at Lew's face for the first time, and something in him stirred. Her eyes were heavily made up, but shadow and mascara only heightened her vulnerability, their coarseness underscored the delicacy of her features. "No one in my family knows about this..."

"Is there someplace we can talk, maybe get a cup of coffee?"

"I'm not going anywhere with you. Besides, I have to do another set." She looked at her watch. "You've got twenty minutes. Make it fifteen, I need to get ready."

Reaching in the passenger seat for a worn leather purse, she used the rearview mirror to apply a coat of lipstick the color of crushed berries. Lew blinked and tried not to think of her breasts.

"What time did you leave the house on Saturday?"

"Acacia or South Cleveland?"

Anger surged, but he controlled it.

"Why'd you go to Gillman that day?"

Laura's mouth opened and her tongue flicked across her newly lush lower lip. Her smile was lewd and cunning.

"I always try to go home on weekends."

"Why that day?"

"Dad said he'd have the brakes on my car checked Monday and I could pick it up later in the week, so I was going to borrow the Dodge to get back to Stanley." She grazed the tip of the lipstick tube with her index finger but he kept his eyes on her face.

"What time did you get there?"

"Around eight-thirty, during breakfast."

"What did you talk about?"

"They were planning to clean the house and my mother was going to spray her roses. Dad had to bring the Cadillac in for a lube job, there was a whole list of chores." Laura's mouth twisted and he thought she would cry. "He's a great father—"

"What about the rehearsal dinner, any mention of that?"

"No." She returned her lipstick to her purse and zipped it shut. "Time's up."

"Can we talk again?"

"Maybe."

"Here's my card. Home number's on the back. Call anytime. I'm sorry I bothered you at work." He reached to touch her shoulder but converted the gesture to a wave.

"Sure." Her raunchy smile flashed once more. "Back to the salt mines."

Laura opened the door and climbed out of the Barracuda, not bothering to lock it. She was wearing spike heels with her jeans. Without looking back she sauntered through the rear door of Jug's, taut buttocks rolling every step of the way.

Chapter Twelve

The night before they left for Peggy's funeral, LaVonne Scott rolled into Gillman flattening everything in her path. Sari answered the door when it rang.

"What are you doing here, gal?" Vonnie's flat drawl made it sound like an accusation as she took in the condition of the front hall.

"I'm Tim's fiancee," Sari replied. She'd returned with Tim to the house on South Cleveland that afternoon so they could get an early start the next day. Kay had prevailed; Peggy was to be buried at St. Augustine's after all.

Vonnie pushed past, dragging a cardboard suitcase behind her.

"His *fiancee*? Why wasn't I told?" As her currant-colored eyes bored into Sari's, Sari struggled to figure out who she was. Vonnie dropped her bag in the middle of the floor and straightened one of the paintings before resuming the offensive. "Where's my son?"

So this was Warren's mother. Tim had said his grandfather had owned a gas station on Main Street in Fillmore and could repair anything he laid his hands on, but Vonnie sold the station the day her husband was buried. No wonder Tim never talked about her. But why had she waited almost a week to come? The police delayed releasing Peggy's body, but surely she knew the funeral was the day after tomorrow.

"He went to pick up fried chicken with Tim, but they'll be back any minute."

"Nothing to eat? What kind of kitchen did Peggy keep?"

"We're leaving in the morning for Walker County, and Warren thought—"

"Don't tell me about Walker County, gal, I've lived there my whole life." As Vonnie started down the hall for the kitchen, Sari retrieved her suitcase and followed her. Vonnie headed straight for the sink and picked up a towel to begin drying cups. "Didn't Peggy have any friends? Where I was raised, folks bring food when a person dies." Let someone come fast, Sari prayed, anyone.

"Can I get you something to drink?" She knew that was a mistake the moment she said it. Vonnie's round face turned to her, pin curls quivering with malice.

"Awfully free with someone else's larder, aren't you?"

"I just thought—"

At the sound of the front door opening she uttered a silent thanks.

"Anybody home?" Kay sang out. Her voice flooded Sari with relief. If anyone could hold her own against this dreadful woman, it would be Tim's aunt.

Vonnie emerged from the kitchen, wiping her hands on the towel. "Who are you?"

Kay stopped in her tracks. She was carrying a large tray covered with plastic wrap. "I'm Peggy's sister, we've met several times."

"What do you want?"

"I brought cold cuts so Warren wouldn't have to worry about dinner."

"My son can provide quite well for his children, thank you." Vonnie folded her arms across her flat chest. "Peggy certainly did all right by him."

Kay gripped the tray with both hands. She wants to slap the woman, Sari thought, and I don't blame her. But Kay was equal to the challenge. Lifting the tray to chest level, she said, "This is awfully heavy, do you mind if I set it down?" Without waiting for an answer she strolled past

Vonnie to the kitchen, calling over her shoulder, "Where are Laura and Tim?"

"Neither one of them lifts a finger to help their father. But what can you expect, the way your sister was raised?" As Kay's eyes darkened, Sari imagined her silently counting to five.

"Speaking of Walker County, mass and burial are at St. Augustine's. My sister Liddie—"

"I forget which one of you gals she is." A crafty look crossed Vonnie's face, and Sari felt a stab of pity for Warren. "There's so many of you Dannhauers it's hard to keep track. She can't be the one who run off when she was fifteen, right after the war—"

Any moment now Kay will grab her by her scrawny neck, Sari thought, and squeeze. But Tim's aunt winked at Sari and affected her sweetest tone.

"All my sisters are married and have children, Vonnie, and they're doing just fine." Vonnie hovering at her shoulder, she made room in the refrigerator for the tray.

"Well, Peggy certainly thought she was doing fine, marrying my son and making him buy her a grand house in the big city, didn't she?" Vonnie's laugh was pure evil, and Kay stiffened. "And look what's become of her..."

Just as Sari thought Kay couldn't bear another moment, the front door opened. Tim and Warren had returned with the chicken.

—

After dinner Sari took her textbooks to the basement and settled at Tim's desk. Summer school had begun and she was determined not to drop her courses, but concerned as she was about keeping up with the work, what she really needed was a break from the tension. South Cleveland was a multistory land mine; anywhere you stepped your foot could be blown off. As she opened her lab manual and flipped to the next lesson, voices drifted through the window.

"—not part of the family, at least not yet, so why does she have to come?" It sounded like Laura.

"Do you have to be so mean to her?" Tim replied. "Just because she's—" The rest of what he said and the beginning of Laura's reply were muffled by a car backfiring in the street.

"—truth. Family is everything, Tim. Remember quiet time?"

"That was a long time ago."

"But we've always stuck together. And Mom would never—"

Never what? Sari wondered.

"Don't talk about Mom!" Tim cried.

"Okay, let's keep this where it belongs." Laura was straining to sound reasonable. "She's not our kind, Tim, and it's not because she's Jewish or from New York, it's the thousand other things that make her wrong for you. I've honestly tried to like her, but—"

"Sari's the best thing that ever happened to me!" Tim dropped his voice, and Sari leaned forward so she wouldn't miss a word. "She believes in me, she—"

"How could you bring her into this home?"

"I love her, Laura, and nothing anyone says is going to change that."

There was a long silence.

"But she's wrong for you, Tim. She doesn't fit." Laura was speaking faster now, and Sari felt her desperation. "You must have known marrying a girl like that would destroy us. Mom would never have—"

Never have what? Accepted our marriage?

"—fine till you brought her home." Laura was relentless. "Mom could be standing here right this minute if—"

If what? If Warren had stayed home that morning instead of going to Stanley to find a place for our rehearsal dinner?

The screen door squealed on its hinges.

"Sari had nothing to do with—"

"—wasn't for her, we would've had that family portrait taken last December. It was going to be just the four of us, but you told Mom if Sari wasn't included, you wouldn't be in it either. I know about the abortion too, did you think Mom wouldn't tell me? Life means nothing to those—"

The door slammed and Tim's feet clattered down the stairs. When he entered the room he kissed Sari on the top of her head, then stretched out facing the wall as she casually turned a page.

"I don't have to go with you to the funeral," she said.

"Don't be ridiculous."

"It's a family thing. Maybe it would be better if I bowed out."

"*You're* my family now."

"I don't blame her, Tim, she—"

"Aren't you coming to bed?"

Sari rose from the desk and switched off the lamp. Slipping on one of Tim's shirts, she climbed into bed. As her pupils adjusted to the dark and the phosphorescent stars began to glow, she sent up a silent prayer. *Just get us through the funeral and back to Stanley...* In the silence she felt Tim's shoulders rise and fall.

"Your grandma's quite a character," she said. "Why'd she wait so long to come?"

"She wouldn't have come at all if Mom's family hadn't insisted the funeral be in Walker County." He rolled onto his back. "She made my grandfather's life miserable. Dad's named after him, you know. Warren Royce begat Warren Dale."

"How old were you when he died?"

"Seven or eight." Tim's arm tightened around her waist and she rested her head on his bare chest. The springy hairs tickled her cheek, and she wondered whether their lovemaking would ever be the same. It was filled with such urgency now, Tim took her with a passion that demanded more than intimacy in the face of violence. Almost angry. "— never went to the funeral," he was saying. "Dad said it was a waste of time and W.R. wouldn't care."

"What was he like?"

"You mean how could he stand being married to Vonnie? We hardly ever visited them. Dad made tracks out of there as soon as he graduated from high school." His yawn was a prelude to cutting the conversation short, but this was the first time he'd really spoken about his father's family, and Sari let her silence prod him. "He never looked back, except to marry Mom and take her away."

"You must remember *something.* "

When Tim finally answered his voice was flat, as if he were reciting words that meant little. "We visited them once, and when he sat down to dinner he had grease under his nails. I kept looking at his hands and waiting for someone to tell him to wash. Mom would never have let us come to the table like that, but no one said anything about it." He yawned again, louder, and she knew he was humoring her. "In fact, no one said anything at all, not even 'Pass the potatoes.' Now can we go to sleep?"

"Was your father close to him?"

"Haven't you noticed? Dad's not close to anyone, except maybe Laura. W.R. left him that big red tool chest in the garage. You know, the metal one with all the drawers? There must be hundreds of tools in it. What a waste." Tim's laughter had an edge. "As far as I know Dad's never even opened that chest. He has his own set of tools, he even stamps them WDS so no one can confuse them with his father's. He caught me in there once when I was in grade school and walloped me."

"Why?"

"How should I know? But he hates grease. Whenever I changed the oil or gave the Olds a tune-up, he'd lean over my shoulder and hand me a tool or say what I was doing wrong, but he'd never roll up his sleeves and do it himself."

"At least he knows what he's doing." She tried to make a joke of it. "When the toilet overflows, my father stands there, bewildered. It would never occur to him to do something as basic as turning off the—"

"Well, Dad's great with his hands. He built the garage at our house in Garfield. He said he was better than any carpenter, so he did the whole thing himself. Even the framing." Tim closed his eyes, snuffing out the painted stars. "He sure knows how to work the problem."

As Sari lay beside him, feeling the tension drain from his shoulders, Laura's accusation came hurtling back. *Mom would never have...* It was easier to accept that she meant Peggy would never have approved of their marriage than that she wouldn't have died if Warren hadn't left to look for a place for their rehearsal dinner. Because weren't there signs that Peggy was coming around, right at the end? Sari tried to recall their final conversations, but all she could think of was the abortion and that uneasy truce on Mother's Day.

When Sari became ill in February they"d thought it was mono, the freshman badge of honor that swept the dorms as predictably as flu. But she was pregnant. Although she'd been using a diaphragm, the doctor made it clear that if she wanted any alternative to carrying the baby to term she would have to go to someone else.

She wanted it, she *wanted* it, but Tim said they should wait. They had to finish school first, build the cabin in Garnet Hill, secure their children's future. They were young, there'd be all the time in the world to have more. The dream demanded sacrifice; did she think it was any easier for him than it was for her? Insurmountable logic, against which the feeble voice that cried *it's ours* was no match.

Tim came up with the money and a name, someone north of Stanley who did them on the side. No one Sari knew had had one—she couldn't even bear to say the word. *Abortion.* The sound of it was awful, blunt and crude. Knowing. They would tell no one.

When they arrived at the clinic at a quarter past five the waiting room was full. She'd heard the doctor's name before; a couple of girls at the dorm went to him for pap smears and said he was gentle, kind of hip. Sari gave her name to the receptionist and waited half an hour with Tim, thumbing through *Family Circle* and *Bride,* hoping she saw no one they knew. Each time the door opened she flinched; they'd arrived on time, but every other patient was called first. Finally she was shown to an examining room with a sheet-draped table. The nurse handed her a paper smock open in front, which covered her only to the waist. Take off all your clothes, she said.

The metal was cold even through the sheet, and there was a bitter smell. Rubber and disinfectant. Sari sat at the edge of the table with her hands in her lap and her feet hanging over the side, avoiding the stirrups. A streetlight shone through the blinds. Except for an occasional sound in the hallway it was very quiet. A car started up and backed out of the lot, casting its beam across her window. *You're in that car,* she told herself, *it's all over and you're driving away...* She'd left her watch in her jeans and was afraid to get up because the doctor might come at any moment. She wanted Tim, wished she'd had the nerve to ask if he could stay. Each time she heard a voice she stiffened, dreading and hoping it was the doctor and this would be over.

Get up and leave.

The first time the thought came she pushed it away, but as the minutes stretched it returned. More insistent. *Get up and leave before it's too late.*

What would happen if she changed her mind, slipped on her pants and told Tim she couldn't go through with it? He'd put his arms around her and say, I'm so glad, I thought we were doing it for you...She felt the roughness of his jacket on her cheek, the safety of his arms enveloping her. It was so cold in here.

The door swung open and it was the nurse, already in her overcoat.

"Doctor will be right with you."

I've changed my mind, I don't want this, I'm going home now... But what if she dressed and went outside and Tim said what about our dream? There was more noise in the hall and a man entered. Tired, cross. This patient was an inconvenience at the end of his day.

"Come down to the end of the table. All the way to the end."

She slipped her feet in the stirrups, not even a drape covering her lower half.

"Wider, wider..."

His exasperation was palpable. As the nurse handed him a syringe and he bent toward her, his eyes had no expression but his breath smelled of wintergreen. Mints. All the time in the world to have more... A pinch. The cold heavy clamp, stretching her out and down.

"This is just to numb you."

A sting like a wasp, an icy rivulet radiating outward and then burning with indescribable pain, the same sensations three times more. *What if something went wrong and this was her only chance?*

"You're not going to make a scene, are you?" Not sympathy, but annoyance. The nurse had gone. "Because if you don't want to be here, you can just get up and leave..."

She lay back and closed her eyes. A cabin in Garnet Hill, with beetle-kill pine and a soaring loft, three children and a goat in the yard... What right did she have to destroy that because she was afraid?

Clank of instruments, snap of a glove, smell of powder and latex. Squeezing her eyes tighter, she willed herself to go to that cabin, a place where there was no pain.

Two days later it was all over the dorm.

The nurse was a friend of a friend of a mother of one of the prom queens, and word spread from there. Sari and Tim decided to marry at the end of the semester, move out as soon as exams were over. The dream would not wait and there would be no shame.

The day after finals Tim drove to Gillman to tell his parents their plans. He left Sari at Rainbow Plaza, where she wandered in circles, staring in the windows of shoe stores and record shops for what felt like hours. When he finally returned, he said Peggy had burst into tears and refused to attend the wedding.

"Then I told them you had an abortion, that we loved each other and nothing could stop us."

"How could you?" she cried. "That was ours, we promised never to tell!"

"They need to see me as I really am, Sari, not who they *think* I am..."

But did they really need to know? Surely Tim's parents could see past the trophies and A's to the boy with dreams of his own, their son, who wanted to be an artist and not an engineer. Sari knew she would pay the price. The Scotts would never accept her.

Though there was little hope her relationship with Tim's family would improve, the following weekend was Mother's Day and they brought a box of chocolate-covered cherries to Gillman on Sunday. Peggy was brittle but began to thaw during dinner, and Sari tried to keep her own anxiety in check. Tim's mother had baked another Harvey Wallbanger cake, and when Sari helped her clear the table Peggy handed her a bottle of Galliano with two inches of liqueur for a cake of her own.

It was the last time they were alone.

"Tim loves my cakes." The water was running, and Peggy's narrow shoulders jerked as she scoured an iron skillet. "He likes the chicken too, but it's always been the cakes."

"I'll never be able to cook the way you do."

"Marriage requires sacrifices." Back to Sari, scrubbing. "Once the thrill is gone, it's nothing but work. And children will break your heart."

By marrying the wrong person?

"I found a recipe for beef Stroganoff," Sari eagerly replied. Why couldn't she defend herself, make Peggy see what a good wife she would be? "Tim says it's one of your favorites. Will you and Warren come to dinner this summer?"

Peggy turned then, and she searched Sari's face as if seeing her for the first time. "You need to shave the meat very thin." She handed her a dishcloth. "It's easier if you let it chill in the freezer first. Not all the way frozen, just firm enough to slice…"

Tim came in and wrapped his arms around his mother. As she hugged him back and turned to the sink, Sari knew the fragile moment had passed.

"Your father's nerves have been acting up," Peggy said. "Maybe it's the stress of leaving Reynolds and starting his own business. Not that he has anything to show for it yet…" She turned off the faucet and wiped her hands on her apron. "When he was on the phone with Public Service yesterday, he blew up at a receptionist who kept putting him on hold. I don't know what's wrong with him. Maybe he'll learn something at that seminar of his."

"What seminar?" Tim asked.

"That Dale Carnegie course on personnel management. Warren read both his hooks and now he acts like it's the second coming. Fourteen Saturdays, starting next week. I can't wait for the session on relieving worry and stress."

Peggy was a mystery to Sari, like her own mother more a force than a real person, and Warren seemed no more irritable than usual. So she took what Tim's mother said as an olive branch. It never occurred to Sari to fear for her.

Peggy untied her apron and hung it on the hook by the door to the utility room, and when she turned, her face was rearranged in a smile.

"Let's see what your sister is doing."

Three days later Warren called and said he and Peggy wanted to take them to dinner. Sari was relieved but dreaded the encounter, as she did all her evenings with the Scotts. Tim's parents picked them up at the rec center and took them to the Carlisle House, a favorite spot when parents came to town because the view was spectacular and the waiters looked the other way if wine was ordered. Peggy was teary-eyed and Warren insisted on small glasses of crème de menthe to celebrate their engagement. Sari was grateful for his gesture. She thought it meant he accepted them as adults.

It was a clear evening, filled with stars. As they drove back in the Cadillac convertible Warren had bought Peggy for her forty-third birthday, Peggy wore a chiffon scarf to protect her hair and leaned back, gazing at the sky. She made Sari and Tim promise never, *ever* to let anyone know they lived together before they were married. It was the last time they saw her alive.

Chapter Thirteen

There was no point talking again to Tim's fiancée, Ray thought, because what could she know? Lew Devine's interview of Scott's daughter had yielded nothing other than they should look into her doper boyfriend, but they checked the creep out and aside from some petty dealing, he seemed to be clean. No, the case would rise and fall on a confession and Ray was being squeezed from both ends. He wanted to learn all he could before questioning Warren, but he couldn't keep critical evidence to himself much longer. Not with Taylor Philips breathing down his neck.

And then Regina Hummel called.

Ray met her over the lunch hour in a small park two miles east of Gillman. At eight minutes past noon, an Audi sedan drove up and a well-groomed brunette in her midforties emerged and hesitantly approached the picnic tables. She was dressed in a navy and white pleated skirt-and-blouse ensemble with a blue belt, spectator pumps and matching handbag, and Ray noted with approval that she wore hose despite the heat. He waited until she was seated at a redwood bench before leaving his car to join her.

"Mrs. Hummel?" Her chin jerked. "I'm Lieutenant Burt. We spoke this morning."

"Yes." Manicured fingers twisted her purse strap as if she were undecided whether to go or stay. "What happened to poor Peggy was awful, just awful. Do you know who did it?"

He smiled to conceal his disappointment. "We're following a number of leads."

"She didn't deserve what happened to her."

"How long did you know Peggy?"

"From the day she started at Llewellyn last summer. We were both in accounts receivable, so we carpooled since the beginning. And we had lunch every day."

"What was she like?"

"Peggy was a great gal, wouldn't hurt a fly." Regina set her purse on the bench and leaned toward him, the index finger of her right hand stroking the reddened knuckles of her left. This was a woman who wasn't too good to wash her own windows, despite the coordinated outfit. "She was shy at first, because she hadn't worked outside the home for so many years. She was really a homemaker."

"Why'd she have to work?"

"To keep up with college tuition after her husband quit Reynolds." As Ray's eyebrows rose, she added, "To become a consultant. It was tough, but Peggy was never one to complain."

"How'd she and her husband get along?"

"She was always upbeat." Regina's eyes slid away and he wished he'd sent Devine. Time was too short to dance around. "Just a great gal," she repeated, and this time he heard the catch in her voice.

"How 'bout the other people at work?" he asked in a softer tone. "She get along with them?"

"Pretty well, with one or two exceptions. There was a Mexican clerk who took his own sweet time delivering mail. Peggy made a comment about him being *poco loco* and next thing we knew, she was called to the supervisor's office and had to apologize. The whole thing got blown way out of proportion in my opinion…"

He'd have to check Peggy's personnel file. "Was she in good health?"

"I know she was on medication because I used to see her take something. I asked about it once, but she said she'd never been sick a day in her life." Ray placed a mental star beside the prescription pills they'd found in the vanity. Had the report on those come back? "—all have our troubles, don't we?"

"She mention any family problems?"

"Nothing but the wedding and her daughter's boyfriend."

The silence stretched and he resisted the temptation to check his watch. Regina didn't look like the type who'd call the cops for attention, so she must have something to say.

"She didn't like him?" he prompted.

"He was a greasy guy with a motorcycle and no job, and Peggy made it clear he wasn't welcome in their home. And there was someone else in the picture, I'm not sure who, but Peggy liked him even less than the boy Laura was living with."

Ray struggled to imagine anyone more repulsive than the speed freak Lew described, and failed. But hadn't he said something about Laura two-timing the creep, another guy on the side? "Why was that?"

"I don't know, maybe they had words. I could tell Laura set Peggy on edge, not like Tim. But we all have our disappointments…"

Now Ray peeked at his watch. Lunch would be over soon and unless he began fishing, he'd leave empty-handed. "You mentioned some difficulty with the wedding."

"The first year I knew her, Peggy just burst with pride about Tim." Regina leaned forward and dropped her voice a notch. "When he began dating his fiancee Peggy tried to reserve judgment, but when she said it was a little Jewish girl from New York, I asked what she planned to do about it. Peggy said, 'What *can* I do? He's head over heels in love with her.' She asked me not to mention it at work."

Swallowing impatience, he cast another line. "When was the last time you saw her?"

"Well, that's the reason I called. Didn't Warren tell you?"

He kept his voice even. "I'd like to hear your side."

"I was at their house that morning. Saturday."

Payday. The mystery woman in peach-colored shorts.

"Why?"

"It was my turn to carpool the week before, and Peggy left her thermos in my station wagon. I knew she'd be out back, working with her roses. It was a gorgeous—"

"What time did you get there?"

"Between ten-fifteen and ten-thirty."

Ray eased his spiral pad from his hip pocket and began jotting notes. "How can you be sure?"

"As I pulled up, I saw a state patrol officer stop a motorcycle and a yellow VW bug at the intersection of Cleveland and Grand. Whatever time that was, I was there."

"How long were you there?"

"I had to ring the bell at least three times before Warren answered. He said Peggy wasn't home, which was a surprise because I knew she couldn't wait to be out in her garden on the weekends." Ray bit his tongue. Let her finish. When she ran out of words, he'd know everything she had to say. "—can't garden in the afternoon because it gets too hot. Plants wilt, so it's best to start first thing or wait till evening, when it cools off. Besides, Peggy said she had aphids and you can't spray roses in the middle of the day. The sun burns the—"

"What was Scott wearing when he answered the door?"

"Khaki trousers and a short-sleeved Hawaiian shirt."

"Hawaiian shirt? Are you sure?"

Regina's lids fluttered as she tested her memory.

"It was kind of loud, really. Dark red with green hibiscus and yellow centers."

"Was he wearing a T-shirt underneath?"

"No. He opened the door only halfway. He was standing behind it and didn't invite me in, but I'm sure I would have remembered. Who'd wear two shirts on a day like that?"

Someone trying to hide scratches on his chest. Had Peggy fought back?

"What kind of shoes?"

"I didn't notice."

But she would have if they'd been black oxfords with an aloha shirt and khaki slacks. Ray bit back his frustration. Why had Regina Hummel waited so long to come forward? If they'd known Warren changed, they could have searched for the clothes she'd seen while they were at the crime scene. Now they would need a warrant, which meant probable cause, and after a week there'd be no trace...

"Did he say where his wife was?" She shook her head. "Remember anything else?"

"I was surprised Peggy didn't call to thank me for returning her thermos. It wasn't like her, but I didn't know anything was wrong till Monday morning. It was her turn to drive, and she always picked me up at six fifty-five on the dot." He'd have to find that patrol officer, hoped to God he'd handed out tickets. "—no answer at her house, so I drove myself to work. When I got there, I tried again. I guess that's why I called you."

Ray snapped to attention. "What do you mean?"

"Well, it was the whole way he described it..."

"Who?"

"Warren Scott. I asked him, 'Is Peggy all right?' and he said, 'I have bad news. We lost her over the weekend.' I said, "What do you mean?' and he said, 'She ran headfirst into a burglar.' At first I didn't know what he was talking about, it sounded like he misplaced her or she was a dog who slipped its leash. And who would describe what happened to poor Peggy as running headfirst into something, like she was clumsy?" For the first time, Ray noticed the circles under Regina's eyes. "When he went on to say she was dead, I felt sick, just sick. I had to leave work. I still can't imagine what it must have been like for her. But you never really know what goes on in someone else's marriage, do you?"

———

"**B**ored?" Lew asked when he walked into Ray's office an hour later and found his partner leafing through a printout from the state patrol. But he gave a low whistle when he heard what Regina Hummel had said.

"—and the officer who gave the tickets bears her out." Ray turned to the sheet of oak tag posted on the wall behind his desk. With a black Magic Marker, he laboriously added two entries to the time line of Warren Scott's whereabouts the day his wife was murdered.

"That tears the case wide open, don't it?" Lew said, peering at Ray's chart. "Together with the clocks..."

Ray pointed to the first notation. "Laura arrives at eight-thirty, while her folks are eating breakfast. They're talking about doing chores—"

"Didn't Tim's girlfriend say Peggy called before that with a message for Laura?"

"Yeah. But they never run into her, so Laura doesn't know she can't pick up the Dodge until after she gets to Gillman. That's why she drives her Barracuda back to Stanley. A big fat zero there." Ray's finger tracked two inches to the right. "The next thing we know for sure, Warren drops Peggy's Caddy at Gillman Sinclair around nine. Right?" He waited for Lew's nod that the service station confirmed the timing. "Laura follows him in the Barracuda and gives him a lift back home."

Now he stabbed at the only entry in red.

"Ten-oh-two. Peggy's watch stops, either from the blow to her wrist or blood seeping into the mechanism."

"Still waiting to hear from your pal at Gillman Mall?"

Grunting in reply, Ray pointed to the numbers he'd just added.

"At ten-twelve we have the state patrol officer ticketing a yellow VW bug at the intersection of Cleveland and Grand for running the stop sign, and a motorcycle for speeding at ten twenty-three." He tapped the next three entries. "That jibes with Hummel saying she was at the Scotts' between ten-fifteen and ten-thirty, ringing with no answer. When Warren finally comes to the door, he's wearing a Hawaiian shirt but doesn't let her in."

Lew nodded, anticipating the best part. "And the piss de resistance..."

"Is the clocks." Ray could barely contain his excitement. "Son of a bitch might as well have shot a home movie when he unplugged 'em and tossed 'em in the garbage can next to her body along with the TV set and the rest of that crap. The radio from the kitchen counter said eleven twenty-two, Laura's Hallmark stopped at eleven twenty-four and the alarm in the master bedroom read eleven twenty-seven. What burglar's gonna hang around the scene an *hour* after whacking the lady of the house, yanking appliances out of the wall?"

"For a guy as bright as Warren," Lew agreed, "he sure made some stupid mistakes. You'd think he'd at least change the time on Peggy's watch to create an alibi, especially after the Hummel broad shows up. She must have come right after he killed her. I guess his first mistake was answering the door."

"Blind panic, Lew. The last thing Scott was thinking about was his wife's watch." Chuckling derisively, Ray tossed the marker on his desk. "No, Warren's real problem is he's such a damn cheapskate. If he'd been willing to risk scratching his Remingtons or silverware, he wouldn't have had to yank clocks out of the wall to make it look like the house was being burglarized."

"What he should've done was set those clocks fifteen minutes or half an hour ahead, to give himself an alibi…" Ray nodded in agreement. "And ain't we lucky he didn't. By the way, did you learn anything more from the Sinclair?"

Lew tried to look nonchalant. "Guy who did the lube job said something interesting."

"Which is?"

"Warren had been bringing the Olds and the Dodge in for a couple years now. Not often, but regular." He reached for Ray's marking pen. "Lube jobs, brake repairs. Seems to know a lot about cars but don't like to do the work himself. You know the type."

"Yeah, so?"

"One time he dropped off the Olds and had quite a little talk with the mechanic about how he wanted his brake pads installed. Guy thought later, 'If he knows so damn much, why don't he do it himself?' They get a lotta guys like that, think they know everything but don't like to get their hands dirty." Lew paused, tapping the cap of the marker against his teeth.

"Funny thing is, Scott really does know what he's talking about when it comes to cars. But guys like him usually want to do the job themselves."

"Jesus, Lew, would you get to the point?"

Grinning, Lew turned to the chart. "Warren went back."

"To the service station?"

"Twice."

"*Twice?*" Ray snatched the pen from Lew's hand.

"A little after ten-thirty and again at eleven forty-five."

"You're kidding! Why'd he do a dumb thing like that?"

"Said it was to check on his car. Looked inside both times, then left."

"Now, ain't that interesting. Why not pick up the phone and call, and why go back twice? I'd say Warren has some explaining to do." His resentment of his partner for holding out on him forgotten, Ray inked in the new times in his careful print and slipped the marker into his pocket. "And didn't he say he got to Stanley a little after noon? What's that Olds run on, rocket fuel?"

"We need to nail down exactly where he was between the time he left the Sinclair and his arrival at the one o'clock practice," Lew agreed.

"You can bet he'll have an answer for every question." In response to Lew's blank look, Ray continued. "Think about it. What's Warren do for a living? He's an accountant. They're detail men, every penny counts."

"But if he left the Sinclair at eleven forty-five, he couldn't have made it to Stanley right after noon like he said. His timing's already so tight, it's not like there's many more answers to give."

"You watch, Lew. He won't be able to resist filling in details. It's a matter of ego." Ray shook his head. "After killing his wife all he could think of was saving his ass. Some of the things he did will be brilliant, and some will be stupid. With a little luck, those details will hang him."

"How do you think it really went down?"

"What do you mean?" Ray leaned forward, momentarily confused. "Laura drops him off, he and Peggy start to do chores. Something happens and he explodes—"

"No, I mean the rest of it. The whole thing."

Ray settled back in his chair.

"There's a four-hour window, Lew, between the time he takes Peggy's Caddy in for a lube and when he shows up at the rec center. He has to account for his time between nine and one convincingly, or he's cooked. And he's got to live with the fact that he went back to the Sinclair twice, at ten-thirty and eleven forty-five. What he doesn't realize is, we *know* Peggy was whacked at ten-oh-two and that he was home when Regina Hummel rang the bell at ten-fifteen."

"Why go back to the service station?"

"The first time? Either to create an alibi or to hide the weapon. My money's on the weapon. When Regina sees him he freaks out, knows he has to get rid of it fast. So he wraps it in something, maybe even the clothes he was wearing, and stashes it in the trunk of Peggy's car. The grease monkey wouldn't have the key. Then he goes back to the house and tries to make it look like a burglary."

"Tearing clocks out of the wall—"

"Which places him at the scene between eleven twenty-two and eleven twenty-seven."

"So why return to the Sinclair at eleven forty-five?"

"The second time had to be for an alibi, Lew." Ray couldn't help admiring Warren's stones. "In case someone saw him when he went back to the house. Hundred bucks says when we interrogate him he'll have a slew of errands he'll say he was out running while those clocks were being torn from the wall, and smack in the middle will be that second trip to the service station."

"He could still be at the house at eleven twenty-seven and the Sinclair twenty minutes later."

"But he doesn't know what we know about the clocks, remember? You watch, when he finds out what time those clocks stopped he'll say the grease monkey was mistaken, he arrived at eleven-thirty."

"A swearing contest..."

"And don't forget, on Warren's side is reasonable doubt. You know what his lawyer will say to the jury? Would you let twelve men put your *own* child in prison based on that kind of proof?'"

"But if he was at the Sinclair at eleven-thirty, he couldn't have gotten to Stanley at noon, like he said that morning. It's a forty-five-minute drive."

"No, he's gonna get creative on us. By now he realizes a field full of hockey players would have seen him arrive at one, so he'll start remembering other stops he made along the way. A trip to the store, this and that, but not a single receipt... That's when he dumped the weapon and his clothes."

"Still seems awfully stupid for someone as sophisticated as Scott."

"Odd combination of dumb and smart," Ray agreed, "but not so different from other amateurs. If they were true geniuses, slobs like you and me wouldn't stand a chance."

Lew laughed. "From your lips to God's ear..."

"Yeah." Ray scratched his head. "And I got a phone call yesterday from Peggy's sister, Kay Butler. Warren was signed up for one of those seminars, a Dale Carnegie—type course that was supposed to start at noon that Saturday in Widmark. She swears he would never have missed it."

"She mention anything about motive?"

"Family tensions over the kids, this and that. When I tried to push, she clammed up. I should have let you handle it." Ray rocked back in his chair until his head rested against the wall. "She sure hates the guy though. When I asked what made her so positive Warren wouldn't have missed his seminar, she told me Peggy said he'd been looking forward to it for months. 'His ticket to success,' Kay called it. And it cost five hundred bucks. I called Dale Carnegie and found out he was registered. The fee was nonrefundable, and they don't take attendance."

"Why didn't he use that as his alibi?"

"Not enough time. Course was set for noon at a hotel by the airport, and he couldn't get there from the Sinclair in fifteen minutes. If he arrived late someone might have noticed. Probably why he decided to go to Stanley in the first place. Where else could he kill a few hours before coming home and finding his wife's body?"

"Oh, and one more thing." Lew pretended to examine his nails. "SBI identified the weapon." The front legs of Ray's chair hit the linoleum with a thud. "Kevin Day says it's a framing hammer. An Estwing, to be precise."

"How in hell does he know that?"

"Ask him yourself. He's from Montana, but he's smarter than your average bear." With that, Lew sauntered out of the office.

Ray slid the autopsy photos from their envelope and peered at the wounds in Peggy's head. An Estwing framing hammer? What a load of crap. And he knew all about that hotshot Day, the Vietnam vet who'd left Butte a year earlier to run the lab at the State Bureau of Investigation. He was even some kind of hero, got lucky and greased a Cong he caught trying to blow up a field hospital, and when the *Post* tried to do a feature story, Day pretended it was no big deal. If there was one thing Ray couldn't stand it was false modesty. But could he really identify the murder weapon? After a long moment he reached for the phone and dialed.

"I understand you're working Scott," he began.

"Lew Devine tells me you were in the MPs, Lieutenant." Day's voice was softer than Ray expected, and he measured each word before it left his mouth. "I was in the MPs too."

"Oh, yeah?" Must've handled lots of dope cases.

"You had it tougher in Korea from what I heard."

"Oh, yeah?"

"You had Greeks and Turks to worry about, not to mention the Aussies…"

"Yeah, it got a little hairy at times." Ray rolled his head until his third vertebra gave a satisfying pop. Maybe the guy wasn't such an idiot.

"I'd like to get together with you sometime, buy you a beer."

Ray's eyes narrowed. "What for?"

"SBI provides support to sheriffs in places like Weaver County, where there's only one deputy."

"Weaver County?" Despite himself, Ray had to laugh. "They got more trout than people up there!"

"Mountain lions too, but the sheriff knows every inch of that county, and I have a lot to learn. You could help me."

Ray let out his breath. "What makes you so sure it's an Estwing?"

"The lab's my turf." He was speaking faster now, and Ray wondered whether Day had thought he was a rube. "We photographed Peggy's bruise and blew it up, and the milled face of the hammer matches the mesh on her skin. Like ballistics, every weapon leaves a signature."

"How's a framing hammer different from a regular one anyway?"

"Our weapon's heavier and has a longer handle to drive those big nails. An Estwing weighs twenty-eight ounces and runs sixteen inches from the head to the base of the shaft." Now Day was firing his words with the confidence of a sharpshooter, and Ray winced at having fallen for his aw-shucks routine. "—double-tempered cross-hatched face to grip nail heads and prevent them from flying, and a forged one-piece steel head with a flattened claw—"

"*Whoa.* Flattened claw?"

"Look in your own toolbox, Ray. I'll bet your hammer's a standard sixteen-ouncer with a curved claw. The ones twenty ounces and up are for pros, who want maximum power per swing and don't worry about hitting off center. They like the extra length because it offers more leverage even though it's harder to hit square." Day laughed. "Ever try pulling out nails with a flattened claw?"

"Now that you mention it..."

"The good news is the weapon will be tough to clean, because blood would have seeped into the vinyl grip. As I say, it's not a tool the average homeowner—"

"I get the picture. But our man's full of surprises." Ray sighed. "Sounds like there's lots of work ahead."

"Whatever I can do, just give me a call. And I meant it about that beer."

Ray looked at his watch. Maybe he'd stop at Ace Hardware on his way home.

Chapter Fourteen

As soon as they left Widmark the terrain flattened and trees became scarce, scattered across the landscape as if shaken from a can. Red barns with tin roofs began to appear by the side of the road, and the horizon was broken by grain elevators and water towers. As clumps of cottonwood in creek beds signaled coming towns, Sari and Tim joked with Laura about blips on the map called Darling, Plutarch, and Pope. Helen had flown back to Brooklyn and they were on their way to Walker County for Peggy's funeral. Any distraction from their destination was a godsend.

As they crossed the state line the difference became more profound. Large pale hands clasped in prayer welcomed them to St. Edmond and the billboard warned, "He Knows." Sari glanced uneasily at Tim, but his eyes were fixed on the road. Each mile seemed to carry them a step backward in time.

They met up with Warren in Fillmore at the funeral parlor where Peggy's closed casket was heaped with yellow roses, and Tim and his sister knelt and prayed before receiving mass cards for the funeral the following morning. Because Warren wanted to speak alone with the priest who would be conducting the mass, they ate dinner at a hamburger stand and tried to locate the site of W. R. Scott's gas station.

Unlike the New England towns Sari had visited as a child, Fillmore lacked a true center. It was dusty and depressing, with unnaturally wide streets and two-story facades on buildings only one story tall. Instead of the comforting hush of a summer evening in a familiar place, nightfall here brought an unsettling stillness. As the sun set, porch lights blinked on and the few pedestrians disappeared, and soon the only sign of life was a motorcycle revving in the distance. Tim finally parked on a side street where they waited in silence until it was time to meet his father.

"I spent the afternoon telling the priest about your mother," Warren began when they gathered at the home of a second cousin where Sari and Laura would be staying. "Listen carefully to what he says tomorrow, because that's how I want you to remember her." He drove off with Tim to another relative's home for the night, and for the first time Sari found herself alone with Tim's sister. Unless you counted that time last winter when she ran into Laura at Doozy Duds.

It had been dead week, the days before finals. Panic percolated through the campus like dirty ground water, and not even the diligent were immune. The library and dorms were wall-to-wall with students cramming, the floor of the lounge at the Student Union was littered with sleeping bags and cardboard cups like the airport when an Easter blizzard stranded thousands of students en route to Mazatlan. Unable to find anyplace sane enough to study, Sari stuffed her laundry in a duffel bag with her books on Sunday night and set off for the Laundromat on Broadway.

Few students patronized Doozy Duds. The dorms and off-campus housing were equipped with their own laundry facilities, and because most residents of the Hill had cars, they went to more modern establishments at shopping centers. Doozy Duds was the refuge of the disenfranchised, the acid freaks who descended on the Hill from Coyote Springs with unwashed children in tow and congregated on street corners scrounging joints and change. It was the last place Sari expected to see Laura Scott.

At half past ten the Laundromat was almost empty. A girl Sari's age in a buckskin jacket with a baby under one arm had just finished loading a garbage bag of clothes in the machine nearest the door, and was settling back to stare at suds breaking against the glass like whitecaps lapping the porthole of a ship. At the far end of the tunnel-like space a young couple sat flipping through magazines.

Thinking about it later, Sari couldn't say exactly how she knew they were together: seated two chairs apart, they weren't speaking when she entered, but their relaxed posture said *cowple*. It wasn't until the girl, slender and wearing a knitted cap, turned to the clean-shaven guy in a jean jacket and laughed that she was sure. Something intimate in that tinkly sound, the way she threw back her head and smiled at him before returning to her magazine. Not wanting to intrude, Sari set down her bag a dozen seats away. Unloading her clothes in a wall-mounted unit, her mind was on her Roman history test.

Another giggle from the far end made her glance up from her text. The girl in the cap was rising to switch her load from the washer to a dryer. Reaching into the pocket of her skintight Levis, she found change and started toward the vending machine, which dispensed miniature packets of bleach and soap. On her return Sari finally recognized her. The only Scott she had a prayer of winning over... "Laura?"

The girl's fingers tightened around the fabric softener and her eyes darted down the row of chairs. Instantly, Sari saw her mistake. Tim's sister didn't want to speak to her.

"Sari?" A wave of resentment swept over her at Laura's trapped look. What had she done to any of them that made it an effort to say hi? After an uncomfortable silence Laura added, "What are you doing here?"

"Cramming for finals." Tim was right; it was going to take time, but if she could just show them she was good for him, get Laura to give her a chance... "I'm glad we ran into each other. I've been wanting to talk."

"I'm in kind of a hurry. I was just about to leave."

But the wet clothes ten yards away and the fabric softener in her hand said something else. And now that Sari was looking more closely, she saw Laura was wearing a tight red cardigan with the top two buttons undone, smoky eye shadow and a hint of blush, a combination that made the mole at the corner of her eye alluring. Something sexual in her embarrassment—defiance and shame at being caught? Laura glanced again at the guy, whose face was buried in a *Popular Mechanics,* and Sari felt her panic mount. This wasn't about Sari, it was about *him.*

"Tim's got calculus in the morning, and I came here so he could study. Tomorrow's Roman history...."

Laura nodded, pretending to listen, looking out the window at the parking lot, *anywhere but at the guy,* and Sari stole another peek. He was older, in his late twenties or maybe even thirty, good-looking in a dark way. Much too clean cut to be the creep Tim had told her about, the pot-smoking biker Peggy couldn't stand. As he flipped through his magazine, his left hand flashed.

A wedding band.

"Well, it's been nice talking to you, Sari, but—"

"I feel like I got off on the wrong foot with your folks." Sari had packed the A-line pattern and yards of polished cloth in the trunk in her closet at the dorm, resolved that Peggy would never learn about her ambition to sew. And now, for just a moment, she held Laura captive. She must have some advice about dealing with her family. "What do you think I should do?"

Laura shook her head, trying to gauge what Sari had seen. Them together, her guy's ring... Suddenly Sari's heart went out to her.

"Mom will come around," Laura was saying, "she's always been protective of Tim."

"I hope it can be different with us." *I won't tell.*

Laura nodded like a puppet. *Just give them time, I won't say anything about this conversation if you won't tell, it'll be our secret...* Never doubting whose secret was the more important one, Sari nodded back. She didn't need to know more.

Laura rushed to her dryer, yanking out still-wet clothes and stuffing them in a muslin sack, fabric softener slipping unnoticed to the floor as she ran out the door. Arms reaching over his head and lanky legs stretching before him, the guy yawned, slowly rose, and sauntered out thirty seconds later. As he passed Sari without so much as a glance in her direction, she saw that his hands were callused and rough.

His livelihood. The rumble of a truck starting up, skidding off in the night. Of course she never told Tim. It wasn't her secret to tell.

And now Sari was in Walker County with Laura, and they'd been given a room to share. After they changed into nightgowns their host's teenage daughter, a strapping girl who'd given birth to the baby she'd just put to bed downstairs, came up to say good night.

"Want to see my stretch marks?" The girl proudly lifted her pajama top, brandishing yards of flesh-colored crepe like combat ribbons. She had seemed almost resentful of their presence, and Sari didn't know whether it was her envy of relatives from the big city or the fact that she'd had to give up her bedroom for the night. It was clear she was still living at home.

"So that's what they look like," Sari said, automatically glancing at her hand for a ring. The girl caught her.

"I know what you're thinking," she said defiantly. "Where's the father?"

"Probably home with his wife," Laura replied.

"If you want to know what that's like," the girl told Sari, "ask *her.*"

"Just shut up!" Laura snapped. A current passed from her to Sari, an urgent reminder of an unspoken pact. *Don't tell.*

Suddenly holding all the cards, the girl walked to the vanity and sat in front of the three-sided mirror. Gazing in the center glass, she began brushing her silky hair back from her forehead.

"One, two, three, four..." she counted under her breath as Laura opened the window and leaned out as far as she could. In response to Sari's unasked question she added, "Laura knows all about married men."

Did she mean the guy at Doozy Duds?

"Eight, nine, ten..." The brush whipped through her gleaming curls without missing a beat. "She was doing it with a married guy in tenth grade. It was so bad, her folks had to leave town."

Off balance, Sari blurted out her question.

"Did Tim know?" The left frame of the mirror caught Laura's reflection. She was on the balls of her feet, preparing to take flight. In her nightgown she looked otherworldly.

"Why else would they move to Indianapolis for a year?" The girl glared at Tim's sister's back, but Laura was in another universe. "You think just because we live in the boonies we don't hear things? For all anyone knows, she's still seeing him."

Under the thin cotton of her gown Laura's shoulders tensed, and Sari knew it was true. She had to defend her.

"Reynolds transferred Warren," she began.

"Like hell!" the girl exclaimed. Just then her baby let out a wail, and she reluctantly rose. "A mother's work is never done," she said with an odd sort of pride. Like stretch marks a baby conferred status, and for the first time Sari felt she understood Tim's sister.

As the door closed behind her, Sari tried to find a way to defuse the tension.

"What was quiet time?" she asked.

Laura turned from the window.

"Quiet time?" she replied, stepping to the vanity. She picked up the brush and began running it through her cropped hair. Free of makeup, her features had an unguarded intensity. "No big deal."

"Tim says your mother had to lie down with a cool cloth—"

Fifteen sixteen seventeen...

"Mom was fragile, that's all it was. When she gave birth it exhausted her. Allison and I were fussy and she had only enough milk for one." She was staring at Sari's reflection but not really seeing her, and for an instant she resembled Warren. "Family was everything to her. A perfect wife, just like her mother."

Twenty-twotwenty-threetwenty-four...

"Who told you about quiet time, anyway?" Laura asked.

"Tim."

Thirtyeightthirtynineforty...

"He had no business telling you that."

"Tim tells me everything!"

The face in the mirror laughed. "You don't know a damned thing."

—

Zigzagging across prairie on gravel roads that intersected at right angles before veering off into more of the same, the trip to St. Augustine's the next morning seemed to take twice as long as it actually did. As they drove in silence past cultivated fields with no sign of human habitation, Sari felt increasingly disoriented. The magnitude and color of the sky rivaled the ocean, and each time they crested a hill she expected to see water.

For miles there was nothing but corn, then finally a steeple gleamed on the horizon. When they drew closer, a red brick church loomed; cars lined the road in both directions. Tim parked the Mustang and, as Laura disappeared in the throng of mourners, grabbed Sari's hand and led her across the crumbly berm.

Two feet into the corn they could no longer see the road, and for the first time Sari felt they were truly alone. The stalks were taller than a man and the rows wide enough to stand in, and Tim kept pulling her deeper until it swallowed them. Now the foliage was so dense all they could hear was the thrum and chirp of crickets and, when they stood perfectly still, a sizzle that seemed to emanate from the broad green leaves. The smell was heady and bitter, like biting into a blade of grass, and they held each other and drank it in until the bell summoned them to rejoin the living.

St. Augustine's was packed with Dannhauers and Peggy's childhood friends, people who had loved her not from a sense of duty but because she was one of their own. An endless stream of fair-haired aunts and cousins filed in, so many that Sari quickly lost track of which of them had brought the casseroles and biscuits and pies for lunch after the service in the old parish house next door. Guard down, Kay Butler looked stricken and unbelieving, but Sari's attention was riveted on Nettie Dannhauer.

Peggy's mother was rail thin and ramrod straight. Her iron hair was pulled back from her face so tightly her skin was white at the temples, and the black taffeta dress that reached from ankle to chin was interrupted only by a string of rosary beads looped around her wrist. Pale lips fluttered inaudibly, and Kay or another daughter was always in sight, ready to rush to Nettie's side at the crook of a finger. She was terrifying in her grief.

Warren assigned his children to the front pew and Sari a seat a few rows back. As Nettie swished up the aisle to the row directly behind the Scotts with a daughter on each side, her muttering escalated to a keening wail. Vonnie Scott sat in the very back wearing a flowery dress and bright pink scarf. She spoke to none of the Dannhauers before or after the service.

Sari had never been inside a Catholic church, and the formality of incense and prayers seemed disconnected from the savage unpredictability of Peggy's death. Because Warren had reminded his children to listen carefully to the priest, she'd expected him to be someone who knew Tim's mother, but to her surprise the man who led the service could not have been more than thirty years old. Following a lengthy sermon about the joys of the afterworld and Peggy coming home at last, he clasped his hands to his breast. As if an invisible curtain rose, the mourners grew still. Now he would say something personal, Sari thought, something to sum up what Peggy meant to those who loved her.

"I never had the pleasure of meeting Margaret Kathleen, but I am told despite her many problems, she always managed to be kind."

Time froze as the congregation absorbed his meager praise; Sari heard Kay gasp. Then everyone exhaled. The service was over.

Chapter Fifteen

Ray had Scott's mouthpiece pegged from the start. Simon Evans had all the pretensions of a gentleman, but the lawyer was a snake at heart.

"I will make Mr. Scott available for one hour this afternoon, Lieutenant," Evans said when he returned Ray's call promptly Monday morning, and Ray wondered whether he put on that lord-of-the-manor accent to impress his clients. "He will not, however, agree to a polygraph. They're unreliable."

Unreliable, my ass.

When Ray called Philips to advise him of the interview, he used a little reverse English and suggested the D.A. handle the questioning himself. Philips declined and Ray knew it had nothing to do with generosity: there was so little physical evidence tying Warren to the crime, the D.A. was in no rush to be blamed for striking out. Of course, if he'd known about the clocks, it might have been another matter... Devine laughed when he heard.

"Your lucky day, ain't it?" Lew said. "I can't believe you haven't told him."

"Haven't had a chance—"

"Why hold back? There's no way the D.A. can queer the interview, Scott either has an alibi or he doesn't."

"Guys like Philips can't resist tipping their hand, Lew, especially when they think they're holding all the cards. I can't tell you the number of times a suspect has left this building after an interrogation knowing more about our case than we learned about his defense. Philips thinks he's running a candy store."

"You're calling the shots, but if it was me, I'd worry about getting my butt in a sling for withholding evidence. What's the story with Peggy's watch?"

"Fritz Smelnic says it *probably* stopped when it was shattered by the blow to her wrist, which puts the attack at ten-oh-two. That means the killer hung around the house an hour and a half after she died, yanking junk out of the wall, and then never even took it with him when he left. Pretty dumb for a burglar, huh?"

"And you don't think you should tell Philips?"

"Not now, Lew, there's always time—"

"Did you keep the fingerprint analysis from him too? Tell me you didn't."

Ray examined the ridges in his nails. "I told him as of yesterday it was inconclusive."

"*Inconclusive?* Jesus, you know the lab said everything was wiped clean and the perp wore gloves! What're you trying to do, get both of us canned?"

At 4:10 on the dot, Simon Evans sauntered into the Hallet County Sheriff's Department dressed in a pin-striped suit, snowy shirt, and silk tie with a repeating pattern so minuscule Ray couldn't have made it out with a magnifying glass. As far as he was concerned, there were two types of lawyers: the polyester kind with the loud neckwear and the fast talkers sporting Italian double-breasteds and monogrammed cuffs. Evans was neither, but that didn't make him any the less indecent. If it wasn't for that off-kilter nose, you might have taken him for a banker, and his client looked like he'd gotten a few nights of sleep since the last time Ray saw him. With his thinning hair slicked back, sideburns trimmed and cheeks as shiny as if they'd just been slapped with the aftershave that came off him in a wave, Warren Scott looked positively sleek. Ray would do something about that.

As instructed, the receptionist showed them to the conference room with the tall windows facing south and west, normally reserved for meetings with state legislators and visiting muckety-mucks. A far cry from the cubicles with wooden chairs near Ray's office in the bowels of the building, where rapists and muggers he could intimidate cooled their heels. With Evans sitting in it would be difficult to lull Scott into any sense of security, but Ray could strip off the kid gloves only if he was wearing them in the first place. Settling directly across from Scott, he fixed his quarry with a polite smile.

Simon Evans wasted no time establishing ground rules. Ignoring Philips, he fastened his flinty eyes on Ray. "We are here on a cooperative basis to facilitate your investigation, Lieutenant. I take it you've not charged anyone with this horrendous crime?"

"No, we haven't." In close quarters Scott's cologne was so strong Ray wondered if he bathed in it. "We're still developing leads."

"Good. As you know, my client discovered his wife's body when he arrived at his residence late that afternoon. He will not give a written statement, nor will I permit this interview to be transcribed." In a tone reserved for Chihuahuas with smaller than average brains, he addressed the assistant D.A. for the first time. "I see you've brought your legal pad. While I have no objection to your presence, I won't allow my client to speak if notes are taken. Understood?"

Philips sputtered, but when he saw Ray's face he capped his fountain pen and placed his pad on the floor at his feet.

"Very good," Evans continued. "Is the young lady with the machine a stenographer? Well, we won't be needing her today."

As Ray excused the court reporter, Evans shot his cuff to consult his watch.

"It is now four twenty-one." He unclasped the gold mesh band and set his timepiece on the table. "We will depart at five twenty-one and leave you to your business."

Ray wasted little time on the preliminaries. Warren was forty-five, born and raised in Fillmore. Upon graduating from high school he enlisted in the army and was assigned to the motor pool as a mechanic, and after his discharge enrolled at the University and graduated with an accounting degree. Married Peggy Dannhauer in Widmark one month after she turned eighteen, and worked at Reynolds Industrial for the next twenty-four years as an accountant. A year before his wife died he left Reynolds to become a freelance consultant. Scott delivered his answers by rote, as a child might recite a poem he was required to memorize. Ray smiled to himself. Let him think he was humoring them. Leaning forward, he began.

"Mr. Scott, what do you remember about Saturday morning?"

"We got up early."

"What time?"

"Around seven."

"What'd you do after you woke up?"

"We decided what we were going to do."

Not the first time he'd had to pull teeth.

"Tell me what you remember of your discussion."

Scott stared at the plaster ceiling. "Chores, clean out the garage. She wanted to prune her roses."

"What happened after your discussion?" The afternoon sun beating through the windows was making the room stuffy, and as Ray wiped his nose he wondered how men could wear cologne. Scott must have poured a bottle of Old Spice over his head before leaving the house.

"While we were having breakfast, Laura came home."

"Why?"

"She's very devoted to her mother."

A twenty-one-year-old girl home on the weekend? But Ray declined the bait. They already knew about the mixup with the Dodge; he wasn't about to waste precious time on a red herring… Philips began drumming his fingers as if he were bored and Ray, distracted, resisted the impulse to kick him. "When did you decide to go to Stanley?" he continued.

"I thought I'd surprise Tim and see his apartment."

"Any talk about that at breakfast?"

Scott hesitated. "I decided to do it later, spur of the moment."

No mention of Dale Carnegie. Good.

"What time did you finish eating?"

"Before nine."

"What'd you do then?" Like watching paint dry, but at least Philips was keeping his yap shut.

"Drove my wife's Cadillac to the Sinclair station. Laura followed and brought me home so I could help with the chores."

"What time was that?"

"Just after nine. Sinclair's less than five minutes away."

"What exactly did you do then?"

"She told me to clean the upstairs bathrooms." A bead of sweat had formed on Scott's forehead, but his hands remained clasped on the table, and Ray once again was struck by the image of an obedient boy.

"Did you?"

"While I was washing a mirror, the nozzle on the Windex broke and I drove to the Safeway at Union and Grand for a new one. I also bought a can of charcoal lighter fluid because we were planning to have a barbecue later that afternoon. When I returned, I finished the job." An odor other than cloves drifted across the table, and Ray shifted in his chair. He wanted to get up and open a window.

"And then?"

"I said good-bye to my wife, got in the Olds, and went to Stanley."

He'd be damned if he'd let Warren get away with that. The woman had a name, didn't she? "What was *Peggy* doing when you left?"

"I don't remember. We just said our normal good-byes." What about those other trips to the service station? Hoping against hope that Warren would blow his own carefully constructed alibi, Ray moved to another topic.

"Any unfamiliar vehicles on your block that morning?"

"Well, I—"

Philips interrupted. "A wood-paneled pickup truck, perhaps?"

Ray struggled to keep his face blank as Scott gave a start of recognition. That's all they needed, to plant the idea of a real intruder in Evans's head.

"Now that you mention it, I believe I did see a truck like that."

"Do you know the owner?" Philips continued. Warren was quick on the uptake but too smart to bite all the way. He'd be nuts to try to blame—

"Matter of fact, I don't."

Warren leaned back and Evans tapped his watch. "Twenty-three minutes left, Lieutenant. Perhaps you'd like to move on."

The time gaps, focus on the timing… Any holes or discrepancies would tell them where he stashed the weapon and his clothes.

"When'd you decide to go to Stanley?" Ray asked.

"After I returned from Safeway, my wife and I discussed plans for Tim's rehearsal dinner. I said I'd check on restaurants."

"Did you drive directly there?"

"Actually, no." He stared at the ceiling again, visualizing that great appointment book in the sky. "I stopped at the Sinclair to find out when the Cadillac would be ready. While I was there, I remembered I'd left a suit jacket in the backseat."

"What time was that?"

"Oh, I'd say ten-thirty… I wanted to make sure the jacket got cleaned, so I picked it up and brought it home." So that was his excuse for returning to the service station the first time. Was the real reason to provide an explanation for being home if Regina Hummel came forward?

"Was Peggy there when you returned?" Ray asked.

"I just tossed the jacket in the front closet and—"

"Did you speak to your wife?" Philips interrupted. What was he doing, feeding Warren lines?

"No. I assumed she was out back. Then I left again." No mention of Hummel. Hedging his bet she wouldn't come forward?

"What were you wearing?"

"Sport shirt and slacks. You saw them."

Ray nodded politely. Plaid flannel and dark blue trousers… Oxfords. Might as well get it on the record. "Did you change your clothes?"

"No, why would I?"

"Are you sure you didn't do anything else between dropping off your jacket and leaving for Stanley?" Philips asked.

Like go back to the Sinclair... Ray prayed Warren missed the cue.

"Matter of fact, I did. I went back to the service—"

"What time was that?" Philips interrupted again. "Eleven, eleven-thirty?"

Jesus, Philips was drawing Scott a road map! Had someone told the D.A. about the clocks? With the service station only minutes away, the difference between 11:30 and 11:45 was crucial. If Warren was there at 11:30, he could hardly have been home pulling clocks out of the wall at 11:27. But if it was closer to 11:45, he just might have made it.

"Why'd you go back the second time?" Ray asked.

"To see if the car was ready. It was right around eleven-thirty, as I recall, maybe a little before."

"Are you sure of the time?" Philips pressed.

With Philips locking him in to the time they'd lost any element of surprise, and worse yet, now it would be a pissing contest between Warren and the grease monkey. Once the clocks came out, Warren would insist he was at the Sinclair at the earliest possible moment and point to this very exchange to show he'd said 11:30 all along.... But maybe Ray could work it to his advantage. The earlier Warren arrived at the station, the more time he had to account for before showing up at Tim's one o'clock practice in Stanley. He jumped in before the D.A. could put his foot back in his mouth.

"Stop anywhere else before you got to Stanley?"

Scott smiled with his teeth. "Now that you mention it, I guess I did. When I left the service station I went to the Walgreen's at Gillman Mall for a pair of clip-on sunglasses." Just across the road from the Sinclair, and on a busy morning, no one would notice either way. "And I looked for a card for Tim's wedding gift."

A square box wrapped in silver paper with tinsely ribbon had been found in the garbage can near Peggy's body, along with the appliances from the house. The gall of him, pretending to shop for a card for a gift he had no intention of delivering!

"Any luck?" Ray continued smoothly.

"No, there were none I liked."

Calm down. Just because he trashed his own son's wedding present...

"What were you planning to give Tim?"

Scott shifted in his chair, smug grin intact. "My wife took care of that sort of thing." Anticipating Ray's next question, he reached in his breast pocket for a set of plastic lenses designed to be clipped onto the bridge of a pair of glasses. "I wear glasses, and I like to use these when I drive."

"Get a receipt for the sunglasses?"

The smile began to fade. "I'm sure I did, but I never keep them."

Warren's nimbleness was impressive. He'd taken Philips's gift of fifteen minutes, which distanced him from the scene of the crime at a crucial time, and accounted for it on the other end by a shopping trip that Ray would have no way of disproving. Two for the price of one, courtesy of your friendly D.A... Sure the clip-ons looked new, but who knew when he'd bought them?

"Any other stops?" Ray asked.

"No. I took Vermejo Boulevard to the Interstate, and then the turnpike straight to Stanley."

"What time did you arrive?"

"I went to Tim's apartment first and knocked on the door, but no one answered. It must have been about twelve-thirty." Just like he'd told Lew, a bunch of bullshit errands no one could verify. And all the while he was disposing of the weapon and clothes. "—thought I heard the water running, so I waited several minutes. Tim's fiancee said she was in the shower.... Then I drove to the rec center."

"And got there when?"

"Around one. You can't help seeing the clock when you walk through the rink. The practice was just beginning." Every moment accounted for, but the fit was too neat. He had to find one loose end—

"Didn't you tell the detectives on Saturday that you arrived *before* the practice?" Philips asked.

Jesus H. Christ.

Scott's eyes lit with triumph as he processed the minor point. "I fail to see the distinction . .

A rank odor assailed Ray and he fought the urge to draw back. He knew Warren was lying about those crucial hours between ten and one, but with his lawyer's meter running, there was no sense going over it again now. Same thing with that Dale Carnegie course; if he asked Warren why he hadn't gone, he'd just spin a line of crap about his son's wedding being more important. And Ray would never hear the end of it from Philips, that by giving Warren a chance to come up with an excuse now—which he would undoubtedly embellish over time—Ray had blown any element of surprise at trial. He had to step up the pace.

"Anything unusual about your house when you drove up?"

"The gate to the backyard was open, though it's wired shut from the inside. I remember saying to myself, 'I wonder why—'"

"What'd you do next?"

"Walked in through the front door."

"Locked?"

"It's always open. I called, 'I'm home,' but she didn't answer."

"And?"

"I went upstairs because I thought she might be taking a nap. When I entered our bedroom I saw the dressers were ransacked, so I went downstairs to look at the rest of the house."

"Where'd you go next?"

"The kitchen, then the backyard. She wasn't there so I went back inside and looked in the utility room. The door to the garage was open, and there she was." Now the room was so quiet Ray could hear a fly on the window behind him. "I reached down, but she was stiff." Scott unclasped his hands and flexed his fingers as if ridding them of a cramp, and Evans reached for his watch and gave it a brisk shake. Was he warning his client? "Then I went to the bath off the utility room to wash."

"What did you think happened to your wife?"

Evans stopped fiddling and the room was suddenly still. From the corner of his eye, Ray thought he saw Warren's lawyer lean slightly forward. Afraid his client would say something he shouldn't?

"I—I didn't know what happened. She looked like she'd been hit…"

Evans held up his watch.

"Eight minutes, Lieutenant." What had Ray missed?

"Do you own a framing hammer?" he continued.

"I believe I do." A muscle in Scott's cheek twitched. "My father left me a tool chest with several hammers, and one of them might be for framing."

"How was Peggy's health?"

"Fine. She was on a new medication—"

Evans thrust out his palm like a traffic cop.

"I'm instructing my client not to answer any questions about his wife's health. Have you no decency? The poor woman's—"

"How's your own health, Warren?"

"I have a nervous stomach. I began seeing a doctor for stress a few months ago and he—"

With his eyes still on Ray's face, Evans dug his fingers into his client's sleeve. "I'll not permit any questions along these lines, Lieutenant."

"Why not?"

"Are you charging him?"

"Not at this time."

"Then his health's not relevant to your inquiry."

"That's for us to decide," Philips replied.

Evans smiled tightly. "Exactly two minutes left, gentlemen. If you wish to spend them quibbling with me over relevancy, that's your call. But he's not answering medical questions. They're privileged."

Leaning forward, Ray summoned his most sympathetic tone. If only he'd gotten something more solid from Kay Butler… "I know there was stress between you and Peggy."

"Look, I put up with her for years." Warren gripped the edge of the table with both hands. "I had no reason to kill her now!"

Evans began to rise, but Ray cut him off.

"Did Peggy carry insurance?"

Now the lawyer was on his feet. "Are you referring to theft insurance?"

"No, I mean life insurance. Was Peggy's life insured?"

"Yes." As his sickening cologne gave up the ghost, Warren's body odor filled the room.

"How much?"

"Don't answer any more—"

But Warren was beyond heeding his lawyer's advice. "One hundred thousand dollars for the children's education!"

"Time's up. My client is entitled to an inventory of everything taken from his house, Lieutenant. I want a copy before we leave."

Ray glanced at Lew. There went the clocks. "We don't have one yet."

"Why wasn't an inventory prepared at the scene?"

"We're still processing—"

"That may be, but I want that inventory at my office no later than tomorrow morning." Evans flashed his shark's grin at Philips. "If it's not there by nine sharp, I'll file a formal demand with your superiors. Understood?"

Ray knew he meant he'd go to the press. But Philips rose, a good six inches shorter than his adversary. After showing Scott every card in their hand, who was he trying to kid?

"Is that some kind of a threat, counselor?" Philips said. With a curt nod, Evans left.

—

On their way out of the Hallett County Sheriff's Department, Warren remarked, "They don't have a thing, do they? I don't know what there was to be nervous about."

Simon said nothing as they passed two plainclothes detectives deep in conversation. When they reached the parking lot, he addressed his client for the first time since the interrogation.

"Next time you're tempted to ignore my guidance, you can find yourself another lawyer. That display of impulsiveness when I told you not to speak just bought you an indictment."

Chapter Sixteen

Two days after he was interviewed by the police, Warren took Sari and Tim to dinner at the Caribou Inn, a rambling lodge in the foothills west of Stanley. The field-rock hearth was unlit and the main dining room half empty that evening in early June when they were shown to a table under a rack of antique rifles. While he examined the wine list, Warren ordered a martini.

"What would you like, son, the red or white?"

Tim shrugged. "Makes no difference to us."

"Are you planning to order fish, fowl, or red meat? They have a wonderful Cornish game hen."

Tim ordered roast loin of elk and Sari the rainbow trout, but after the first glass of Burgundy, Warren was the only one who touched the wine.

"What's happening with the investigation?" Sari asked when the wine steward left. The papers had carried only the barest of facts and they'd been told almost nothing, not even how or when Peggy died.

"Simon Evans says they don't have a suspect."

"Evans?" Tim asked.

"My lawyer."

Lawyer? Sari thought. When did he hire a—

"—detective in charge of the case is a real bumbler," Warren was saying, "so we have to face the fact this may never be solved. A pickup truck was parked down the street, and they haven't even looked for the driver. Can you imagine how incompetent they must be?" He turned to Tim. "But that's not why I brought you here." Their food was arriving and he waited until they were alone again. "I want to share some personal things about your mother, Tim. Things you may not remember or maybe never knew."

So that's what this was about. Memories. Sari let out her breath. Warren must have realized how impersonal the priest sounded, how confusing and upsetting his single comment about Peggy was. Now they would talk about good times, and tonight Tim could close his eyes with the knowledge that his childhood was real, his parents' marriage had been loving and strong. Maybe he would even be able to sleep.

"How's the elk?" Warren asked Tim, cutting into his venison.

"I know the priest couldn't say much because he didn't really know Mom…"

Warren looked perplexed. "I told him to say what he did because that's exactly the way I want you to remember her. Despite her troubles, she tried to be a good mother." He swirled his game in its Madeira sauce before lifting a forkful to his mouth. "Don't you remember when we lived in Garfield, that house with the backyard that opened onto the field? I had to take time off from work to care for you children. I was going to get in on the ground floor of Grant Pharmaceuticals, but the money went for her medical expenses." He carved another morsel from bone. "Do you have any idea how much I could have made if I'd invested in Grant Pharmaceuticals fifteen years ago?"

Tim set down his fork.

"And that wasn't the only opportunity I lost," Warren continued. "She was never able to contribute. I had to take jobs beneath my abilities just to keep food on the table. I may not have been a perfect father, but I did the best I could." He reached for his wine. "There were so many companies I had an inside track in. If it wasn't for her, I would've really been able to get somewhere."

"I knew she had problems," Tim said, "but—"

"Bad genes. Whatever was wrong ran in her family, not mine." Warren bit into a scalloped apple, then gestured at Tim with his fork. "Sometimes I worry about you too."

Was it Peggy's genes that made her seem two different people, Sari wondered, animated one moment and despairing the next? Maybe that bizarre procession of dishes the first night had nothing to do with them, her aloofness on Mother's Day wasn't the rejection it seemed. Was illness the reason she gave up her art? And where did Allison's death fit in?

"—used to spend hours in front of the TV with her on weekends," Warren was saying, "watching golf and tennis with the sound off. Don't you remember any of this, son?" Under the table cold fingers clasped Sari's. She glanced at Tim. His expression was a mixture of fascination and dread. *Warren was killing her twice.*

"One day she cooked every recipe in the book," he continued. "I got home and felt like I was in a cafeteria. And she kept harping on the smallest things, stuff that goes on in any marriage, but she could never let it go. Quite a temper, but you probably don't remember that… We were stabilizing her on a new medication when she died and I had to force her to take it."

"I—I didn't know any of this…"

"All those opportunities are gone, of course, but I intend to make up for lost years. For the first time, I have the chance to do what *I* want."

Unable to look at Warren's face, Sari focused on his hands. Guided by fingers as supple and strong as the ones in her lap, severing flesh from bone with surgical precision. It was then that she noticed his wedding ring was gone. He'd been wearing it at the funeral.

"I never knew you felt that way," Tim said. Left hand now clenched beneath the table in a fist, staring at his father as if he were a stranger. An adversary.

"I wanted you to know what she was really like." The matter-of-fact tone was more unsettling than what he was saying. "Know how you were conceived, Tim? I didn't want any children after the twins, but she tricked me. We were using the rhythm method and she said it was safe. If I had my way, you never would have been born."

"And aren't you lucky I was?"

Startled, Warren stared back at his son.

In the dim light their resemblance was uncanny. Two pairs of opaque eyes challenging each other, tension whitening their lips.

"I've always been there for you, son. You know that." Warren nodded slightly, inviting acknowledgment. When it didn't come, his voice took on an edge. "But you had your problems with her too."

"Please—"

"You know the toughest part of raising kids? Not when they're young, but when they grow up and you have to let them go. When they're small they take everything on faith." Polishing off his wine, he signaled the waiter for the dessert tray. "They have a marvelous Black Forest torte, Tim. Sure you don't want a slice?"

—

When they returned to Stanley they went straight to bed. But two hours later Sari roused to the short, tense rasps that told her Tim was awake.

"He must have hated her," he said as if they'd been in the middle of a conversation.

"That's not what he said."

"It's what he meant."

He rolled to the wall and she reached for his shoulder. "Their marriage was difficult because of her illness, not to mention losing a child. That's not the same as—"

"I'm surprised at you, Sari, you always thought my father was a monster."

That stung, but she let it pass.

"This isn't about me, Tim." What did Warren mean about taking everything on faith? "Why did he say he worried about you? Did you ever—"

"That's not what he said!"

Wasn't it? She struggled to remember the rest.

"He said you had problems with her too. What did he mean?"

"I wouldn't expect you to understand."

Suddenly it was too much. Sari slid to the edge of the bed and reached for her nightshirt. There was nothing she could do, their dream was slipping away...

"Where are you going?" he demanded.

"The couch." Fastening buttons, biting back tears. "There's a test tomorrow, and I need sleep."

"Don't leave." The anguish in Tim's voice stopped her. "It's happening too fast, Sari, everything's out of control..."

"But I'm on your side, can't you see?" She sank to her edge of the mattress. "I'm not the enemy." Letting him pull her to him, joining him under the sheet.

"Then don't ask," he whispered.

———

Twilight was Ray's quiet time.

Sitting with Marion on their patio he watched the color fade from the sky. With the mosquitoes sluggish and the air balmy and soft, it was the perfect time to tote up the day's victories and defeats. As he sipped his iced tea, he wondered whether Warren was relaxing in his own backyard, gloating over just how little the police really had.

"Those kids don't know nothing, Marion. Philips is grandstanding, trying to pressure Scott, but he's barking up the wrong tree."

Marion set her needlepoint in her lap. It was getting too dark to read the pattern on the mesh and she didn't want to go inside for her glasses. Besides, Ray needed to talk. The past two nights he'd been muttering in his sleep, and when she pressed his shoulder he woke with a violent start and seemed not to know where he was. She knew all about Peggy Scott, of course. He filled her in on his cases every evening while she fixed dinner and he set the table. But something more was bothering him than his lack of progress, and as she watched his head tilt back Marion knew his posture had little to do with fatigue.

"What are they like?" she asked, gathering skeins of thread.

"Scott's kids? Boy's a longhair but something of an athlete, probably gets decent grades at school. Paints pictures like a professional." In the strobe of the garage Tim's stricken face flickered, and Ray jerked his eyes open. "Should have protected his mom."

"He wasn't there, was he?"

"His girlfriend and a dozen hockey players swear he was in Stanley, but—"

"Then how could you expect him to save her?"

Ray was surprised at her vehemence. Must come from not having one of her own, he thought, and replied in a conciliatory tone. "Tip of the iceberg, Marion, I can feel it."

"He's not responsible for what his father did."

"What do they say, 'Acorns never fall far from the tree.'"

She slapped her packet of needles on the table. "Ray Burt, what's got into you?"

"Nothing."

"What's his daughter like?" Safer ground.

"Lew's got the hots for her. She don't look like much to me, but he's been at loose ends since Cindy moved out. Never could keep his dog in his own yard, but he knows better than to screw up a case."

"Didn't you say she was there that morning?"

"A wasted trip." And a long way to go to get your brakes changed… Didn't they have service stations in that college town? "Once she got home, she turned around and headed back to Stanley. None of those kids knows a thing. Hell, the boy almost lost his lunch when I showed him the body."

"But you just said—"

Ray's throat closed, and he blamed it on the ice cube he swallowed. What was it with this case that made him feel the other shoe was about to drop? "Tell you the truth, he's a little hard to figure. Boy his age should've been able to protect his mom." Marion reached for his hand,

and his gut slowly unclenched as they watched the first stars and a sliver of moon emerge from the sky. He didn't like to think what he might have become without her.

Ray had met his wife the day he was discharged from the army, pushing forty and sure about everything but the opposite sex. They married soon after. Pragmatic, Marion liked to say she was, with the tiniest streak of romance. Her dreams? Ray never knew; it wasn't something men had to think about back then, but she seemed content enough. She wanted kids but after two miscarriages it wasn't in the cards, and now she crocheted receiving blankets for every new mother in the neighborhood. On rare moments he admitted to himself he was glad they were childless. He didn't even want a dog, for Chrissakes. Too many strays at work, he said, to come home and find one underfoot. If Marion saw through his grousing, she had the grace not to make an issue of it. Now he squeezed her hand, and she smiled sympathetically in the dark.

"This case is really getting to you, isn't it?"

"It's those kids, they're just trying to make the best of a bad situation. That's why I don't like hauling them in front of a grand jury. We can win on the clocks anyway." He didn't have to explain because Marion knew the case better than Philips. When she added two and two she came up with four, more than he could say for most D.A.s. Plus she knew how to keep her yap shut. "Know what really bugs me, hon?"

He took her silence for interest and proceeded without waiting for an answer.

"What'd he do with the weapon and his clothes? When Regina Hummel came to the door he was wearing khakis and an aloha shirt. Red with green flowers. But six hours later he has on dark trousers and a flannel shirt, with a T underneath. And black oxfords." His lips pursed. "I always figured he stashed them in Peggy's car and then dumped them on the way to Stanley. But the grip of the hammer would have been soaked with blood and it had a steel shaft. He wouldn't have been able to burn it. 'Course, Vermejo's lined with so much trash, he could've tossed them out along the way and they'd never be spotted. Only time those ditches are cleaned is when the Fremont River floods—"

"Let's go in, dear." Marion rose, balancing the plastic pitcher and glasses on a tray with her needlework. "The mosquitoes are starting to bite."

"You go ahead, I'll be along in a minute."

Ray tried to visualize the route Warren took to Stanley that Saturday. As he mentally drove along the railroad tracks east of the Fremont a familiar queasiness began to take hold, and he told himself he should be inside helping his wife with the dishes. Powerless to obey his better judgment, he extended his legs and gripped the arms of his deck chair. He was trying to recapture a moment that was just out of reach, had been teasing him for days. It shimmered and slowly came into focus.

As his foot began to tap in time to the oom-pah-pah, oom-pah-pah of a railroad band on his cement patio in Gillman, Ray tasted fruit punch and smelled cigar smoke drifting from the poker players. What could happen in a crowd of three thousand people? Only when shouts from the parking lot drowned out the thump of the tuba did the camera zero in on the pulp of the woman's face gleaming wetly under festive lamps…

Furious at the memories that had once again betrayed him, he jumped from his chair and hurried inside to Marion.

—

When Ray knocked on the door at the second floor landing of 655 Locust at seven the following morning, the raven-haired girl he remembered from the crime scene peered out. Sari was her name, Sari Siegel. Tim's fiancee.

"Is Tim home?"

"Why do you want him?" The crack expanded, but she stood blocking his way. In cutoffs and T-shirt she looked all of fifteen years old. But her olive skin and high cheekbones were striking, and Ray wondered how she fit into the family of fair-complected Scotts.

"I'm Lieutenant Burt from the Hallett County Sheriff's Department. We met, remember?" As she widened her stance and folded her arms across her chest, he suppressed a smile. Mother cat protecting her young.

"I need to give him something."

"Can't you give it to me?"

She couldn't weigh more than ninety pounds soaking wet, and there she stood, as if she could hold off a horde of Mongols. But something in her eyes made him think twice.

"Well, Miss Siegel, I'm afraid I have to give it to him myself." She surveyed him warily. He would have to give her a darn good reason for bothering Tim. "You want whoever did this to be caught, don't you?"

She hesitated, then stepped away from the door without inviting him in.

Ray followed her inside and looked around. Not a bad place, small but neat despite the thrown-together look that came from foraging at garage sales. Hockey trophies stood on a table beside a stack of textbooks, and more volumes lined a handmade bookcase across from a daybed covered with an Indian-print spread. An old poster for an antiwar demonstration hung by the entrance to the kitchen, which was tidy despite the lingering smell of burnt toast. He wondered why Tim didn't live on campus and what the girl was doing there so early in the morning. Kids must be fixing it up for after the wedding....

"Tim?" she called. From the bathroom Ray heard the sound of water running.

"Maybe you could help me while we're waiting." He had to breach her armor. "Our job is to eliminate suspects, Sari, not just arrest them. So if you know anything that would help us nail down what time Tim's father arrived Saturday, you'd be doing him a favor." No dice. "You mentioned you weren't expecting him to come..." The water stopped and he spoke faster. "Didn't you tell me something about that?"

"I guess it was meant to be a surprise."

"A surprise?" He kept his tone noncommittal. "Isn't that the usual thing, parents of the groom giving a rehearsal dinner?"

"I've never been married before."

Her bravado rang false: his interest quickened. "But Peggy never mentioned it?"

"Look, she called to leave a message for Laura. Maybe they decided later."

"And Warren came by while you were in the shower, right?"

Once again her expression was unreadable.

"How'd he know you were in the shower?" Ray pressed. "Did you tell him that first, or did he ask if that's where you were?"

Bingo.

"Did he say anyplace else he might have been before he went to the rec center?"

Tim entered the room shirtless. His damp hair was shoulder length and redder than his mother's, but his torso was muscular and fit. Recalling Peggy's delicate wrist and the smashed bones of her left hand, Ray's bile rose. Why hadn't he been where he belonged? Didn't he know he was supposed to—

"What do you want?" The boy's voice cracked on the last word, and Ray handed him the manila envelope, suddenly ashamed of his own antagonism.

"I'm serving you with a subpoena to testify before the Hallett County grand jury the day after tomorrow." Tim held it with his fingertips like it was radioactive, and Ray's resentment of the D.A. swelled. Philips should be doing his own dirty work. "I'm sorry, son."

The girl snatched the envelope from Tim and stepped between them. "Please leave." As she strode to the door and opened it wide, Ray sensed the steel in her spine. *"Now."*

"Make sure he reads that, miss. And if you think of anything else, call me."

She stared back with mute hostility, and Ray wondered what made her so distrust someone she should be turning to for help.

—

S ari latched the door before handing Tim the envelope. "What did he mean, if you can think of anything else?"

"Nothing," she replied. "He was just asking about the rehearsal dinner."

But the detective's questions had reminded her Warren was supposed to be at a seminar that day. She'd even asked him about it. What had he said?

Tim peeled open the flap and removed two sheets of legal-sized paper. When he gazed at them without comprehension, she took them back.

"It says you have to be there two days from now," she read.

"Where?"

"The courthouse in Gillman. At three in the afternoon. To give testimony concerning the events of May 17, 1980."

"I'd better call Dad..." He turned to the telephone and she went to the kitchen to think.

A Dale Carnegie seminar, that's what it was. Peggy had told them about it on Mother's Day. She tried to recall her conversation with Tim's father at the rec center. Why hadn't Warren gone?

"—have to meet first with his lawyer." Tim was standing at her elbow. "That guy Evans. Dad's making the appointment now."

"Want me to come?" Why hadn't she said anything about the seminar to that detective?

"I'd better go alone." He reached into the laundry basket for a T but instead chose a long-sleeved shirt with a button-down collar though his chest was beading with sweat. The phone rang and Sari took the message; it was Evans's office telling him to be there the next morning at eight. As Tim buttoned his shirt, she came up behind him and slipped her hands under the cloth.

"Do you want to talk?" she asked, running her fingers up his smooth back to his shoulder blades.

"About what?"

"The past two weeks."

He pulled away. "We put off the wedding, what's left to say?"

"I want to know what's going on."

"Leave it alone, Sari, it doesn't concern you."

"Doesn't *concern* me? Everything about you concerns me!"

"If you care so much, back off." Beneath his warning she smelled fear. "You're only making it worse..."

"You don't need to do this alone."

He tucked his shirt in his pants and buckled his belt. "I'm going to the rec center to work out."

As the door slammed behind him, Sari sank onto the daybed. There were still moments when Tim turned to her in the night and buried his face in her hair, and she could believe when this was over they would pick up where they'd left off and march toward their dream. But as often as not he pushed her away now; he was closing off in ways she couldn't define. If what it took to get him back was pretending nothing had changed, wasn't that a small price to pay?

Chapter Seventeen

The corner suite on the ninth floor of the Security Trust Building held a reception area just large enough to accommodate a desk and two wing chairs, but the grayhaired woman simply nodded and kept typing when Tim arrived. Through one door he saw a conference room lined floor to ceiling with books; the other was closed. The woman never announced him, but after ten minutes the second door opened and Simon Evans appeared in shirtsleeves, silk tie tightly knotted though it was not yet eight in the morning. He waved Tim in without a greeting.

Evans's office was furnished with massive pieces suited to his imposing stature, and its only remarkable feature was a controlled clutter that reminded Tim of the art room at his junior high. Lithographs of storm-tossed schooners covered the wall above a table piled high with paper and loose-leaf notebooks, and ceramic mugs of pencils and pens bristled like sea urchins on every available surface. Navigating around knee-high stacks of books and journals, Evans cleared a leather chair across from his desk and gestured for Tim to sit.

"Isn't Dad going to be here?"

"It seemed sensible for us to meet alone." Simon leaned back and locked his hands behind his head, but any notion of informality was dispelled by his next words. "I don't have to tell you how serious his situation is, do I?"

"No."

"Convening a grand jury means he's almost certain to be indicted. A grand jury will indict a leg of mutton if—"

"Indict? For what?"

Simon dropped his hands and planted his feet on the floor. Could the boy really not understand what was at stake? "For the death of your mother."

"What would the charge be?"

"First degree murder." He leaned across the desk, forcing Tim to look at him. "Do you want to help?"

"Of course."

"Then pay close attention. When you're called to testify you must tell the truth, but that doesn't mean you have to give them everything they want. Do you follow?"

Tim nodded, expression guarded. Good, Simon thought, he's thinking.

"If they ask a question and you know the answer, tell them as little as possible. If yes or no will do, say only that. If you don't know the answer, say so." His pewter-colored eyes bored into Tim's. "Never answer any question that isn't asked even if you know what they're after. *Especially* if you think you know what they want. Am I making myself clear?"

"Will you be in the room?"

"Outside, in the hallway. If you're less than one hundred percent sure of the answer or it requires an explanation, tell them you need to consult your attorney and leave."

"What will they want to know?"

"I imagine they'll ask what time your father arrived at the rec center that morning." Tim stiffened, and Simon concealed his apprehension by leaning back. If there was any place the boy could hurt them, it was here. "Do you know when that was?"

"I think so."

"What time did he arrive?"

"Before the one o'clock practice."

"Can you be more specific?"

"No."

Simon tented his fingers and smiled tightly. He could press Tim further, but the answer was satisfactory enough. If the boy had the wits to stick to it. "They will also ask about your parents' relationship. I take it they got on well together?"

"Except for religion. Mom was Catholic and Dad's a Prot—"

"What would you say if the district attorney asks, 'Does your father have a temper?'"

"He's very... controlled."

Tim smiled and Simon's stomach fluttered. If the boy thought this was going to be easy, he'd be no match for Philips, even on his worst day. They'd best get it all out on the table now.

"What do you mean?"

"Dad's philosophy is 'Let's work the problem.' Tackle details in their order of priority and fix things then and there. I guess that's why he became an accountant."

"Did you ever see your parents fight?"

"Dad gets angry about politics and things he reads in the newspaper. He's intense that way, but he never reacts to what goes on at home. If my sister or I argued with each other he made us go to our rooms." Simon frowned, but Tim ignored the warning. "He hates wasting time. He never goes to a store unless he has at least two reasons for it, and they'd better be good ones."

"Would you describe him as spontaneous?" The question was unnecessary given Tim's last answer, but Simon wanted to see how suggestible he was.

"He never does anything without a list. Each morning he writes his plan for the day in the notebook he carries in his back pocket. By Wednesday he knows exactly what he's going to do the next weekend."

Simon gazed at the ceiling, trying to reformulate the description into more appealing terms as his mind raced ahead. Was he giving Tim too little credit, was it possible he understood the effect of his answers without letting on? And Warren had made no mention of a notebook, precisely the sort of development every lawyer dreads. The last thing he wanted was to focus Tim's attention on what could be a smoking gun. Finally he replied, "I'd stick to 'He's very disciplined and orderly.' Did your parents socialize with other couples?"

"We spent a lot of time with Aunt Kay and Uncle Bud because they live five blocks away. But Dad doesn't like Bud."

"Why not?"

Tim shrugged. "Nothing puts Dad in a worse mood than an evening at the Butlers'. He'd say to Mom, 'I thought we left Walker County twenty years ago—'"

"Let's talk about the grand jury." Whatever game Warren's son was playing, it was time to get down to business. Simon fixed Tim with his most forbidding stare. "You'll be in a large room with a group of ordinary-looking people dressed in casual clothes and suits, not wearing robes or sitting on a raised platform. But don't be fooled. They will approach their task with the mind-set that your father is guilty. You must never, under any circumstance, think they're trying to help him."

"If they already think he's guilty, why do they want to talk to me?"

"Because the district attorney wants as much information as he can get without giving anything in return. Don't help him. Understood?"

—

"What was Evans like?" Sari asked when Tim returned two hours later.

"Tall, graying. He wore a suit. You know. .. ." Tim went to the refrigerator for orange juice and drank it straight from the pitcher. Two gulps, not pausing to swallow or taste as it went down. "There was a wood-paneled pickup truck parked down the block. If they looked for the owner, Dad never would have been charged."

"Is that all he said?"

"And I have to tell the truth."

Thank God, she thought, *for Simon Evans.*

The next afternoon they drove to the Hallett County courthouse. Carved ceilings and glossy oak banisters attested to the stately building's age, but the fan in the hallway outside the grand jury room did nothing to dispel the June heat. Tim wore a tie and the polyester sport coat from his high school graduation because Evans said nobody ever dressed inappropriately by wearing a white shirt. Tim had agonized over it, but in the end the sport coat was his only choice. If he wouldn't wear his wedding suit to Peggy's funeral because he couldn't bear the thought of getting married in the clothes he wore to bury his mother, how could he betray her by wearing it now?

As she waited for Tim on the oak bench in the hallway, Sari watched Simon Evans. He sat by himself on a wooden chair near the jury room door. His lined face was grave. He never even glanced at his watch. How could he sit so still?

For the first twenty minutes there was no sound from the room. She imagined they were asking Tim his age, address, where he went to school. Suddenly the door opened and Tim stepped into the hall. As he bent and whispered in Evans's ear, Evans nodded once and Tim went back in. She tried to read from Simon's face what the question was, but the lawyer never looked at her.

Tell the truth, she thought. What could be easier?

After that the questions must have been more complicated, because Tim kept coming out of the room. Each time Evans nodded or shook his head, and once he cupped his hand over his mouth and gave a longer answer. The examination lasted more than two hours. As Sari rose near the end and walked to the water fountain a few feet from the door, Tim emerged. She strained to hear.

"—framing hammer?" Evans was saying.

"—never works with his hands…" Tim replied.

The next day Warren Scott was indicted for first degree murder.

When Sari and Tim were instructed to attend the bail hearing, she found herself looking forward to it. Evans wanted them there to show support for Warren, of course, but for her the hearing had a much more important purpose. Warren's antagonists would now have their chance to speak. His arrest had stripped away the pretense that the police were spinning their wheels, and she wanted to learn what they knew.

Five days after Tim testified before the grand jury they were back at the domed courthouse. With Laura they waited in the hallway for Evans, too jittery to exchange anything but small talk. It was out of their hands now, Sari knew, and she busied herself straightening Tim's tie.

Three minutes before the hearing was set to begin, Evans arrived alone. Impeccable in a black pin-striped suit and custom-made shirt, he moved at a measured pace that inspired confidence despite his close timing. A professional focused on his job, she thought as he held himself back from anything but the most perfunctory personal contact. With a nod to Sari and a tight-lipped smile for Laura, he gave Tim's shoulder a squeeze and led them into the courtroom. Entering through the double doors, she was relieved to see Aunt Kay and her husband Bud, but when Kay pointedly looked away, the room suddenly felt cold. Evans led them to the front row, across the aisle from the Butlers.

Blinking to adjust to the dimness, Sari took in the large square chamber. The north-facing windows were tall but heavily draped, and the ceiling and walls were trimmed with the same dark wood as the elevated bench. A polished rail with swinging gate separated the well of the court from the spectator section, two long tables and a lectern occupied the center of the room, and a raised gallery with a dozen empty wooden chairs stood along one side, angled as if their invisible occupants were anticipating the drama about to unfold.

As Evans passed through the gate and set his briefcase on the table opposite the jury box, the flags flanking the bench twitched and the men on the other side looked up. A sudden hush, and they resumed whispering. When Warren's lawyer continued to ignore them, Sari peered at his adversaries.

The leader seemed to be the short man in the gabardine suit with a silk handkerchief in his breast pocket. Taylor Philips, Evans had said. Rounding his table with a self-important strut, the D.A. spoke into the ear of the squat mournful-eyed man who'd served Tim with the subpoena. The detective nodded vigorously in response. The other two were nondescript, assistants of some sort. As the prosecutors shuffled through the contents of a dozen manila folders neatly arranged across their table, Evans withdrew a single legal pad from his briefcase and set it in his lap. Slowly uncapping his pen, he rested it on the pad.

Sari squeezed Tim's clammy fingers and peeked across the aisle at Kay Butler, who was seated directly behind the D.A. Tense, watchful. Why was she sitting on the other side—Just then a door to the right of the bench opened and Warren was led in by two burly deputies in taupe trousers and short-sleeved midnight-blue shirts. Sari heard the toe of Laura's bone-colored pump hit the rail to the left of Tim as her foot swung back and forth. Warren was clad in an orange jumpsuit and black tennis shoes. Wrists cuffed, face pale but composed. When he saw his children, he raised his hands in a half-wave before being led to the jury box. Sari glanced at the prosecution table in time to catch the detective staring at her curiously, but he quickly dropped his gaze. The bailiff cried "All rise" and the rest happened too fast.

The D.A. argued against bail because he was working up to a death penalty case and the circumstances were brutal, a defenseless woman beaten to a pulp in her own garage. As Philips grew increasingly strident and began thumping the lectern, Sari sneaked a look at Tim's father. He sat in the jury box as unconcerned as if it were a different Warren Scott they were talking about. Evans's hand was making small round motions over the pad, and she realized he was doodling.

He knows he's going to win.

She glanced at the detective again. The set of his lips telegraphed disgust; the redness rising from his collar said even more. Warren's knock on the door, the unexpected rehearsal dinner...Why was he so sure Tim's father killed Peggy? What did he know that they hadn't been told?

Suddenly Sari yearned to hear Evans slip. What did she want him to say? "Your Honor, I am deeply troubled by my client's story. This man showed up at his son's hockey practice with a bruise on his head, totally unannounced, instead of attending a Dale Carnegie seminar…" *What was the matter with her?* Releasing Tim's fingers, she pressed her hand to her own burning cheek. Five seconds before Philips ran out of steam, Evans capped his pen and smoothly rose.

"Your Honor, Warren Scott is a pillar of this community. He has an exemplary record as a father, a husband, and an employee." In a conversational tone he addressed the court from his place at the defense table, but as his powerful voice filled the chamber, Sari's head began to pound. Turning, he gestured at Laura and Tim. "His children are here in this very room, behind him every step of the way. It's a shameless cruelty to continue to incarcerate him."

"Tell that to his wife." Philips jumped to his feet and pointed at one of his assistants, who handed him a manila envelope. Approaching the bench, he extracted with a flourish a handful of eight-by-ten-inch glossies. "Look what he did to her!"

Evans rounded the table before Sari even saw him move. Positioning himself between Philips and the gallery, he exclaimed, "Isn't it enough for these poor children to see their father in handcuffs and jailhouse overalls? Must the district attorney further traumatize them by waving sickening photographs in their faces?" He turned to them now, and as the throb in Sari's head began to resonate in her stomach, she thought she might be ill. Exemplary father? What about telling Tim he wished he'd never been born? And why was it so important to Warren that she back him up about being in the shower? They were window-dressing, it was just a game. And now they were trapped in his story like fleas in amber… "You children should leave," Evans was saying. "There's no conceivable reason for Mr. Philips to inflict this on you." He pointed to the door, and the chamber was silent as they filed out.

As Tim and Laura headed down the hall, Sari felt a hand on her shoulder. It was Kay. She'd slipped out of the courtroom after them.

"You know something, don't you?" Tim's aunt spoke in a low voice, as if she didn't want the others to hear. "I was watching you while Warren's lawyer spoke."

"I know only what I already said."

Kay's eyes burned. "Do you know what it's like, Sari, to not be there for someone when they need you most? I should have done something before it was too late."

"What do you mean?"

"I knew there were problems and did nothing to protect her." Her chin quivered with the effort of containing her torment. "She didn't tell me everything, but I always suspected...."

"Warren told us she was ill."

"Is that what he said? How very convenient." Tears began to spill down Kay's cheeks. Angrily, she brushed them away. "I'll be damned if I let him sweep her life under the rug. But I can't do it alone, Sari, I need your help."

"What makes you so sure—"

"Think back to that day." Kay moved a step closer. "Warren always has a plan. He'd never have gone to Stanley spur of the moment, not Warren, and especially not when he had that damn seminar. Is there any doubt in your mind he used you and Tim—"

"Used us for what?"

When she'd gone to the library that morning, she'd been so engrossed in her reading she lost track of the time. She'd looked up and it was a quarter past twelve...

"For God's sake, use your head!" Kay said desperately.

Warren said he'd come to the apartment around 12:30 and knocked on the door while she was in the shower. But she'd jumped in and out, and if he waited several minutes as he'd said, he would have been difficult to miss.

"You and Tim hold the key..."

She'd gone to the rec center right from the shower and arrived just before the one o'clock practice. Warren was already there. There was only one route from the apartment to the center, straight down Broadway. How could they not have seen each other?

"—must have said something to you that day, or maybe it was the way he acted." Kay's voice was rising but she was beyond caring whether anyone else heard. "*If you know anything at all, you owe it to Peggy*—"

"Sari?" Tim took her arm. "Let's wait with Laura."

Kay turned to him. "You have to tell the police what you know."

"I don't know what you're talking about. Come on, Sari."

"Tim, didn't you love your mother?"

"Of course I did!"

"Then where's your loyalty?" Kay cried as Tim led Sari down the hall. "Didn't she mean *anything* to you?"

That afternoon the judge granted bail and Warren posted a surety bond. He was home in time for dinner.

———

Simon Evans had to admit the circumstances were brutal, a defenseless woman bludgeoned to death in her own garage. But what judge would deny bond to a white man from Gillman, that haven of the middle class, with no confession or criminal record and his bright-haired children sitting teary-eyed in the front row? Not in Simon's lifetime.

He had Philips pegged the moment he laid eyes on the D.A. How well he knew the type: an officious peacock in love with his own looks, too busy gazing in the mirror to survey the judicial landscape. But judges and juries were rarely swayed by blowhards with weak cases regardless of the cut of their suit. And Philips was pitifully green, an amateur. He traveled with a gaggle of minions, junior D.A.'s and rumpled cops, the more the better as far as Simon was concerned. He rejoiced each time one of Philips's assistants had to dig through a file to feed him an answer.

The bail hearing was just the warm-up.

After that Simon attacked from every direction, filing motions for a bill of particulars specifying the evidence and to suppress the results of fingerprint tests, quash the indictment, halt the ongoing grand jury proceedings, and exclude witnesses from the courtroom during hearings. He even moved to dismiss on grounds the definition of premeditation in the first degree murder statute was unconstitutionally vague.

"Why are you wasting time?" Warren demanded late one afternoon as Simon packed his briefcase after the judge denied another motion to suppress. "You never win." Simon waited until Philips and his assistants gathered their files and exited the courtroom. When the door swung shut behind them, he addressed his client.

"Don't *ever* question my strategy in the presence of the opponent. If you wish to know why I'm doing something, you can wait until we're outside the courthouse." Simon said nothing more until they reached the parking lot. As he stowed his briefcase in the boot of his Jaguar, he continued. "I'm wearing them down by attacking their weaknesses."

"Attacking their weaknesses?" Warren's lips twisted with contempt. "I'd say you're exposing ours. I might feel differently if you won once in a while."

Simon slammed down the lid and turned to face him. "Now you listen, and listen well. Nothing could be less important than winning these motions. What matters is they're coming at Philips from all sides and he never knows what's next. By making him defend, I'm reversing the momentum. Every motion diffuses his efforts, erodes his confidence, prevents him from getting on top of his case."

"Do you know what you're talking about? Look at all the people on his team!"

"I'll spell it out for you, Warren, but only once. Simon's words were clipped. "Diffusion of responsibility can destroy the tightest case. The more people assigned the greater the disarray. Disarray is one short step from panic, an even shorter step from losing. I will win this case and Taylor Philips will lose."

"You think he doesn't care about winning?"

"He doesn't know what winning is. He's more concerned about his own career than what happens to you Right now he's trying to figure out who to blame for botching the investigation. And if you're quite through questioning my expertise, I have better things to do than explain myself to a disagreeable lout in a parking lot."

Simon got behind the wheel and drove off. Edith was grilling lamb chops for dinner, and he was ravenous.

Chapter Eighteen

On her way out of biology lab ten days after the bail hearing, Sari literally bumped into the squat detective. She had spent all week dissecting a fetal pig and was just taking a breath of sun to rid her lungs of the formaldehyde when he suddenly appeared. Halfway up the steps to Hale, forcing students to fork around him like a log in a stream.

"Miss Siegel." His smile was as natural as the expression on her pig. Pickled innocence, obscenely frozen in time.

"We didn't have much of a chance to talk the other day," he continued, "back at your apartment."

He'd planned it so Tim wouldn't be there; maybe he'd been planning this since the day he served that subpoena. What made him think if he got her alone she'd be disloyal? Turn around, walk back into Hale as fast as you can, exit through the side door, and what could he do… But she had nothing to hide. She clutched her lab books to her chest, hating him as the smell of death wafted from their pages.

"There was nothing more to say," Sari replied.

He took off his Stetson and mopped his broad brow, looking old and ridiculous among these athletic children in sneakers and shorts. She tried not to feel sorry for him.

"Jeez, it's hot," he said. "Can I buy you a pop?"

Did he think she could be bribed?

"No, thanks. I have to get home—"

"I'll walk you. Partway." Tacitly acknowledging they shared some secret, a mission that did not include Tim. Two minutes and they'd be at the fountain at the Student Union. She would end it there.

"I had a talk with Tim's aunt the other day. Kay?" A test stroke. "She and Peggy were real close, they talked every day."

She forced him to lengthen his stride.

"She said Warren was planning to start a seminar that morning. Saturday. A Dale Carnegie—type thing." The marbled composition book in which she wrote her lab reports slipped and he caught it with an awkward motion. "Didn't you tell me something about that?"

She'd never mentioned that seminar, she was sure. And he couldn't force her to say anything she didn't want to. *Don't get involved,* her mother said, *if you really love Tim...*

"I don't know what you're talking about." Mind racing to that morning, struggling to remember what Warren said while revealing nothing to this man whose eyes were suddenly shrewd. *How was that seminar...*

Sari reached for her notebook and he surrendered it.

"That day was the first session," the detective continued. "The class started at noon and Kay said he wouldn't have missed it for the world." More confident now, slicing at a sharper angle. "You sure he didn't say anything about it?"

Warren said it was postponed.

"Positive," she replied. She started walking again, forcing his stubby feet in those hot-looking boots to keep up. Or had he said they'd given him a rain check? No, Warren specifically said *postponed...*

"Because if there's a reason why he didn't attend, we could check it out."

With one phone call she would know whether Warren told the truth.

"You're going to feel awfully stupid," she said, "when they find that pickup truck."

"What pickup truck?" But she was rewarded by a deep flush creeping up from his bolo tie. Warren must be right; there really was a suspect and the cops weren't even looking. And if he was right about that—

"The one parked across the street," she answered.

"You really believe that?" Businesslike, professionally indifferent. He was angry. "If you do, it makes everything pretty simple. Doesn't it?"

He put his Stetson back on his head, stuffed his stained hanky in the pocket of his polyester coat. They were at the fountain, kids were lobbing Frisbees through the glistening spray, this was almost over... There was no way to know whether Warren knocked on their door that morning, but he'd said that seminar was *postponed*.

With one phone call she would know whether he lied. "Life tends to be that way," he continued, "if you don't question what you hear."

Tipping his hat he left her standing there, suddenly cold in the late-day sun.

—

Hugging her books to her chest, Sari walked faster and faster, and by the time she reached Locust she was leaping up the steps. The Wings practice began at four and Tim wouldn't be home for half an hour. She threw the window open all the way, drank in the squeals of students splashing in the College Townhouse's pool and the faint smell of meat grilling on a hibachi on the opposite balcony. A barbecue on a Thursday afternoon in June. Nothing had changed...

Turning from the window, she walked past the phone to the kitchen and drew herself a glass of water. Dehydration, that's what it was, and spending all afternoon bent over that ghastly pig. They'd been carving since Monday and what was left was shrunken and rubbery, like the remains of a very small smoked turkey. She returned to the living room and set her composition book on the windowsill, weighted open so the pages could air out. A drop of formaldehyde had landed on her data, fanning the ink in lavender petals. There was no reason to call Dale Carnegie.

Sari stripped off her T-shirt, stuffed it in the laundry basket in the alcove, and pinched a shriveled leaf off one of the coleuses. She should shower before Tim came home, get rid of the pickled smell on her fingers, and think about what she would make for dinner. But the thought of food was unappealing and the black phone stared at her from its place on the shelf above his hockey trophies. Dale Carnegie would be a Widmark exchange, and all she had was a Stanley phone book.

That detective was obviously grasping at straws to come to her now, after all these weeks. The case must be falling apart for him to come to her *at all,* hoping she'd implicate Warren. If she called Dale Carnegie they would simply confirm what Warren told her, the seminar had been postponed, and tonight she and Tim could laugh about how foolish the whole thing was.

She went to the kitchen and peered in the cupboard. Kraft macaroni and cheese, too hot to worry about anything else. Poking in the refrigerator she found a bowl of bean salad that wasn't too old… When was the last time she'd fixed Tim a real dinner? She'd bought a book with chicken recipes, but with school she hadn't had time to try them out. Her eyes wandered to the window. Beneath the table to its left lay the phone book. The number wouldn't even be there, she should hop in the shower before Tim got home. But would it hurt to look?

The Stanley directory was skinny, its pages evenly divided between yellow and white, and she flipped to the commercial listings. First the C's, then the D's. Not there. All that agonizing over nothing. Slapping the book shut, oddly disappointed, she slid it back under the table and headed for the shower. As she wrenched the faucet to the left and waited for the water to warm, it occurred to her she could call information. But that was a toll call and Tim might see…

Turning off the faucet, Sari draped a towel around her shoulders and walked back to the phone. To whom was she accountable for a twenty-five-cent call? She'd gone this far, hadn't she, and even if she got the number it didn't mean she had to call. Before she could change her mind she'd dialed information.

"Widmark, please… Dale Carnegie." She waited. "No, not a person, it's a business. One of those self-improvement places."

Realizing she didn't have anything to write on, scrambling for a pencil, reaching for her composition book… "Yes, thank you." Scribbling the number in the left-hand margin of the first blank page, a neat little D. *Carn.* on top. Easily erased. Tim need never know. And she could still change her mind. So long as she didn't dial, things would remain exactly the way they were.

She was staring at the phone when she heard a cheery whistle and footsteps clatter up the stairs. With guilty relief she dropped the receiver just as Tim walked through the door. He flung his sweaty practice clothes on the daybed and strode across the room for his kiss.

"I should come home early more often," he said, slipping the towel off her shoulders.

Feeling betrayal written all over her face, she turned away.

"I was just about to hop in the shower," she replied.

"How was your lab? You look a little pale."

How trusting he was.

"It's nothing." The first lie; was this how it began? "We're finishing up that fetal pig, I can still smell it."

Walking past him to the shower, hoping the water would rid her of more than the smell. Tim following her in, reaching for her from behind as she bent to strip off her shorts, kissing the nape of her neck. She couldn't bear the deception.

"You smell pretty good to me." he said.

Turning on the faucet again, stepping into the tub.

"I'm getting my period." The second lie; couldn't he tell?

"That never made a difference before."

Slipping from his gentle grasp, the first time she'd ever pushed him away. Trying to make a joke of it. "Making love to a fetal pig would be a real first…"

Sari turned her face up and let the cold spray envelop her.

—

At the mid-afternoon break on Friday Sari went to the pay phone. She'd thought about it all night, hadn't eaten a bite since yesterday's lunch or heard a word of the morning lecture. She didn't know why she'd never told anyone Warren said the seminar was postponed; she'd hugged the knowledge to her chest, tucked it away to examine later and never did. Until that detective came. Because what she was contemplating now felt like a complete betrayal of Tim.

She'd wrestled it back and forth. If Warren lied about the seminar, he lied about why he came to Stanley, and that could only mean he killed Peggy. But if he told the truth she could set her fears aside and put that Saturday where it belonged. Believe he came to their door as he said and she'd somehow managed to miss him, that Peggy's death was a horrible tragedy caused by an unknown intruder. And Tim would never know her doubts… All she had to do was call.

She couldn't bear to touch her fetal pig; kept in a cooler overnight, today it seemed clammier and the smell sickly-sweet, like the time she mixed all the starters in that perfume kit in third grade. The shortage of specimens meant there were three students per pig, so she filled in diagrams for her lab partners and when the instructor reminded them next week they'd be pithing frogs she didn't even care. In ten minutes she would know the truth.

The pay phone was three feet from a pop machine, and as she lifted the receiver she turned to the wall to mute the jiggle of change in the slot and the whump of Coke and Dr Pepper. Fumbling for her composition book, inserting her coin, glancing at the penciled number, watching herself almost with contempt—she'd memorized it, hadn't she?—dialing and half hoping no one would answer. Closed for the summer.

"Thank you for your interest in Dale Carnegie, how may I help?"

Pert intonation, like a stewardess. Pageboy cut, collar-like wings and tailored navy blue pants.

"I'm interested in signing up for a course."

"We have several seminars. Are you interested in customer relations or supervision and management?"

All wrong, she had no idea which one Warren signed up for, and they were wasting precious time. Sari took a deep breath and began again.

"I read something in the paper about one that started in May." Much better. "Which was that?"

"Oh, you mean our fourteen-week Personnel Development Course."

"What day did it start?"

"All our seminars are held on Saturdays."

"I mean, what date did it begin?" Students were heading back to the lab.

"I can look it up, but it's halfway through and a new course will be starting in—"

"Please"—trying to keep the desperation from her voice—"just tell me what day it *began.* "

The hallway was empty by the time the woman returned.

"May seventeenth. At noon, by the airport. Right on schedule."

—

Dinner, she had to fix dinner. Reaching in the freezer, Sari grabbed the first thing she saw. Fish sticks. Checking the refrigerator for tartar sauce, opening the jar and sniffing, deciding it was not too yellow to eat. Tim had another practice and wouldn't be home until after seven.

As soon as she'd returned to the lab she erased the number from her book, and the greasy smudge accused her all afternoon. Happy now? Couldn't leave well enough alone, had to find out for herself... The only thing she was sure of was that she couldn't tell Tim. At worst Warren's lie meant he'd murdered Peggy, which would destroy Tim; at best, it showed she doubted his father and therefore *him.*

Carrying the card table to the window, Sari covered it with a gingham square and set it with unnecessary knives and spoons. It still looked bare, so she ran downstairs for a spray of salvia and Clary sage from the yard next door where they grew wild. Planting them in a water glass, she was pleased with the effect. They could eat as the sun set. There would be no need for light.

At twenty minutes past six she heard Tim tromping up the stairs; no whistle this time, and the jersey under his arm looked as fresh as when he'd left.

"Why are you home so early?" she asked, meeting his kiss.

"Surprised?... I deputized our star defenseman to lead the practice." Tim's cheek felt cool against hers and his gaze took in the table and flowers. "What's the occasion?"

"Today we buried our fetal pig."

"Thank God. I missed you." His kiss stung, and she was the one who broke away. "I'm starved…"

She arranged fish sticks on a baking sheet and slid them in the oven, got what was left of the bean salad from Tuesday out of the refrigerator, mixed the limeade. Tim was so undemanding; even her mother said she'd never seen anyone so grateful for a peanut butter sandwich. He must never know what she'd done.

"Not hungry?" he asked as she filled his plate, taking only a couple of sticks for herself.

"Just tired, I guess." She flinched, then glanced at Tim to see if the unfortunate choice of words registered.

Feeling okay, Dad? Warren on the daybed, head in hands. *I'm fine son, just a little tired…* Stop it, she warned, right now. Before he thinks something's—

"—wrong, Sari?"

"No, not a thing."

"Nothing exciting today besides the last rites for your pig?" He pushed away his plate. The bean salad was untouched, the breading on the fish sticks had congealed in an unappetizing sheen.

"I thought you were hungry," she said.

"Did you get the note I left in your lab book?"

"Note?"

"I put it there last night." Did he see the number? "Don't tell me it fell out."

"I didn't see any note." Even if he recognized *D. Cam.* he wouldn't know what it meant. She reached for his plate and he pulled her into his lap.

"Don't tell me I've got competition…"

Tim's eyes were unreadable. Could he possibly know? She rose and brought their dishes to the sink. As he followed, she began filling it with soapy water. Maybe he thought it was a guy.

"The only competition you have to worry about is the frog I'll be pithing—"

"Why did you call Dale Carnegie?" he asked.

She turned off the water and faced him. This was Tim. They'd agreed there would be no lies.

"Your dad told me that seminar was postponed. I needed to find out for myself."

"You want to crucify him, don't you?"

Not what-seminar or have-you-lost-your-mind, or even what-did-they-say.

"I had to know the truth," she replied. She reached out, but he pushed her away.

"I know he's innocent, isn't that good enough?"

"Tim, I—"

"Don't force me to choose, Sari, you're tearing me—" Pain, unbearable pain in his eyes, the pulse in his throat beating wildly. She'd wanted to protect him but it had gone all wrong.

"Your father has nothing to do with us—"

He wasn't listening, didn't want to hear.

"I believe him," he cried. "Why won't you?"

She stumbled past him and out the door.

—

Sari wandered the campus for hours. Sobbing, not caring who saw as she pushed her way through the throng gathered outside the chemistry building for the weekend movie, numb to the happy innocence of couples strolling into dorms arm in arm. All the way to the east end of the campus, as far as the stadium across from Swenson Tower where Tim had physics. Suddenly exhausted, she lay in the middle of the practice field staring up at the stars. For the first time since she'd met Tim ten months before she felt invisible, and it was an odd relief.

As her tears subsided, she tried to think rationally. Now so many things made sense. Peggy not telling her Warren was coming, his insistence that he'd knocked after she said she'd been in the shower. Kay was right; he wouldn't have missed that seminar for anything... It came down to two things: Warren had lied about Peggy, and it was over with Tim. She couldn't live with or protect him from his father's lies. Not if she loved him.

The stars were very bright and the grass was cold against her bare legs. If only she could lie there forever, not have to return to the wreckage of her life. If only she hadn't made that call... She closed her eyes, picturing the cabin and the goat. A garden and three children. Were they a lie too?

She began to shiver, sat up and hugged her knees. She'd left the apartment with two quarters and her house key, not even a jacket. The only thing to do was go back to the apartment, pack a suitcase and find a place to stay until she could figure things out. God, where would she go? Not back to New York... Slowly she rose and started across the silent campus.

At Locust she stood on the corner, staring up at the darkened windows of the second-story porch. She remembered the day they moved in, how ecstatic she was at their first place. Back when the number of rooms was more important than their size...Tim must be asleep; it was past midnight. She mounted the steps as quietly as she could, telling herself to remember the feel of worn carpet and the musty odor. When she leaned on the door to insert her key in the lock it swung open.

He was sitting on the daybed with his face in his hands. The room was pitch dark, but she knew he was awake. He said nothing as she let herself in.

"Tim?"

Something lay in his lap, cradled in his elbows. A long white tube. She sat beside him and took one of his hands in her own. It was very cold.

"Tim?" She wrapped her arm around him, and the tube rolled to the floor as he turned to her.

"I thought you'd left," he whispered. His face was wet against her shoulder. "I looked everywhere, I thought you were gone."

"I went for a walk." The rest could wait.

"Don't leave. Without you there's nothing."

"Don't say that…."

"My family means nothing to me, Sari." He hugged her tightly and she began to feel lost in his familiar scent. "Nothing in my life is worth a damn without you."

"Let's talk in the morning," she said, and pulled him from the daybed.

"I have something to show you." Switching on the lamp, he handed her the tube. It was loosely rolled and bound by a rubber band. "Open it."

The pastel portrait was of a black-haired girl standing in front of a cabin with a bouquet of poppies. The chalk made good use of the rag paper, bold strokes of color picking up surface fibers to enrich the textures of petal and skin. The intensity of the girl's smile rivaled that of the poppies, which seemed to catch and reflect the light, while softer smudges of chalk made her cheeks and lips glow with pleasure. A girl in love with life and its endless possibilities, and most of all in love with the person who'd captured her at that moment. Her dark eyes were wide with wonder, and for an instant Sari was reminded of her mother in the photograph with the soldier.

"Do you like it?" he asked.

"I—I don't know what to say." It was their dream, it lived… Not too late after all. Her future was there with him. "It's beautiful."

"I've been working on it for months. For your birthday."

"I love you, Tim, so much I can't—"

He pulled her to him and the beating of his heart stilled her fears.

"Shh…" His fingers were gentle on her lips. "We'll work it out, I promise."

Chapter Nineteen

It was worse than a kick in the nuts.

"What do you mean, you're dropping the charges?"

"Just what I said, Ray. You blew the case."

It was the Friday before Labor Day and they were in the D.A.'s office. The searing heat had given way to hail earlier in the week, destroying Marion's vegetable garden and vanishing as quickly as it came.

"*I* blew the case?"

"Want me to cite chapter and verse about that farce you called an investigation?"

"You can't be serious…"

"Four words." Philips ticked them off on the fingers of one hand, ending with the gold signet ring on his pinkie. "Weapon, motive, clothing, and alibi. This case has holes big enough to drive a tank through."

"Scott's alibi's shit and you know it. Regina Hummel placed him at 4990 South Cleveland *after* he whacked his wife. We have the clocks to prove—"

"You mean we *might* have been able to prove it if you'd sent Peggy's watch to the SBI like you were supposed to. Now all we have is an approximate time of death, which spells reasonable doubt. What the hell did you think you were doing, giving it to some idiot jeweler in a shopping mall? Once he took the damn thing apart, we couldn't produce it to Evans for his own testing, couldn't even get the SBI to say it stopped because of the blow to her wrist. You're lucky I'm not charging you with obstruction of justice!"

"Any jury in the world would believe Peggy Scott died when her watch was smashed."

"What makes you think a judge would let it go to a jury? Did you get your law degree in Korea too?" Philips was pacing the floor, warming to his own theatrics. "And you focused on the husband too early."

"There was no evidence of a burglar." Ray *knew* what happened. Hadn't he charted every step Warren took that morning, predicted his alibi to the minute? "That theory was baloney from start to finish—"

"No evidence of anyone skulking around or entering the house the back way? How the hell would you know, Ray? There were so many unidentified footprints, General Sherman might as well have marched his troops through South Cleveland."

"But it *had* to be an inside job. Nothing was taken from the house. The condition of the drawers alone—"

"I don't give a crap what's in his drawers."

"No burglar in his right mind would—"

"Since when does a burglar have to be in his right mind to surprise a homeowner and kill her in a blind panic? You're a disgrace to law enforcement."

"It had to be Warren."

Philips stopped short.

"Oh, yeah? What was his motive? You know, that stupid *detail* juries care so much about." He stabbed his forefinger at Ray. "I guess it was too much to ask you to drive out to Walker County and dig into his background. What is it, a few hundred miles away? You never even called the local sheriff, did you?"

"There's still time..."

"Your time has run out."

Ray tried to clear his head. Where was Philips getting his

information? "Maybe she was ragging him about something. He's so tightly wound, he'd never—"

"I don't care if Peggy Scott was the biggest bitch God ever made. Do you think a jury's going to believe her husband put up with her for twenty years, then lost control all of a sudden and bashed her brains out for no reason at all? You found nothing to explain why a man like Warren would explode."

Now Ray remembered the interrogation, how helpful Philips had been to Warren. The D.A. had even fed him cues for an alibi. Was it possible that even then he was afraid of trying this case?

"If I had more time, I could—"

"—dig it out? From whom? You never sweated his kids. And you blew his interrogation, you never took the gloves off. Why didn't you get a confession?"

White-hot rage elbowed aside the nausea that had paralyzed Ray from the moment he'd heard the case was being dumped. It was a setup. He was the fall guy. *Philips never intended to try this case.*

"We don't beat confessions out of suspects anymore." He struggled to keep his voice calm. "The Supreme Court won't let us."

"What about the weapon and the bloody clothes?"

The only things Philips hadn't thrown in his face were the charcoal fluid and the Windex bottle. Next thing Ray knew, he'd be heaving that wood-paneled pickup truck. "Vermejo Boulevard's fifteen miles long and the Fremont River is dirty and deep. With more men I might've been able to do something…"

"Stop making excuses for yourself. Scott's an accountant, how did you describe him? 'A man who never gets his hands dirty.' Would a guy like that carry bloody clothes around town? No, Ray, it just won't wash. And you didn't follow important leads."

"Leads?"

"You never found the pickup truck. I'm not going into a two-week trial and have Simon Evans shove that truck up my ass every five minutes. And you never talked to that Mexican who complained about Peggy at work, right? I can hear Evans now, Where's José? Where's José?' And does José own a pickup or have a friend who does? I don't know the answer, Ray, and the reason I don't is because *you screwed up!*"

"This isn't about the evidence, is it? It's about you being afraid to square off against Warren's mouthpiece."

Philips froze. When he turned, his face was a mask of fury. "You can kiss it all good-bye, Burt. When I'm finished you'll be lucky if they let you retire. I'm putting Sergeant Devine in charge of the investigation, whatever's left of it. Now get the hell out of my office."

—

When Simon Evans called Warren to tell him the charges were dropped, his client's only question was who could he sue. "They can't get away with this," Warren fumed. "You're my lawyer, what about my rights?" Simon leaned back in his leather chair and closed his eyes. It never ceased to amaze him how naïve the average American was about his own justice system. "Let me tell you a fact of life, Mr. Scott. Just because the D.A. is afraid he can't prove your guilt beyond a reasonable doubt doesn't mean he can't defend his office against a suit for false arrest or malicious prosecution."

"But they should pay! Aren't I entitled to justice? Isn't that what courts are for?"

"If you want justice, go to a whorehouse. If you want to get fucked, go to a courthouse."

Simon hung up. He was reasonably certain he'd never hear from Scott again. Unlike some of his clients, Warren didn't strike him as a repeat offender. And he was just as glad not to have to go the distance with him anyway. He couldn't stand that cheap cologne.

—

Tim's father told them the charges were dismissed and he was moving to Seattle to start a new life. Laura was talking about going east where she didn't know a soul. It's almost over, Sari thought, we'll be able to pick up where we left off.... But Kay's words were seared into her brain.

Warren would never have gone to Stanley spur of the moment, not when he had that seminar.

The only explanation for Warren's behavior that day was he hadn't been planning to come. The way he acted at their apartment made his desire to visit as implausible as stopping by when he knew Tim would already be at the rec center. Of course, she'd handed him that piece on a silver platter: hadn't she rattled on about having taken a shower before he even said he came to the door? Kay was right; he'd used them. And that could have been for only one purpose. But it was too late now, and anything she might have done would have destroyed Tim.

Together they walked down the Hill to find Warren something to celebrate the end of the case. They saw the poster at the same time, a life-sized portrait of a hound leaping over a chain-link fence with the caption *"Free at Last!"* Tim said it seemed so perfect.

And then it hit. Free of what?

Without speaking, they chose a card instead.

—

Ten days later Sari's parents came to Stanley for the wedding. The afternoon before the ceremony she and her father walked down the Elm Street Mall. Sari could hear him tick off the attractions in his head: blue sky, sunshine, lots of trees, rustic. Foothills and wooden storefronts. Picture postcard of a place. In fifteen minutes they'd exhausted every geographic and cultural possibility Stanley had to offer.

"Quite a town you've got here, Sari," Max said.

He meant, didn't anyone read anything besides the *Courier?*

"It's not so bad." She joined him on the bench outside the courthouse where she and Tim were to be married.

"Not bad at all." Don't be fooled; this is no paradise. "I know things haven't been easy between you and your mother, but we've always been able to talk. Kept the lines of communication open. Haven't we?"

"Uh-huh."

"I've never lied to you, have I? And neither has your mother."

There was more than one type of lie. The ones you spoke, and the truths you didn't. But it was too late for the luxury of self-righteousness. "Not unless you count pretending the bruised spot on a banana is honey," Sari agreed.

"So you'll believe me when I tell you I know these people."

"What people?"

"The Warren Scotts of the world." He'd met Tim's father only the night before, with her mother for a drink at the hotel. Was she about to get the Jewish version of what was wrong with folks out here?

"I know only one of them," Sari evenly replied.

"Fine, let's talk about him. That man may have killed his wife."

"The charges were dropped!" She'd never told them about Dale Carnegie, or Warren's claim that he'd stopped by their apartment. Just that the police never found the guy with the pickup truck.

Turning, Max took one of her hands in his own. The gesture was so uncharacteristic it alarmed Sari more than his next words.

"You think I've forgotten your call, when your mother was here in May? You said you knew things, things you'd never—"

Fury rode to her rescue.

"And you told me to forget it, to mind my own business!"

"His family will never accept you." He squeezed her fingers and for an instant Sari was six, shivering in the protection of his lap after falling in the pond in Sloatsburg. But his next words severed all connection to that comforting memory. "How many people have you invited for the ceremony tomorrow? Ten, twenty?"

Pulling free, she rose from the bench.

"I'm not marrying the Scotts, I'm marrying Tim."

"Whatever led Warren to act must have affected his son." She started to walk away, up Elm toward Broadway. "I have nothing against him personally, but—"

"Tim is not his father!" she cried, and broke into a run.

—

The next day they were married at the courthouse. When they assembled for a group picture on the stone steps, Sari stood between Tim and his sister, with Warren and her parents on opposite ends. She stiffened just as Kay Butler snapped the shot. Laura had whispered in her ear, "Now *you're* the only Mrs. Scott."

Chapter Twenty

R ay could have ended his career with Peggy's murder but it would have meant giving up half his pension. He couldn't do that to Marion, not with the mortgage and their cabin in Torrance needing a new roof. And what about their plans to buy a used motor home, spend six months touring Lake Louise and the Cascades? Swallowing what was left of his pride, he agreed to transfer to the juvenile crimes division of the Hallett County Sheriff's Department for his last years before retirement.

Ray hated everything about juvie with a passion that surprised him, the car thefts and petty vandalism, the slashed tires and joyriding. Not to mention curfew violations; curfew violations were *big*. After six weeks he was so bored he went through every file in the office, even the ones that had been closed for years.

The cabinets in the storage closet adjacent to the juvenile division were crammed with reports from school hoard psychologists cautioning society against boys who were now adults, educators throwing up their hands and trying to avoid being sued by shunting failures to a criminal justice system so disaffected and overburdened, it made only cursory efforts to follow up. Most of the closed files were clumsily redacted, with names of miscreants blotted out by overzealous clerks with Magic

Markers who misunderstood the meaning of laws sealing juvenile records and obliterated any information that might possibly be of future use. Occasionally Ray found things that chilled him to the core, tales of boys skinning live squirrels or drawings that provided windows into the violent fantasies of adolescent minds. As he examined one distressingly lifelike sketch of a blindfolded woman reclining on a bed with a breast cut off and a gaping hole where her privates should be, he reflected that some of these boys were dangerously sick.

He ran into Lew Devine once in a while, but they didn't have much to say to each other. The day after Ray was thrown off the Scott case he'd called Lew and invited him to Las Margaritas for a drink. That was before Lew was promoted to lieutenant, of course, and placed in charge of Investigations.

They'd sat at the bar, though the place was empty and they could have had a booth. Balancing the heels of his Tony Lamas on the brass rail, Lew ordered a Coors.

"Tough break, Ray..."

"I'm sure it's all over the Department by now." He signaled for a Jim Beam.

"Little early in the afternoon for that, ain't it?"

"It's the right time," Ray replied. "Change your mind and have one with me?"

"I'm going back to the office after this."

"Oh, yeah, I forgot. You're in charge of the Scott case now, aren't you? What was it Philips told the press, 'The charges were dropped because of newly-discovered evidence?'" Ray laughed. "What evidence was that, Lew, the phantom pickup truck?"

"Look, I know you're sore—"

"Damn right I'm sore! I never expected that from you."

Devine stared into his beer. "What're you talking about?"

"C'mon, Lew, I may have been born at night, but it wasn't last night. How long were you feeding him reports behind my back?"

"I never—"

"Cut the crap. Philips is too lazy and dumb to read the file himself.

The only reason he knew about that truck was because you told him. Come to think of it, there was only one mention of it in your report. Who was it told you about that, the woman across the street?"

"Yeah." Unable to meet Ray's eyes in the mirror, Lew was staring at the reflection of the neon beer sign behind the bar.

"Why didn't you write it up?"

"Wasn't important." He shrugged and took a long pull on his Coors. "No one else reported it, and she never really saw the driver."

"Then how the hell did Philips find out?"

"Look, Ray, he asked me to keep him posted. What was I supposed to do?"

Ray turned on his stool and stared at his former partner until Lew had to look back. "You were supposed to tell me, goddammit, like I would've done for you! Not set me up to take the fall."

"I had no idea what was coming."

"What'd you think, all of a sudden Philips figures you're the reincarnation of Sherlock Holmes? He wants to be your pal? Christ, didn't you learn anything from me?" He signaled the bartender for another whiskey. "I should've seen it coming. His blood turned to piss the minute Evans entered the ring, and now the whole thing gets swept under the rug. What'd he tell you to do with the investigation, Lew, work it a couple months and then let it die a quiet death?"

"Something like that…"

"There's never gonna be an arrest, is there?"

"No." Devine gave a short laugh and stepped down from the barstool. "Not unless Evans finds that pickup truck."

"Jesus." Ray tossed back his drink and raised his hand to order a third.

"Why don't I give you a lift? At least let me take you back to your car."

"You've done enough already. I can get myself home."

—

It took Taylor Philips three years to exact his ultimate revenge.

The last Monday in April of his final year on the force, Ray received a memo from the sheriff saying the SWAT armored car would not be available to the Gillman Rotary Club that coming Friday. "For security purposes." His stomach flopped. Must be a mistake, he thought, he'd been the keynote speaker at Law Day for ten years now. The Ray Burt show was the only thing that made his tenure in juvie bearable.

Ray's romance with the Rotary had begun with a phone call from the used car salesman who lived down the street, a nodding acquaintance who needed a speaker for that month's luncheon. At Marion's urging Ray went, taking with him a bulletproof vest in case they ran out of questions, and before the applause died from his first presentation the Rotary booked him for a return engagement. He didn't have to be a genius to realize props were a key factor to his appeal, so he began bringing technicians who owed him a favor and could explain fingerprinting, the effects of poison and, on one all too memorable occasion, autopsy techniques. Last year's Law Day luncheon had reeled in more than a hundred local businessmen with the lure of a blood spatter analyst.

Now SWAT was the law-enforcement flavor of the week. Although more phenomenon than necessity in Gillman, where domestic terrorism of the political variety was unknown, the sheriff had nevertheless purchased an armored vehicle. Ray had been given permission to drive it to the Rotary Club and it promised to be the event of the season.

Now he told himself to buck up, that his popularity transcended props, but deep down he knew what those good old boys really loved was the toys. While he was racking his brain for a substitute for the armored car, his phone rang. It was Wendell Horsley, the club's president.

"I want you to know you're still welcome to come Friday as our guest."

"Glad you called, Wendell, I've been looking forward to this all—"

"—hate to bump you, but we just found out this morning."

"*Bump* me?"

"Since the SWAT car won't be available, the SBI volunteered its surveillance van. They're sending a—"

"What—"

"—got the name of the fella right here." Ray ran a finger under his collar so he could breathe. "Kevin Day. Ever heard of him?"

Ray slammed down the phone and dialed before he could think better of it.

"You son of a bitch!"

"Excuse me?" Day replied.

"It wasn't enough to stick me with snot-nosed kids and whiny parents, now you gotta humiliate me in front of every businessman in Gillman? The Rotary is *my* gig."

"Lieutenant Burt? I don't know what—"

"Don't hand me that crap! We both know what this is about."

"Now, hold on a second. I got a phone call from the director of the SBI instructing me to be at the Moose Lodge Friday at noon, with no explanation. If you think I'm in cahoots with someone to discredit you, you're dead wrong, and if you'll give me five goddamn minutes to check it out, I'll get back to you."

When Day called twenty minutes later, Ray let it roll through to the switchboard. It wasn't until the gal at the front desk poked her head in the door with a message that it was urgent that he picked up the phone.

"I got nothing to say to you, Day."

"That may be, but you better get down here fast, because you have a lot to learn between now and Friday."

"What are you talking about?"

"You were right, Taylor Philips screwed you, but we'll go him one better. How would you like to unveil the SBI's state-of-the-art mobile crime lab? It cost only six hundred grand." Ray was speechless. "It's as big as a bus so it takes a little getting used to. In fact, we call it a cross between a Greyhound and a bloodhound... That's an inside joke, Burt, but you can use it. Still there?"

"*Jeez*-us!"

"When I reminded my boss the whole point of a stakeout is *not* to let the target know he's being watched, he nixed the surveillance van and blamed the whole thing on pressure from your D.A. How soon can you get your butt down here so we can start figuring out what makes this Winnebago run?"

"Are you pulling my leg?"

"Not on your life. But you're buying the beer."

The following year Taylor Philips retired from the D.A.'s office having never lost a trial, and joined Hamilton & Portnoy, his father-in-law's firm. Ray's blood pressure soared when he saw the headline in the *News:* "Star Prosecutor Joins Montgomery Street Firm—From Black Hats to White Shoes." Philips posed for the camera with his arm around his toothy wife, a cuddly child of indeterminate sex in front of each parent. A dozen more kids and he could have been a Kennedy.

Chapter Twenty-One

When Sari graduated from college a year early and told Tim she wanted to go to law school, his initial reaction was to laugh.

"Did Simon Evans impress you that much? Or maybe you want to make sure the bad guys get what they deserve…

His grades had slipped from A's to C's and with them plans for graduate school. But engineering had been Warren's dream and not Tim's, so the loss did not seem so great. He spent more and more time at the hockey rink and Sari saw him with his sketch pad only once, at the bench beneath the coleuses in the flat on Locust. But his blunt pencil robbed the leaves of their delicate vitality and the next morning she found the sheets in the trash. He would paint again, she told herself, he just needed time to heal. The cabin in Garnet Hill had never seemed so far away.

"That's not it at all," she replied. "I just think it would be nice to be in a profession where you can do the right thing, be part of a solution."

"The right thing?" They were sitting on the daybed, and Tim drew Sari to him and gave her a hard kiss. "My little idealist."

"No, I'm serious." She pulled away. "I've already registered for the admission test."

"Without telling me?" The pretense of humor was gone.

"I'm spinning my wheels, Tim. I can't keep working at the campus bookstore, waiting for you to—"

"Minimum wage isn't good enough?"

Like all their arguments, it started in one place and slid sideways. Was that because his mother's death hovered like a shroud but they never uttered her name?

"Even if I get accepted, I wouldn't start till after you graduate. By then…"

He shook his head, knowing he wouldn't be able to talk her out of it.

"Go ahead, be a lawyer. Maybe you'll learn nothing is black and white."

—

When Tim graduated the following spring, he went to work full-time for the contractor for whom he'd framed houses during high school and college vacations. He gave up coaching but continued to play for the Wings, and between hockey and his job he had little time to dwell on the past. Construction wasn't so different from engineering, he joked. It would be a stop-gap measure to keep food on the table until he could get his start as an artist.

Sari began law school the same day Tim was made foreman of his crew. The first day of classes she and her fellow freshmen were herded into an auditorium and told, "Unlike your brethren who have chosen to become doctors, we are going to teach you to think." As she struggled to reconcile idealism with the meat-grinder reality of legal education, she reminded herself why she was there. To learn how to clarify right from wrong, she thought, and gain the tools to achieve justice for survivors… But it was far more personal than that. She needed to know every step of the process so she could understand where the fault lay in botching Peggy's case. If Warren had evaded justice through the assistance of Simon Evans and an inept prosecution team, would her coming forward have made any difference?

Instead of lecturing, Sari's teachers interrogated students in the modem equivalent of a trial by ordeal, hunting down sacrificial lambs on the basis of an attendance roster. Every concept was fair game, and once she stopped envying the odd philosophy student or two who enjoyed matching wits with professors over abstractions, and the backbenchers who'd given up any hope of a decent grade, she began to relish the challenge. The first semester became a model for those that followed: she took it one day at a time, on the edge of her seat, willing the accusatory gaze to fall on anyone but her but able to hold her own when it did. For the first time in her life, school was a battleground rather than a refuge, and now it had a real purpose.

Every night when she came home, she reviewed her lessons with Tim.

"I don't know how you keep it all straight," he'd remark, fighting back a yawn. "But that's lawyers for you. Truth is whatever they're paid to say."

His assessment was uncomfortably close to the mark. What she was learning was that truth took a backseat to staking positions and formulating arguments to support them. But she couldn't bear the bitterness in his voice.

"I called the Institute of Art, Tim. They're offering scholarships—"

"At least construction's an honest living."

At the end of the first semester Sari received the highest grades in her class. But she wasn't fooled; she'd succeeded simply because she could not afford to fail. Saying nothing of her plans to Tim, she began scanning the job boards for second-year internships in the office of the local D.A.

When Kay Butler invited them to a hockey game the following March, Sari was jubilant. Kay's son Todd was captain of his team, but the occasion was the least of it; this was the first time they'd seen Tim's aunt since their wedding. Sari prodded Tim to accept, and they met at a rink in Widmark for the quarterfinals.

As they settled in the stands, Kay hugged Tim. "Remember all those Saturdays we spent watching you? Nothing but trophies."

Tim winked at Sari. "Believe it or not, we actually lost once or twice. Dad would say, 'Your passing's off, your grip's too wide. Why didn't you check that guy into the boards?'"

"Warren likes to win." Kay's smile was tight, but Tim was watching the rink. Tim's aunt was thinner now and the skin around her eyes was translucent.

"You know what I remember?" Tim continued. "You saying, 'Don't worry, wait till next time. You're still the best little guy I know.' And the pain would be gone, just like that. Mom never knew what to say to make it go away. She acted like the game didn't happen or we lost because I wasn't trying hard enough. When she was there at all."

"Don't criticize her, Tim, it's not easy to be a mother." Kay's arm dropped from his shoulders. "But you children meant everything to Peggy."

"Remember when I had appendicitis and you picked me up from school?"

"You were one sick pup…"

"I told the nurse Mom was visiting relatives, because—"

"How's Laura?" Kay interrupted. "I never hear from her."

"She's working at a bookstore in New York." The game had started and he leaned forward. "She loves the city, nothing could bring her back. Dad's fine too."

The silence stretched and Sari waited for Kay to ask about Warren. Seattle was rainy and cold, he had difficulty attracting clients and was thinking of moving to Arizona. The farther away he stayed, the better.

"I've been meaning to ask you something, Tim." At the false brightness in Kay's voice, Sari glanced again at his aunt. The opposing team had almost scored a goal, but Todd's goalie pounced and covered the puck with his glove. That should have stopped the play but a brawny defense-man skated right into him. "When your father showed up that day in Stanley—"

"That was almost three years ago," Tim reminded her. In accordance with the cardinal rule of hockey, a player on Todd's team grabbed the aggressor by his jersey and punched him in the face. He toppled to the ice, ending the scrap as quickly as it began, but Tim kept staring at the spot where he had fallen.

"What was the reason he gave for missing his seminar?" Kay continued.

"Sari's the one he spoke to." As Tim's nails dug into her palm, Sari felt his tension mount. How could Kay do this to him?

"It's been so long," Sari protested. "Who can remember?"

"I hope he didn't say it was postponed, because I checked with Dale Carnegie. The course started on schedule." Kay's eyes bored through Tim as the whistle sounded and the game resumed. "What exactly did Warren say?"

Sari answered before he could respond. "Tim told the police everything he knew. It's behind us now."

"I see your mother's face every day. Don't you, Tim?"

"We need to move on with our lives," Sari replied. His hand lay cold and heavy in hers.

"You think it's that simple?" Kay asked. Now her piercing gaze was leveled at Sari. "For me it will never be over."

"We can't change the past…" Sari began.

"I see." Kay nodded slowly, and then rose. "So that's all she meant to you," she said to Tim.

"Kay—" Tim rose to block her passage to the aisle.

Tim's aunt pushed her way past them.

—

Tim was earning enough after his first year with the construction company that they were able to afford a ranch-style starter home in a subdivision northeast of Stanley. He built a split-rail fence and Sari spaded mushroom compost into the dense clay of their yard, and the marigolds and zinnias they planted that spring bloomed with faces as massive as a man's fist. At Tim's insistence they scoured three counties for a Harrison's yellow rose, and when they finally found one in a private greenhouse west of Gillman he told her it grew wild on the prairie of his mother's birth. From the Dumb Friends League they adopted a German shepherd they named Champ.

"Sure you wouldn't rather have a goat?" Sari asked as they loaded Champ in the backseat of the Mustang.

For a moment he looked blank, then there was a flash of the old Tim.

"He'll be better practice for those three kids," he replied. He leaned over and kissed her. A lingering, tender kiss, and in it she tasted something she hadn't felt in a long while. They were going to make it. They were finally leaving the dark days behind.

Tim had stopped coaching but continued to play defense for the Wings. He'd been coming home with welts and bruises for years and now Sari began to notice a change in the pattern of his injuries. Fights were an accepted part of hockey, but when he returned from one league game with his nose taped and another with a dozen stitches bisecting a copper brow she knew it was something more.

"You're too old for this," she said.

"Don't you like the Frankenstein look?"

"What are you now, the goon?"

"I do it for the team."

"Break your nose once more and the cartilage will be destroyed." She grazed his misshapen knuckles with her forefinger. "Is it worth giving up your art?"

"When's the last time you saw me paint?"

"Does that mean you'll never do it again? Is that what you want?"

He laughed. "I'll let you know when I figure it out myself."

Six weeks later Tim's team was in the semifinals. Sari was sitting in the third row of the stands, behind the Plexiglas at center ice. The Wings were two goals ahead when one of Tim's teammates shot the puck at the goal and the goalie leaped on it. Making no effort to control himself, Tim skated straight into the goalie. As the other side's defenseman, who had six inches and seventy-five pounds on Tim, skated toward him, Tim yanked off his helmet and threw down his gloves and stick. The enforcer grabbed Tim by his upper sleeve, slammed him into the boards and began punching him in the face. Tim stayed on his feet but made no attempt to defend himself.

Sari screamed, "Tim!"

Each time the enforcer pounded Tim, his head smashed into the Plexiglas in front of Sari. Standing on her seat, she tried to climb over the barrier to him. As his front teeth shattered and blood began to gush from his mouth onto his sweat-soaked jersey she could feel every blow.

Leaning as far as she could over the shuddering Plexiglas, she reached for him.

"Tim!"

For an instant he looked up and their eyes met. His words were faint but unmistakable.

"Can I stop now?"

Chapter Twenty-Two

The transfer to juvenile gave Ray too much time to think. Marion knew by heart every mistake he'd made, every lead he should have run down, every reason no one but Warren Scott could have done that dreadful thing years ago. When he came home from work he would set the table and talk while she finished cooking dinner. She would place herself on automatic pilot, stirring pots and tossing salad, making comforting sounds while he relived the case that destroyed his career.

"You know what's always bothered me, Marion?" he'd say. "We never found that hammer. Nothing else was missing from the house or the garage. He could have burned the clothes, but what'd he do with that hammer?"

"Wouldn't it make sense for a burglar to take it with him?"

"Maybe, but most burglars don't carry weapons. They're cowards, you know. When your typical burglar's confronted by a member of the household his first thought is to get away without being seen." He stood at her shoulder, watching her season the pork chops. "Even if he strikes, he hits only once. Not several times."

The kitchen wasn't big enough for them both and Ray made her nervous, hovering there like that. So she'd clear a space for him on the far counter and go to the pantry for an onion. The largest she could find. "Mince this for me, dear?"

"All he cares about is getting away. The last thing he wants is to commit an even bigger crime. Most burglars just run." He drew a cleaver from the knife drawer. "And the first thing he does is make sure nobody's home. He calls and lets the phone ring or hits the doorbell. If nobody answers, he checks the backyard."

"Maybe Peggy was taking a nap."

"In the middle of chores?" He snorted. "But let's say she was. She hears a noise and surprises him in the garage. Then he hits her four or five times, let's say, with something he picks up. There's lots of things he could've grabbed, pipes and boards laying around. Which brings us to an interesting question..."

Marion knew her lines by heart. "Fingerprints?"

"Fingerprints. All we found was glove marks, everything else was wiped clean. Household items are full of prints and they last a long time. That means the killer wiped whatever he took and *then* wore a pair of gloves to carry it to the garage. A burglar who's savvy enough to use gloves ain't gonna wipe junk for prints, Marion. There's no need."

She peeled the onion and handed it to him without responding.

"If he was wearing gloves to avoid prints, he wore them when he hit Peggy. And if he was wearing gloves there was no reason to take the weapon with him." Proud of his logic, he began chopping the onion. "Can you feature a burglar taking a weapon, covered with blood, out of a house in broad daylight? In that neighborhood, at that time of day? And we know it was an Estwing framing hammer, because that's what Kevin said..."

Marion certainly didn't intend to look that gift horse in the mouth. She slapped two pats of margarine in a pan. It had been Kevin this and Kevin that for the past three years, but after Ray's falling-out with Lew Devine, Day was a godsend. When her curiosity finally got the better of her and she told Ray to bring him home for dinner, she was relieved to see their guest was mortal, a little shaggy around the ears and with lapels just wide enough to confirm there was no woman at home. Glancing over at the carving board, she saw the onion had been reduced to mush.

"How 'bout a couple stalks of celery, dear?" she said.

"Of course the clocks completely blow that cockeyed alibi of his." Ray went to the refrigerator and began rummaging in the vegetable bin. "Put them together with the woman who came to the door, and you see how he thinks."

"How who thinks?"

"Warren Scott! Aren't you listening?" He continued without waiting for an answer. "Let's take his story first. He says Laura followed him to the Sinclair around nine so he could leave Peggy's Cadillac for a lube job. Laura takes him back home, drops him off a few minutes later. You with me, Marion?"

"Yes, dear." The onion was too soupy to brown properly. What was she going to do with it? She certainly couldn't serve it with pork chops.

"The next thing we know is Regina Hummel drops by, and we've got damn good confirmation from the state patrol that happened between ten-twelve and ten twenty-three. At that point Scott's wearing a Hawaiian shirt, red with green flowers. Different clothes than he's got on later when he goes to Stanley. You follow?" This time he waited for her nod. "Now, Scott says he went back to the Sinclair at ten-thirty to find out when his wife's car would be ready, and again at eleven-thirty. But the owner says he got there the second time around eleven forty-five, which tallies with the times on the clocks he pulled out of the wall. If Philips hadn't shot his yap off, Warren might not have realized how crucial that second fifteen minutes was."

"Didn't he say he went to the service station to pick up his jacket, then dropped it off at home?"

"Why bother if the car's gonna be ready that afternoon anyway and he's not going to the cleaners till Monday? At the very start I wondered if he went to the Sinclair the first time to create an alibi. Hummel showing up in the middle of him whacking Peggy must've freaked him out, and Warren would've wanted to distance himself from the scene in case she came forward. In a he-said, she-said dispute, you tend to believe the guy, but he had no way of knowing she could corroborate the time by a patrol officer handing out tickets. But the more I thought about it…"

She couldn't just throw the onion out. And what was she going to do with all that celery Ray was mincing?

"…the more I was sure it was to stash his weapon and clothes. Once Hummel saw him in that shirt, he would've been desperate to get rid of it. And while he was doing that, he would've been thinking about how to cover up what happened. So he comes back to the house and starts yanking clocks out of—"

"And you couldn't search his car…"

"Not without a warrant. It's like a house, you can't just barge in without one unless the owner consents. And by the time we had probable cause, it would've been useless. A man as meticulous as Warren would have washed and vacuumed that Cadillac half a dozen times." Ray's frown made Marion wonder if he was more disturbed at his failure to secure a warrant than he was willing to admit. "But maybe that wasn't how it happened at all. Let's go back to scenario number one. Alibi." He decapitated another stalk with a resounding *thwack.* "Hummel's bad enough, and of course he don't think about Peggy's watch while he's bashing her face and she lifts her arm to protect herself, much less the effect of the clocks… But he needs both an alibi and a reason for being home, first when Hummel comes to the door and later at eleven-thirty, in case he's seen at the house or we put two and two together. Which we generally do."

She knew this was the part he enjoyed most. "So?"

"So what could be better than going *back* to the service station to ask about his wife's car? Busy as they were Saturday morning, he thought no one'd notice what time he arrived, and in case anyone says he saw Warren at home, he can say he was there just long enough to throw his coat in the closet. Kill two birds with one stone that way." Ray chuckled grimly. "Only problem was, we could corroborate the times Hummel and the folks at the Sinclair saw him that morning. That explains his trips back and forth, but he still needs to fill in the time between when he left the station and arrived at Tim's one o'clock practice. So he says he ran a bunch of bullshit errands, none of which he can prove, and then stopped by Tim's apartment." He stared at the celery with a look of distress, and Marion wondered if he'd suddenly realized the futility of his task.

"Only thing I can't figure is, where does Tim's girlfriend fit in? Was she really in the shower, and if she wasn't, why cover?" Shrugging it off, he resumed chopping. "It's a neat little package: Warren needed to fill in that extra fifteen minutes by running errands, and the errands prove what time he arrived at the Sinclair, because if he didn't get to the service station by eleven-thirty, how would he have had time to go to Walgreen's before he went to Stanley? If that snake Philips hadn't encouraged him to say he arrived at the Sinclair fifteen minutes earlier than he actually did, I'll bet we never would have heard a word about wedding cards or clip-on sunglasses."

Marion whisked the pan from the stove and dumped the onions in a bag under the sink. "Done with that celery, dear?"

"Remember how those sunglasses always drove me nuts? The only thing Warren said he bought that morning, no wedding card for Tim. He couldn't show us a receipt, but when he whipped them out in the middle of his interrogation they looked new. And you know what we found in that trash can in the garage?"

"An old pair of clip-ons..."

"You guessed it. Scott says the burglar stole them from his bedroom, but if he left the house that morning *before* the burglar came, why didn't he take his glasses with him?"

"Maybe he just forgot, Ray." Would he notice she didn't use the onion, and what on earth would she do with that mountain of celery on the carving board? She'd have to make a pot of soup tomorrow, which meant buying a fresh chicken in the morning.

"—too bright and hot that day to drive without them. He's in a blind panic when he tries to make it look like a burglary. So he gathers a bunch of cheap junk to throw out, stereo turntables and ice makers, stuff he don't care about in case he never sees it again, and one of the things he grabs is his clip-ons. When he leaves the house later he can't go back for them, so he has to buy another pair. But when and where did he do it?" Nagged by that thought, he shook his head and turned back to his wife.

"That and the damned Windex bottle..."

"Windex?"

"Remember how he said the bottle broke while he was cleaning the johns, and he had to go to the Safeway for another? That would have been between the time Laura dropped him off and Peggy was killed."

"So? He had an hour, didn't he?"

"But when we looked later, the only Windex bottle we found was brand-new, and there was no bottle in the garbage either. The seal on the nozzle wasn't even broken! No, it's not the timing that bothers me, Marion. Or even the fact that he never used the Windex. It's the details."

"Hmn?" If she was going to make soup tomorrow, she would need carrots, more onions, maybe a turnip...

"It's like the clip-ons, why mention them at all? I mean, neither one by itself has any significance to the case. But they're so damn specific, they couldn't have come out of thin air."

"So?"

"So what that tells me is Windex and clip-on sunglasses were on Warren's mind for some reason when I questioned him. And I just don't know why."

—

The next evening it would start all over again.

"I always knew there was something fishy with that charcoal fluid. Have I told you about that, Marion?"

She knew there was no point saying yes, I've heard about the lighter fluid a hundred times. "What's that, dear?"

"Warren went to Safeway that morning to buy the Windex and a can of charcoal fluid. He said they were planning to have a barbecue when he got home that afternoon, but he stopped and ate a late lunch in Stanley. Remember?"

She nodded absently. She'd give him five minutes, no longer.

"Whoever killed Peggy was drenched with blood. It splattered all over the wall, there was even spots on the ceiling. According to Forensics, with each blow blood and brains splattered up behind the killer. So his clothing and shoes had to be blood-soaked."

Marion mentally revised the dinner menu. No burgers tonight. Maybe she'd throw some nice white chicken on the grill.

"Scott changes his clothes before he leaves the house and burns them on his way to Stanley. That's why he buys the lighter fluid, not for a barbecue he never expects to have because he already ate. He pulls off Vermejo and burns his shoes and clothes in a ditch. There's plenty of places to do it. That's why we never found them. But the hammer wouldn't have burned...."

"If I was Warren Scott, I'd stick my clothes in the washing machine. Didn't you tell me the garage was right off the utility room?"

"We looked in the washer and dryer. But that was hours after the fact, he had plenty of time to take them out before he called us."

The next night Ray picked up right where he left off. "Even if he washes his clothes first, he can't get all the blood out. So he has two reasons to drive to Stanley: he gets rid of his clothes along the way, and while he's gone from the house the phony burglar has plenty of time to commit the crime."

"You're giving him an awful lot of credit, aren't you, dear?"

"Warren's smarter than you think. Remember, he's an accountant. To them, it's all in the details. But no matter how smart he thinks he is, when it comes to crime he's an amateur. You know the real tip-off?"

Marion closed her eyes. She'd been waiting to hear about the drawers again for a week now.

"The drawers in two of the bedrooms were all pulled out the same distance. No burglar does that. Unless you start with the bottom drawer, which they never do because jewelry and cash are always on top, when you get to the top drawer you can't look in it unless you pull it farther out or push the bottom ones in. Try it sometime, you'll see I'm right." She nodded. He'd proved his point at least a dozen times, with every chest of drawers in the house. "Not only that, but the drawers in the master bedroom weren't ransacked per se, he pulled them out and set them on the carpet. Your average burglar won't take the time to ransack drawers, he pulls them out and dumps their contents on the floor."

Marion turned just in time to stop him from emptying the silverware onto the kitchen counter. Laying a gentle hand on his arm, she said, "You don't have to show me again, Ray."

"After he dumps them out, he sifts through the items to see if there's anything he wants to take. He don't care about neatness because he's in a hurry to get outta there."

She nodded and sent him out to light the barbecue.

Once he called her while he was eating lunch at his desk.

"Marion, you know what I just figured out?"

"What's that, dear?" She reached for her sewing basket. Maybe she could mend those trousers he tore the other day crawling under the Chrysler...

"The Windex. Remember how he said he bought a bottle at Safeway that morning because the other one broke? Well, why didn't he buy the clip-on lenses at the same time if he knows he's driving to Stanley that day?"

"Yes, dear."

"I'm so glad I figured that out. It's been bugging me all this time."

Chapter Twenty-Three

B y Sari's final year of law school, Tim had retired from the Wings. Construction was booming and he was now supervising three crews handling jobs across the northern half of the state. He worked until late every evening and on weekends, was sometimes gone as long as a week. The responsibility seemed to give him a sense of control, and she wondered whether he looked forward to the long drives because as he drove, his mind was free to wander.

More and more, Tim was a stranger. Because Sari was working after classes as a law clerk, their hectic schedules reduced their time together to rare evenings when they shared a meal. On the few occasions when she tried to reach him on the job, she was invariably told he was out with a crew.

"When I pass the bar," she told him one night, "you can cut back on these crazy hours. And if you want to go back to school—"

"And give up the overtime? No way."

———

W hen Sari got off work early one afternoon in April she decided to drop by Tim's job site and surprise him. They were building a development on the east side of Stanley and the proximity of the project provided a rare opportunity to see him during the day. The frantic pace was temporary, she told herself, just two more months...

"Where's Tim?" she asked Randy, his second in command, after a friend had dropped her off. He shrugged and Sari looked across the muddy field. At one end stood the skeleton of a multi-unit housing complex, with hard hats scrambling over the scaffolding like kids on the monkey bars, and at the other end another crew was by a bulldozer. She searched in vain for a lanky figure in the green plaid shirt Tim had worn that morning. Had she been mistaken about his schedule? "Isn't he here?"

Randy seemed uncomfortable. "I'm filling in."

"Will he be back later?"

Randy glanced down at some papers in his hands.

"Isn't he on this project?" she continued.

The driver of the bulldozer had jumped down and was approaching them. As Randy turned and waved Sari registered his relief.

"How long has this been going on?" she pressed.

"A couple of days..." Now he was embarrassed for her. As he began conferring with the hard hat, she turned back to where the crews parked but saw no sign of the Mustang.

When Sari called the contractor's office and was told they hadn't seen Tim in two weeks, she started to panic. Was he having an affair? She could handle anything but that. But Tim's increasing remoteness had seemed a product of isolation and emotional fatigue, and surely there would have been some sign... Confronting him would be futile; he had an answer for everything, and wasn't that part of the problem?

As the garage door squealed open at one in the morning and Tim crept upstairs, Sari pretended to be asleep. He sank to the edge of their bed and remained motionless for an eternity. Then she realized he was watching her in the dark. He was breathing softly, as if he were afraid to wake her, and the long low sighs seemed drawn from a well of sorrow and not remorse. As he slipped under the covers beside her, he buried his face in her hair.

The next morning she called the person who knew Tim best.

"Kay? It's Sari."

"What can I do for you?"

Sari flinched at Kay's coolness. She had planned to ask about Bud and the kids, how Christmas had been, and Kay's clipped words brought their encounter at the hockey game back in a rush. But Kay was Tim's closest tie to his mother. No matter how angry she was at them, she had to *care*.

"It's about Tim. I'm worried."

"Is he ill?" The question was more polite than concerned. Kay was a minute from hanging up.

"I can't reach him anymore."

There was a long silence, and when Kay responded her tone had softened.

"I'm not surprised."

"Has anything like this happened before?"

Kay hesitated again. "Tim had some adjustment problems when he was younger, but he worked through them. I'm sure he—"

"What kind of problems?"

"Peggy was very artistic when she was a child." Sari bit back her desperation; as long as she could keep Kay on the line, there was hope. "—won quite a few prizes at county fairs."

"I didn't know that." But she remembered those stunning portraits of Tim and his sisters tucked away in the photo album in Gillman.

"Pencil and ink, mostly. I always wondered what might have happened if she hadn't stopped." Why was Kay telling her this? "That's where Tim gets his talent."

He'd brushed aside questions about Peggy's art. And so much else… "He never really talked about it."

"There's a lot about his mother he didn't know."

Now Sari knew Kay's digression was intentional.

"Why did Peggy stop drawing?"

"For his fifth birthday I gave Tim a box of colored chalks, and he wore those sticks to nothing in less than a week. Warren built him his own little desk, but the walls were much more fun and Peggy was fit to be tied…" Kay's voice caught and Sari knew there was more she wanted to say. But Tim's aunt no longer trusted her. "You need to get him painting again."

"He hasn't opened his sketch pad in—"

"A clever girl like you will find a way."

———

The spare room at the southwest corner of their house was too sunny for a bedroom, but the light was ideal for a studio. With each carton of textbooks and trophies Sari moved to the garage, she became more certain she was doing the right thing. Since Peggy's death Tim had shunned all outlets for his creativity. Almost as if he were punishing himself…But now she would help him reclaim his art.

When Tim asked why she was cleaning out the back bedroom, she said she thought she'd seen a mouse near one of the cartons. Because their subdivision backed onto a field he asked no questions, and the next evening laid traps baited with peanut butter. When he saw her hemming bright yellow curtains by hand she told him spring was in the air. After the hard winter the daffodils and tulips leaped from the ground, and wasn't the Harrison's yellow in bud for the first time? Tim's birthday was two weeks away and she had one thing left to do.

"I need the Mustang next week," she told him. Tim was so proprietary about the car that unless he gave her a lift, she always took the bus.

"What for?"

"A job interview in Widmark," she lied. "Firms are hiring for the summer."

"When?"

She thought fast. "Wednesday afternoon. You'll be working."

"I'll take you."

Sari smiled to conceal her irritation. Although they'd bought the Mustang together, it was registered to her. What's mine is *yours*, Tim said, but that meant nothing in terms of the car. He wouldn't even let mechanics work on it.

"Afraid I'll get a flat?"

His laugh was strained. "I'm more concerned about you driving thirty miles an hour on the turnpike and getting rear-ended."

If she never drove, whose fault was that?

"Forget it," she replied, "I'll take the bus."

The following Wednesday Sari skipped classes and took the bus to downtown Widmark. As she made her way from the bus station to Markson's she imagined Tim's face when he saw what she had done. If it took every cent she'd stashed away, it would be worth it.

"I want a set of paints," she told the wispy-haired man at the largest art store in Widmark.

"What sort?"

"Oils, I guess." In response to his skeptical frown, she quickly added, "The best you have."

Following him through a narrow aisle lined with oil crayons and pastels, Sari was overwhelmed by the raw sensuality of the pigment. She reached for a violet chalk. "Go ahead," he said, inviting her to try it out on the scratch pad hanging from a shelf, but she was remembering the ink drawings Tim had made while he waited outside her Italian classes in Chapel Hall. Glorious flowers and birds, all the more captivating because they were imagined and not real. .. Was she too late?

"Winsor & Newton," his voice carried from a display in the next section, and she joined the clerk at the wire racks of plump aluminum tubes emblazoned with a griffin crest. "A gift?"

"For my husband. He's an artist, but—"

"—he hasn't painted in a while."

"Yes," she whispered, "exactly."

"Well, then, you'll want to get him a white and a black, and at least one each of the primary colors. But they're pricey."

"That's okay."

She reached for a tube with an emerald band. Sap Green, it was called, and she was back in the cornfield outside St. Augustine's with Tim, drinking in the broad bitter leaves. She turned the tube over and examined the label. Quinacridone gold and brominated copper in linseed oil. Not chemicals. *Elements.*

"This one," she said, handing it to him, and reached for another. "And this…" Phthalo Turquoise, an azure so deep and cool you could dive right into it. The pool at College Townhouses on a blazing morning in May. Before it all went wrong.

"—looking for primary colors, this one's more versatile," he was saying. He pointed at Winsor Blue, a darker shade with a shot of vermilion.

"I'll take them both."

She added Cadmium Red and Indian Yellow more for the sound of their names than any other reason, then accepted his advice on Titanium White and Indigo, a transparent black with the ability to capture light. Her final selection was Carmine. The shade closest to the poppies in the pastel portrait of the smiling girl at the cabin.

"Unh-uh," he said, returning it to the shelf. "He wouldn't be happy with that."

"Why not?"

"It's a fugitive color."

"What do you mean?"

"Winsor & Newton classifies its oils in degrees of permanence. Carmine's the only one graded C." He handed her a tube of Permanent Alizarin Crimson. "This one is the recommended alternative. AA. It'll last long after Carmine fades."

"No." How foolish to fear the choice of color could shorten the life span of a dream… "Carmine." Exasperated, he led her to the brushes, and she compromised with mongoose bristles instead of sable.

"Does he have an easel?" They'd already selected a linen canvas, oil-primed and stretched, and were standing in front of a display of vertical oak frames.

"I'll never be able to carry it on the bus," she protested, but they were collapsible and she chose one she could lift. With almost no money left, she was on her way to the checkout counter when a compact wooden case with a leather handle and brass clasps caught her eye.

"What's that for?"

"Carrying paints."

Propping the easel against a shelf, Sari opened the box. The lid held two Masonite palettes and the base was divided into compartments for brushes, paints, and solvents. It looked like a medicine chest. For healing tools.

"This too."

"Frankly, you'd be better off getting him another brush. I can show you an Isabey that'll last forever...."

"You don't understand. *We need this.*"

—

When Tim's birthday finally came, Sari baked him his first cake since they'd been married. The orange layer was modeled on one of Peggy's creations, the frosting message lopsided but clear: *I love you.* As she set the candles in their holders, she felt nervous for the first time since she'd gone to Markson's.

"You didn't have to do this," Tim said.

"Afraid you can't blow out all twenty-five of them?" There was something strange about his smile, and it took her a moment to realize he was on the verge of tears. "What's wrong, darling?"

"It's nothing, I just—" He reached up and hugged her. "This is the nicest birthday I've ever had."

"It's my fault. I should have done this every year." "You've been in school, and working—"

"Too busy for what's really important."

He squeezed her tighter.

"Can we go back?" he whispered.

"We don't have to," she said, "we can move forward." It was time to start a family, she thought. They should never have waited this long. "Come on, I've got something to show you."

She led him upstairs to the door to the back bedroom. "Go ahead," she said, "open it…"

The sun was just beginning to set over the foothills. It bathed the northeast corner where the easel stood pinkish gold, and the empty canvas seemed to glow. Tim took a step inside and came to a dead halt.

"Happy birthday!" she cried. But he stared at the canvas as if it were stained.

"It's linen," she said. Was it the wrong size?

Now his eyes turned to the pine box on the table against the opposite wall. He crossed the carpet and slowly lifted the lid.

"Winsor-Newtons," she said. "The man at Markson's said they were—"

"—the best." As Tim reached for one of the tubes and turned it over in his hands, the dying sun caught the label. Sap Green, the marriage of copper and gold. His thumb grazed the cap and lingered there. He wanted to open it. "Nothing but the best," he murmured.

"Should I have gotten pastels?" Maybe she could return them. "Or watercolors, you used to—"

He replaced the tube in the box and closed the lid. Snapping the brass latches shut, he turned to her.

"That part of my life is over, Sari."

"You don't have to give up everything you love."

She took a step closer but Tim's expression in the half-light made her stop. The pinpricks of jet in the center of his eyes were widening.

"Is that what you think it is, a penance?" His laugh was curt. "Not all Catholics are saints. Didn't you know about nuns?"

"Tell me." Anything to help her understand.

"My first-grade teacher was a Sister named Jeannette-Marie. She had Laura two years before, but I was her favorite. Like Mom, she thought cleanliness was the highest virtue—"

What did this mean now?

"—so every day before recess she had us clean the floor under our desks. She'd come down the aisle with the classroom monitor, and we'd sweep up paper and dust and crayon peelings and put them in their basket. Then we could go out to play."

Tim was leaning against the wall with his arms crossed, and Sari could no longer see his eyes. The ten-foot gap between them yawned.

"As Sister came down the aisle that day she spotted some paper under the desk next to mine. When she began to scold the other boy, he said, 'Timmy did it! I saw him.'"

"How awful," she began, but he was lost in the memory.

"I remember feeling paralyzed, not knowing what to do, but suddenly Sister came to my rescue. 'What a wicked lie! Our Timmy would *never* do that…' The other kid kept insisting no, I'd pushed the paper to his side, but it only made her angrier. I can still see him standing there, outraged, tears running down his cheeks as she made him stand in the corner while we ran off to play. I even remember his name, it was—"

"But she stood up for you, Tim." The canvas was dimming. "You must have adored her, it was wonderful—"

"You don't understand. That boy was telling the truth." His plaintive tone pierced her. "I pushed that trash under his desk, and she *knew*. I haven't thought about it in years, maybe not since that day…"

"Why now?"

"I hated her."

"Who?"

"Jeannette-Marie. She made me lie because I was so afraid to disappoint her. The image she had of me."

Who was he so afraid to disappoint? Whose image had he lied to protect?

"But you were what, Tim, five or six years old?" She wanted to go to him, to still that haunted voice. "And it was such a small thing, a scrap of—"

"She knew me so well, that I'd never embarrass her with the truth. It was so much easier to pretend."

The air seemed to part as Tim stumbled past her to the door. At the threshold, she felt his eyes seek hers.

"You know why I can't paint. Sari? Because when I close my eyes, I see *nothing*."

Chapter Twenty-Four

Ray's reward for juvie was retirement on two pensions. Not bad for a skinny kid from North Junction who enlisted during the Depression at age sixteen, was with the occupation forces in Japan and discharged as a master sergeant after serving as an MP in Korea. There was no doubt he'd earned his twenty-year army pension, but he was less proud to cash the checks from the public employees retirement fund. After two decades with the Hallett County Sheriff's Department he should have felt he earned it, but the final years had been a running sore. Who could be proud of going from head of Investigations to little more than a desk clerk?

As Ray was packing his personal belongings on his last day of work, Lew Devine stopped by.

"Buy you a beer, Ray?"

Ray peered in his bottom drawer a third time.

"Don't think so, Lew." Devine was Chief of Investigations now, with a bigger office than Ray ever had. D.A.'s prize gumshoe, widely rumored to be poking the boss's wife. But that was Lew. Still letting his little head do all the thinking.

"Oh, come on, Ray. Enough's enough. Is it really my fault you got stuck in juvie?"

Ray rose and looked his old friend in the eye. "Let's have that beer." He stuffed a sheaf of papers in the carton that contained all that was left of his tenure at the Hallett County Sheriff's Department and grabbed his hat.

Las Margaritas was quiet that time of day, and they sat in a vinyl booth in back. Devine ordered two shots of Jim Beam.

"Ever hear from Cindy?" Ray asked.

"Nah, she moved to Grand Falls years ago. Got a new stallion, I guess."

"I hear you ain't done too bad in that department yourself."

Devine bared his teeth in a parody of a wolf's grin. "I never talk out of school, Ray, I'm a regular gentleman." He raised his glass in a silent toast. "To all the roses waiting to be plucked…"

"Remember that gal in the Scott case?"

Devine's glass stopped just short of his lips. "Jesus, that's ancient history now. Why'd you bring that up?"

"Just wondering what happened to his daughter. You had more contact with her than I did. Wasn't she a real babe?"

Devine belted down his drink and signaled the bartender for another.

"Can't say I recall." He laughed uneasily. "Hell, back then I thought anything in a skirt was a babe."

"I bet you'd remember if you tried. You told me she was the sexiest thing you ever saw." Lew's face colored even in the dim light of the bar. "Never wrote up your interviews with her, did you?"

"What're you driving at?"

"Not a thing. Just wondered what happened to her." The bartender brought two more whiskeys although Ray's drink was untouched.

"Damned if I know. But come to think of it, she was a hot number. Long legs and big tits, right, Ray?" Devine closed his eyes and leaned back with a smile on his lips. "No, you're right, I'm not likely to forget that taste of honey long as I live."

"Where's she now, Lew?"

"Said she was moving to New York."

"How long did you keep seeing her after you dumped the case?"

Devine sat up. "What is this, Ray, the Spanish Inquisition?"

"Calm down." Ray tossed back his drink. "Couldn't care less how many times you plowed her, I just wanna know what she said."

"Not a goddamned thing!" Devine reached for his SWAT cap and started to stand, but Ray's grip was iron. "Did she tell you what he did with the clothes?"

"What the hell you talking about, are you nuts?" He tried to pull away but Ray wouldn't let him.

"What about the weapon, Lew? He went back to the Sinclair to put it in the Caddy, didn't he? After the case was dumped I talked to the grease monkey, and he said one of the times Scott came back he fiddled with the trunk. I want to know what the hell she told you!"

"She didn't know a thing, Ray. I never sweated her, I swear."

" 'Course not, Lew, you were too busy poking her. Taylor Philips get a piece of the action too?" He released Devine's arm and tossed some bills on the gouged table. "You make me sick."

Grabbing his Stetson, he walked out.

—

That night Ray came home stinking of Jim Beam and went straight to the basement. When he emerged a couple of hours later, he mumbled he wasn't hungry and staggered up to bed. Marion guessed he was entitled; after all, it was his last day after twenty years on the job. And here he was now, wide awake and stone sober at three in the morning. "I'm glad to be out of that cesspool."

"Hunh?" Marion lifted her head from the pillow. "What's the matter?"

"Nothing. Just glad to be here with you."

"Good." She aimed a kiss at his shoulder and rolled over. "Now go back to sleep."

"You know what I can't stop thinking about, Marion?" Silence was never a deterrent. "That stuff in the trash can."

"What trash can?"

"In the garage at 4990 South Cleveland. Remember?"

Sweet Mary, mother of God! Marion sat up and lit the lamp on her nightstand. "What are you talking about?"

"He threw junk in the trash to make it look like a burglary, but all he took was cheap stuff like an old black-and-white TV that belonged to Tim and a gift wrapped in wedding paper. He trashed his own son's wedding present!"

"Ray Burt, I've had it with the Scotts." She jerked back the covers and planted her feet on the carpet. "I never want to hear another word about them, do you understand? That case is going to kill you!"

"He threw out his own kid's wedding present! How cold can you get?"

She headed for the bathroom. "I don't care about Warren Scott or anyone in his family."

"You can't mean that, Marion, someone's gotta care. What about his kids?"

She stood in the doorway, belting her flannel robe. "Those kids are grown now, Ray, they've got all sorts of people to care about them. Warren Scott's boy is not your son." The floor creaked as she padded down the hall to the kitchen.

Ray switched off the light and pulled the comforter over his head. For such a sensible woman, sometimes Marion came out with the most ridiculous nonsense. It had nothing to do with Tim being his son. As he fell asleep, a black-and-white TV with a broken antenna flickered in his head and finally went blank.

Chapter Twenty-Five

For the first time in three years, Sari could wake up and follow the day wherever it led. Law school was over, bar review didn't start for another two weeks, and she was in their front yard feeding the roses in the late May sun. Tim was already out of bed when she awoke, and by the time she'd showered and changed into gardening shorts and a T-shirt he was out back. Perfect day to tune the Mustang, he called over his shoulder on his way to the garage.

As she slipped off her sandals and began scoring the earth at the base of the Harrison's yellow, Sari thought back over the past four weeks. Tim's birthday had marked a turning point. The following morning he'd said he wanted to quit his job, maybe apply to the Institute of Art. He'd been angry and frustrated because he lacked direction but was ready now to face the future head-on. *Thank God,* she'd thought, and when she found the easel and paint box neatly stowed behind the trash cans in their cul-de-sac she retrieved the paints and stored them in the garage. As the days passed, she focused on finals and stopped waiting for the sky to fall. Once the bar exam was behind her she could seriously think about what she wanted to do. There was an opening in the local D.A.'s office, and though there would be half a dozen applicants with grades as good as hers, she had a decent shot.

Now she measured the fertilizer in a cup and began applying it to the base of the shrub. The ground was already warm from the sun and a faintly bitter aroma rose from the soil as she sifted through the grainy clumps. Was it too old to use? She sprinkled it in anyway, then circled to the backyard for a hose to soak the roots. As she was uncoiling it, she saw the Mustang in the driveway with the trunk open but no sign of Tim. They could go to a greenhouse for more rose food once the car was tuned, pick up a flat of snapdragons… Hopping across the sizzling asphalt, Sari ducked under the half-open door to the garage. As the soles of her feet embraced the cool cement, she drank in the heady odor of motor oil.

"Tim?" she called softly. A couple of tomato plants would be nice too. Now that the danger of frost was past, they could plant them in the clay pots Warren had left them along with his father's tool chest when he moved to Seattle. "Honey, are you there?"

Catching a movement in the corner of her eye, she turned toward the back wall, where the tool cabinet stood. He must be looking for an instrument to tune the car.

"Tim?"

In the dimness she saw him rise. He was holding something large and heavy in both hands.

"I thought I threw this out," he said. Bronze clasps glinted dully as he lifted the object for her to see. Mindful of her bare feet, Sari took a careful step forward. "What's it doing here?"

It was the box of paints.

"I put it there." She tried to read his face, but the light from the half-open door did not reach it. "I thought you might—"

"I tried, Sari, I've really tried. But you just won't let it go."

His tone was mild, but as Tim set down the paints and wiped his hands on his khaki trousers, something stopped her from taking another step.

"What are you talking about?"

"Laura was right. Our marriage could never have worked."

"I don't know what—"

"—think I don't know what you're trying to do with these goddamn paints? That one minute hasn't passed in the last seven years—"

"Tim, I—"

"He didn't do it, Sari. Why can't you let me forget?"

"I never said—"

"Just living with you is accusation enough. You were supposed to be on my side, remember?" He took a step forward. His face was shadowed but his fists were clenched at his sides. "You never believed in me, did you?"

"Am *I* to blame for what happened? Tim, I love you…"

"If you really did, you wouldn't keep dredging up all this shit."

Sari wanted to turn and run toward the light, but her toes were rooted to the cement. His coldness paralyzed her.

"This craziness has gone on too long, Tim, it's time we got help."

"You're destroying me!"

He turned and reached for something behind him. As he straightened and came toward her, Sari threw up her hands to shield her face.

"*Don't!*" she cried.

Tim froze in shock and she fled the garage.

—

From the field behind their house Sari watched Tim drive off five minutes later. Ashamed of her panic, she brought Champ inside and spent the rest of the day cleaning the refrigerator and cupboards. When she'd thrown out almost everything there was to eat she tackled the floors. She thought about calling her mother, but Helen had been against the marriage from the beginning, and what could Sari say? *We were in the garage and all of a sudden I was Peggy?* If anything, Tim had been more frightened than she by his near loss of control. Each time she thought she heard a car she ran to the window but it was never him, and she spent the night on the living room couch with Champ at her side.

When Tim returned at seven the following morning, he calmly announced he'd contacted a lawyer about a divorce.

It wasn't until he began packing a suitcase that Sari realized he was serious.

"I know you didn't mean to hurt me, Tim. You don't have to leave because you're afraid—"

"All I want is the Mustang," he replied.

"After what we've been through, the only thing you care about is the car?"

He tossed an armload of shirts in his bag. "I'm leaving before it's too late."

"The past seven years mean nothing to you?"

"You can have the house, just give me the car."

Fury cleared her head. They'd saved for that Mustang and bought it together just before the earth opened under their feet. It was the last reminder of what they'd had, it stood for their commitment to each other in the face of all odds...

"No."

Champ at his heels, Tim followed her into the kitchen. "What?"

"You can have this house and every stick of furniture in it, but not the car."

"It's only worth three hundred bucks!"

"At least it's paid for." But their two mortgages were the last thing on her mind. "And it's in my name, remember?"

"You don't even know how to drive the damn thing. It's a stick shift, you've never even changed a tire—"

"Then it's time I learned."

"If this is some kind of game to keep me here, I'm not going to play." As angry as she, Tim reached for the keys on the hook by the refrigerator but she grabbed them first. "At least let me get my stuff out of the trunk."

"It looked empty yesterday."

"There's a jack—"

"What if I get a flat?"

"You won't have a flat because you're never going to drive it!"

Tim stormed off without the keys. As Sari fell asleep that night with one hand on Champ's coarse ruff, his words rang in her head. Had she really destroyed their marriage? She'd tried so hard to pretend his father was innocent for Tim's sake, and all along it made no difference. They would have been better off if she'd come forward with the little she knew. At least then Warren would have had to answer, and they could have known the truth. All of it.

Two days later she received a call from Tim's lawyer. All Tim wanted, "in full settlement of any property claims," was title to the Mustang. She told the lawyer Tim could have half the proceeds from the house when she put it on the market, but the car was already sold. That afternoon she stored the Mustang in a garage in Stanley and placed a classified ad for it in the local paper. She tore the Harrison's yellow rose out of the front bed and accepted a job clerking at the first law firm she contacted in Stanley.

Champ began growling and nipping at strangers. He smashed the glass top of the coffee table by jumping on it, defecated on the rug, urinated on her mattress. When Sari scrubbed away the stains, dragged the mattress to the backyard to air out, and returned it to the box spring with the clean side up, he peed on it again. Although she came home each day at noon to walk him and allowed him to sleep with her at night after bar review class, as soon as she left the next morning he howled for hours with the certainty that she would never return. She heard nothing from Tim.

Her mother wanted to visit, but Sari kept saying the time wasn't right. Champ's behavior was so erratic she was afraid he would attack Helen, but in those first months after Tim left, the dog was the only creature in whom she could confide. When anyone called about the Mustang she said it was already sold. After the bar exam, she collapsed in bed and didn't leave the house for three days.

—

With the bar exam behind her and mortgages to pay, Sari needed a permanent job. The D.A.'s office now had two openings, but criminal work was suddenly unpalatable. So she applied to law firms in Widmark and, on the strength of her résumé, was interviewed by the most prestigious. At Cooper Nash & Hall she was reduced to monosyllables by a hugely pregnant blond lawyer who glowed as if she'd swallowed the sun. By the time two other partners took her to lunch she was incapable of speech, and they ended up discussing pending cases with each other over a taco salad Sari only picked at. The firm's kindness in paying fora cab back to Stanley only heightened her sense of inadequacy. She was equally tongue-tied at Kenton & Bell.

Then Spenser & Trowbridge called. The largest and most exclusive firm on Montgomery Street, the place where the classmates she liked least had clerked. Steeling herself for another rejection, Sari rode the bus in from Stanley. If the other firms didn't want her there was no way she'd get an offer from S&T.

The hiring partner, Cameron Knight, was just what she expected. From an empty desk in a corner office uncluttered by the debris of a working attorney, he greeted her with all the animation of a glacier. The only jarring note was the life-sized wooden Indian in a grass skirt that stood directly behind his chair. As he began with an abridged version of the standard pleasantries, Sari reminded herself all she cared about was a paycheck large enough to cover her debts. But Knight wasted no time getting to the point.

"I notice you didn't clerk for our firm while you were in law school..."

"I had no interest in working here," she replied.

"I also see from your resume that you were Order of the Coif. What's the cutoff for that, top ten percent of the class?" Sari nodded, wondering how long it would take a quick study like him to realize she didn't belong at S&T regardless of scores. "What was your class rank when you graduated?"

"I never picked up my final grades."

"Do you think you were in the top three," he pressed. "Top five?"

"If I thought that, I would have looked at my grades." Knight peered at her in silence, and then his fleshless lips twitched. Five other S&T partners grilled her that day, nobody offered her cab fare to Stanley, and it was well after dark when she finally caught the bus home. At seven the next morning she received a call from the hiring assistant who said, "Mr.

Knight would like to know how soon you can start." Later, Sari wondered whether her screw-you attitude was just what they were looking for.

She gratefully slipped into a demanding routine that gave her little time to feel or think. She could have written it out on half a sheet of legal paper: Walk to bus stop at six each morning, arrive at S&T by seven, consume packets of miniature bread sticks at desk for lunch. Perform research, review contracts and draft memoranda on procedural issues, above all else plan her work to have a stack to bring home on the weekend. Leave office at six in evening, arrive in Stanley by seven, walk Champ, fall into bed. She tried not to dream.

At home she never answered the telephone, which rang less and less often, and opened her mailbox only when it was too full for the postman to cram anything more in. All the coleuses died. It was so simple to stop watering them, and when their gaudy leaves blackened and shriveled in the bay window Tim had built, she tossed them in the trash with a sigh of relief. She saw no friends. In fact, she had no friends.

The only time she allowed herself to feel was when she was with Champ. Isolated during the day and starved for attention, he lunged without provocation at dogs and pedestrians but was devoted to Sari, attuned to her every mood and affectionate beyond comprehension. She told herself he was too large for her to handle, but she knew the real reason she was unable to control him was that she empathized with him. Champ was so human, his misery so raw and unrelenting, he was a constant reminder of what they both had lost. When she finally decided to put the house on the market and move to an apartment in Widmark, she knew the real reason wasn't the hour-long commute. It was so there would be no room for another pair of eyes to ask, *Why have you driven him away?*

Instead of eating crackers at her desk, that fall Sari spent her lunch hours touring Widmark with a real estate agent. They went from high-rise condominiums with swimming pools and security doors to upscale singles roosts where residents paraded through the lobby in jogging bras and bicycle shorts. But nothing appealed to her. Returning to S&T at the end of another futile trip in November, a stone fortress facing Edwards

Park caught her eye.

"Let's stop."

"Why?" the Realtor asked.

"There's something about it I like."

"If I were your mother, I wouldn't want you living here." The Realtor slowed without stopping. "It's not safe." Sari gazed at the three-story building with red tile roof and wrought iron grilles on balconies that were more decorative than functional. "What's wrong with it?"

"It's too close to Randolph Avenue. There's a halfway house a block away and Edwards Park is dangerous." She hesitated. "It's not a place where you'll be able to make friends."

"Why not?"

"The neighborhood's filled with homosexuals. The only men your age aren't interested in girls."

Perfect.

"Let's see if anything's for rent."

The moment Sari entered the Belvedere, she was struck with nostalgia. Except for the roof and the forty-foot Douglas firs that surrounded the building like watchtowers, it bore a striking resemblance to the apartment building on Willow Street where she was raised. The shadowy front hall echoed and smelled of wax, and when she closed her eyes and inhaled its musty grandeur she knew she had come home. The air shafts, a standard feature in New York tenements since the turn of the century but virtually unknown out here, left no doubt. A second-floor unit was for sale and, ignoring her Realtor's disapproval, Sari arranged to see it the next day.

The apartment had oak floors, ten-foot ceilings, mosaic tile in the bathroom, and French doors overlooking a secluded courtyard at the side entrance on Bancroft. Safer than the first floor, mumbled the Realtor, resigned to what she was convinced would prove a dreadful mistake. But from Sari's perspective, the amenities only improved.

The warren of storage lockers in the basement surely must have originated in a nineteenth-century madhouse. Their varnished doors were marked by letters and secured with padlocks, ventilated by chicken wire at the top eight inches and lit from the winding corridor by a single forty-watt bulb. The laundry room was even stranger, a narrow sloping chamber on the north side of the basement lined by washers and dryers that were surprisingly modern. Its barred windows were set too high in the wall to see out of, and it was impossible to imagine hanging wash from the wire clotheslines strung six feet high the length of the room. An adjoining chamber featured iron sinks suitable for dissolving bones in lye, exposed pipes, and an inexplicable drain in the cement floor. But the real selling point was the boiler room.

"Why on earth do you want to see that?" the manager asked.

"Would you mind getting the key?"

It was just as Sari hoped. A flight of cement steps led to a subbasement that housed an enormous boiler. It chugged away, throwing off billows of steamy heat, fully capable of blasting the Belvedere into outer space. She made an offer on the second-floor unit the same day.

—

All that was left was Champ. Sari placed another round of ads in the paper, contacted law enforcement agencies, spoke to anyone who might be willing to take him. As a last resort she appealed, through his lawyer, to Tim, but he refused to help. He's your problem now, he told her, you're the one who wanted a dog in the first place.

The Stanley Humane Society promised to do everything they could to find Champ a home. "How does he get along with children?" they asked.

"He hasn't been around them much."

"How is he with other dogs?"

She hesitated. "He's afraid. But he's very affectionate, he's just had a rough time lately."

They promised to start Champ in his own cage and give him a chance to become accustomed to other dogs before trying to find him a home. "It's our policy not to let owners know what happens to their pets," they warned, "so don't expect to hear from us. But that won't mean we couldn't place him…" She gave them all the money she had, everything except what she had to pay the movers. Blood money.

The day before the van arrived, Sari retrieved the Mustang from the garage and took Champ for one last hike. She sat for hours talking and hugging him until the sky began to darken and it was time to start down the trail. Then they climbed into the Mustang and drove a few miles out of town to the Humane Society, a rambling structure that looked like a farm. When they parked and walked up the path to the woman waiting by the front door Champ was so eager, so happy to be on this adventure, Sari knew he thought she was taking him someplace special. She handed the woman the leash, knelt and hugged him one last time. Burying her face in the acrid fur of his throat, she whispered, *I love you,* then rose to leave.

Champ threw back his head and howled. It was a hideous sound, feral and human at the same time. He knew he was being betrayed. And Sari knew exactly how he felt, that his howling came from a place deep within his core, that it was the worst pain a living creature could endure. She stumbled to her car and drove two miles, then pulled to the side of the road and wept. She knew she would hear that howl forever.

Chapter Twenty-Six

For the first two years of his retirement, Ray tried to put Peggy Scott out of his mind. He and Marion were getting older, and some mornings it was harder to climb out of bed than others. They went to the cabin in Torrance for weekends when the weather was warm and talked about going to Lake Louise. Marion developed cataracts and a touch of arthritis and he had a mild coronary, but they settled into what should have been a comfortable routine.

During that time, Ray helped his wife dig a circle in the backyard for a peony bed, finished paneling the basement and cleaned out the garage. He sorted his tools for the first time ever and hung them on hooks attached to a wooden Peg-board, then oiled and sharpened the lawn mower. Having exhausted the domestic chores, he searched for a hobby. He bought a set of golf clubs and became pen pal to a thirteen-year-old Korean, and when the boy stopped writing back, he gave up golf and took a class in bonsai. He spent more and more time alone in his basement.

Alternating between short-lived enthusiasms for each new hobby and lows so fathomless even Marion couldn't plumb them, Ray dreamed over and over that he was lying in a field of glass, unidentified, until his bones bleached white. And for the first time in their marriage he expressed an interest in Marion's family. Awakening in the middle of the night, he asked, "Whatever happened to that cousin of yours?"

"Who?"

"You know, the one who had the little girl with braids?"

"I haven't heard from Joyce in twenty years. You never liked her anyway."

"Well, what was her daughter's name?"

Marion stared at the ceiling. "Her name was Alicia and she probably has children of her own by now."

"Where do they live?"

"I have no idea, Ray. We were never close, you know that."

"I just think it'd be nice to stay in touch."

It was on the tip of Marion's tongue to say, if you're so interested in family, why don't you get in touch with your own? For all she knew he could have relatives living in Gillman, not that he'd recognize them if he bumped into one in the street. And here he was with no one but her.

Because Marion was used to running the household her way, adjusting to Ray's retirement was twice as difficult for her as it was for him. She regarded the Scott case as his hobby and humored him with it the way another wife might have brought home a book about tying flies for an amateur fisherman. She put her foot down just once, the day after he retired from the Sheriff's Department.

She was at the sink, peeling carrots for the pot roast they were having for supper, when Ray set a carton on the kitchen table. With a backward glance, she resumed peeling. "What's all that junk?"

"Just stuff from my desk." He began unloading the box. First came a stack of manila folders and some loose papers, then a wooden plaque from the Police Athletic League. She looked over her shoulder again in time to see him unpack an enormous ceramic mug labeled *Old Fart*.

"I always wondered what happened to that. What've you been using it for, pencils?"

Ray nodded absently, then reached in the bottom of the carton and carefully withdrew its final contents. Swinging it in an arc from shoulder to knee, he crossed the floor to show his wife.

"Ain't she a beaut?"

As he raised it again, Marion turned. With the light flashing off its steel shaft, the milled head made a swift descent. Gasping, she raised her hands to her face.

"My God! What are you doing with that?"

Ray dropped the hammer to his side; it glanced harmlessly off his thigh. "Didn't mean to scare you. It's an Estwing, just like the one that killed Peggy Scott." As he turned it over in his hands, the metal gleamed and a wingshaped yellow logo contrasted jauntily with the blue of its molded vinyl grip. "Kind of pretty, isn't it?"

"Where on earth did you get that?"

"Ace Hardware years ago, after Kevin told me what the murder weapon was." He opened the drawer next to the silverware, where they stored screwdrivers and measuring tape. "Been keeping her in my desk ever since."

"It's morbid, Ray. I don't want that thing in my kitchen."

"It's not the real one, honey—"

"I know that. Just get it out of here." So he stored the hammer in the basement with the other mementos of the Scott investigation he'd squirreled away over the years.

One April morning in his second year at home, Ray watched his wife scour every knife and spoon in the house and then attack the china closet as if it were her worst enemy.

"You're gonna wear a hole in that thing if you don't stop."

She rubbed the back wall of the cabinet even harder with Murphy's Oil Soap. "What difference does it make?"

"Why don't we take that trip we always planned, to Lake Louise?"

She shot him a fierce look. "You never had any intention of taking me there."

"How 'bout a trip to the cabin? The fish should be jumping out of the water."

"You hate fishing, Ray." She sat at the dining room table, the fight suddenly drained out of her.

"Oh, yeah? How long you known that?"

"About as long as you've been obsessed with the Scott case." She reached for his hand. "So what's new with it? You haven't brought it up in a while."

He sat across the table from her. "You don't really want to hear…"

"Are you kidding?" Marion laughed. "If we charged the Scotts rent all the years they've lived with us, we'd be millionaires."

"Since you asked, I've been thinking motive. You gotta have some sense of what made him tick. Way I figure it, Warren was a time bomb."

"Then something must have set him off."

""She told me to clean the upstairs bathroom.'" Ray replied.

"Beg your pardon?"

"That's exactly what Warren said. Peggy had him home on a Saturday morning swabbing the john. That's when the nozzle on his Windex bottle broke. When he got back from the Safeway, he 'finished the job.' I keep wondering what job he meant."

"It wouldn't hurt you to scrub the shower once in a while either, Ray."

He winced. "An accountant ordered by his wife to clean the john on his day off? And Peggy's sister said he was planning to start a self-improvement course that morning." He shook his head in mock sympathy. "I guess his wife showed *him* who was boss."

"It had to be more than that." Hands bracing her knees, Marion slowly rose. "Cup of tea?"

"I can't say he seemed abnormal at the house that day," Ray continued as he followed her into the kitchen, "or at the interrogation. But there was something queer about him. One minute he's mean, like, "I can keep a grudge for a long time,' and the next it's like he's on some kind of a sedative. The guy showed no genuine emotion."

"Maybe he was medicated." Marion filled the kettle with cold water and put it on to boil. "Didn't he say he went to a doctor for stress, a nervous stomach?"

"I wanted to interview the doc, but Philips backed off when Evans spouted some mumbo-jumbo about privilege."

"You talked to people who worked with Warren at Reynolds, didn't you?" The kettle began to whistle and she went to the pantry for the Lipton's. "What did they say?"

"That Warren thought he was smarter than everyone else and couldn't make friends with a puppy. All in all a nonemotional, controlling type of individual with a temper that flares three minutes at a time and then everything's okay. In fact, he had a nasty bruise on his forehead that day."

"What about Peggy, what was she like?"

"Her sister hinted about family problems, and when I pressed for specifics, she dummied up. She hated Warren like poison, but I got the feeling there was more she couldn't bring herself to say."

"What did Warren tell you about his wife?"

"When we interrogated him his comment was 'I put up with it,' or something, 'for twenty years. I had no reason to kill her now.'"

Marion handed Ray his tea. "Well, there you have it."

"Have what?"

"If you want to know why Warren Scott murdered his wife in 1980, you need to know what he was living with since 1960."

"Well, I sure as hell won't find it in Gillman."

That night when Ray went to the basement he pulled out his Rand-McNally road atlas. Turning to the map of the neighboring state, he began studying the southwest corner.

—

The *News* carried it on the front page of the metro section in the spring of 1986. A bold headline: "Tough on Crime: Former Prosecutor Hitches Ride on Beltway." Ray read on. Taylor Philips had stayed at his father-in-law's firm just long enough to finance a run for Congress, a Republican in a district where a popular incumbent from the same party was retiring after thirty years for health reasons. Ray flung the paper to the floor. Probably befriended the old guy and sat back waiting for him to die…After a moment his curiosity got the better of him and he reluctantly retrieved the paper. Yep, there it was at the bottom of the page, a reference to Philips as the retiring politician's protégé. Starting from the beginning, he read the article through slowly.

At the press conference from his sanctuary in Ponderosa Hills, Philips pledged to fight crime. And not just street crime. "I'm committed to making this country a safer place for us all to live. The silent majority, the backbone of our nation, has been routinely ignored. When a housewife in Metcalf is afraid to get in her car and drive to the supermarket for a quart of milk after dark, it's time we sat up and took notice…"

A *quart of milk in Metcalf?*

How about feeling safe in your own garage in Gillman in broad daylight? Not that Philips's wife had to worry. She probably had a thousand-dollar alarm system and a pack of Dobermans. Not to mention a husband who could afford to hire someone to do a clean hit instead of resorting to an Estwing framing hammer. Stomping into the kitchen, Ray slapped his hip pocket for his wallet and grabbed the keys to the Chrysler.

"Gonna take the New Yorker for a spin," he told Marion.

"Want some company, dear?"

"Nah. Engine's a little rough." He crossed his fingers and begged his car's forgiveness. Eighteen years old and all she asked was oil, gas, and her five-thousand-mile tune-ups. "Thought I'd check her out on the highway."

"When will you be back?"

"Couple hours."

"Would you bring home a quart of milk?"

"Okay." What was it with housewives and milk?

Ray puttered past the Gillman Sinclair and drove north on Vermejo to the turnpike, then opened her up and allowed the purr of the V-8 to soothe him. He caressed the vinyl steering wheel and sank deeper into his seat. He was almost at the turnpike when he caught himself peering once more at his watch. *Turn back now,* he thought, *you don't have to do this…*

Six years had passed, but Warren's route that morning wouldn't have changed, though the traffic back then would have been lighter. As Ray turned onto the turnpike he sped along with his eyes straight ahead, intent on reaching his destination as fast as he could without breaking the speed limit. After all, he was creating an alibi. After the sharp descent into the valley, the storybook town took shape and he exited where tract housing yielded to the tiled roofs of the University campus. The New Yorker purred west to Broadway and turned halfway down the Hill at Locust. Forty minutes on the nose. Which meant that if Warren left the Gillman Sinclair when he said he did, he reached Stanley between 12:15 and 12:30. That jibed with his story about knocking on Tim's door but left damn little time to browse in a Walgreen's for a wedding card and a pair of sunglasses before he left. If he'd been at Tim's apartment at all.

The two-story brick next to the College Townhouses was still a Heinz-57 sort of place, with additions slapped on every which way. How did it ever pass muster under zoning laws? Circling to the Broadway side, Ray gazed at the enclosed porch jutting out from the second story. Cold as hell in winter…He cut around to the entrance near the Townhouses and rattled the knob, but the door was locked.

Closing his eyes, he remembered a single flight of wooden steps, the worn hall carpet relieved only by a bright woven mat at the threshold to 2A. "Welcome." He saw the little brunette as she opened the door, the look in her eyes as she stood there blocking his way. Was it hostility or dread? As the red-haired youth emerged from the back of the apartment, the girl stepped between him and Ray, determined to protect the boy. Protect him from what, and how could Ray not have realized they were living together? He'd felt some connection with her at the bail hearing; when he waylaid her on campus a week later he'd tried to plant a seed, hoped for that one little piece that would lead to Warren's downfall. But once again he'd underestimated her resistance… Suddenly he knew he hadn't even scratched the surface of that Saturday in May. Was it too late to finish the job he and Lew should have done?

As he started back to Gillman, he thought about calling Kevin Day. Unlike Devine, as Day rose through the SBI ranks he always found time for a friend. After their standing ovation at the Rotary Club the year he retired, Ray told Kevin he wished he'd given him Peggy's watch because his boys could have taken it apart and figured out whether it was running when her blood seeped in the mechanism. What was it Kevin had said?

"Don't beat yourself over the head with it, Ray, the important thing's the weapon. That and the motive. Sure would be nice to know what lit Scott's fuse...And when they went to lunch to celebrate his retirement, Kevin said he envied him. "You're a private citizen now, Ray, you can do whatever you want. You don't have to worry about blowing a case by going in without a warrant or forgetting to read some mutt his rights. If you ever find that Estwing, just give it to me and I'll make sure it gets in the right hands. No questions asked."

As Ray exited the highway, an image of Taylor Philips standing in front of the Rotary Club with his pants down flashed before his eyes. The image was instantly replaced by that of Tim's dark-haired fiancée, but now Ray recognized fear in her rigid stance. He pressed the gas pedal, suddenly in a hurry to be home.

Chapter Twenty-Seven

During her second month at S&T, Sari was sent to file papers at the County Courthouse. On her way out of the clerk's office she saw a knot of people huddled in front of a courtroom and poked her head in just as the recess ended. Trapped by the bailiff's pounding gavel, she settled in the back row as a cop about Tim's age took the stand.

As the defense attorney led him through his story, Sari learned the officer had shot an unarmed teenager during a traffic stop and the boy had bled to death on the sidewalk. Her gaze swiveled to the front row where a slump-shouldered clan observed the proceedings. As she watched, the man in the middle bowed his head, and his stoicism abruptly turned to grief. Wondering whether he was the victim's father or the cop's, Sari slipped away before the cross-examination began. But the next morning she returned.

This time she sat closer to the front, trying to locate the precise center of the pain that pulsed through the courtroom like an invisible tide. Today the testimony related to the officer's training and the bowed shapes in the front row remained as silent and vigilant as totem poles. The third day, when a woman two seats in from the aisle gave a great hiccuping gasp at a description of the rubberized pants the paramedics employed in an attempt to arrest the boy's shock, Sari looked over and imagined she was that woman. That night she was able to cry for the first time since Tim left, but her anguish seemed voyeuristic and shameful. She did not return.

The S&T partners respected Sari's capacity for legal analysis and were just as pleased that she demonstrated little inclination to be sociable. Her relationships with other associates were cordial but limited to work, and after polite but repeated rebuffs they stopped inviting her to events outside the office. As time passed she rose through the ranks of the corporate department, eventually specializing in banking law. *It's only money*, she told herself as she haunted the library at night researching lending limits. It wasn't as if lives hung in the balance How could she ever have imagined working for a D.A.?

The Belvedere was her refuge. She took the bus wherever she needed to go and paid a small fortune to keep the Mustang in a garage eight blocks away. She still couldn't bear to part with it; the Mustang represented the first step toward the dream, the last tangible reminder of her marriage. At home she kept her walls bare and her windows free of plants. When she returned from work, she locked the door and didn't go out until the following day. On the rare occasions when she saw neighbors in the hallways she waved, but when they knocked she didn't invite them in. The Belvedere was peculiar that way: a door was always whispering shut as if someone had come or left just moments before. When she rang for the elevator it hummed softly but invariably arrived empty.

Sari's goal each day was to be so tired at night that she could sleep without dreaming. If she didn't immediately succumb, a switch would be thrown and a reel would unwind, a home movie projected on the ceiling above her bed whether her eyes were open or closed. It always began with that Saturday in May. A blazing sun and turquoise pool. Warren peering at himself in the mirror, then slumped on their couch with his face in his hands. The funeral in Walker County, the dinner at the Caribou Inn... On and on, each frame more painful than the one before. The last time she'd seen Tim's face lit with joy, the last time he smiled as if he really meant it—that very Saturday at the hockey practice, when he came off the court after running the slalom with his ball and stick... She could stop the film in 1980 or let it roll to that terrible moment in their garage before he left. If it ran that far, there was no chance of sleep.

Occasionally, she would receive in the mail a crumpled clipping about an art show somewhere in the Southwest, in an envelope printed in Tim's hand with no return address. Wagon Mound, Bullhead City—the postmarks ranged as far west as Tonopah, Nevada. Each time she would run to her atlas and try to imagine where he was living. Then she would be gripped by shame, tear the clippings to bits and flush the envelopes down the toilet.

—

B lizzards were Sari's favorite time to jog because the frigid air slapped her awake and then anesthetized her, synchronizing body and spirit. She rarely allowed herself to feel cold or pain, and when she did it was comforting because those were sensations she could control. Each morning she jogged ten miles before dawn, regardless of the weather or how poorly she'd slept the night before, clad only in cotton sweatpants, a thin shirt and a down vest she'd worn in college.

Renouncing hat and mittens, she wore the same pair of sneakers long after her toes worked through the nylon and canvas. As she ran, she fantasized she was in a war zone picking her way through a mine field, on a solitary trek across the Sahara, or sailing the ice pack in Antarctica. Sometimes she was the only living creature on earth. She emerged from those runs stoked with a power that saw her through the rest of the day.

First her right knee plagued her, then her feet. She knew she walked with a limp because the chairman of the tax department, whose office was down the hall from her, kept asking what was wrong. She finally said she had a wooden leg because his refusal to accept that she was fine irritated her. As the years passed her feet tingled and became misshapen, with joints protruding in angry knobs. Instead of vacations she scheduled surgery, one foot at a time, and then a double-header on her knees. Bones were broken and reset with pins and screws and deadened nerves carved away. When it came time for more surgery on her right leg, it was the third Christmas in a row she lay on her couch watching the snow swirl in the little courtyard on Bancroft Street, downing saltines with painkillers until she could hobble and finally run again.

—

One frosty November morning in her fourth year at the Belvedere, Sari bumped into a roly-poly man sporting a shaggy dog with clipped ears and docked tail. She'd seen him once or twice while picking up her mail, and though they'd nodded she knew nothing more than that he lived on the third floor with a spare, keen-eyed fellow who left for work the same time she did in a vintage Mercedes with California plates.

"You won't tell on us, will you?" the man drawled.

"I beg your pardon?"

"The dog." He gestured at the brindle-coated beast. "He's not as fierce as he looks, but taking him out the front's a definite no-no under the condo rules. But drifts are piled at the side entrance and the ramp's so icy…"

Flustered by his friendliness, Sari bent to fasten a shoelace that didn't need to be tied. "I wouldn't think of telling," she replied.

"Where on earth are you going at this hour?" His voice was as soft as his eyes, and she guessed he was from somewhere down south.

"For a jog."

"But it's freezing."

"That's why I like it."

"Are you dressed warmly enough?"

"I go out like this all the time."

"Well, be careful. It's awfully dark."

"I'll be fine." She stroked the shaggy beast's belly and was surprised at how soft it was. Not coarse, like Champ's. "What's his name?"

"Jacques. After all, he's a Bouvier de Flandres." He wrinkled his nose and they both laughed. "And he's been so obnoxious lately we wouldn't even be on speaking terms this morning if it weren't for John. I'm Dan, by the way."

"Sari."

"Come up for a drink sometime. We've been taking bets on what you do for a living. John thinks you're a shrink-in-training, but I say you're a lawyer."

"You've been reading my mail!"

"Just what doesn't fit in the box." He gave a lazy wink. "You wouldn't believe what the biddies in 1C read, not to mention the rummy down the hall from you. Brown paper wrapping used to be so *affordable...*"

An artist with a studio on Carey Street, Dan had moved to Widmark from San Francisco where John had made a fortune as a stockbroker. He began timing his walks to coincide with Sari's runs and she came to look forward to seeing him on her way out in the morning. When the two men invited her over for Thanksgiving dinner, she baked a pecan pie from a recipe in a magazine and John, who Dan claimed detested sweets, insisted on keeping the leftovers. The pair knew all there was to know about everyone in the building, even the elderly managers, Minnie and Les, who holed up in their basement apartment with vodka from dawn to dusk, and Sari sat on their couch for hours at a time just listening. Because attachments only interfered with the numbness she craved, she told them nothing about Tim. She didn't realize the narcotics of isolation and exhaustion deadened indiscriminately, killing her capacity for pleasure along with pain.

—

Only once did Sari miscalculate her endurance. On a bitter morning a month after she met Dan, she set off on her run long before the sky blanched from black to gray. It had snowed heavily the night before and the air crackled with cold. Ice imprisoned bushes and trees and the wind swept the shimmering dust into knee-deep drifts on the path through the park, but she warmed up quickly as she ran and felt a surge of exhilaration when she realized the cold had kept everyone else inside. Having completed her normal circuit, she decided to take an extra turn around Edwards Park to celebrate the solitude.

A mile from the Belvedere, Sari was seized with a fatigue so sudden and complete it was as if she'd been tripped by a wire. The moment she slowed she was overwhelmed with cold. The sky was still dark, the branches along the path so thick she could barely see the moon. Her thin socks and torn sneakers froze to her feet. Closing her eyes, she sank to her knees in the soft snow.

And then she thought she saw Tim.

The man stood to the left of the path at its darkest point, where it curved past the deserted maintenance shed in front of the fence enclosing the Botanic Garden. He wore a bulky jacket, and the wool scarf wrapped around his ears and throat obscured all but his eyes and mouth. As she watched, he took a half-step forward and smiled. That taut, graceful motion could have been only Tim's... Rising on one leg, Sari held out her arms to him. But now the muffled figure seemed taller and she couldn't be sure. As she drew back, his features seemed to coarsen, and suddenly she thought he was Warren. She stumbled to her feet and fled across the park, abandoning the icy path for the knee-deep powder of the central basin. When she reached the Belvedere, she took a scalding shower before catching the bus to work. It had to have been her imagination, she kept telling herself; who would be lingering in the park before dawn in weather like this?

The next morning was no colder than the day before, but now the winter pierced Sari's vest and every shadow held menace, every Dumpster seemed to conceal a crouching man. She forced herself onward, but by the time she should have begun her final lap through the park she was shivering so violently she let herself return home. The morning after, she thrust her feet into her sneakers and out the door, but she didn't feel warm again until the crocuses poked through the earth in March. Now she knew the backlash of exhaustion, that the pendulum could swing without warning from omnipotence to defenselessness, shattering her illusions.

Chapter Twenty-Eight

B ecause Ray normally skipped the society columns, it was Marion who called the item in the *Gillman Camera* to his attention. The weekly rag was good for little more than garage sales and lining a cat box but big on public works announcements.

"Isn't that where the Scotts lived?" she asked.

Pointing to a story accompanied by a photo of a bulldozer tearing up a suburban intersection, she passed Ray the paper. *Grand Avenue Getting Grander—Improvements at South Cleveland,* the headline read. He reached for his glasses.

A shopping center was going up directly across from the Scotts' house, and the county commissioners had condemned the corner lots on both sides of Grand Avenue to widen the road: 4990 South Cleveland and several of its neighbors were slated for the wrecking ball to accommodate the anticipated increase in traffic.

So it had come to that.

"Progress," he snorted, and passed the paper back without looking at the photograph. "Since when is demolishing a bunch of homes an *improvement?*"

"What'd I tell you, Ray?" Marion replied. "Life goes on."

That afternoon he drove his wife to a garden supply shop and watched her fuss over the selection of a new rake.

So protective of tender growth was she that she always waited until the bulbs were completely up before clearing away the winter's debris. I should've given her kids, he thought, she would have been a good enough parent for both of us... Back home, he waited until he heard the screen door slam and Marion's good-natured ranting at the weeds in the backyard before he carried the half-empty kitchen basket to the trash by the carport. Carefully retrieving the *Camera*, he brushed away coffee grounds and smoothed its wrinkled pages before stowing it under the sink.

When the lady down the street picked Marion up an hour later for their weekly stint on Gillman General's volunteer brigade, Ray spread the paper across the kitchen table. In the lower left corner of the photograph he could just make out the grape-stake fence surrounding the Scotts' backyard. Nine years and it was still there.

On the seventeenth day of every May since Peggy Scott died, Ray had made a special point of driving past 4990 South Cleveland. For the first six years, that is. Warren had put the house on the market the week after the charges against him had been dropped and hightailed it to Seattle as soon as it was sold. August was a tough time to move real estate; the for sale sign had been up for quite a while. Was that when Ray had begun taking a detour on his way home from work? Just keeping tabs, he'd told himself, though for what reason he could not explain.

When he finally spotted the Mayflower van, a Toyota at the curb, and a young matron with curly blond hair tied up in a kerchief in the front yard, Ray heaved a sigh of relief. That's what the place needed, a new family with frisky kids to fill the rooms with joy and sorrows of their own. Four walls, some windows, brick and trim—sentimentality was Marion's department. When the woman planted flowering quinces on either side of the stoop and her husband climbed a ladder to touch up the fading butternut trim, Ray silently approved. They installed a lock on the gate leading to the backyard and kept the garage door all the way closed. He told himself Peggy's house was in good hands.

But something happened, and less than a year later that family moved out. This time Peggy's house stayed on the market so long, Ray wondered if there'd been talk. Sometimes that happened; a place where a tragedy occurred could take on the reputation of being jinxed. After six months the Realtor sent out a landscaper, who planted a hedge between the front door and the garage, and a painter, who transformed the trim from butternut to a trendier avocado. What would Peggy have made of that? An older couple with no children moved in and stayed for two years before they, too, departed. After them came a series of renters, and the avocado faded to olive gray. That was when Ray stopped driving by.

Now he padded upstairs to reread the sports section of the *News,* but it didn't hold his interest. He pulled out the mower, but he'd fertilized the lawn two days earlier and Marion would wonder. Finally he reached for his car keys. A few weeks short of the ninth anniversary, but he owed Peggy that much. His last respects.

Grand Avenue was choked with traffic. In the past five years strip malls had sprung up, giving the once-residential area a decidedly commercial character. What had he expected, the world to stop while he took his own sweet time trying to nail Peggy Scott's killer? And a lousy job he'd done of it too. He should have pushed harder. Someone must have known *something...* As he reached the dusty intersection where the workers had parked their bulldozers before knocking off for the day, Ray suddenly wished he hadn't come.

Who was he trying to kid?

It was over. Peggy's murderer had walked.

And he'd walked because *Ray* had blown it. Instead of pissing and moaning about Taylor Philips and Lew Devine, he should have kept his focus closer to home. *This* home.

He pulled to the curb and climbed out of his car. Despite the quinces and hedge, 4990 South Cleveland had never lost that naked look. Why *this* house? he'd wondered the first time he saw it. It seemed so obvious now; whatever lit Warren's fuse had originated right here. He gazed up at Peggy's bedroom window, picturing the gathered curtains of eyelet lace. The vanity with the flounce, the crystal perfume bottles... a world a fairy-tale princess might inhabit. Not exactly the room of a forty-three-year-old housewife with a daughter she couldn't control, and who took prescription pills but claimed she'd never been sick a day in her life—

What in God's name did that family have to hide?

Furious at himself, Ray jerked his car door open, jammed the key into the ignition, and stomped on the accelerator. No witnesses except the killer and his victim? Bullshit. There had to have been a houseful. And somewhere out there was the weapon...

If he was going to find that hammer and what lit Warren Scott's fuse, he needed help.

Chapter Twenty-Nine

It was in the produce section of a supermarket, the Saturday before her twenty-ninth birthday, that Sari's cocoon began to unravel. She was reaching for a plastic bag for lettuce when she caught sight of a tall woman in a green linen jacket, stooped over the zucchini six bins away. Something in the jut of her chin was familiar, and Sari peered at her reflection in the aluminum splash panel behind the glistening vegetables in an effort to place her. Just then the woman looked up and, eyes widening as they met Sari's, dropped her squash and wheeled off. Without thinking, Sari pushed her aluminum cart in pursuit. It was Kay Butler.

Tim's aunt was leaner than she remembered; her flesh had been pared back to reveal the planes of a face that was pure Dannhauer. But the years had stolen more than pounds. With Kay's broad shoulders bowed and her hair faded a mousy gray, the vitality that had once been so striking now seemed a casualty of bitterness and grief. But as she strode past the dairy case and headed for the canned goods her gait was as brisk and purposeful as ever, and Sari struggled to keep her green jacket in sight. Kay glanced over her shoulder once and Sari reached blindly for a can of soup. What would she say if Tim's aunt confronted her?

I didn't come forward because I had no choice.

Tim couldn't afford to lose his father too, couldn't Kay see that? If Sari's doubts had indeed destroyed her marriage, what would it have done to Tim if Warren had been tried and convicted? When Kay turned left at the end of the aisle, she hurried after her. It was so unfair of Kay to blame them for the D.A. dropping the case, when all she could have said was she would have heard if Warren knocked and the business about the seminar being postponed. Neither of which was *proof.*

Kay was canvassing the shelves too quickly, as if she sensed she was being followed. Near a midsummer display of back-to-school supplies, Sari saw her chin thrust forward once again with the fierceness of the woman in the hallway outside the courtroom of the Gillman Justice Center. She must recognize me, Sari thought. Why else would she look so agitated? *Where's your loyalty,* Kay had asked Tim, *didn't your mother mean anything to you?* Anger rising in her throat, Sari swerved to the center of the aisle, but Kay was gone.

In the section fronting the meat department she searched for a jacket the color of grass. Leave it alone. … . Suddenly they were two cart-lengths apart, and Sari drew to a stop. The woman turned from the shelf of laundry detergent and faced her.

"Do I know you?" she demanded. The freckles were now the mottling of age, but her eyes were still piercing.

"I'm Sari. Tim's wife." The set of Kay's lips confirmed the introduction was unnecessary, and Sari's cheeks burned as her quarry set a quart of bleach in her empty cart.

"How is Tim?" Kay asked.

"We divorced years ago." Kay's eyes held pity and regret, but not surprise. "How are your kids? Todd must be finishing college—"

"You should have taken my advice."

And denounce Warren? She couldn't mean getting Tim to paint again, what a disaster that had been… Suddenly Sari wondered whether Kay had known how Tim would react. Did she want him to go over the edge?

"Actually, I—"

"Peggy may have had her doubts," Kay continued, "but I always liked you. I thought you were good for Tim." Her voice rose and a woman comparing fabric softeners glanced in their direction. "Did your lies help him?"

"I never lied to the police." But the words rang hollow in Sari's ears and Tim's aunt was staring at her with contempt. Was there really a difference between lying and not telling what you knew? Kay's wheels squeaked on the linoleum as she prepared to turn. But, abruptly, she stopped.

"How do you sleep at night?" she hissed.

That was enough.

"Do you remember that day at the courthouse," Sari asked, "when the judge granted Warren bail?" Kay remained silent, but she gripped the handle of her shopping cart so hard her knuckles turned white. "You asked if I knew what it was like not to be there for someone when they needed you most. Remember?"

Kay's chin began to tremble, but still she said nothing. "Well, I was there for Tim. Where were *you*?"

Kay's hands flew from the bar and she fled down the aisle, abandoning the solitary bottle of bleach and her cart.

Two days later Sari was at her desk reviewing loan documents, when the phone rang.

"Happy birthday!"

She sucked in her breath. The voice was strangled and tinny, straining to be heard above a familiar roar.

"—always think of you today. Can you believe either of us made it this far?"

"Tim, where are you?"

"New York. Times Square."

"Are you okay?"

His laugh was cut short by a metallic screech. Sari closed her eyes and tried to picture him at a pay phone in a sooty station below Forty-second Street. Was his hair still fire, or had it faded like Kay's?

"—knew you'd end up at a fancy firm," he was saying. Just hearing his voice was enough, it didn't matter what he said, and she immersed herself in its comforting cadence. "You were hard to find. Why'd you leave Stanley?"

"I sold the house. I sent you half the money, remember?"

"Whatever happened to the Mustang?"

"Long gone..." Could that car possibly mean to him what it did to her? "I got nothing for it, if that's any consolation."

"—get my letters?"

"No." Didn't he care what happened to Champ, how he'd been living? "Oh, you mean the clippings. I'm glad you're painting again."

"—where you live. The Belvedere, right?"

Sari felt a twinge of apprehension. It couldn't have been Tim in the park that day, she was sure it was her imagination... Of course he knew where she lived. He'd been sending her clippings, right?

"How's your sister?" she asked.

"Laura's here in the City, but I guess you already know that. Haven't you talked to Dad?"

"Your father?"

"He's operating his consulting business out of Arizona, but he's in Widmark all the time. I spoke to him just last week and he asked about you. I'm surprised you haven't run into him."

Could that have been Warren in the park?

"What are you doing in New York?" she replied, trying to regain her balance.

"Talking to galleries about showing my paintings."

Was there a hint of accusation in his tone? Was he saying she'd held him back, that their marriage had stifled his art?

And just like that, Sari was back at the Caribou Inn. What was it Warren said? Do *you have any idea how much I could have made if...*

"For the first time, I have a chance," Tim continued, "a real chance to make people see what I can do..."

I intend to make up for lost time. But this was Tim talking, not Warren. What he'd said about his father being in town had thrown her for a loop.

"—twenty thousand bucks," he was saying. His voice was rising and

Sari heard a metallic clink. Coins dropping down a chute. "Galleries won't take me seriously without it."

"I don't have that kind of money, Tim."

"You can get it if you want to. All you have to do is pick up the phone."

"I never ask my parents for help, and you—"

"—already have. Your dad threw me out on my ass. Yesterday, as a matter of fact." He waited for that to sink in. "So I'm coming home. Maybe I'll stay with you a few days, we've got lots of catching up to do."

Sari swallowed her queasiness. If Tim knew where she lived, Warren must too. And where she worked.

"Tim, I—"

"Don't tell me you don't have room. I know your building."

Buy time, he'll run out of quarters any moment... "I'm buried with work. My firm's a real sweat—"

"With your brains, you never needed me. It was just a matter of time before you found that out yourself." Could he really believe she was better off without him, or was that just what he told himself? "Maybe I did you a favor—"

"Well, I'm glad things are okay. It's really nice of you to—"

"You know, Sari, I never wanted to have children."

I want to tell you things you may not remember, or maybe never knew...

"Tim—"

"I never even wanted that dog. Champ. It was all your idea."

"Please—"

"There are things I haven't said, not to anyone. I'm coming to Widmark."

—

Trembling, Sari hung up and immediately dialed another number.

"Mom? What the hell is going on?"

"Happy birthday, darling. Your father and I were planning to call tonight."

"I just heard from Tim, he said he saw you yesterday. Why didn't you tell me he was in New York?"

"You know how I hate to bother you at work." What did it matter that yesterday was a Sunday? "—came for a little visit," Helen was saying, "we had a friendly talk, he left. Nothing to be concerned about." She paused to mark the end of her comments on that subject. "I was just talking to your brother. He's still working on his master's. That will be his ticket to a *real* teaching—"

"How did Tim look?"

"Tired, older. Under a certain amount of strain." Sari heard her mother cast about for a cigarette in the credenza beneath the phone. "He brought us a very nice box of pastries. Italian, from the Village. Did I tell you Andy Cohen's wife is pregnant?"

"I don't give a damn about Andy Cohen! Now, will you tell me what happened?"

A drawer slammed shut, and when the inevitable match was struck, Sari knew she would finally get the real story.

"Tim wanted your father to lend him money, and he offered his portfolio as collateral."

"What did the stuff look like?"

"Illustrations like you find in textbooks. He had some of them printed on cards, a promotional sort of thing. He's quite talented, you know."

"Was that all?"

"No, there were a few others. Portraits." Her mother paused again, caught between her desire to have everyone around her believe they were liked and the brutal frankness that was her true nature. "The people looked like they just got out of Auschwitz." Sari heard her grind out the Kent. "What are you doing for your birthday, darling, going to dinner with friends?"

—

When her secretary came to the door with a stack of loan documents half an hour later, Sari was still at her desk, staring at a blank legal pad. She stuffed the papers in her briefcase, said she had an appointment, and went straight home, where she sat on her couch waiting for the room to darken. How could she have been so naive as to think the past was behind her?

As the light through the French doors faded to nothing, the phone rang. Why hadn't she changed her name while she still had the chance? But if Warren knew where she lived and worked, he could find her no matter what she called herself. The phone rang again, and when there was a knock at her door she wondered if it was Dan. She was supposed to go to their place tonight; she hadn't told anyone it was her birthday, but somehow they knew and were going to surprise her... When it was pitch dark she went to her bedroom and lay down fully clothed on top of the quilt, waiting for the reel to play. But the ceiling remained blank and her eyes finally closed.

When the alarm went off at a quarter to five the next morning, Sari awakened to the vision of Warren Scott's face. In sneakers and sweatpants she detoured around Edwards Park in the mist, choosing dark streets over the tree-lined path to Seventh Avenue. In the light of day it seemed foolish to worry about Warren tracking her down after all these years. What threat could she possibly pose? But the notion that he knew where she lived, could pick up the phone and call or show up at her door, haunted her. Her lock could be opened with a piece of plastic, she'd used her credit card to get in more than once when she misplaced her key... By the end of her run she'd decided that regardless of whether her fears had any basis in fact, she would not make it quite so easy.

When she reached her office she called the phone company.

"I'd like to change my number and have it unlisted."

"There will be an extra monthly charge for that service..."

Her next calls were to a locksmith and to a partner in the tax department.

"I need a will, Nick." What was sillier, a grown woman with a last testament, or one without one? And she was a lawyer; it made absolutely no sense not to take advantage—"For whom?"

"My birthday was yesterday and I realized I'm not a kid anymore."

"I hear you."

"Something simple, as plain vanilla as they come." "Any rush?"

Noon would be fine.

"If you point me to a form, I'll—"

"No, I'm glad to do it," he insisted, "just give me the name of your executor."

When she spoke to the partner with whom she did most of her bank work, she tried to make her request sound jaunty. "How'd you like to be executor of the smallest estate the firm's ever handled?"

"So long as I don't have to give money to any of your crazy left-wing causes."

"No offense, but I only need to plug in your name."

"Nothing wrong, is there?"

"Of course not. Just thought it was time I grew up." For three hours Sari sat at her desk, drawing up status reports on every client for which she had responsibility. Then she threw herself into her work, trying to accomplish as much as she could in what remained of the day.

The next morning Ray Burt showed up at her door.

Chapter Thirty

As he stepped off the elevator at the forty-fifth floor of the second-tallest building in Widmark, the one shaped like a giant mailbox, Ray was determined not to be impressed. In the lobby the first thing he saw was an enormous bouquet of salmon and bloodred roses, three times the size of anything he'd ever bought Marion. His gaze swept from the crystal vase at the receptionist's desk to a trio in Italian suits and silk ties chatting discreetly before a wall of glass overlooking the foothills. On a smog-free day you could see seventy-five miles south to Curtis Peak, but Ray's enjoyment of the view was marred by the thought that Taylor Philips had thrown the Scott case to preserve his no-loss record so the D.A. could join a firm like this.

"May I help you, sir?" The girl at the desk was young but polished, with perfect teeth and diction to match. Her taffy-colored hair was pulled back from her face with enamel barrettes shaped like butterflies, and her crimson nails hovered near the most complicated telephone Ray had ever seen.

"Does Sari Scott work here?" As he leaned forward, he sniffed the roses. They had absolutely no scent.

"May I have your name, please?"

"Ray Burt."

"Does Ms. Scott know what this is regarding?"

"I'm an old friend."

The receptionist spoke softly into the receiver, and then fixed him with a dazzling smile. "Miss Scott will be right out."

He'd forgotten how small she was. But he recognized her stance as she strode across the lobby to greet him, her slender shoulders drawn back with the same defiance she'd displayed the day she stood between Ray and her fiancé when he'd served that grand jury subpoena. As she extended a delicate hand, he saw her nails were bitten to the quick.

"Mr. Burt?" Her voice was soft and clear and she looked him straight in the eye. Nothing to hide, that gaze said. "I'm Sari Scott."

"Is there a place we could talk?"

Her fingers went limp, but perhaps that was his imagination. "Let's go to my office," was what she said.

Following her through the labyrinth of Spenser & Trowbridge, Ray was struck by how trim she was; two of her could have fit in that high-necked blouse and navy skirt that grazed the tops of her knees. This was a girl who kept in shape. Good-looking and proud, nothing cheap about her…She walked quickly, maybe to hide a slight limp. Sports injury?

The oak desk that dominated Sari's office was awash in paper; drifts of it covered the carpet like late-melting snow. Though her floor-to-ceiling bookcases were crammed with black binders, there were no photos on her desk or plants basking in the light from the tall windows. But the room felt more lived in than disorderly, and Ray was willing to bet it would take her less than ten seconds to lay her hands on anything she was looking for. Clearing a seat across from her desk, she gestured for him to sit before sinking into a leather chair that dwarfed her.

"Would you like a cup of coffee?" she asked.

"No, thanks." Ray studied her face. Despite her efforts to downplay her femininity, Sari Scott was a beauty. Unspoiled by makeup, her features had an exotic look and her lustrous hair was chin length, thick and shiny as a boy's. But there was an arrested quality to her, and the fine lines around her mouth and smudges under the eyes spoke of pain at odds with her polite smile as she waited for him to say why he came.

"You probably don't remember me, Miss Scott."

"I'm sorry to say I don't." But apprehension flickered in those dark eyes, and he knew she wasn't being truthful.

"There's no reason for you to, it's been ten years. I investigated your mother-in-law's death."

She didn't seem surprised. But how could she possibly have known he would come?

"As you know," he continued, "Peggy Scott's murder has never been solved. I thought maybe you could help." The girl's lips twitched as if she were suppressing a laugh, but her eyes remained wary and Ray told himself he must be imagining it. This wasn't at all what he'd expected. "It's been a long time and memories fade, but do you think you could answer a couple of questions about that day?"

Her silence began to irritate him. If she thought she could outwait him, two could play that game.

Finally she replied, "It was so long ago."

As she blinked, her features contorted. Pain, or something else? Leaning forward, Ray continued in a softer tone. "But you remember, don't you?"

She nodded, slowly.

"You and Tim were getting married the following week, right?"

No response. Was it fear?

"And your father-in-law showed up at your apartment that morning while you were in the shower. Later he said he was in town looking for a place for the rehearsal dinner… Stop me if I'm wrong."

Still nothing. Was it Warren she was trying to protect? Or his son?

"But he wasn't supposed to be there, and when he showed up you knew that wasn't why he came. He was supposed to be attending a seminar, one of those self-improvement things. Right?" Her silence was unnerving but he had to find a crack. He sensed a basic honesty in her, an unwillingness to lie. Ten years ago she must have been a scared kid who would've done the right thing if given half the chance… And Warren's alibi had been so crucial to his defense. "You knew he couldn't have stopped by your apartment, didn't you? Because you would have heard him knock."

Her chin jerked, and Ray cursed himself for not having taken more time when she was eighteen. Sari Scott couldn't tell a lie if her life depended on it. But suddenly she drew herself up.

"I showered before I went to the rec center. That must have been when Warren came. I don't know when Peggy was killed, but—"

"So why didn't you believe him?"

Her eyes narrowed and Ray flogged himself. Great move, putting her on the defensive just when she was about to open up. But maybe what she didn't know was more important than what she did. He rolled the dice again.

"You probably never heard about the lady who knocked on the Scotts' door right in the middle of the murder, according to Peggy's watch."

"Her watch?"

He'd found his opening.

"They never even told you what the weapon was, did they?" Now that his foot was in the door, he pushed harder. "Or about the clocks pulled from the wall. Warren had plenty of time to get to Stanley, but it was too late for Dale Carnegie so he used his son instead."

A direct hit.

"You asked about that seminar, didn't you?" he said. She was very still. "What'd he tell you, that it was postponed?" He took his third gamble. "Want to know the rest?"

He almost had her; if there was one thing Sari Scott yearned for, it was to break free of the past. But something was holding her back.

"Tim had nothing to do with it," she said softly.

Ray slowly let out his breath. Tim he could deal with. "He's not the one I'm after. I think you know that."

"What do you want from me?" The words were defiant, but beneath the pose was a woman with nothing more to lose.

"You're my ticket to the Scotts."

"Tim left me four years ago."

"Maybe the truth would have saved your marriage."

"Do you think I haven't thought about that every day since she died? What makes you think any of them will talk to me now?"

But he had her, and they both knew it. Sari Scott was remorseful over Peggy's death. Was that why she was hiding in this mausoleum with flowers that had no smell? No matter what led her to punish herself, if she didn't help him the weight of that day would drive her straight into the ground.

"We'll come up with a plan," he promised.

"You never found the owner of that pickup truck, did you?"

Ray winced, then smiled to cover it. How Warren must have gloated after the charges were dropped! Was that truck going to haunt him to the end of his days?

"—help you, I'll want something in return," she was saying.

"What's that?"

"An open mind. Whatever we find, we share. And that truck moves to the top of the list."

Thank God she hadn't asked whether he was acting in an official capacity after all this time. "Fair enough. But if we discover it was Warren, I want you to promise to do everything in your power to help me convict him."

"I'll think about it."

Ray rose. Slipping his card out of his billfold, he set it on the corner of her desk.

"You should be glad you got away from that family, Ms. Scott. That could have been you one day, on a cement floor."

When Sari returned to the Belvedere that evening the locksmith was waiting to install a dead bolt. As his drill bit a hole in her door frame, her mind raced. Two minutes after he arrived she'd recognized Burt. Even without his Stetson and bolo tie, the flat face and knowing eyes brought her right back to the house in Gillman. *Not so fast, miss, I need a word with you...* When he served the subpoena on Tim, he'd asked whether she wanted whoever killed Peggy to be caught. And at the fountain when she played dumb about the seminar. *Life tends to be simple when you don't question what you hear...* Had anything ever been simple again?

Throughout Burt's visit Sari had been inundated with voices from the past.

Don't do anything, her mother said, *someone else will handle it.* Would she be barricading herself in an apartment now if she hadn't denied her own perceptions? Then Laura, locked with her in the mirror the night before Peggy's funeral. *You don't know anything.* But if that was true, why were they so afraid? Finally Tim, and his plea was not so easily silenced.

If you care about me, leave it alone.

Although Sari had no illusions that Burt's investigation was still active, she realized the full extent of his bluff only when she picked up the card he'd left on her desk. The yellowing pasteboard bore the official seal of the Gillman Sheriff's Department, but the office number ending in "00" was crossed out and what could only be a home exchange neatly penciled in. If that tenacious flatfoot was offering her an opportunity to learn who killed Peggy and why, what difference did it make in what capacity he acted?

When Sari was small her family had taken trips to New England on the New York, New Haven & Hartford Railroad. As they boarded the train at Grand Central the passenger cars were always waiting, a long cylinder of silver chambers lodged benignly in their underground berth. But for the return trip they would stand on an elevated platform and watch as the locomotive came barreling down the tracks. She loved the oily smell of the rails and the sting of gravel kicked up by the furnace-like wind. *Don't get too close,* her mother warned, *you don't want to fall...*

Once again, Sari was leaning over that platform. But this was no longer a game: she could allow the monsters of her past to crush her or put them behind her once and for all. Tim or no Tim, she could finally know the truth. Call him, she told herself, *call.*

When she dialed the number, she asked for Lieutenant Burt. The motherly voice that answered held a hint of curiosity but didn't ask Sari's name. Did Burt's wife abet him in that small deception, the belief he was still a genuine detective?

"I lied about that seminar," she began.

"What?"

"When you questioned me on campus after the bail hearing. You asked whether I knew anything about the seminar, and I said I didn't know what you meant." She twisted the telephone cord. "You were right. Warren told me it was postponed. I checked later and found that was a lie. That's when I should have—"

"It wouldn't have made any difference, Sari." Was he trying to make her feel better? A solid discrepancy would have strengthened the D.A.'s hand, they could have used it as a wedge. "Warren knew if you told us he said that, he could always say you were mistaken. An accountant with a slick lawyer and reasonable doubt versus an eighteen-year-old kid. You tell me who a jury's gonna believe?"

All these years, the damage to her relationship with Tim …For nothing.

"Maybe we can do together what neither of us could do alone. Are you with me, Sari?"

"Name your time and place, Lieutenant. I'll be there." Sari hung up the phone and closed her eyes. If Warren lied, how much did Tim know?

Chapter Thirty-One

"Meat loaf?" Marion Burt set another ten-ounce slab of ground beef on Sari's plate without waiting for a reply. "Ray said to fatten you up." As her husband rolled his eyes at their other guest, she whispered in Sari's ear, "Ninety-eight percent lean. He's had a *coronary.*"

"It's delicious...."

"Quit hogging the potatoes," Marion admonished Ray. "Kevin looks like he could use another helping." As their host obediently passed the oven-browns, Sari sneaked a look at the man seated directly across the Burts' dining room table.

There was nothing remarkable about Kevin Day except for his size. Well over six feet tall and with a chest as broad as the trunk of an oak, he had arms long enough to reach across the table with the bearlike grace that accompanied all his movements. His blue-black hair, parted and neatly combed to one side, was graying at the sideburns, and the five o'clock shadow obviously began before dawn on his broad face.

"You're a lucky man, Ray," he was saying, and Sari found herself staring at his hands to avoid his gaze. His hands were pale and square, the fingers well formed and blunt. He cut his meat into precise rectangles with his knife and fork, which he set on the edge of his plate between bites, and he chewed slowly with mouth closed. As her eyes traveled to his lips, he winked; she turned away.

"Just stack them on the counter," Marion said as Sari helped her carry dishes to the kitchen. "I'll run them later."

"You're awfully sweet to invite me to dinner." Marion had made a fuss over the small bouquet she'd brought, but it was a nice fuss, one that made her feel the gesture was unexpected but appreciated.

"Ray's quite taken with you, dear."

"I don't know why, we just met last week."

"Don't sell yourself short." Marion patted her arm. "And he thinks the world of Kevin…"

As she carried coffee cups to the dining room, Sari examined Day more critically. When Ray mentioned he was inviting an old friend who happened to be the assistant director of the SBI, she'd expected a rumpled gnome with Coke-bottle glasses and a nervous laugh, closer to Ray's age than her own, or a testosterone-laden gunslinger so full of himself, no one would be able to get a word in edgewise. If Kevin Day noticed her surprise when they were introduced, he kept it to himself. It wasn't his fault their host thought it would be cute to play matchmaker. But what lay beneath the off-the-rack navy jacket and muted tie?

"Cobbler?"

Marion cut generous slices hot from the baking dish, crumb topping yielding to plump blueberries and indigo syrup.

"Frozen," she whispered to Sari, "the real ones are out of season."

Ray drained his cup and cleared his throat. Nervous, Sari thought, despite his assurances that the investigation was viable if not all but complete. Who was he trying to kid? There was technically no statute of limitations on murder, but they all knew a prosecution a decade after the fact would be virtually impossible. And what was Peggy to him but a dead housewife from Gillman? To pull in the assistant director of the SBI—

"—down to business," Ray was saying. "Each of us has something to contribute. Sari knows the family, Kevin's got the crime lab and"— he chuckled grimly—"if I could have cracked the case alone, I would've done it ten years ago. So let's begin with our star witness. What do you remember about that day?"

Sari took a deep breath, then let it all out. Putting words to the memories for the first time, she found every detail as fresh and vivid as if she'd captured it on film. Each memory triggered another. The sparkling pool next door reminded her of the precise time she'd left the little apartment on Locust for the library, sweat trickling down her neck told her the height of the sun as she climbed the stairs upon her return. And the memories she'd never been able to erase, the glimpses that said little to a disinterested observer but had revealed so much to her: Warren's blank expression when she'd asked about his seminar, his lack of interest in the apartment he'd come to Stanley to see, his furtiveness as he probed the bruise on his forehead in their hall mirror...

"Any chance Tim knew something?" Ray asked.

"No." She shook her head emphatically, banishing that moment on the lawn when Warren pulled Tim close. Their purpose was to discover who killed Peggy and why, not cause trouble for Tim. "They weren't a family that talked." Marion poured more coffee. "What do you mean, dear?"

"To Warren, life is a problem to be worked. If he was involved in Peggy's death, which you have yet to prove"—she glanced at Day in time to see him blink and stare into his cup—"he wouldn't have implicated his son. And if Tim had any reason to distrust his father, I would have known."

"I'm sure you would," Marion said with a fierce look at the men.

"And just for the record, we may be divorced but if I thought my ex had anything to do with a cover-up, I wouldn't be sitting here now helping you slip a noose around his neck."

Ray threw up his arms in mock surrender. "Okay, okay. Hands off Tim."

"Your turn, Ray." Now that she had him on the defensive, Sari was driving their bargain home. "What do you know about that pickup truck?"

"Only one witness saw it, and she wasn't credible. Downright unbelievable, in fact."

"Why?"

"I don't know how to say this, but women are lousy witnesses." He appealed to Day and Sari saw a flicker of amusement on the SBI man's lips. "Right, Kevin?"

He shrugged. "Their estimates can be . .. off."

"They're blind as bats!"

As Marion opened her mouth in protest, Day jumped to his friend's rescue.

"What Ray means is, women process and record information differently than men." He smiled at Sari but she wasn't about to invite his patronizing generalizations. Realizing he would get neither validation nor a rise out of her, he smoothly switched tactics. "Did you have trouble finding your way here tonight?"

"I wouldn't be surprised if she did," Marion sputtered, "with Ray's directions..."

"I stopped at a gas station." Sari hesitated. "Twice. But I have problems with east and west, even with the foothills as a guide."

"The second time you asked for left and right, and landmarks instead of mileage. Right?" She didn't need to nod. "The same thing happens with heights and distances. An investigator asks, was the man who attacked you taller or shorter than me, and narrows it down from there."

Sari rolled her eyes at Marion and got a nod of disgust in return. Now would come the sop to their feminine egos. What did Burt think, she was so desperate she'd fall into the arms of any unattached male?

"But you're more accurate and precise than men when it comes to sensory data," Day continued as Ray watched the exchange with an approving smile. "Men remember words, women the way they were said. One's every bit as important as the other."

"So what was wrong with the description of the truck?"

Ray took over. "Woman across the street said the side panels were eight feet high. For a contraption like that to make it down the Interstate in a moderate wind without tipping over, it'd have to be rigged with sails! Where was the last prairie schooner *you* saw?"

"Is that why you didn't look for it?" Sari directed her question to the SBI man. Ray would have been responsible for the botched investigation, but there was no reason for their host to take all the heat. "What about now?"

"Without a year or make, odds are worse than a needle in a haystack," Day replied. As she bristled at his smile which was clearly meant to charm, he added, "But I haven't begun yet."

Ray heaved a sigh. "Tell us about Tim's sister," he asked. His attempt at matchmaking having come to naught, Sari knew he was trying to salvage what he could from the evening. And it would probably be the last time Kevin Day let himself get talked into dinner at the Burts'. "She had nothing—"

"—to do with it," Day finished, "but she may know something helpful. Laura was in Gillman that morning. What makes her tick?"

"She was seeing a married man while she was in high school, but Warren 'worked' that problem by moving the family to Indianapolis for a year. Apparently it was quite a scandal." Sari hesitated. "Laura was dating two guys at the time Peggy was killed."

"I remember that speed freak in Stanley," Ray said. "Who else?"

"I saw them together just once." She heard a tinkly laugh, saw Laura throw back her head with pleasure in that scruffy Laundromat. What difference would it make if she told now? "He was wearing a wedding ring, I guess that's why she didn't want anyone to know. But she seemed really stuck on him. And there was something else, the night before the funeral..."

"What?" Ray prompted.

"I don't know why, but I thought he might be the same guy Laura was seeing in high school."

"So?"

"So nothing." She hesitated again. "To tell the truth, I felt kind of sorry for her."

"Why?"

"Because she wasn't Peggy's favorite." Sensing their confusion, she added, "They had another daughter. Laura's twin."

Ray leaned forward. "What happened to her?"

"She died when she was small. A congenital defect." The men exchanged a look that said, *geez, can you believe the things women think are important?* "I'm not saying it means anything, but you asked."

"No," Day replied. "Keep going. How do you think their child's death affected the Scotts?"

"From what I gathered, it sent Peggy into a tailspin." Something about that dinner at the Caribou Inn, what had Warren said? *Whatever was wrong ran in her family, not mine.* Sari shook her head. "It wasn't something they talked about."

"Any idea where Warren is now?" Ray asked.

"Arizona. He may be running his consulting business out of his home."

"Feel up to a shot at Laura?"

"You mean do I feel like letting Laura take a shot at me?" She laughed. "I think I'll pass."

"I thought you liked her," Marion said.

"I tried, but the feeling wasn't mutual. She basically told Tim bringing me into his family would destroy it."

"Go back to that morning," Day said. The change of subject was a relief. Warren's alibi—"

"—stinks," Ray interrupted.

"Yeah, I know." Day smiled sympathetically at his friend. "But if he wasn't at Walgreen's at Gillman Mall, where else could he have been?"

"If he went to Stanley early and knocked on the apartment door like he said, you would have seen him. Right?" Ray turned to Sari for confirmation.

"Unless he really did come while I was in the shower. But even then—"

"What?" Ray pressed.

"He would have been hard to miss. He said he hung around a few minutes, but I was in the shower just long enough to get wet. And we would both have taken Broadway to the rec center." She shook her head. "I've told you all I remember. I was so distracted that morning, I—"

"Why was that?" Day asked.

"Our wedding was in a week. I was trying to make a good impression on Tim's parents, but Warren was always so aloof I never knew what to say to him. And then I was clumsy, I bled all over his car..." As the SBI man's eyes bored into hers, Sari forced herself to continue with the embarrassing story. "He drove us home in his Oldsmobile, and when I got in, I stepped on something and gashed my heel." Catching Marion's sympathetic nod, she tried to laugh. "All I could think of when we got to the apartment was cleaning his car, and that he'd tell Peggy and she'd think I was a klutz. She already knew I couldn't cook."

"I'm sure it wasn't your fault," Marion began. "I can't imagine you being—"

Day was leaning across the table. "Did you clean the Olds?"

"He wouldn't let me."

"What did you step on?"

She tried to picture the interior of Warren's car.

"A wooden yardstick was tucked under the seat, and when I kicked my heel back it snapped. I offered to replace it, but Warren said he got it free at a hardware store."

Day looked disappointed. "Remember anything else?" She shook her head, the humiliation of that morning still fresh. Why did she care whether she let the SBI man down? She owed something to Ray, not—

"If you had to guess Warren's motive," Day continued, "what would it be?"

Sari shrugged. But it was the first time anyone had asked, and suddenly her opinion seemed important. "Peggy was ill. No one would say exactly what it was, but she'd been that way a long time, and it continued up to her death."

"No one kills his wife because she's sick," Ray scoffed, but Day was interested.

"What makes you think that's what it was?"

"Warren said it made their life difficult. From the time the kids were small." She remembered what Tim said about quiet time. "Peggy would lay in a dark room with a cold cloth for hours at a time, and they weren't allowed to make noise."

"She sounds depressed," Marion suggested. "The death of a child..."

"I think it was more than that. Tim said there were times when she wasn't around at all." She felt foolish. Overdramatizing, her mother would say. "But how it could have triggered her murder, I don't know."

They batted around other scenarios, ranging from an affair—all agreed Warren was too cold and Peggy lacked the energy—to insurance money, and the discussion slowly wound down. Marion offered seconds on the cobbler, but it was getting late and Sari had to work the next morning.

"Was Warren wearing clip-on sunglasses that day?" Ray asked.

"I don't remember. Is it important?"

"Probably not. He said he went to Walgreen's for them, and it just stuck in my head." He glanced at Marion, who reached across the table and patted his hand. "Sometimes my imagination doesn't know when to quit."

"Speaking of quitting, I think it's time I called it a night." Sari rose. "Marion, thanks for a marvelous dinner." Day walked her out and whistled when they reached the curb. "Vintage Mustang, what a car!"

"Not quite what you were expecting?"

He looked her up and down. "I would have guessed a Toyota. Corolla. Two-door, AM radio, no air-conditioning. If power steering was optional you'd tell them to leave it off."

His answer stung, but she wasn't about to give him the satisfaction of showing it. "Looks like you guessed wrong."

"How often do you drive it? The license tags—"

"As a matter of fact, I've been keeping it in a garage."

"Why take it out now?" He was close enough for her to smell his aftershave, but it was a clean scent. Pine or juniper.

"I thought it was time." As his eyes widened with recognition, she felt a surge of panic. The last thing she wanted him to think was that she was grieving over her marriage. "I mean, how else could I get here? And speaking of timing, why do you care about the Scott case? Other than your devotion to truth, justice, and the American—"

"Ray got screwed." In the glow from the streetlamp Kevin Day smiled tightly. "And no matter what you think of me personally, Ms. Scott, I hate to let a murderer walk."

Chapter Thirty-Two

A sking herself for the hundredth time how she let Burt talk her into this, Sari watched the eastern part of the state hurl past. But that Sunday in early September was a splendid day for a drive. The sky was baby blue and the foothills shimmered in the haze; the only hint of fall was the rich corduroy of fields. As the hills shrank in the Chrysler's wake the land flattened and sun devils danced, dust clouds shooting from the earth like bantam tornadoes. On the plains the sky began at the ground.

When Ray had suggested the trip to Walker County two months earlier, Sari told him she couldn't take time off from work.

"What," he scoffed, "Spenser & Trowbridge does a bed check on weekends?"

"If you're going to poke around old newspapers and tour cornfields, there's no reason for me to tag along…"

Since that dinner at the Burts' they'd spent many evenings together, all, to Sari's relief, without Kevin Day. Ray shared his entire file with her, except the photographs, and in return she told him everything she knew about the Scotts. When she declared Tim off-limits, Marion backed her with "No woman should be asked to bear witness against her husband," and that was that.

The initial allocation of responsibilities left Ray to focus on motive and weapon, and gave Sari the apparently hopeless task of devising a strategy to identify the pickup truck. That fell apart as early as their second dinner, and future sessions were devoted to three-way brainstorming. Ray proclaimed an early victory when he ambushed Sari one July evening and asked her to speculate on what lit Warren's fuse.

"The wedding. Peggy hated the idea, and it pushed them both over the edge."

"That's what you want to believe," Ray replied.

"Why would I—"

"If it was your fault, maybe you'll get it right next time."

"Get what right?" His smug grin was more irritating than usual.

"Your next relationship with a guy."

"There won't be a next time, Burt, and I'm not making it up. Even Regina Hummel said Peggy was upset about our marriage."

Ray shook his head like a dog with a snout full of water. "Red herring, like the pickup truck. But you're using it as an excuse to hide from the world."

"I am not!"

"What are you whipping yourself for, blowing it with Tim?"

At that Marion intervened. "Ray Burt, lay off!"

On less tense occasions, Sari veered from detached amusement at Burt's list of what-ifs to dread at what they might find when they actually began to look. Ray seemed content to endlessly rehash details, but as the summer drew to a close, he pronounced himself ready to move. The first step, he said, would be to go to Fillmore.

"What do you expect to find?" Sari asked.

"I don't know. We questioned people about tensions in the Scotts' marriage, but nobody seemed to know much. They didn't have any close friends other than Peggy's sister Kay." He reached for a dish towel to dry the dessert plate Marion handed him. "Warren and Peggy both grew up in Walker County. Maybe someone remembers when they were courting." His words must have sounded unconvincing even to himself, because he tried again. "Never hurts to poke around in a suspect's past.

Should've done it years ago."

"You don't have to go just because Taylor Philips threw it in your face," Marion objected.

"Philips?" Sari asked as he flashed Marion a warning. Elected to Congress, the former assistant D.A. was already raising his sights to the Senate. "He's long gone. Even if you find what you're looking for, he won't be the prosecutor."

"Nothing to do with Philips," Ray mumbled. "This time I'm not making any mistakes."

"He's a jerk," Sari replied, "he's going to lose that Senate race."

"The only time *I'll* vote Democrat…" But he flashed Sari a grateful smile.

By the following week, Ray had their itinerary planned, right down to the motel in Walker County with the lowest economy rates. Two nights was a long time, Sari protested, but when he countered they could drive to Fillmore on a Sunday and be home Monday night, she ran out of excuses. On the appointed morning she parked the Mustang at his house and they set off.

Now they were hurtling past cornfields, where the horizon was interrupted only by grain elevators gleaming silver in the sun and green and yellow combines that littered the landscape like giant Tinker Toys. Sari settled back in her seat and willed herself to focus on cows grazing at the bottom of stream beds, where growth was greenest, and not on the last time she'd made this trip. As stands of junipers and Russian olives crept up on weathered homesteads and the asphalt shimmered with mirages, once again she felt herself being drawn back in time. When she looked in the rearview mirror again the foothills had vanished.

"Want me to drive?" she asked.

Ray's hands tightened on the wheel and Sari instantly realized her mistake. He'd obviously washed and waxed the Chrysler for their trip, vacuumed the soft-knit nylon and fine-grained vinyl upholstery, and rubbed the interior paneling until it gleamed like burled walnut. Why entrust the love of his life to someone who drove a Mustang that hadn't been tuned in years?

"You want to?" he replied.

"Not on your life!"

He relaxed his grip. "Does that poor old Mustang at least belong to triple A?"

"What for?"

"Never know when you'll need them."

"What are you, my mother?"

"Sounds like you could use one. What do corporate lawyers do for fun?"

"Tear wings off clients."

He glanced at her shrewdly. "Kevin likes movies…"

"Let me guess. *Sands of Iwo Jima?*"

"Now, don't start with your pinko crap."

She flashed him the peace sign. "What's with the two of you anyway?"

"Me and Kevin?" The question caught him off guard. "Just old friends, and speaking of which, you could do a lot worse. He's a great—"

"Not in the market."

"When you gonna quit carrying the torch?"

She twisted in her seat. "Look, Burt, so far I've resisted the temptation—"

"Someone's gotta loosen you up."

"—to dissect your primitive brain. All I ask in return is that you steer clear of my personal life."

He chuckled. "Got your Irish up, didn't I?"

"My *Irish?* Some detective you are."

"Where you from anyway?"

"Brooklyn."

"One of my best friends—"

"—is a New Yorker. Can we stop for lunch before one of us says something truly unforgivable?"

Just past the state line they pulled up at the Diamond R Bar & Grill. When Ray opened the door, cigarette smoke and fried onions assailed them, Stetsons outnumbered John Deere caps, and not one of the burly men hunched over cups of joe gave them so much as a look. The vinyl barstools were all occupied, but as they waited at the threshold a man who could have played tackle for Nebraska and a woman almost his size rose from one of the knotty-pine booths across from the counter and left.

"Yee-haw!" Sari said under her breath as they slid into their seats.

Strip basket, pork sandwich, cheese sticks, fries, announced the menu board over the grill. The corn-fed heifer behind the counter ignored them as she hauled her catch from the fryer beneath a mural of a cowboy lassoing an eight-foot bottle of Coors.

"This your idea of a joke, Burt?"

He shrugged. "When in Rome…"

"I didn't realize Romans fried their cheese."

Through the doorway to the rear, Sari saw a pool hall with four regulation-size tables and a hinged bench running six feet above the ground the entire length of the room. A dozen pool sticks hung in a glass case over the bench with a handwritten sign that read "Private Cues." Resigned, she turned back to the menu board.

"Trying to corrupt me?" she asked.

When Ray ordered a double cheeseburger with onion rings, she wondered when his last meal away from Marion had been. After briefly contemplating what fried fish on a bun in a landlocked state might taste like, she asked for the same. Moments later, the waitress brought their food in red plastic baskets, wiping sweat from her untamed chestnut brows with a dish rag. The thin bun disintegrated after the first bite but the sodden layers of beef congealed into a delectable mass.

Ray heaved a sigh of contentment before wolfing down the rest of his burger. "Honest-to-God farm-fed beef, not that feed lot mush."

"Treat me right and Marion will never know." Sari took a smaller bite and slid her onion rings to the center of the table. "You're from here, aren't you?"

"Might as well be," he replied in an offhand tone. "Born in North Junction, eighty miles from McComb." In response to her blank look, he added, "Northeast of here, just over the state line."

Squirting ketchup on an onion ring, she ignored his pained expression. "That's why you care so much about this case?"

"Maybe."

"I'll bet Peggy reminds you of someone."

He reached for a ring, fastidiously avoiding the ketchup.

"Thought you weren't gonna play shrink."

"Was your father a rancher?"

"Nope."

"Did he—"

"Worked the railroad hump yard in North Junction. Biggest switchyard in the world." He smiled at her bewilderment. "Incoming rail cars are sorted and hitched to trains heading out to every part of the country. They call it a hump yard because it operates on gravity, with the cars rolling from hills into receiving bowls, but in my old man's day crews did the work."

"You must have been proud." Ray's eyes went flat, and Sari realized how patronizing the words must sound. "I mean—"

"Not a single one of those trains could have run without Ray Burt, Sr." There was an edge to his tone, but as he continued she realized his curtness had nothing to do with her. "He didn't want to be a switchman, of course, there were dozens of those. No, he wanted to be *yardmaster*."

"What happened?"

"First you gotta take the test for brakeman. Which he did, over and over. End of story." He grabbed the check and was fishing in his pocket for the tip before she could protest. Swallowing her questions, she followed him out.

In another five miles they came to a water tower with *Fillmore* painted on it in tall black letters. It had been ten years since Peggy's funeral, but as they drove through the town Sari recognized the wide streets and two-story storefronts. They had a make-believe look, their breadth and height endowing them with the illusion of prosperity. She tried to find the funeral home where Peggy's body had been brought but they lost their way on side streets, where cosmos and marigolds paraded in gaudy thickets along the asphalt. On the outskirts of Fillmore once again, grass sprang from dust as prairie reclaimed town.

With the light waning, Ray drove to the Homesteader Motel,

perched on a gentle crest half a mile east of the business district. Without being asked, the woman at the desk handed them keys to two rooms and Ray an AARP discount, and they unloaded their overnight bags from the trunk.

"Bright and early tomorrow?" he said.

"What's the plan?"

"We'll figure that out in the morning."

Leaving him in the doorway to Room 11, Sari unlocked 12. The latch was flimsy enough to open with a paper clip, but judging from the muck in the fifteen-by-twenty-foot swimming pool ("Absolutely No Pets Allowed") there were no other guests to worry about. When she opened her door a wave of insecticide hit, and she swatted a large black fly that had been following her since the Diamond R. As she lit the twenty-five-watt wall sconces, she wondered once again what she was doing there. All she knew was that since Ray Burt came into her life she hadn't had a single nightmare.

—

R ay plopped on the bed, exhausted. He slipped off his boots and unpacked his small bag, hanging his nylon windbreaker on the rack by the door. Then he splashed cold water on his face and lay down again to stare at the stucco ceiling. What would be their first move? As he closed his eyes he heard a whistle and a thrum, and the steel track under his thin leather soles began to vibrate. A mouth yawned wide, its teeth the color of marigolds...

He awoke with a start. It was eight o'clock and the room was pitch dark except for quarter-moons above the wall sconces and the arc cast by the dim bulb in his bedside lamp.

"Where are you?" Marion's voice was high-pitched with worry when he finally placed the call through the switchboard in the front office.

"Fillmore, honey. Everything's fine. I checked into a motel and fell asleep, that's all."

"Is Sari with you?"

"Of course. I mean, in her own room. Long drive but she's a real trooper."

"Did you have dinner yet?"

"Yes, dear." At this hour, nothing would be open even if he was hungry.

"Did you find what you need?"

"We just got here, Marion, it's Sunday night and everything's buttoned up tight." He sighed. "I'm not even sure what we're looking for."

"You'll find it, Ray, you always do." Her confidence buoyed him and he was pierced with longing for her, wanted her right beside him in the motel room. How many years had it been since they'd spent a night apart? Too long to remember.

"I've got a plan." He spun it out as he spoke. "Tomorrow morning we're going to the local newspaper to learn all we can about the Dannhauers and the Scotts. Then we'll find Leeper."

"What's in Leeper?"

"That's where Peggy was born." He closed his eyes. "If we can see what she saw while she was growing up, maybe we'll know why she left."

"I thought you were looking for information about Warren."

"Whatever Peggy left, she took with her. And that may tell us more about why she was killed than anything else."

"You're not making sense, Ray."

"I'm tired, honey. Call you tomorrow, 'kay?" He was asleep a moment after his head hit the sandbag of a pillow.

Chapter Thirty-Three

The next morning they coasted down the hill to the two-block-long center of town. The New Yorker was decidedly out of place but drew only polite smiles from an elderly woman behind the wheel of a battered Ford and a farmer in a pickup who touched his fingers to his cap.

Ray was secretly relieved when Sari said she thought a walk would jog her memory. Dissembling did not come naturally to her, and he needed all the flexibility he could get because Fillmore was anything but a level playing field. When it came to families with roots you could trace back a hundred years, doors that might crack open for one person would be slammed shut in the face of two. If people were willing to talk at all.

They separated at the *Walker County Sentinel* office, agreeing to meet in an hour at the Frontier Café directly across from the single-story frame building the paper shared with the County Historical Museum. Outside the office a fellow ten years senior to Ray in overalls and a Farmer's Co-op cap leaned against the wall, smoking an unfiltered cigarette. He nodded as Ray tipped his Stetson and stepped past him through the threshold.

When Ray asked for 1980 editions, the girl at the front desk said the paper had been in operation only five years. It had succeeded the *Fillmore*

Square Deal, which had been published since the turn of the century.

"Where can I find copies of the *Square Deal,* dear?"

"Next door, at the museum. You have to go outside and come in through the door to the right, but they'll have what you're looking for."

Exiting the newspaper office, Ray almost collided with the old man in overalls. He tipped his hat again, feeling more than a little foolish, and entered the museum through the screen door.

The woman behind the counter was in her late sixties. Her rouge complemented the carnation pink of her pantsuit and a flowered scarf softened the wrinkles at her throat, but her eyes were razor sharp. Ray opted for the direct approach.

"I'm looking for copies of the *Square Deal* from the spring of '80."

"Any particular story?"

"I know the date, ma'am, I'm sure I can find what I'm looking for if those issues are available."

"We have newspapers from longer ago than that, but it might be easier if you told me the name of the family you're interested in." Her steel-rimmed spectacles flashed, and he wondered how long she could contain her curiosity. "We keep files on county folks."

"What sort of files?"

"Photographs, wedding invitations, funeral notices, and such." For the price of a name, they could be Ray's. "Who are you interested in?"

He threw himself on her mercy. "Do you have any information on the Scotts?"

Beneath that tight perm the wheels spun.

"That wouldn't be the *W. R.* Scotts, now, would it?"

He gave her the satisfaction of a nod, though her fingers were already on the file. Had someone else asked? Or had she been expecting this day to come?

But the folder bulged with memorabilia in no particular order, and Ray sensed he was the first stranger to intrude on this piece of Walker County's past. Settling on the wooden bench at the entrance to the museum with the file on his knees, he began with the original license granted to W. R. Scott to conduct business as a garage in 1928 and a handwritten copy of a deed to an unimproved lot on Washington Avenue. Glancing up, he saw the man in overalls help himself to a cup of coffee from the hot plate behind the counter. The file shifted in Ray's lap and a six-by-twelve-inch cardboard folder fell to the floor. When he retrieved it, Ray came face-to-face with Warren Scott at seventeen.

"You kin of the Scotts?" The clerk's inquisitiveness had finally gotten the better of her.

"An old friend. I was passing through town and thought I'd look them up."

"Phone book's right over there. Lucille Scott still lives on North Third…"

"Lucille?"

"W.R.'s sister."

"Maybe I'll give her a call." They both knew he wouldn't, but Ray was beyond caring how badly he tipped his hand.

"Where'd you say you were from?" the clerk asked.

"Widmark." The penciled brows arched, then she nodded to herself.

Returning to the photograph, Ray searched for the man in the boy. It must have been Warren's high school graduation picture because the name of the studio was embossed in gold script in the lower right-hand corner of the folder. Feldmann's, in Loving. Scott's chin was tilted toward the camera, and his flat eyes gazed past the photographer's shoulder. His forehead was high and his hair slicked back, and the soft wave at his receding brow created an impression of maturity. Straight nose, ears close to the head, smile playing on narrow yet sensual lips but stopping short of the eyes. A pleasant-looking youth, maybe even handsome, but not a face you'd remember unless you had reason to.

Peering closer, Ray tried to get some sense of Warren's physique. He was decked out in a double-breasted pinstriped suit and tightly knotted silk tie, the kind a banker might wear, but his jacket was too wide for his shoulders and the elongated points of his snowy collar accentuated a reedy neck. Not a farm boy or an athlete, but he projected a confidence, almost an arrogance, that was arresting. A boy who couldn't bear to let his father's present become his future… Closing his eyes, Ray let loose the memory that had been taunting him since they'd left the Diamond R.

It was early spring and he was eight years old, tapping his boot to a rousing polka from a nine-piece railroad band. He was dressed in his best clothes to witness the opening of the McComb station built just to the north of its demolished wooden predecessor. McComb was the division point on the main line of the railroad and the workers had been freed from their duties that day to lead three thousand visitors on tours of the depot. As Ray's father disappeared in the direction of the poker tables on the balcony in the atrium, his mother wandered outside to watch the dancing. Her cheeks were flushed with excitement. It wasn't often that Polly Burt was allowed to socialize.

Ray had wandered through the depot, hopping from one group to the next as they toured baggage and express service and dormitories for the crew. But when they reached the telegraph office he stopped dead in his tracks. The McComb station was among the first to replace the Morse code dots and dashes with a modern signaling system, and he couldn't tear his eyes from the winking lights whose flashes controlled the movements of a mighty railroad. Then and there he decided his future lay in manning that system, and he ran to the parking lot to tell his mother. Elbowing his way through the dancers he searched for silky black hair, but shouts drew him to a knot of men at the far end of the lot.

As he stood on the periphery of the crowd, Ray glimpsed his father struggling in the grip of two burly rail workers. Eyes the color of pitch cast madly about as he thrashed and growled like a dog, and Ray shrank back before he could see him. A few feet away, a raven-haired girl knelt with her head in her hands. Another woman gently pulled her upright and dabbed at her with a bit of cloth, and as she straightened Ray saw dark stains on her blouse. He stared at her face. The nose and mouth were a crimson pulp and one of her eyes was sinking into her swollen cheek. As the other looked straight at him, she cried, "Ray!" He whirled in shame and fled.

"—all right, mister?" The museum clerk was leaning over him with a cup of water and an expression of concern.

"Not used to this heat, I guess." He gratefully accepted the water and handed the file back. He'd better get a grip on himself, there was too much at stake to—

"—anything else? Some other family you might be interested in?"

He surrendered to her knowing look. "The Dannhauers."

She returned so quickly with the other folder Ray wondered just when she'd guessed why he was there. No longer bothering to busy herself with the surrounding stacks, she retreated behind the counter where the man in overalls stood sipping his coffee.

According to her obituary, Nettie Alt was born in Walker County in 1907, married prosperous farmer George Dannhauer in 1925 at St. Augustine's Church in rural Leeper, and bore him five girls and a boy. Margaret Kathleen was the youngest. Although the weddings of three of Peggy's sisters at St. Augustine's received extensive writeups and the death of the son in Normandy was recounted in heroic detail, the file contained no mention of Peggy's marriage to Warren Scott. Her obituary from the *Square Deal* in May 1980 said she was bom and raised north of Leeper and enjoyed painting and gardening, and maintained a happy home for her husband and children before passing on a Saturday morning in Gillman. It didn't even say she was murdered.

Ray closed the file and returned it to the woman behind the counter.

"Still need those copies of the *Square Deal*?" She rubbed it in a little, just to show she knew. "What date was it you were interested in, May of '80?"

Why pretend? "I guess not."

"Thought so." She glanced at the man in overalls. "Anything else?"

"No, thanks." Ray searched for an opening. "Nettie Dannhauer must have been quite a woman."

"She surely was. Worked her fingers to the bone raising those children after George died. Of course, Nettie came from good stock. Her people, the Alts, were the finest folks around. Family always came first." She looked defiantly at the old man, who was staring into his cup. "I remember their boy Tom's death like it happened yesterday. That's what killed George Dannhauer."

"Oh?" Ray wondered what that farmer would say if he got him alone.

"How's that?"

"He was one of the first boys on that beach. He died a *hero*. That finished off George, and Nettie was so distraught they had to bring in a nurse. Peggy was little more than a babe in arms."

"Did you know Peggy?"

"She was the apple of her mother's eye. Nettie could have fed the entire family on what she spent on drawing lessons for Peggy, and then Warren Scott came home from college and swept that girl right off her feet." Her eyes narrowed with scorn. "I'm surprised Nettie let him in the house."

The old man set down his cup and shuffled out. Must know something, or why leave so fast? Ray forced his attention back to the woman.

"She didn't like Warren?"

"W.R. ran a service station. The Dannhauers were devout Catholics, and the Scotts attended First Methodist. Nettie's boy worked the farm and her gals married in the faith, and most of them settled right here in Walker County. But not Peggy." Her voice rose, and it carried more than indignation. "I don't know which was worse, her marrying a Protestant or leaving home. Things sure are different out your way."

Ray cast for words to break the tension. "But some come back, don't they?"

"They surely do, one way or another. But nothing good comes of leaving home." Squaring her narrow shoulders, she leveled him with her steel-rimmed glare. "Cut yourself off from your roots and you wither and die."

He thanked her and quickly left. If he was lucky he'd catch that farmer and see what he could find about Warren Scott... Glancing up the street, he spotted him on the bench outside the Frontier Cafe.

"Nice town you've got here," Ray began.

"We try." The old man fanned himself with his cap.

"Mind if I sit?"

"Figured you might." Shifting to make room, he waited for Ray's next move. But two could play that game, and after a moment the farmer offered, "You've got to take with a grain or two of salt what Aggie over there at the museum says."

"How's that?"

"Some folks think the Dannhauers walked on water. Others might disagree." Ray kept his mouth shut. "But no man takes his life because his boy dies a hero. If that was the case, half the farmers in Walker County would've strung themselves up in their barns after the war."

Now Ray was completely lost. "What killed him?"

The man shrugged. "Oldest gal, the one before Kay, left two months after her brother died. Some folks think fifteen's a mite young to be with child, others say the fact she ran off with a married man pushed George over the edge. That's what some folks think, anyways, but I say neither one of 'em had a choice." For the first time, he looked Ray square in the eye. "Nettie was high-strung, when she had spells she wasn't around for George the way a wife should be. But that was a long time ago and I expect it's not what you're interested in."

Ray shook his head to clear it. Could he really-be saying *that*?

"Did you know the Scotts?"

The man nodded slowly and continued fanning himself with his cap. "W.R. was the son of a minister, his folks were one of the first families in Fillmore. Spent most of his time in his shop because Vonnie didn't like him underfoot. Prob'ly just as well."

"Why do you say that?"

"Vonnie was a cold one. When their younger boy died, she didn't turn a hair."

"Accident?"

"No, sir." He paused, milking it for what it was worth. "Born with a hole in his heart. Didn't make it past the age of two."

"What about Warren?"

"Couldn't wait to hightail it out of Walker County."

"Why was that?"

The old man looked surprised, the first emotion to register on his face. "I don't know where you're from, mister, but this was a dust bowl in the thirties. If Fillmore wasn't the county seat it would of dried up and blowed away. Boy as ambitious as Warren had better things in mind than trying to earn a living the hard way, like his daddy."

"Where'd he go?"

"Enlisted in the army first chance he got, then after the war he went to the University. A&M wasn't good enough."

"Sounds like he didn't get along with his old man."

"You could say that." He hesitated. "Warren always thought he was too good for Walker County. Handsome boy, girls flocked to him at dances even though he was never on a team. He always said he was waiting for the right one." He chuckled. "Way he talked, we all figured he'd marry some gal he met out in Widmark. It was a real surprise when he came home and picked Peggy Dannhauer."

"What was she like?"

"Pretty little thing, but quite a temper. Any man who married her would have had a lot on his hands. She was moody, high-strung like her mother. One minute bubbly, the next sad. No, I don't envy Warren a bit." He rose, set his cap on his head, and lifted two fingers in a salute. "Enjoy your stay in Fillmore."

Ray followed him into the dusty street. "Where is Leeper?"

"Leeper?"

"It's not on my map."

"That's because it don't exist. Never was much of a place."

"Did there used to be a town?"

"Before the war, but nobody's lived out that way in years. I don't think there's even a sign anymore. Just cornfields. Drive north of Fillmore on Route 2, follow the sign to St. Augustine's, then go west. You'll run into whatever's left."

—

"So what did you find?" Sari asked.

She'd located the funeral parlor, now a lawyer's office, and thought she recognized the place where she and Laura had spent the night before the funeral. But Ray was uncharacteristically quiet over sandwiches and pie at the Frontier Café, and when she asked if he learned anything useful, all he said was they'd talk about it on the way to Leeper.

"Everything and nothing," he replied once they were under way. "Vonnie had a younger son who died of a birth defect."

"What kind?"

Her interest took him aback. "Something with his heart."

"So that's what Warren meant…"

"Come again?"

"That's how Laura's twin died, but he told us whatever was wrong ran in Peggy's family and not his. I wonder if she blamed him for their daughter's death."

"Fifteen years would be a hell of a long time to carry a grudge." Ray's mind seemed to be elsewhere.

"Did you learn anything more?" she prompted.

"Old news better forgotten."

"I thought Peggy's family was the pillar of Walker County."

"Tim ever tell you his granddad killed himself?" He didn't need to look to know the answer. "And he had an aunt who got herself pregnant and ran off with a married man. Apparently Nettie went wacko."

"What?"

"Had a chat with an old gomer outside the cafe. He hinted Peggy's father knocked up her sister but I find that hard to believe. Dannhauer was the most prosperous farmer around, old guy's probably holding a grudge. That's how small towns are. Nothing but gossip."

"Mean or not, gossip usually has a grain of truth."

"Things like that just don't happen in families like the Dannhauers," Ray insisted.

But was it so hard to believe? Sari pictured Nettie being escorted down the aisle of St. Augustine's by Kay, her other daughters the crook of a finger away.

"He wasn't talking about Kay, was he?"

"No, he said the oldest daughter."

"I thought Kay was the oldest. Tim never mentioned—"

"What any of it has to do with Peggy, I don't know." He was clearly impatient with the subject.

"True or not, if they're still talking about it fifty years later, you can imagine what it was like growing up. I don't blame her for leaving."

They were north of town now and the New Yorker was the only car on the road. As they drove in silence, Sari looked over at Ray. He was staring straight ahead at the blacktop like the wooden Indian in the window of the museum.

"What's eating you?" she asked.

"It's just a women's myth that you can start over someplace else."

"We all leave home for the same reason."

"Oh?" He aimed for mockery but missed. "And what might that be?"

"Break free of our parents, create something of our own. Isn't that why you left?"

When he made no response Sari focused on the scenery. The rolling prairie alternated with dense swaths of sunflowers, corn, and milo awaiting harvest. They seemed to be in the middle of nowhere.

"Are you sure we're going in the right direction?"

He shrugged. "You tell me."

"Why did you leave North Junction?"

"Enlisted." Ray flexed his fingers, but from the way he hunched over the steering wheel she knew his tension emanated from a deeper source. "I know what you're saying," he continued, "but we're stuck with who we are. Look at Peggy. If Warren hadn't taken her from Leeper, she'd still—"

"And she might be alive if she'd married a missionary and moved to China. Ray, you promised to keep an open mind about the investigation. So far we don't have a shred of proof he did it."

"You've been divorced what, five years?"

His tone was accusatory, and Sari wondered what set him off. "I don't regret any decisions I've made."

"Not even marrying Tim?"

"Tim wasn't responsible for what happened. If I'd said what I knew, brought it to the surface—"

"A better this or a better that, it's always easier to blame yourself." His anger bubbled over. "Is that why you make excuses for him?"

Now she was boiling mad herself.

"And what can't you forgive yourself for, Burt? Don't tell me every murdered housewife means this much to you…"

He slammed on the brakes and the Chrysler skidded to the shoulder. Bracing her hands on the dashboard, Sari stared through the windshield. The road had abruptly ended, forking east and west. A small hand-painted sign on the west fork read "St. Augustine's Church. W2N3W1," like the combination to a safe.

"Are you okay?" she asked.

Trembling, he nodded and cranked the ignition. The sedan bounced as they turned left onto an unpaved road and followed the route to another Y, this one forking north and south. When they turned right the surface changed from gravel to crushed limestone, crumbly like chalk. After a slight rise there was another fork, and in the distance a redbrick church faced a vast field of corn eight feet high.

Sari glanced again at Ray, but he was breathing hard and she dared not speak. When they reached the church he pulled to the shoulder and switched off the engine.

"I didn't mean—" he began.

"The end was hard for me to accept."

He let out a deep sigh and looked at her for the first time since she'd asked him why he left North Junction. "Sounds like your marriage was over before it began."

"I loved him so much, Ray. I guess it wasn't enough."

"You never had a chance." His voice had softened, and his sympathy was harder to accept than anger. A divorced woman in love with her ex, the love that knows no shame. "How could you be his wife when you had to be his mother?"

Sari opened the door and stepped out. This was the same spot where she and Tim had stopped before Peggy's funeral, and she longed to run into the cornfield and find him. The air sizzled as her feet sank in the berm, she could taste those bitter leaves… She took another step and turned.

"You know what I keep thinking? We're never going to see the

Delaware Water Gap."

"Delaware Water Gap?"

"When Tim and I drove east the Christmas before we were married, we passed through the most beautiful place on earth. A gap in the Poconos where the Delaware River flows, with thousand-foot bluffs rising out of nowhere. We got there at dawn after driving twenty hours straight, and it was so stunning I sat in the car and wept. And I know I'll never see it again. Not with him."

"Tim's the only guy with a driver's license?" She stared. "Seems to me you could go with someone else, when you're ready..."

What if that day never came?

"Want to see the church?" he finally asked.

Shaking her head, Sari climbed back in the car.

"Let's find Leeper," she said.

After another mile of gravel and limestone the road turned sharply north, and a grain elevator flanked by storage bins and a decrepit wooden shed materialized beside a set of iron tracks. A wooden post with faded crosspieces marked rails overgrown with weeds and brush. Just beyond, a narrow white board was mounted on poles three feet high, all but obscured by a stand of sunflowers. Ray stopped the car, and Sari walked up to the hand-painted sign to brush the foliage aside: LEEPER.

If the town had ever been more than a whistle stop there was no sign of it. Past the tracks a barn sagged in a field of tall weeds, and a one-story building of dark brick stood at the end of the gravel road on the right. The howl of a dog pierced the silence.

They crossed the rails and parked in front of the building. The bricks were blackened, as if there had been a fire; sunflowers reached as high as the boarded windows, and a porcelain-enameled stove lay on its side next to broad steps leading to the entrance. Engraved in capital letters two feet high in bleached stone above the door were the words "Leeper School."

As they stood together at the edge of the road, Sari closed her eyes and imagined she heard children squealing. A ten-year-old boy chased a girl with pigtails that blazed like fire around the school yard, her high-pitched shriek carrying over the others as a rubber ball flew back and forth. Then a bell rang and the children lined up in a double row before marching up the steps to the schoolhouse. The pigtailed girl stood at the edge of the yard and shielded her eyes from the sun. She stared off over the fields to the south and east, wind ruffling her skirt and pressing it against her thin white legs. She took a step forward, as if she were about to fly into the corn. Then she ran back to join the others. She was the last one in.

Sari hiked through knee-high bramble and cockleburs to the privies behind the school. They lay on their sides, gray wood slats long reduced to tinder as clumps of chartreuse sunflowers, violent in their intensity, marauded through the brush. To the north she could see the railroad crossing and the grain elevator. In the other three directions lay prairie and sky, with nothing in between.

Chapter Thirty-Four

Wheeling her cart to a stop, the waitress set a tray of sliced unagi roll at the center of the table, ducked her chin, and sped off.

"You didn't have to take me to lunch," Sari said.

"I don't recall my arm being twisted," Kevin Day replied as he unwrapped his chopsticks.

Ray must have told him about her taste in food, Sari thought, or why else would they be at Sumi's? When they arrived the dining area was just starting to fill. The cashier personally led them to a prized booth, but Day was twice the size of any man in the room and Sari supposed the woman's attentiveness was a product of amusement at the odd couple they made.

"I'm surprised you've heard about this place," she continued.

"Didn't you know? Cops never eat with forks and spoons." He waited for her to select a slice of roll before following suit, and when she helped herself to pickled ginger and a healthy dab of green horseradish he did the same. His deliberate movements suited chopsticks and she wondered what would happen if she speeded up the tempo.

"You look more like a steak-and-potatoes guy to me." She watched him calmly swallow half a glass of water as he underestimated the strength of the wasabi. "But about that pickup truck..."

It had been three weeks since her trip to Fillmore with Ray. On the way home they'd plotted what Burt optimistically called Phase II of the investigation, which entailed a joint trip to New York to interview Laura, and Sari perhaps paying a visit to Kay Butler. She had misgivings about dropping in on Tim's family unannounced but agreed it was unlikely the Scotts would cooperate if forewarned, and it seemed fruitless to contact Tim. That left the pickup truck. With nowhere to turn for advice but Kevin Day, she'd called him the day before and he suggested discussing it over lunch.

The waitress was returning with bowls of miso soup. As Day gracefully retrieved tofu from the steaming broth with his chopsticks, Sari concealed her annoyance with a smile. He was wearing a silk tie and the nick above his left ear confirmed her suspicion that he'd just had a haircut. He was trying too hard to impress her.

"Ray tells me you're from New York," he said.

"Brooklyn. Where people never ask you how you are unless they need to know. How about you?"

"Montana. Where it's too open to hide."

"Why'd you leave?"

"To join the SBI after I finished college at MSU on the GI bill. My marriage was busting up and it seemed the thing to do."

The waitress brought his udon, and as he tucked his tie into his pin-striped shirt Sari wondered how quickly he would abandon his chopsticks for a fork and spoon.

"How long were you together?" she asked.

"Nine years. We were high school sweethearts, but when I got back from Vietnam nothing was the same. Eighteen's too young to get married anyway."

"Kids?" Day shook his head, and she realized she was hungrier than she thought. So they'd outgrown each other... Cutting into her teriyaki salmon, she lifted a pink morsel to her lips.

"—decide on law school?"

"I fell into it." The salmon was so good, she felt sorry for him, sitting there with a bowl of noodles he couldn't have expected. "I'm a corporate lawyer."

"Not a believer in the Holy Grail, eh?"

Why did he have to be so irritating?

"Do you know any lawyers like that?" she replied.

"I've met a few idealists, until they got the crap kicked out of them in court."

"I learned early it's better to keep your mouth shut than be humiliated." She punished her impulsiveness with a piece of sashimi, but Day's eyes were alive with interest. "Don't stop there," he prompted.

Now Sari was stuck. She'd never even told *Tim* about the chart. If she changed the subject he'd know he struck a nerve, and if she told him what she'd been thinking he was sure to laugh. But who cared what Kevin Day thought?

"I have an older brother and we used to fight a lot. When my parents came home from work, my mother always took Sam's side." Avoiding his eyes, she teased a shred of salmon from crisp skin with her chopstick. "I guess she got sick of hearing me whine 'It's not true' and 'It's not fair,' because she posted a chart in our front hall, and every time I said either she made a big black mark."

"You're kidding!" She strained her ears for derision, but Day's outrage seemed genuine.

"Five checks were supposed to earn me a star. I never let it get that far but she kept that chart in the hall, where everyone could see it, for months to make sure I learned my lesson. I must've been a real brat."

"It sounds like your mother was afraid."

"Of what?"

"I don't know. Loss of control, the usual stuff…"

"My mother?" Sari laughed. "You've got it all wrong. One night when I was ten, my dad was away on business and we heard screams across the street. Mom ran out of the apartment in her nightgown to rescue a woman who was being mugged. She didn't even have slippers on, but she chased the guy off and stayed until the cops came."

"Physical courage has nothing to do with lack of fear, Sari." He'd stopped eating his udon, and she was surprised to see his bowl was empty.

"She isn't afraid, it's just easier to care about—How did we get onto this subject?"

"We were talking about keeping a lid on the truth. Your mother's chart, convincing yourself of what you really don't believe to maintain someone else's illusion...I learned to hate lies by listening to body counts in 'Nam. That's why I'm a cop." Day waited until she could no longer look away. His eyes were more black than blue. "I believe in justice. If Warren Scott kills his wife and gets away with it, we all lose."

"You sound like Burt." With a Ph.D. in psychology. "How'd the two of you become friends?"

"In my book Ray's a first-class detective." Did he really believe that, or was it just loyalty? Maybe she'd been a little hasty in her assessment. "Hindsight's always twenty-twenty," he said, his tight-lipped smile closing the subject.

The waitress brought another pot of tea, and Sari tried to lighten the mood.

"So how does a first-class detective locate a pickup truck ten years after the fact?"

"With more luck than skill, I'm afraid. Even if the description weren't so outlandish, there must have been hundreds of trucks with wood side panels in metro Widmark in 1980. If I were you I'd focus on evidence that might be in your own hands." He cut off Sari's protest by refilling her cup. "I know you want to believe Warren is innocent"—why, because she'd defended Tim?—"but every detail counts. Professionals solve cases through observation and deductive reasoning, not emotion. When we can fit each piece into the larger picture we'll have the answer."

It was Day's complacency that was so annoying, she decided, and his lack of a sense of humor. Her eyes wandered to a table in the middle of the floor, where a middle-aged couple was just being seated. Time to call the SBI man's bluff.

"Can you deduce what they're going to order through the details you observe?"

He craned his neck, then grinned confidently.

"As a matter of fact, I can. The man will order fish and the woman meat."

"That's it?" She was truly disappointed. "I could have guessed that from their appearance. He can stand to lose a few pounds and she looks like she doesn't care. Besides, meat and fish aren't very specific."

"Then I'll take it a step further." He turned to look again, eyes narrowing in apparent concentration. "The man will order a combination plate like yours, with salmon teriyaki, gyoza, and sashimi but, unlike you, he will finish his sashimi. The woman will order tonkatsu, which is a pork chop with a sauce reminiscent of the Chinese hoisin."

"That's absurd. How much do you want to bet?"

"I wouldn't dream of taking advantage of you." Day's color was rising, and Sari suddenly realized her disbelief in his abilities irritated him as much as his self-assurance provoked her. "But I'll tell you what. If I'm right, you'll forget about the pickup truck and focus on that morning. Try to remember anything else Warren said, where he might have—"

"Afraid to admit you can't figure out where eight-foot slats fit into the larger picture?"

"Let me worry about the pickup." But he was breathing harder, and she found herself wondering what it would be like to look up at his face in the throes of a different passion. "If the truck fits, I'll find it." He was scanning the room for their waitress.

"Don't you want dessert?" Sari asked. As she reached for the tea to refill his cup, he leaned back on the bench and laughed. "I mean, if you're in no particular hurry..." Accepting the tea, he slowly sipped.

"Ray says you live near Edwards Park. That's not the safest neighborhood."

"My only regret is that the Belvedere doesn't have a garage. Now that I'm driving again, I have to park on the street."

"Outgrown the bus?" But his smile was encouraging, not at all smug.

"A car is much more convenient." Sari wasn't about to admit how rusty she'd been, that awful moment the week before when she shifted into reverse in the supermarket parking lot instead of stepping on the brake. "But one of my neighbors almost caught someone trying to break into the

Mustang the other night."

Day leaned forward. "Has that happened to you before?"

"No, but everyone else in the building has been broken into or vandalized at one time or another. He must have been after the radio, it's the only thing that really works."

His eyes remained somber. "What does a corporate lawyer do for recreation?"

Exactly what Ray had asked, but this time Sari felt no urge to be flippant.

"The highlight of my week is Friday." As Day stared into his cup she added, "Morning, not night. That's the day I stick my wash in the machine in the basement before I go out for my jog. I switch it to the dryer when I get home."

"Sounds about as exciting as my life, except I do laundry on Saturday. Maybe—"

They looked up to see the waitress.

"Dessert?" Day said. "Five bucks says they have green tea ice cream."

If he asked her for a date, what would she say? He wasn't anything like Tim, it was too soon, she didn't even like him. . . . And what if he didn't?

Flustered by her own ambivalence, Sari slid to the end of the bench. "I need to get back to my office."

As they walked to the cash register, the meat-and-fish couple waved. The man was about to dig into a salmon teriyaki combo and the woman had ordered a pork chop. "Do you know those people?" Sari asked.

"They work with me at the SBI. We come here once a week."

She let him pay the check, and as she drove off in the Mustang she saw Kevin Day laughing so hard he was shaking.

Chapter Thirty-Five

Two weeks later, Ray found himself in an aisle seat on the emergency exit row of a Boeing 727. As he gripped the armrest he couldn't help resenting Sari. His first trip in a plane since his discharge in '52, and looking down on clouds still made him want to toss his cookies. But after snickering at his suggestion that they drive to New York, to add insult to injury at the last minute Sari had backed out. And here he was, banking over Flushing Bay and about to land, armed only with his wallet and a slip of paper with Laura Scott's address.

Sari had called from her office at seven that morning to say a deal supposed to close Monday had been moved up to that afternoon, a Friday, and when Ray suggested putting off their trip till the following week, she urged him to give her ticket to Marion. That's when he knew the girl had cold feet, that work had nothing to do with her decision not to come. She didn't want to tangle with Tim's sister. But just before they hung up, she told him to ask Laura when was the last time she saw the fellow who worked for the glass company. "Come again?"

"A suggestion from your friend at the SBI," she replied. "He called it a hunch."

"Packed away the sackcloth and ashes, eh?"

"Our dealings are strictly professional. And don't forget to ask about that pickup truck."

As for bringing his wife, there were certain things a man had a right to keep private, like the reaction of his large intestine to being twenty thousand feet in the air. By the time the 727 landed and he hailed a cab, he still hadn't figured out his approach, but the ride into town provided a welcome distraction. Ray was never more grateful to be living in a landlocked state than when he caught a glimpse of water beneath his feet.

Laura lived in a trim brownstone on a quiet block in Greenwich Village. In this city of noise and trash and stench, everything was relative but everyone was a stranger. The cabdriver was swarthy and monosyllabic and Ray was in the uncomfortable position of having to trust his sense of direction and the accuracy of his meter. As they sped down an expressway so crowded and chaotic he could have reached out and touched the rusting paint on the cars swerving past, he couldn't figure out what depressed him more: the refineries belching black smoke into the already smoggy air or the ratty assortment of vehicles on the road. The cab stank of cigarettes and it was even worse when he opened a window. Naming his majestic Chrysler a New Yorker must have been Detroit's idea of a sick joke.

Laura's block had two dozen brownstones indistinguishable from her own. The only variation seemed to be in the scabby iron railings on the front steps, whose elegant swirls and geometric motifs enclosed tiny squares of cement at the entrance to street level apartments protected by security gates. One of Laura's neighbors had planted a spindly tree in a pot in the middle of the cement and another had geraniums spilling from a window box. The spots of color in this sea of gray were touching in their optimism, but Laura's house issued no invitation. Its shuttered windows were unadorned by flowers and the concrete beside her stoop was bare.

Ray's ring went unanswered. Laura's home address had been surprisingly easy to obtain, courtesy of directory assistance and a couple of lines Lew Devine taught him years ago to use on women of a certain age. Ray knew this was the right house because the white square in the brass holder under the doorbell read *Scott.* He rang again, peering into the hallway. But heavy curtains covered the glass panels flanking the wooden door and, frustrated, he walked two blocks to grab a bite on Bleecker Street.

As he munched a hot dog with sauerkraut, he watched an astonishing array of people parade by the steam cart. Everyone seemed to be in costume. Halloween was days past, but from the looks of these folks, the party was far from over. Too bad Lew wasn't there to enjoy the spectacle....

That reminder brought him up short. He'd come to New York for a reason, not to rubberneck like a tourist. He stood in the middle of the sidewalk trying to get his bearings, and then to kill more time walked a couple of blocks east to the place where Laura worked. The gilded sign read "Lonesome Laddies." Two muscle men in matching leather pants and vests sauntered out the door, and Ray averted his eyes. The one carrying the black and gold bag from the shop gave him a knowing look as he passed. When they rounded the corner, Ray peeked in the window.

What on earth was Laura selling? The contraptions baffled him: paddles and chains and something that looked like a swing with the bottom of the seat cut out. Why would a girl like Laura work in a place like this?

Ray bought a copy of the *Daily News* at a stand and retraced his steps. Settling on a stoop across from Laura's, he watched the neighborhood from the protection of his paper. A couple of delivery men blocked traffic for ten minutes, eliciting a barrage of horns and curses from motorists who leaned out their windows and shook their fists. An indifferent looking cop wandered over, scratched his head and left. A man passed by with the strangest dog Ray had ever seen, a head like a Rottweiler grafted onto the body of a Springer spaniel. Other than that it was quiet, with little foot traffic except a mailman whose heavy jacket could have doubled as body armor.

Ray was so engrossed in the football scores he almost missed the woman in the dark coat trudging down the street with a sack of groceries. She stopped in front of Laura's house to reach in her purse for keys, slowly climbed the stairs and disappeared. The brownstone swallowed her so completely he would never have known anyone was home if he hadn't seen her go in. He waited five minutes, then rang the bell.

"Excuse me, ma'am, does Laura Scott live here?"

She opened the door just far enough for him to catch a slice of face and torso. "Who wants to know?"

Her eyes were leaden and her delicate nose, slightly upturned at the end, was sunk between coarse and bloated cheeks. As Ray's gaze traveled past the fleshy throat to breasts straining against an ash-colored blouse and a belly that bulged over the waistband of tight black pants, he judged her to be in her mid-forties.

"An old friend. Do you know when she'll be home?"

She chuckled and he smelled cigarettes. "I don't think you're a friend of Laura's."

"If you'd just tell me when she'll be back—"

She laughed again, a crude noise deep in her throat, and the door opened a little wider. Now her voice was teasing. "Bet you wouldn't know her if you ran into her on the street..."

Younger than Ray first thought, and he searched for a girl with luminous eyes and chestnut hair. The hair was a duller shade, but—He stuck his foot in the threshold just as she tried to slam the door shut.

"I have to speak to you." He pushed against the heavy wood, but she was stronger than she looked and she had the momentum. He gave the door one hard shove. "Please let me in!" Suddenly it swung open and he found himself in a dim hallway facing what had become of the sexiest girl Lew Devine ever saw.

"What do you want?" Laura asked.

"We need to talk about your mother's death."

She froze, then lifted a finger to twist a lackluster strand of hair behind her ear.

"Her death?"

Slow down, he reminded himself, at least you're in. "I'm just trying to clear up a couple of things."

She rolled her shoulders, straining her blouse to the bursting point, then linked her hands at the small of her back and thrust her hips forward. As she leaned against the wall with one knee spread, Ray found himself mesmerized despite his revulsion. Laura used her body angrily, as a weapon and a shield.

"I told the other one everything I knew…"

Breaking her hostile gaze, he looked around him at the papered walls. The decor was oddly formal but there were no pictures. When he spotted the framed pen and ink drawing of a group of people posed in two clusters, he stepped closer. The figures were remarkably realistic, almost photographic in grace of limb and texture of skin, but their expressions were curiously blank. Suddenly he recognized the man on the far left as Warren Scott. He stood with his hand draped over the shoulder of a girl who looked about fifteen years old and whose head was slightly bowed.

"Is Tim the artist?"

"Yes."

The woman stood to the far right, flanked by a wide-eyed boy. Her eyes were half closed and she was so distant from the man the portrait would have seemed more natural had it been cut in two.

"Amazing…"

Laura's expression had softened. "He was twelve when he drew it."

Ray stared at the drawing. Something tugged, an association, but he couldn't place it. Turning to Laura, he continued in a gentler tone. "You came home that morning, didn't you?"

"So?"

"You said your parents were planning to do chores. Did they talk about your brother's wedding?"

"You mean the rehearsal dinner?" Her fingertips grazed her thigh, elongating the curve. For the first time Ray sympathized with Lew. Against this one he'd never stood a chance. "Someone had to arrange it."

"But your mother wasn't even planning to go to the wedding."

Laura's hand dropped to her side. "What gave you that idea?"

"She told a friend at work."

"Regina Hummel? Maybe that's what she wanted her to think." She smiled scornfully. "Mom wasn't about to risk losing Tim. She was making a dress to wear to the ceremony."

Ray dimly recalled a blue satin gown on a dressmaker's form in Peggy's sewing room the day of the murder. Could Hummel have been wrong about other things too? They had the cop giving the tickets, they had the clocks...

"Did you see a pickup truck that morning?"

Laura shrugged. "Dad told me—"

Dad told me?

"—to have him park it away from the house. Mom would have gone ballistic—"

"Who was the driver?" Her insolent smile threw Ray further off balance, and he struggled to recall the question Kevin wanted him to ask. "Where did he work?"

"Bluebell Glass." As she arched her back her breasts flattened, and he forced himself to focus on her face. Thank God Marion wasn't here...

So there really was a pickup truck, and Warren knew all along who drove it. A friend of Laura's. Lew had thought she was two-timing the speed freak she'd been living with, but Ray was so obsessed with nailing Warren he'd blown the lead. If they'd eliminated that red herring, Taylor Philips would have been forced to prosecute.

"What was he doing there?"

"He came to pick me up. I drove my car to Gillman so Dad could have the brakes replaced. Mom thought I'd need the Dodge to get back to Stanley, but the transmission was out. She tried to reach me—"

By calling Tim's apartment that morning. What was he missing, why would Peggy have cared?

"—didn't want her to know I was meeting him, so I drove the Barracuda home to Stanley. It was worth it to avoid the hassle."

If it was the guy Sari had seen, he was married. Was that enough to—

"Why would your mother have been angry?" he persisted.

"She never liked any man caring for me."

What was he missing?

He'd blown the case, given Philips the excuse he needed, and now he was standing there, gaping like a trout with a knife shoved up its ass. Calm down, calm down… So Laura didn't want her mother to see her with a man Peggy disliked. Was that so strange for a twenty-one-year-old girl? All it meant was the truck was a false lead…. Now he had to pick up the pace—before she threw him out.

"What happened to the hammer? Do you have it?"

Coarse laughter spewed from her throat.

"I keep it in a little black bag." Her tongue flicked, obscenely pink. "I'll bet you have one too. Mine's under the bed. Where do you hide yours?"

"Did your father put the hammer in the Cadillac?" Ray took a step forward, blinding himself to all but her eyes. "He burned his clothes but it wasn't so easy to get rid of the weapon, was it?" She flicked her tongue again and he stepped closer, moving as if to reassure a cornered animal. "Why are you protecting him, Laura? Didn't you care about her?"

"You know nothing about my mother!"

"I know your father killed her, and so do you."

"He loved me." Her face twisted with the effort to hold back tears.

"So did she."

"She was ashamed of me. The only one who cared was Dad…."

Laura slumped against the wall with her shoulders shaking and her face in her hands. For the first time, Ray noticed how slender her wrists were, the unadorned fingers as small and delicate as a child's. He reached out again, then dropped his arm to his side.

He left her like that, shuddering in the dim hallway.

—

Trudging up the Avenue of the Americas in search of a taxi to the airport, Ray was more angry and disgusted at himself than at Laura Scott. He'd fumbled from the start by not recognizing her, and then it went so fast he never regained control. And it was absolutely inexcusable for him to blow the lead about her two-timing the creep. If they'd nailed down that pickup truck…Maybe he really was too old for this. At least Sari hadn't been there to see the mess he'd made of things.

The sun was setting and the street swelled with the noise and fumes of rush-hour traffic. As he stood on the corner watching cabs speed by, he gave a bitter laugh. Way to go with that hammer, Ray... What had he expected, Laura to admit she had the weapon and hand it over? But there'd been a moment when he was so close, he could almost taste it. He ran through the exchange once more.

The pickup truck was a hopeless failure and he had no idea what to make of the business with the wedding. Where he'd almost scored, however, was with the hammer. Had Laura ever actually denied she had it? Maybe it wasn't her taunt about the hammer at all. Maybe it was with the drawing, something about the style... Squeezing his eyes shut, he willed his brain to focus. A boy trapped inside a crystal ball pounded on the glass, but that wasn't it either. Finally he gave up and hailed a cab.

Warren had trumped him again. He'd known all along who the driver of the pickup was, that the truck had nothing to do with Peggy's murder. How he must have gloated when Taylor Philips brought it up at the interrogation! Settling back in the seat as the taxi began making its way to the airport, Ray felt the weight of failure deep in his bones. He would fly back to Widmark with nothing to report but the elusive driver was an old flame of Laura's who drove a glass truck.

Chapter Thirty-Six

Sari's secretary entered the conference room on the fifty-first floor bearing a stack of pink message slips. As she handed them to Sari, she bent to her ear.

"There's a call for you from a Mr. Ray Burt. I told him you were tied up but he said to interrupt. Shall I put it through to you here, or do you want him to call back?"

Sari glanced around the table. To her right sat the president of the lead bank of her firm's biggest client, a holding company whose forty other subsidiaries were also clients of Spenser & Trowbridge. Across from them sat the president and chief financial officer of one of the bank's largest borrowers, Petroglyph Energy Corporation, which was closing on a forty-million-dollar line of credit as Harrison Spenser, chairman of the corporate department, hovered on the sidelines. The dozen others were lawyers for Petroglyph, bank officials, and associates and paralegals from S&T's corporate and oil and gas departments who were assisting in the closing. The documents had been signed and the borrower's counsel had just handed her his opinion to review.

"Have the operator put it in the phone booth." Smiling at the others, Sari promised to be right back and hurried across the lobby to the glass cubicle behind the receptionist's desk. Opinion in hand, she pulled the door shut.

"Sari?"

"Where are you, Ray?"

"La Guardia, about to get on the plane. Jesus, I can't believe you were actually raised here. No wonder you—"

"I'm in the middle of a closing. I have to go right back in."

"What's with the name?"

"Can't we talk later?"

"I ask for Sari Scott and the girl says, 'You mean Sari *Siegel?*' When did you change your name? The last time I called, you were still—"

At the tap on the glass, she looked up. "Did you review that opinion yet?" Spenser asked, opening the door. "The bank needs to wire the funds to Petroglyph's account in the next twenty minutes or we'll miss the deadline."

She pressed her palm to the receiver and held the opinion for him to see. "Be right there..."

As Spenser rolled his eyes and headed back to the conference room, she returned her attention to Ray just in time to hear him say something about Laura working at a sex shop. She glanced at her watch and began skimming the first paragraph of the opinion.

"—not gonna believe this, but she knew the guy in the pickup truck. He was waiting to meet her after she dropped off the Barracuda. An old boyfriend her mother couldn't stand."

"What?"

"Warren made him park down the street so Peggy wouldn't see and blow her stack. But when Peggy told Laura she couldn't take the Dodge back to Stanley, Laura had to cancel her rendezvous and drive the Barracuda home. See, she didn't want her mother to know she didn't care about borrowing the Dodge because her boyfriend was picking her up. The truck was a red herring, and they knew it all along. And you know what else?"

Sari peered across the lobby to the conference room, where the bank's president was standing by the telephone and Spenser was making placating gestures. As she watched, her mentor opened the door and started for the phone booth.

"—planning to go to the wedding. Peggy was working on her dress when she was killed. Laura lied when she said her mother would never—"

Spenser yanked open the door. "You're holding everything up. Whoever it is can call back." He stalked to the lobby, where he stood with his arms crossed.

"Ray, are you sure she—"

"There's more." He paused, clearly relishing the suspense. "You said Kevin wanted me to ask about someone who worked for a glass comp—"

Spenser rapped on the window again, his face contorted with anger. Sari opened the door and thrust the unread opinion at him. "I don't care how much money's at stake, leave me alone!" Bewildered, he backed away.

"Guess where he—"

A metallic drone intruded. *"Yout time is up. Please deposit another six quarters."*

"Sari—"

And all she heard was the dial tone.

—

Spenser was furious and the client was barely on speaking terms with her, but Sari felt as if the weight of ten years had been lifted from her shoulders. Laura had lied. She'd let Tim believe Peggy would never accept Sari, knowing all along she was planning to attend the wedding. Their marriage could have worked: it was Peggy's murder and Laura's malice that had doomed it. As she drove home that night, she wondered what time Ray's plane would land. Maybe she'd go to his house and surprise him, take him and Marion to dinner...

A moving van blocked the loading zone at the Bancroft Street entrance to the Belvedere. Wondering what was going on, she parked on Ninth.

"Sari! I'm glad I caught you."

Her neighbor Dan was carting a stereo speaker up the ramp from the basement.

"I haven't seen you in weeks," she replied. "Where've you been?"

"Charleston. House-hunting."

The news hit harder than she'd expected. "So you finally convinced John to move."

Dan hoisted himself into the back of the van and Sari handed the speaker to him. "After what happened there's no way we could stay. You know, I always bitched about that damn dog, but now he's gone..."

"What are you talking about?"

He jumped down as a burly fellow wheeled a dolly stacked with cartons up the ramp. "A week ago Wednesday I let Jacques off the leash like I always do, and he ran up the path toward the playground. When I whistle he always comes." Sari nodded. Dan's morning routine was as predictable as her own. He timed the Bouvier's walk to coincide with her return from her run so they could watch the sun rise together, and that was when he let the dog roam. The road curving through the park was closed to traffic from dusk to dawn and the only pedestrians were joggers and fellow dog walkers.

"—took off into that stand of pines by the water fountain and I followed on the footpath. When I got to the San-O-Lets across from the swings, I looked but didn't see him. I thought maybe he'd found another dog to play with, so I kept calling. It wasn't until the sun came up that I found him." Dan's soft eyes filled with tears. "Jacques was lying on the grass at the side of the road. It's a cruising spot, you know, even though they have it posted. I thought a car hit him."

"I'm so sorry." As Dan lifted his hands to his face, Sari impulsively put her arms around him. "Don't say any more unless you want to."

"We took his body to the vet and he said Jacques was killed by a blow to the base of his skull. It was no accident, Sari." They moved aside as a man with stringy hair joined his partner and began loading cartons in the van. "I told John I'll never be able to walk in that park again."

"Do you have any idea who did it?"

"He was such a friendly dope, always running up to strangers. He must've pissed someone off..."

"So now you're leaving."

Dan tried to smile. "I've wanted to go back to South Carolina practically since we came to Widmark. We never lived anywhere for more than five years and it was my turn to pick the city. I didn't want it to happen like this."

"I'm really going to miss you."

"We'll send the address as soon as we move in." The blue eyes became shrewd. "But something tells me it won't be long before you pick up stakes, Miss...*Siegel.*"

"You've been reading my mail!"

"Just what—"

"—doesn't fit in the box."

"Your maiden name, I assume?" He nodded for her. "John owes me a C-note. When I saw the change I said to him 'Hallelujah! She's finally over the bastard, whoever he was.' But that wasn't the only clue."

"Oh?"

"You've lost that hunted look. You're peppier, you've overslept a couple of times lately, and the circles under your eyes have shrunk. If I didn't know better I'd think you were getting laid."

"You do know better."

"I told John the other night, 'You watch. She'll be moving on.' Too bad I won't be around to collect on that one."

"Where will I be going?"

He shrugged. "All I know is, it won't be because you're running from someplace else. The Belvedere is a refuge, not a haven."

—

From her French doors Sari watched the moving van drive away. For the first time since she'd moved in five years earlier, her apartment felt cramped, and she threw open the windows to let in air. It was Indian summer, and the balmy days and nippy nights only added to her restlessness. She hadn't heard from Ray since he'd called her office but now it was too late to bother him at home. She showered and put on a nightgown, then settled on her living room couch to watch the stars emerge.

Dan was wrong, she wasn't ready to leave, but nothing had been the same since her trip to Walker County. She couldn't stop thinking about Peggy, but now she was no longer just Tim's mother. When Sari closed her eyes, she saw flashes of a girl growing up in Leeper, a town no longer on the map. Was that flat horizon what had made Peggy trust a man who betrayed her when she became a burden? Had she reconciled to her son's marriage because at the very end she'd remembered how it felt to yearn for something more?

Sari had been so sure she knew the answers, and now nothing made sense. For Tim's sake, she'd denied everything she knew about the day his mother was murdered; she'd pretended to believe in a random act of violence by the faceless owner of a wood-paneled pickup truck. Now Ray said the driver wasn't a stranger at all, but a boyfriend of Laura's—maybe even the man she'd seen in the Laundromat. Warren had let Tim believe the red herring and Laura had convinced him their marriage stood no chance...

Switching on the lamp, Sari fetched the phone book. Wait till morning, she told herself, it's past ten... But she couldn't. She had to know why.

The phone rang four times before a sleepy voice answered.

"Kay? It's Sari." A low gasp. "Sari Siegel."

"Bud-"

"Don't call your husband. This is between you and me." Hearing her own ragged breaths, Sari summoned a courage she wasn't sure she felt. "Your choice, Kay. Talk now or I'll be on your doorstep tomorrow."

"It's nothing, dear!" Kay sang out in response to a grunt. "Just Martha. I'll take it in the other room and be off right away..."

Sari listened for the hollow rush of another extension. When she heard a masculine mutter, "Can't you ladies talk tomorrow, for Pete's sake?" she waited for an irate click before continuing.

"I have to know what happened that morning."

"Didn't Laura tell you?" Kay replied.

Tell Sari what?

"I know all about the pickup truck," she bluffed.

"Peggy knew why he was there."

"Who?"

"Gary Ames. Laura met him in high school, when he came to install sliding glass doors for their patio. He couldn't stop sniffing around, just like the rest."

"Maybe they loved each other."

"He was married." But Sari knew it must be more than that. "And Laura was easy. No man was safe around her."

"But she was twenty-one when Peggy died, she wasn't even living at home...."

All of a sudden Kay's resistance crumbled.

"Don't you know what shame is? It destroyed our mother and it was happening all over again."

She still wasn't getting it; there had to be something else.

"What did Warren think?"

"Don't you see?" Kay was sobbing now. "He started while Peggy was sick..."

Quiet time. Closed doors, whispers. Warren saying the toughest part of raising kids is having to let them go. Tim pretending he didn't see or hear...

Were they all in on it?

"Did Tim know about the pickup truck?" Sari asked.

"Tim knew everything."

Chapter Thirty-Seven

A t seven the following morning Sari set off in the Mustang east on Randolph Boulevard, past the tattoo parlors and used car lots. The day had dawned wet and gray, and though the haze was lifting the sun cast a pitiless light on the trash-filled strip bisecting Widmark. Motels billed the Chateaux, 7 Star, Ahwanee, and Biltmore heralded the city limit, and Chinese restaurants offering only takeout competed with drive-through package stores for customers who, even at this early hour, lined up for service. When she passed the Army Hospital and the Korean nail parlors, pawnshops and thrift stores surrounding the base in an ersatz community for generations of war brides, she feared she'd overshot her mark. Could Tim possibly be living here?

As lodgings became seedier and "Weekly Rates" signs were replaced with "*Low* Weekly Rates," trailer parks cropped up behind the Taco Bells and instead of cars the used lots advertised pickups. Burger Kings finally gave way to Dairy Queens, gun shops, and irrigated farmland, but it wasn't until Sari reached the Interstate that she knew she'd missed the address.

Sari had spent a sleepless night, alternating between compassion for and anger at Tim. When she left for her jog at five that morning she was seething. How could he have let her believe the pickup had anything to do with Peggy's murder? How dare he endorse Laura's story that their marriage could never have worked? But now she understood what their dream meant to him: the one-room cabin with no doors. Three kids sleeping together in a loft under a soaring roof with exposed beams... No matter what coming forward would have done to Warren, she should have laid her suspicions on the table and let the police sort them out. Then their marriage would have been based on truth and not fear. Then they would have had a *chance.*

By the time Sari reached the park on the final leg of her run, she knew she had to see Tim. As she dressed she considered calling Ray but remembered the fatigue underlying his excitement when he called from the airport. Seven in the morning the day after a strenuous trip was too early, period. And this was personal. Digging into the carton of Ray's files he'd lent her back in July, she found the scrap of paper with Tim's address. She'd been annoyed when she first came across it, wondered if Ray was holding out on her, but now she was grateful for his doggedness.

Just before the Interstate Sari made a right turn and doubled back. A mile and a half west of the highway she caught sight of the mint-green balconies of the Crestview Apartments, a sprawling two-story structure whose sign still bore the outline of Capri Courts.

Sari parked the Mustang next to a hatchback Accord with a bashed-in fender and red and gray primer paint. One of these days I'll get rid of it, she thought, but an odd loyalty to her car tugged. Never even a flat, perhaps not so remarkable considering Tim's fanatical maintenance schedule and how few miles she'd put on it since the divorce, but that wasn't the real reason she kept it. All that was left of the good times... Quit stalling, she told herself, and pushed open the door that said Office. Unit 8, the man in the chicken-wire cage said with no curiosity. Mounting wooden steps, she rapped on the hollow door at the end of the balcony.

Laughter brayed from a TV set. She knocked again, louder. The noise abruptly stopped, and she found herself holding her breath. A barefoot Tim in blue jeans and a paint-stained T-shirt opened the door.

"Sari!" His eyes widened, but the surprise seemed overdone. Had he spoken to Laura or Kay?

"Can I come in?"

The flames in his hair had gone out and his eyes were duller than she remembered, but maybe she'd imagined their glow. And he seemed thinner, his features had coarsened like his father's. Could five years account for such a change? He reached for her hand, but she drew back and he moved aside so she could step past him into the living room.

Clothing and shoes were scattered across the worn carpet, and a plate of half-eaten food sat on a coffee table. Even at this hour the place smelled of fried hamburger. Sensing her reaction, Tim shrugged at the mess. But Sari was transfixed by what she saw on the stucco walls.

From massive canvases wrathful faces stared back, a hostile gallery of androgynous subjects silenced in midsentence. The oil portraits were distressingly lifelike, meticulous compilations of subtle flaws of feature and complexion, jaded eyes and scornful lips poised to devour the viewer. Sari turned to the landscapes. Bleak broad plains in shades of umber and rust, unfamiliar mountains a brooding backdrop. She stepped closer to examine the only pastel. Smaller than the others, bold color and energetic sweeps conveyed a passion the oils lacked. A girl was running from a stand of pines under a cobalt sky from which the stars were beginning to fade into a clearing knee-deep with snow. The girl's face was a blur, but her head was angled so Sari could see a scarf covering her eyes. She was barefoot…

"I wasn't expecting company."

She turned. "How have you been?"

"Okay." He gestured at the portraits. "I sold a couple of paintings in New York, and when the money ran out I came home."

"The last time we talked—"

"—you said you didn't want to see me. What changed your mind?"

"Mind if I sit?"

Tim cleared a spot for her on the couch and pulled up a folding chair.

"You were right," she told him, "we have to talk."

His lips were smiling, but there was a tightness around his eyes.

"About what?"

"That day. Our marriage. It was over so fast we never even said good-bye. I don't blame you for leaving, Tim, I—"

"You should. I blamed you for things you had nothing to do with."

"I want to talk about that."

"I've been doing a lot of thinking." He reached for her hand and held it in his familiar way, with his thumb stroking her palm. As he leaned forward, Sari smelled a musky sweetness that brought her back to their first dinner at Chico's. Suddenly she wanted to touch the tender spot beneath his left jaw. "I've never stopped loving you, Sari. Leaving was a mistake..."

She closed her eyes and saw Tim as he was that first day at the rink, gliding effortlessly across the ice. There the two of them were, arm in arm and laughing as they ran up the steps to the flat on Locust the day they moved in, already planning a family of their own. Three kids, a cabin in Garnet Hill. Them against the world...Then it was gone and they were in Room 8 of the Crestview Apartments, before a gallery of jeering strangers.

She pulled her hand from his. "This isn't why I came."

Tim leaned back and folded his arms across his chest. "It's your dime."

"I've been in touch with Kay." Behind the mask his eyes burned. "I know who drove the pickup truck, that it had nothing to do with what happened that day. I know everything." Why had she come when she still couldn't say the word *murder*, much less what Warren had done to Laura so many years before?

"If you know it all, why are you here?"

"Because no matter what happened, *we* could have made it!" She had to reach him, even if it meant going back to that day. "Your mother was planning to come to our wedding. She was even making her own dress. Laura told you later, didn't she? And the seminar ..."

Tim's grin widened and Sari's anger surged.

"You knew your father wouldn't have missed it," she continued. That terrible night when she ran out of their apartment, determined to leave

Tim, and the laughing-eyed portrait he gave her when she returned…

He shrugged.

"You gave me that drawing so I'd keep my mouth shut."

"If that's what you want to believe."

"Did you lie for him?"

His eyes flickered. "I wasn't sure what time Dad arrived at the rec center. When I testified before the grand jury, I gave him the benefit of the doubt. What did fifteen minutes matter? And you never denied he came to our door."

"But you had no doubts, did you? You knew he did it."

Tim rose, his chest heaving as if he were holding something terrible inside. And yet she wasn't afraid. No matter what his father had done, Tim would never harm her.

"It had nothing to do with you, Sari. I didn't use you."

"But you told me you believed him, you let me sacrifice the truth to protect him, when all along you *knew*—"

"Anything I did was to protect my family." He was remorseless. "If I had to I'd do it again."

He stepped back and Sari rose. How could this stranger have been her husband?

"What family was that? Your mother didn't deserve to die."

—

Skidding on gravel, Sari backed out of the parking lot and turned west on Randolph. She had to talk to Ray. Now she knew Warren killed Peggy and Tim had covered for him. And she knew, too, the awful secret at his family's core. But she wanted to believe him when he said he'd never used her, that he'd given his father the benefit of the doubt. Wouldn't she have done the same?

When she saw the sign for the Interstate she slowed. The highway was unfamiliar, but it obviously went south and with luck she could be in Gillman in thirty minutes. She'd stop for a box of doughnuts and the three of them would put their heads together over a pot of Marion's coffee and figure this whole thing out. Without another thought, she took the entrance ramp.

Zipping past the orange-and-white-striped cans that channeled the sparse southbound traffic, Sari immediately regretted her impulsiveness. Every local highway was in a state of repair and this stretch of the Interstate was no exception. Kicking herself for not having consulted a map, she studied the exit signs to reassure herself she was indeed traveling in the right direction. Now the Mustang was bucking, but the sooner she got to Gillman...

At sixty miles an hour Sari hit the chewed-up pavement just past Mohawk. Too late a sign warned of road repairs, and scraped asphalt revealed an interminable stretch of heavy-gauge wire mesh. With a violent thump she stomped on the brake as the Mustang left the blacktop. The car lurched to the right and she fought for control. Telling herself not to panic, she took her foot off the accelerator and bumped another hundred yards before she could steer to a stop on the shoulder.

With trembling fingers she switched off the ignition. As trucks whizzed past, she examined her options. Maybe it was the shocks, whatever those were, or the struts. Or it could be as simple as a flat; something had to give after all those years of loyal service. For the first time she regretted not joining the triple A. Once she reached Gillman, Ray would have the last laugh.

Sari got out of her car and walked around the hood. The right front tire was completely flat. It must have blown when she hit the rutted surface, or maybe she'd picked up a nail on the boulevard. She smiled in relief. This she could handle, AAA or not. The last time she'd been in Gillman Ray had demonstrated how to use a tire iron and a jack, a paternalistic exercise she'd endured more out of affection than interest. And she knew Tim kept a spare because she'd seen it in the trunk. Reaching through the driver's window for the keys, Sari circled to the rear of the car.

First she lifted out the spare, bouncing it once as she'd seen a mechanic do years before. Seemed springy enough. There was the tire iron just where Ray told her it should be. Lug nuts, think lug nuts. A truck slammed by without slowing. She certainly wasn't going to count on a good Samaritan coming along… But the jack was nowhere to be found. In frustration she banged down the lid. Now she would have to wait for help.

As she sat behind the wheel and tried to remember where the button was for the emergency flashers, something came to her. When they were in Walker County, hadn't Ray shown her a special place for tools? The Chrysler had one, and maybe the Mustang did too. She grabbed her keys again and circled to the rear. Opening the trunk, she removed the rubber mat from the plywood flooring that concealed a snug well. Almost giddy with relief, she reached in. As she lifted out the jack, her fingers brushed against something solid. She set the jack on the ground and thrust her hand back in.

The foot-and-a-half-long package was bound in clear plastic and duct tape. Hefting it in one hand, Sari peered through the sheath. Whatever was inside was heavy and weighted at one end, and it was wrapped in what appeared to be cloth. As she looked more closely, she made out the wavy outline of green flowers on a red background… And suddenly she knew just what it was. She gasped and dropped the parcel in the trunk. There it sat, its contents mocking her from the swathing of plastic and tape.

Take it to Kevin, she thought, her heart pounding, he'll know what to do. He would finish the job she and Ray should have done a decade ago. Then Tim's face rose before her, pleading with her not to destroy what he'd sacrificed everything to protect. She reached for the tire iron and slowly circled the Mustang. At the left headlight, she came to a halt.

Eighteen-wheelers flying past, Sari swung once and the light shattered with a rewarding crunch. It was more than letting her believe in something he suspected was a lie… Another blow and sharp pellets stung her thigh through the thin cotton of her sweats. Tim's deception went far beyond that.

She raised the iron over her head and brought it down, two-fisted, on the windshield. The glass bowed under the first blow; the second left the windshield in smithereens. He'd hidden the weapon Warren used to kill Peggy; he'd known damn well his father committed the crime!

Breathing harder, Sari crossed to the shoulder. Putting her hip into it, she swung the tool like a golf club, and the right headlamp shattered.

She'd been riding around for years with that shirt and hammer in her trunk.

Sari circled the Mustang again, oblivious to slowing traffic as drivers gawked at the wild-haired woman on the rampage. With a tinkle the taillights collapsed, and she moved to the side windows. Pop, pop, *thwack*. *At* the front of the car now, she stared down at the bucking bronco on the grille.

Freedom.

The next blow traveled all the way up her arm to her neck, and she knew she'd feel it for a week. The second hit that horse dead on, leaving it a mangled metal scrap. The third—

"Lady, what the hell are you doing?"

The officer stood to one side, just out of reach, and as Sari turned she saw the white sedan marked State Patrol parked on the shoulder just behind the Mustang. Its red lights were flashing. Another officer in tan trousers and a trooper hat slammed his door and headed her way.

"I—had a flat tire."

"A *flat!*" The first patrolman looked at his partner, not knowing whether to arrest her or laugh. "Jeez, if that's what you do for a flat, what happens when the transmission blows?"

"I don't give a shit what happens to this car."

"You're going to have to take a sobriety test, miss. But first I want you to hand me that tire iron. Slowly, please ..."

As she gave it to him her arms were trembling.

"How much have you had to drink?" the second one asked.

But now the laughter was exploding from Sari's chest, and she began to shake uncontrollably.

"I'll call a tow truck," the first officer said. With the weapon safely in custody, he moved closer. "But whatever that Mustang did, it's no way to treat an antique."

"I don't care what you do with the damn thing," she cried. "I just want what's in the trunk!"

He looked at his partner.

"Lady, if you promise not to hit it again, we'll take it off your hands."

Chapter Thirty-Eight

Four days later Ray tossed his canvas overnight bag in the trunk of the New Yorker and gently closed the lid.

Two changes of underwear, his windbreaker, and a heavy wool shirt lay at the bottom of the bag along with his nylon shaving kit. He'd be traveling through the high country and nights could be cold this time of year. He certainly wasn't about to take the desert for granted.

Standing in the driveway with his arm around Marion's waist, he savored the last moments before hitting the road. Their lawn was covered with leaves, and the asters and chrysanthemums lining the front walk were putting out one last burst of color, plum and rust overshadowed by an impossibly brilliant gold. Indian summer was drawing to a close.

"Are you sure you don't want me to come?" Marion drew her cardigan tighter across her chest as a breeze cut through the thin wool. "I'd feel better if Sari was with you..."

"I'm going to do what I have to, Marion." He squared his shoulders to still his momentary doubt. He hadn't even told Sari or Kevin his plan. "No more, no less."

"And I'm going to sit here and worry until you come home. You'll call every night, won't you, Ray?"

"Every night." He stooped to kiss his wife's cheek and then enveloped her fragile bones in a firm embrace, carefully because her arthritis was getting worse. Inhaling her fragrance, Ivory soap and the clean scent of violets, he whispered "I love you" too softly for her to hear.

Climbing behind the wheel, Ray ran his fingers over the supple leather of his seat. He'd spent the previous afternoon waxing and buffing the New Yorker, and her burgundy metallic finish shone as fine as the day she rolled off the assembly line twenty-two years before. He'd repainted her three times but remained faithful to her original color. Buoyed by the confidence the Chrysler always instilled, he reached for the ignition.

"Are you sure that car's going to make it?"

He looked up at his wife with a flash of annoyance. "She's in better shape than you or me, Marion." They continued the litany, old phrases coming unbidden to their lips.

"That Chrysler's going to be the death of you, Ray Burt…"

"I only hope I have the privilege of being carried out of her feetfirst, my dear." He pulled the door shut and smiled up at her. "See you Friday night." With a jaunty wave he backed out of his driveway and set off for Tucson.

The November morning was crisp and clear, the sky a scoured blue. But as Ray drove south he was nagged by the pen and ink portrait in Laura's hallway. It reminded him of something else, and he was unable to place it. That was the trouble with getting old. Not the aching joints or difficulty hearing, or all the times you had to get up in the middle of the night and pee, but the inability to recall simple things like where you'd seen a drawing like that before. Shaking his head, he focused on the trip ahead.

If he made the Springs by eleven he'd be in Jemez in time for a late lunch. After that Pawnee and El Morro Pass, hook up with the Interstate and then down to Albuquerque by nightfall. A long day of driving, but he wanted to get to Tucson as fast as he could. He should have raked the yard before he left, was already thinking about the chores awaiting him when he returned… Where had he seen that goddamned picture?

Suddenly he regretted not having a dog. Marion had wanted one for years, but he always said it was too much work. She'd stopped asking and now Ray wished he'd listened because she shouldn't have to be alone, not at her age. And this trip had really upset her. Their argument two nights before had been a corker.

"You're going *where?*" she'd asked.

"Tucson."

"I heard you the first time. I want to know what on earth for?"

"I have to see him face-to-face." Ray ran his finger down the Interstate on the New Mexico map in his Rand-McNally.

"Have you lost your mind?"

"I have to do it, Marion." She knew all about the Estwing and the shirt Sari had found, both now being tested by the SBI lab. But what if the blood wasn't Peggy's? Or if Warren somehow tried to pin the crime on Tim? Tim's presence at the rec center that morning was documented, but Ray wouldn't put anything past Warren. No, without a confession they'd never have enough to make first degree murder stick. "You want to put this behind us, don't you? It's the last piece, all that's left to do."

"Why?"

"Warren has to pay for what he did. I want to look him in the eye after all these years and—"

"I forbid it!"

Ray looked up from the atlas in surprise. "You forbid it?"

"I've stood by for ten years while you indulged yourself with the Scotts, and—"

"*Indulged* myself?"

"I encouraged you, I'll be the first to admit it, because Sari's a lovely girl and I know how much you think of Kevin Day. But you're not a young man anymore, Ray. Why are the Scotts so much more important than your own family?"

"My own family?"

"You've paid more attention to Peggy and her children than you ever have to me. Why do strangers come first?"

"They're not strangers—"

"That's exactly what I mean, they're more real to you than I am."

He pulled the tight bundle of anger close. "You're being ridiculous."

"I'll tell you what's ridiculous, a sixty-eight-year-old man who's had a coronary driving to Tucson to confront a suspect in a murder that happened a decade ago. *That's* ridiculous."

"Honey, I'll make you a promise. After this, it's over. No more Scotts, I swear." And if he could make Warren confess, that truly would be the end. Ray grabbed Marion's chin, forcing her to meet his eyes. "I can't let him go to his grave thinking he got away with butchering his wife. If I do that, my life has meant nothing."

As he drove east on Grand Avenue, Ray's thoughts returned to the portrait. It wasn't the composition, he decided, but the style. India ink, so accurate it was almost like a photograph... As he was about to turn onto the entrance ramp it came to him. He hung a quick right, made an illegal turn at a gas station, and headed back to Gillman. Ten minutes later he pulled up to the Hallett County Justice Center and, praying he wouldn't run into Lew Devine, parked in the visitors lot and entered by the side door.

"Imelda!" he cried as if the zaftig gal with the bouffant were a long-lost buddy instead of the most important woman in the juvenile division, if not the entire Sheriff's Department. She'd been there almost as long as Ray, and no one dared call her a secretary.

"Well, if it isn't Ray Burt. I would've thought you and Marion would be in your Winnebago by now, up in Lake Louise."

"On my pension we're lucky to be eating franks and beans." They laughed together easily, and he felt a wave of nostalgia for the old days when they were in Investigations. He tried to remember whose toes Mel had stepped on to earn her demotion to juvie but quickly gave up. It was all the same, only the names changed... He smiled winsomely. "Just passing by, thought I'd stop in."

"Marion kick you out?"

He tried to look sheepish. "You know how it is, she's set in her ways, and sometimes I get under her feet. Thought I'd come by, see a few familiar faces."

"Anyone in particular?" Imelda was nobody's fool.

"Matter of fact, I was wondering if I could look at a file."

"Not the Scott case, is it?"

"No, no. Something's been on my mind, you know how that is. I think it may be in the closed files."

"You're retired, Ray, you don't have to worry about those things anymore."

"That's exactly why I want to look, so I can quit worrying. They still in the back office?"

Imelda tossed him a ring of keys. "Gilardi's out and Babbitt's never around. You've got the place to yourself, but don't make me regret this…"

He kissed her plump cheek. "Be in and out before you know it."

Her fingers fluttered over her hair, and she winked lewdly. "That's not what Marion says."

With a blush and a bounce to his step, Ray strode down the hall to the room where the inactive case files were stored. Surveying the wall of cabinets, he thought of all the hours he'd spent fighting the humiliation of his transfer and of the endless boredom of chasing shoplifters and kids on joyrides, but nostalgia swiftly yielded to the task ahead, and he tried to decide where to begin. If he was right, what he was looking for would be at least fifteen years old.

Although they'd begun converting adult files to microfiche just before Ray retired, no one had touched the juvenile cases. Those were still arranged by numbers approximating chronological order. Starting with the ones from 1970, he carted them by the armload to the wooden table in the center of the floor and began thumbing through them. The slimmer the file, the skimpier the documentation underlying the complaint and the less effort expended by the juvenile division in pursuing it. No wonder so many kids slipped through the cracks until they were mature criminals…

As he opened each folder he could tell at a glance it wasn't what he was looking for, but every time he recognized a case he was heartened. He wasn't crazy, it was there somewhere. He looked at his watch, dreading the prospect of another dead end and impatient to be on the road.

On his third trip to the drawers Ray spotted a sheet of heavy white paper protruding from the edge of a file. When he saw the case was from 1973, he skipped over the others and pulled it out. The folder contained a one-page memo from the principal of Gillman Elementary School, a three-page report from the part-time psychologist employed by the school district, a series of barely legible notes, and a pen-and-ink drawing of a woman reclining on a bed. He spread the contents across the table.

The drawing was unsigned and torn from a ten-by-fourteen-inch sketch pad. At first glance it was arresting both for its remarkable realism and the sophistication of the artist's technique. A study in detail. The woman was lying gracefully with her head on a pillow and a cloth over her eyes. She looked peaceful, as if she were resting and her dreams were not unpleasant. Her nude body was perfectly proportioned and accurate to the smallest detail, with two exceptions. Her left breast had been severed and there was a gaping wound where her genitalia should have been.

Ray reached for the principal's memo. The portrait had been found by a Mrs. Grady, the art teacher at Gillman Elementary, in the sketch pad of a sixth-grade pupil. She had instructed her students to draw pictures of their mothers for Mother's Day, and the artist had apparently drawn an extremely skillful but otherwise normal picture of his mother and turned it in for the assignment. Because he was the most talented child Mrs. Grady had ever taught, when he left his sketchbook behind after class that day she could not resist the temptation to peek.

Immediately alarmed at the potential implications of the drawing, she brought it to the principal, who called the boy's parents in for a conference. When the parents arrived, they agreed to have their son evaluated by the school board shrink before the end of the year. The boy never showed up for his appointment and, when the shrink was closing out his files in June, he attempted to contact the family. Unable to do so, he informed the principal, who asked him to prepare a report detailing the psychological significance of the drawing. The principal, apparently a fellow traveler of Taylor Philips, referred the matter to the Sheriff's Department to absolve himself and the school board of further responsibility. Disgusted by this bureaucratic passing of the buck, Ray scanned the psychologist's report.

The gist seemed to be that the artist, a twelve-year-old boy referred to simply as "the subject," was one sick pup who hated his mom. With no opportunity to interview him and based solely on the psychologist's training, twenty-six years of experience in the field, and the drawing itself, the doctor had analyzed the figure in the mutilated portrait. The cloth over the eyes, which he called a blindfold, implied the mother was both vulnerable and inattentive to what was going on in her family, perhaps intentionally so. The gaping hole signified her inability to produce anything of value, reflecting abdication of her role as the woman in the family and the artist's powerful sense of personal worthlessness. The severed breast suggested she was unable to nurture her children, perhaps as a result of illness, and the artist's consequent hostility toward her.

The meticulousness and technical proficiency of the drawing and the length of time it must have taken to complete demonstrated the highly developed nature of the boy's fantasy and the potency of his rage, the psychologist had concluded. He added, almost as an afterthought, that the blindfold might also symbolize the boy's unwillingness to be seen, or the willful blindness of the women in her son's life to his needs and a larger hostility toward members of the opposite sex. No doubt secure in the knowledge that his report would render this child someone else's problem, he recommended immediate follow-up by law enforcement authorities. But the investigating officer's scrawled notes testified to his own cursory attempts and to the ultimate discovery that the family phone had been disconnected when they'd moved to Indiana.

With the exception of Mrs. Grady, all names in the file had been crossed out, including those of the principal and the psychologist. Holding the report up to the light, Ray tried to read beneath the crude strokes that covered the child's name. Each word had one syllable that began and ended with a consonant. Toward the bottom of the page the felt tip had started to run dry, and he made out the letters

"*Stt*".

With trembling hands he returned the empty folder to the cabinet. He pressed the sketch and reports to his chest and zipped his windbreaker over them. One arm around his waist to secure his prize, he grabbed Imelda's keys and locked the door behind him.

"Find what you were looking for?" she asked.

"Nope. Just my imagination."

"Well, don't be so hard on yourself, Ray. You were quite a detective…"

… *in your day,* he finished silently. "Thanks for the keys, Mel," he murmured.

"Don't be such a stranger," she called after him.

He had to find a phone and call Sari.

Chapter Thirty-Nine

Sari had been in the glass conference room off the forty-ninth-floor lobby since six that morning, preparing for a marathon closing on a debt restructuring for Continental Energy Company and its dozen wholly owned subsidiaries. Her secretary and three paralegals were with her, and junior associates had been running in and out with certificates to review and last-minute revisions to the mountain of documents to be signed that day. The deal had been in the works for three months. Hers from start to finish, but now it took every ounce of willpower to focus. Since Ray's trip to New York the week before, her work seemed like so much paper and ink.

"There's a call for you."

She glanced up to see the receptionist at her shoulder.

"A client?"

"Kevin Day. I can tell him to call back."

"No, I'll take it outside."

Sari followed the girl to the booth across the lobby and closed the door.

"Am I disturbing you?" he asked. "You're probably knee-deep in—"

"Not at all." She was surprised at how glad she was to hear his voice.

"Are the results back?"

"You were smart to leave that package intact. The shirt and hammer both tested positive for blood. They're being typed to confirm it's Peggy's."

She shivered. "Great! What about fingerprints?"

Kevin hesitated. "None yet, he was either wearing gloves or wiped everything clean. But I'm calling because I found something interesting on the plastic. Got a second?"

"Sure."

"There was a fragment of what appears to be a price tag on an interior fold of the sheeting, with the letters "I-D-E.' Sound familiar?"

"Not offhand."

"Well, just calling to check." He paused. "By the way, are you doing anything tonight?"

"Aside from recovering from what will probably be a ten-hour closing?"

"I knew I shouldn't have called you at work…"

"Don't be ridiculous. I'd rather talk to you than—" She stopped. What was she saying?

"—bite to eat? I could pick you up whenever you're through."

"Who knows when that will be? I'd better take a rain check."

"Sure." But Sari heard the disappointment in his voice. "Some other time."

"I'll call if I have any ideas about "I-D-E.'"

"Sure."

An associate handed Sari another stack of documents, but her thoughts kept returning to Warren. An hour and a half of his time that day, between 11:30 and the beginning of Tim's one o'clock practice, had never really been accounted for. Where had he been?

Skimming a certificate of representations and warranties, she tried to recall every moment of that Saturday. Ray had said Warren told them he'd gone to the Walgreen's at Gillman Mall for a pair of clip-on sunglasses and a card for their wedding present, but there was no evidence of that. And how long would it have taken him anyway? It was only forty-five minutes to Stanley, depending on traffic, which left half an hour. He'd claimed he arrived early and stopped at their apartment, but she'd doubted that from the moment he insisted he waited for a matter of minutes. If he wasn't there, where else might he have gone?

I-D-E, I-D-E...

As she handed the certificate back to the associate with a couple of corrections, Sari tried to remember their conversation. At the rec center they'd talked about Dale Carnegie and the rehearsal dinner. Nothing there. Now they were in the Olds, driving up the Hill to the apartment with Tim. She stepped on the yardstick, bled all over the backseat, and felt like an idiot, then babbled her head off about cleaning the mess... The paralegal was looking at her strangely: Sari realized she'd been staring at one page without reading it. Smiling stiffly, she rose from the table and walked to the wall of glass. As she gazed north at the highway to Stanley, she suddenly had it.

McBride. The yardstick said *McBride.*

Warren must have stopped at that hardware store on his way to the rec center. What if they could prove he bought the plastic and tape there, *after* he killed his wife? She had to call Kevin. Whirling from the window, she reached for the phone.

"Miss Siegel?"

She looked up. The conference room was filled with representatives of her client and its subsidiaries and half a dozen attorneys from various banks. With an apologetic smile she mumbled she would be right back and fled to the phone booth in the lobby.

"Kevin?" She couldn't seem to catch her breath. "I think I know where he went."

"Who?"

"Warren Scott. That morning. What if we could prove he bought the plastic and tape in Stanley *after* he killed Peggy?"

"What are you, a magician?"

"The yardstick in his Olds came from McBride's. That's the—"

"—biggest hardware store in the state. 'If we don't carry it, no one does.' But even if the plastic came from there, he could have bought it anytime, and that yardstick could've been sitting in his car since God knows when."

"Warren said it was a spring promotion, they were just starting to give them away. And when else would he have come to Stanley? Widmark's full of hardware stores."

"It's a real long shot, Sari."

She hated that tone of voice; it sounded like her mother.

"But what if we could prove he was there that day and bought the plastic?"

"How?"

"A receipt."

"It's been ten years, Sari, stores never keep them that long. And if Warren paid cash—"

"He wouldn't. He never carried cash, he always used credit. An accountant, remember? Why put money down when you can pay thirty days later and take advantage of the float?"

"You're talking about a needle in a haystack…"

Suddenly she was furious. "And what exactly do you have?"

"A hammer and shirt covered with blood—"

"—which you haven't identified and maybe never will. No fingerprints—"

"—yet, but we're not finished."

"If Warren wore gloves when he pulled clocks out of the wall, do you really think he'd be so stupid as to wrap the weapon in plastic with his bare hands? We're back to where the wrapping came from. And I say it was McBride's."

"I can't subpoena Warren's credit card records. You're a lawyer, you know that."

"But we can go through the receipts." She turned and saw her secretary outside the booth. "It's only one day's worth."

"If they still have them. And if they're willing to cooperate. But it would be a tremendous amount of work, and I don't see—"

"It's the only way we can prove intent."

"Intent?"

"Even if we have him cold with the forensic evidence, Warren will argue manslaughter. Heat of passion, no malice. He'll be out in five years or less. If we want to nail him for first-degree murder, we'll have to prove he took deliberate steps, after the moment of passion was past, to conceal his crime." There was a tapping on the glass, but Sari turned to face the wall. "The way it stands now, we don't even know he's the one who wrapped the weapon and shirt and stashed them in Tim's trunk!"

"You have a point, but we'd have to sort through thousands of—"

"If you can get us access to McBride's records, I'll do it with you tonight."

"I thought you were busy."

"After work." She paused. "I'm going to do this, Kevin, with or without you. But I'd rather we do it together."

Chapter Forty

On his way out of the Sheriff's Department, Ray stopped at the first pay phone he found. Tim was dangerous and Sari had to be warned. The mistake they'd made for the past ten years was assuming he'd felt guilty for not saving his mother, but now they knew he'd hidden the hammer and shirt. And what if the shrink was right and he hated Peggy? Maybe there was more than one secret Tim was trying to protect.

"—sorry, Mr. Burt," the officious voice was saying, "but Ms. Siegel is in an all-day closing. She can't take any calls."

Not knowing whether to be angry or relieved, Ray bit back his retort. Spenser & Trowbridge was a glass fortress guarded by men with watch fobs and three-piece suits and pimply boys wheeling mail carts, and as long as Sari was tied up in her closing, she would be safe. The risk would come later when she was alone… Glancing at his watch, he saw it was already past ten. He would speak to her long before she left for the day, and what he'd discovered made it all the more imperative to confront Warren and wrap this case up. Unwilling to delay his departure a moment longer, he climbed back in his car and set off south on the Interstate.

Traffic on the four-lane blacktop was lighter the farther he was from

Widmark, and Ray pushed the New Yorker past the speed limit to make up for lost time. Curtis Peak, already covered with snow, jutted dead ahead over the black crags of the Hobart Range. Pine-covered buttes gave way to mesas stained burnt orange, mustard, and chartreuse by scrub oak and buck brush, and leaves glistened like rain. But Ray was oblivious to their glory. At Bent City he headed toward the Conejos Peaks. It was past two in the afternoon when he reached Jemez, gassed the New Yorker, and coasted down Bishop Avenue to Carmine's.

The waitress was a swaggering hundred-and-seventy-pounder, tired and tough and not yet thirty. When she took Ray's order for iced tea and a soapapilla burger and brought him a Pepsi instead, her crooked teeth dared him to complain. He looked for the pay phone and found it at the end of the corridor to the rest rooms. But a man with more hair on his face than his head was already using it.

As Ray waited for his food an old man in a satin baseball jacket hobbled in, hoisted himself onto the next stool and ordered an enchilada smothered with green chile. When the waitress returned with the man's coffee Ray said, "Nice town."

She shrugged her meaty shoulders. "County seat."

"How come they call it Huerfano County?" Ray looked over his shoulder again, but the phone was still busy. Relax, he told himself, she's in an all-day closing… He could call Kevin, he knew that, but he wanted to handle this on his own. He would complete the job he'd started years earlier, without any help from the SBI.

"Spanish for 'orphan.' " Untying the dishrag from her waist, she strode to the kitchen window and returned with two steaming plates. The fried bread was crisp on the outside but chewy in the center, and at the first bite oil ran down Ray's chin. Chile and Cumin pierced his tongue, and the chopped beef, cheese, lettuce, and beans blended together in a delicious mess that took him straight back to North Junction. Wiping his fingers on a napkin from the dispenser on the counter, he tried again.

"Where'd it get that name?"

"I don't know." Her biceps bulged as she folded her arms across her chest and retreated to the far end of the counter. Now a chunky gal was tying up the phone, but from the way her little boy was squirming in her grasp, Ray knew she wouldn't be long. The man in the baseball jacket forked a mouthful of enchilada and swirled it in chile before lifting it to his chin. Ray waited until he swallowed before asking again.

"Why's it called Huerfano anyway?"

"Like she says, it means 'orphan.' Lost one." The trembling fork dipped back to his plate and rose again, dribbling chile onto satin. "All orphans sooner or later. But them Spaniards kidnapped Indians, put 'em to work in the gold mines over to the Conejos Peaks. When I was a kid they found bones in chains in the mine shafts."

"What's the county south of here?"

The man exchanged a glance with the waitress, who stalked off to the kitchen.

"Las Animas. That means 'spirits.' See what I mean?" He cackled, all enchilada and gums.

Ray left two bucks on the counter and grabbed the phone before anyone else could use it. This time he waited almost five minutes before he was connected with Sari's secretary.

"It's really urgent," he said.

"I'm sorry, Miss Siegel can't be disturbed."

"Would you tell her it's Ray Burt?"

"She's in a room with two dozen people, up to her elbows in paper. All I can do is make sure she gets the message when she surfaces for air."

"Tell her to stay with friends tonight, it may be a matter of life and death." Hearing the skepticism in the secretary's sigh, Ray forced himself to slow down. "I don't care what it takes, you've got to get that message to her."

"I will, Mr. Burt," she promised in the tone of a woman long experienced in dealing with people who thought their problems took priority over everything else. Ray knew he would have to try again later.

—

He continued south, trying to focus on the scenery and not his concern for Sari, but the shrink's words kept running through his head. "Larger hostility toward members of the opposite sex" at the age of *twelve*? Tim had never hurt Sari, but if he was willing to hide the hammer that killed his mother and a shirt stained with her blood in the trunk of his Mustang and drive around with them for years, what would he do if he learned they were gone? All-day closing, Ray reminded himself; she'd be fine. He breathed deeply and tried to think about the gomer with the enchilada at Carmine's. Orphans and spirits. If that don't beat all...

South of Jemez, Indian names began to alternate with the Spanish. Here the mountains were flat-topped and black, and the desolate terrain was enlivened only by splotches of scrub oak. No farms huddled behind tree lines; all was exposed to the elements. The New Yorker glided down the road, drawing Ray deeper into the afternoon shadows. A long way from Walker County and even farther from North Junction.

He was still making good time, should be up and down El Morro Pass in another hour, but for the first time he let himself feel fatigued at what lay ahead. A long haul to Albuquerque. He'd think about the next leg, the two hundred some odd miles to Hatch and even more desolate stretch across western New Mexico to Lordsburg, after a good night's sleep.... Suddenly he was tempted to turn around.

He should have driven to Sari's office as soon as he discovered the drawing, but he could still be back in Gillman by nightfall. He could bring her home with him, put this trip off until they could arrange adequate protection for her, and wouldn't Marion be glad? But even as he ran through the options, Ray knew it was too late. He could no more have reversed his course than he could change any of the things that had set him on this path. It was fifty years too late.

Entering New Mexico at El Morro, he pushed on to Wagon Mound. There he stopped at Texaco for gas, drank a cup of Styrofoam coffee, and checked out the snacks. He compared his watch to the clock on the wall and tried to picture what you did in an all-day closing. Thirty-nine types of beef jerky, a dozen kinds of peanuts, and too soon to call again; his message would just get shuffled to the bottom of the stack. He chose a slab of jerky the size of a tongue depressor, one hundred percent all-natural beef locally smoked with chile and garlic salt. When he was a boy they ate jerked buffalo. And Marion wasn't there to tell him how unhealthy it was.

Picking through a rack of tourist brochures while he waited for the key to the washroom, Ray spotted one for a ghost town called Shakespeare. Desperados Sandy King and Russian Bill had been hanged from the timbers of the Butterfield Stage Station dining room after stealing a horse to flee town when King shot the index finger off a clerk at Smyth's Mercantile Store. Rough justice, but in those days it sure was quick. No waiting ten years to face your accuser... He pocketed the brochure. A nice souvenir for Marion, just the kind of thing she liked.

The sun was going down and it was getting cold. He opened his trunk and reached for his overnight bag. His lumberjack shirt was clear at the bottom under the nylon kit, the price of refusing to allow his wife to pack. The last thing he'd wanted was Marion poking around that bag. Stuffing his underwear back in, he closed the trunk, buttoned his wool shirt to the collar, and headed south for Albuquerque.

As he drove, he tore open the cellophane bag with his teeth and bit into the stick of meat, relishing its harsh tang. The jerky was tough and dry. The texture reminded Ray of North Junction but the first bite took him straight to the Philippines, the blood and bone of the tanneries while he was stationed there. At sixteen he'd run away like a coward. The army wasn't near as tough as life back home.

He'd told Marion he was an orphan, that both his parents died when he was small and he had aunts in North Junction, but they'd lost touch and there was no reason to return. That part was true—once he enlisted he'd never looked back—but the rest was a lie, the only lie he ever told his wife, the only really important one anyway. The truth was his mother died two years after he entered the service. The only reason he knew was that the last two allotment checks to Polly Burt had been returned to him in the Philippines in 1940 in an envelope marked "Deceased." What happened to his old man was another question. Ray never knew and never cared. Reaching for the radio, he found a country-western station to help him focus on the long road ahead.

Chapter Forty-One

It was past seven that evening when Kevin met Sari in the deserted reception area of the forty-ninth floor. He whistled at her fawn-colored suit.

"That's an awfully nice outfit." He was dressed in a pair of corduroys that were frayed at the knees, a flannel shirt and a windbreaker. "Sure you want to wear it in a storage locker that hasn't been opened in eight years?"

"I didn't have time to take the bus home and change. I don't have a car anymore, remember?"

"We can stop at your place on the way."

"You'll use any excuse .."

"Suit yourself, but don't say I didn't warn you." He looked at the messy conference room behind them. "Is that where you've been stuck all day?"

"Yes."

"Need to go back to your office and check your messages?"

Sari shook her head. "I'm out of here."

As they climbed into a 1960 Thunderbird in mint condition parked outside the building's entrance on Lincoln, she tried not to look impressed.

"I guess you do like old cars."

"Honey, this ain't old. It's a *classic.*"

They said nothing as they sped to the turnpike. When they made the turn onto the highway west, she looked over.

"You probably think what I did to Tim's Mustang was a crime."

"Not at all." He stared out the windshield. "I'm only sorry it wasn't another part of his anatomy."

"Where exactly are we going?"

"McBride's has a storage unit out on Jessup. The owner said he'd get ahold of the keys and leave them with the store manager. They're open till eight and we can pick them up on the way." Kevin's lips twitched with amusement. "He suggested we bring a Coleman."

"What's that?"

"I guess you've never been camping. It's a lantern. It's going to be pitch black inside."

"Good."

"I thought we might stop for a bite after we pick up the keys…"

"We can celebrate if and when we find what we're looking for."

When they reached the hardware store, Kevin ran inside for the keys and emerged with a battery-operated lamp, two folding chairs and a brown paper sack. Sari eyed the bag suspiciously.

"What's in there?"

"They don't sell beer, but I got the next best thing." He passed it to her: half a dozen jumbo candy bars were nestled in a pair of Ragg socks and a set of white overalls, size extra small. "You'd never forgive me for what that shed will do to your skirt. They were out of Chuckles, but before tonight's over I'm sure we both can use some Snickers."

The shed was as isolated and filthy as Kevin had warned. He politely turned his back as Sari slipped off her pumps, panty hose, and skirt and put on the overalls and heavy socks. Then they lit the lantern and looked around them. The shed was stacked floor to ceiling with cartons of all sizes and shapes and there was a strong odor of mildew. Some boxes had contained large appliances, others shipments of nails and tools, and more than a few appeared to have suffered serious water damage.

"Talk about storing your records in a shoe box," she began.

"Sure you want to do this? There's probably spiders, maybe even black widows…"

"Let's just hope those cartons are marked."

"They should be by month and year. The owner said to expect a week's worth in each box."

Kevin unfolded the chairs and moved one of them to the far corner of the shed, then stood on it with the lantern in one hand to read the inscription on the side of the carton closest to the ceiling.

"Why are you starting there?" she asked.

"You have any better ideas?"

After that she shut up and helped. It took them almost two hours to locate the boxes for May 1980, but when they did, they were grateful to see cash register and credit card slips stapled to the handwritten receipts.

"It's going to be fun deciphering these." Kevin held one up to the light. "Do you suppose "C-H-S' means cheese? I could use a pizza about now."

Sari handed him a Snickers bar. "The night is young."

The receipts had been dumped in no apparent order. As they sorted through them, she made piles for each day. He reached for a stack and began dealing them out like a hand of solitaire.

"This will take forever," he complained. "Can't we get something to eat and come back?"

"Quit whining." But her tone was affectionate, and Kevin leaned back and smiled at her in the dark. "By the way, you never told me how you knew Laura's boyfriend worked for a glass company."

"When I went back and read Lew Devine's notes, I knew we'd paid too much attention to one part of the description at the expense of the other. The lady across the street said the pickup truck had wood panels eight feet high, but she also said it was a "pretty blue.' The shade was distinctive enough to make an impression on her."

"Because she was a woman, you ruled out her being color-blind—"

"—and lopped two feet off the panels. When I realized she was describing a truck rigged to transport glass I looked in the yellow pages. Bluebell Glass's trucks are still robin's egg blue, but nowadays they're rigged with a steel frame instead of wood slats to support the panes."

"Pretty smart. Of course, that's what I'd expect from a *professional*."

"Since there was no construction going on in the neighborhood and those companies never deliver on Saturdays anyway, that meant a personal call by the owner or one of his crew. The rest was a lucky guess."

"I've already learned not to bet against you." Kevin's logic was impressive but Sari tried to keep the disappointment from her voice. The truck had been a blind alley after all, and what made Warren explode that day seemed destined to remain a mystery.

The stack for May seventeenth was rapidly towering over the others for that week. "It *would* have to be the first Saturday every do-it-yourselfer on the Front Range remembered he had a yard," Kevin grumbled. But he was sorting through the slips at a rate almost twice as fast as Sari's.

"Are you really reading those?"

"This may come as a surprise, my dear, but I've been doing this for twenty years. It's not my first storage locker."

"But some of the handwriting is awful." She passed him one slip. "What do you think this says?"

" 'H-A-M-M'… either *hammer* or *hamburger*, I'm not sure which. Can't think when I'm hungry."

She snatched it back and kept sorting. Forty-five minutes and three Snickers bars later, they'd narrowed their search to a thousand receipts. Kevin divided the pile and handed Sari the smaller share. It was almost midnight, and the lamplight was making her eyes water. They had long since abandoned the chairs and were sitting cross-legged on the floor.

"Why don't you lie down in the T-bird while I finish this?" he suggested. "You're exhausted."

"We're almost done."

He laughed and stood, stretching his long arms over his head. "You are some piece of work."

She held another slip to the light. "We can ignore everything but the ones with credit card receipts. I'm telling you, Warren never carried more than five bucks in his pocket."

"You're right, the others don't have names anyway." He reached for another handful. "I think you should come home with me tonight."

"Not as romantic as I would have liked, but I admire your candor…"

"I'll sleep on the couch. I don't think you're safe."

"It's been ten years and nothing's happened yet. Why worry now?"

"Tim must have assumed the hammer and shirt were still in the Mustang."

"So? They were probably there since the day after Peggy was killed, and Tim thinks I got rid of the car years ago."

"But you drove it to his apartment. What if he saw it in the lot? Or even before that. You've been driving it for months."

"I'm not leaving the Belvedere. I have plenty of neighbors."

"You're being stupid, Sari. I know you value your independence, but—"

"My God!"

"What?"

" '*Hamm, plas,* and *dct tp.*' This may be it. And '*clp-on sngl.* '" She peered at the credit slip, and when she spoke again, there was a quaver in her voice. "The MasterCharge receipt was signed by Warren D. Scott. Why do you think he bought another hammer?"

"To replace the one he'd used two hours before to kill his wife. He didn't know whether he could trust Tim to lie for him."

Chapter Forty-Two

It was close to midnight when Ray reached Albuquerque, checked into a Motel 6 off the Interstate and collapsed. He'd driven five hundred miles on a soapapilla burger and a half-ounce stick of jerky, but he felt no hunger and was dead to the world for two hours straight. Then the sound of squeals and moans thrust him bolt upright, and with heart pounding he stared into the dark until he realized the couple next door were watching cable. Stripping to his skivvies, he relieved himself and climbed on top of the bedspread. This time sleep evaded him.

Ray turned on his lamp and peered at the clock. How could he have forgotten to call Sari? Groping on the floor beside the bed, he fumbled in his trousers for the unlisted number in his wallet. As her phone rang and rang, he cursed her unwillingness to indulge in an answering machine. But she must have gotten his message, and weren't there a couple of guys in her building she was close to? Probably spending the night on their couch... He settled back on his pillow and tried to sleep.

Now his thoughts turned to Marion. It was too late to call her and there was so much they'd never said. Reaching in the drawer of the nightstand, he found a Motel 6 pad and a cheap ball-point. He'd write a short note and give it to her when he got back to show he'd been thinking of her even if he didn't call. He penned his wife's name at the top of the page, then stopped. He'd never written to Marion before. What do you say in your first letter to the woman you've been married to for thirty years, the only woman you ever loved? He closed his eyes and thought, and suddenly the words came and Ray wrote until his fingers cramped and there was nothing more to say. He folded the sheets and stuffed them in his nylon kit. Then he withdrew a slim plastic folder from the bottom of his bag.

In the dim light of the motel room Peggy Scott's features flickered in the old photographs. The gouge in her temple and the claw marks across her nose defiled her pale skin like the hateful strokes of a child with a blunt pencil. But it was her eyes he could not escape. Her left one was swollen shut and the lids glued together with congealed blood, but the right bulged at the camera in mute outrage. Had she seen it coming?

In the next photograph she was lying as Ray first saw her. Facedown on the concrete with her head cradled in her arms, one slim white leg bent at the knee and tucked neatly under the other as if she were curtsying. Hair so matted with blood no auburn was visible, and if you looked too quickly and ignored the cement floor, you might have thought she was a teenage brunette at a slumber party. The last photo was a close-up of Peggy's left arm, the knuckles of a graceful hand smashed and the face of her watch a web of cracks. Two minutes past ten.

Returning the photos to their folder, Ray reached for Tim's pen-and-ink portrait. Though the subject was on her back instead of facedown and a cloth covered her eyes, her resemblance to the woman on the cement floor was unmistakable. Both appeared to be resting, peacefully if you overlooked the blood on one and the mutilations of the other, and free of pain. But the poses were deceptive; the images horrific. The wounds in Tim's family ran much deeper than the gouges in his mother's skull, and they would be the key to forcing Warren to confess.

Ray closed his eyes and pictured the evidence Sari had found. The Estwing was just the way he'd imagined it, with the added bonus of one key characteristic. The rust-colored stains that had seeped into the blue molded grip of the framing hammer obliterated the yellow teardrops radiating from the logo near the base of the handle, but they highlighted the letters stamped in the steel shaft. Now he knew why Warren was afraid to dispose of it.

He'd been wrong about the shirt. It hadn't been burned after all, it was crusted and stained with such a vast quantity of dried blood it had rotted in places. The gaudy green flowers were splattered with it and the pattern further distorted by marks where it had been wrapped around the hammer while the cloth was still wet with Peggy's blood. That was why Warren went to the Sinclair the first time, just as Ray thought. After Regina Hummel showed up he had been in a desperate hurry to hide the hammer and shirt, and what better place than Peggy's car?

Why hadn't Hummel noticed the blood? That always bothered Ray, but now he understood. The fabric was dark red to begin with and Warren hadn't opened the door all the way. Only his left shoulder would have been exposed in the crack, and most of the stains were on the right side of the shirt. And finally all the rest of Warren's moves that morning made sense.

On the way to Stanley Warren had burned his trousers and shoes. Later that day he wrapped the gruesome bundle in the trunk in plastic and taped it; he could have burned the shirt then, but even he must have been too squeamish to touch it. Much more efficient to keep the original package intact until he could palm it off on Tim the following day. *Need a little favor, son. Don't ask...* That hammer screamed Warren's guilt.

Ray smiled as he imagined Taylor Philips grilling him in that smartass tone of his. "How the hell do you know that hammer belongs to Warren Scott?" And Ray would wait a moment and casually say, "Because it's got his *initials* on it." Philips would turn the hammer over and there they'd be, W.D.S., stamped right into that steel shaft still crusted with his wife's blood. Suddenly he remembered Philips was long gone from the district attorney's office. On his way to the Senate now, but that didn't matter because Kevin would find someone who would prosecute. And once Ray delivered the confession...

Now sleep came too quickly and with it the claustrophobia of a murky room furnished only with a table and chair. Something slammed into the wall and as the door flew open a woman rose from the chair wrapped in a flannel robe, hair streaming down her back in a cascade of jet. The giant in the doorway stumbled to the table, knocking over the chair, and the shouting began, the unintelligible slurred words that always preceded a beating. Ray ran to the woman, tried to stand between her and her attacker, but he kept slipping, couldn't stay on his feet. The floor was slick with something thick and wet. When he looked down he saw an enormous buffalo tongue, severed at the root.

"What're you staring at, you little bugger?" Bloody fists upraised, the giant advanced on him. "Want to know what it's like? *Want a taste?*" He lurched another pace forward. "You can't do anything about it!" Through rotting teeth he roared with laughter as Ray ran past his mother's body through the door into the night.

Four hours later, he awoke with a coppery taste in his mouth: he'd bitten the inside of his cheek. It had happened many times before, a chronic annoyance that was the only residue of his nightmares. Quickly he packed and checked out, wishing he were on his way home.

Chapter Forty-Three

Sari rolled over and squinted at her alarm clock. Twenty past three, and she'd gone to bed only an hour before. She raised herself on one elbow and wondered if she'd imagined the muffled thud. Settling into her pillow, she told herself to forget it and go back to sleep.

Then she heard a whimpering, like a dog begging to be let out. The sound was coming through her open bathroom window. It must be traveling up the air shaft from the unit below.

"Please…"

Did the girl in that unit own a pet?

"No!"

The voice was charged with fear. And then a chilling scream.

Sari jumped out of bed and ran to the bathroom window, but the shaft was dark. Dashing across her bedroom to the courtyard side, she saw a light come on in the opposite unit one floor up. An anxious face met hers.

She grabbed the phone and dialed 911.

—

When the police left three hours later, a group of residents remained huddled in nightclothes in the meeting room adjacent to the managers' basement apartment. Minnie had produced her industrial-sized coffeemaker, which Dan once claimed she'd filched from an AA meeting, and dispatched Les to the all-night grocery for doughnuts. They'd been interviewed and told what the detective in charge thought of the Belvedere's security system. Or lack thereof. He minced no words when it came to the junipers and Douglas firs surrounding the building.

"Did you know her?" Sari's neighbor in 2C asked her. "When they carried her to the ambulance, I thought at first she was you."

Sari shook her head. All she knew about the woman in the unit directly below was she lived alone and sometimes played loud music late at night. She'd seen her picking up her mail—petite, dark hair.

"I warned her about buzzing guys in," his roommate claimed, "but she told me to mind my own business."

"I don't care what you do to the junipers, no one's laying a finger on those firs." The widow in 1F-G jammed a Camel into her cigarette holder with trembling hands. Her husband had built the Belvedere and she was occasionally seen returning from the grocery store in a chauffeured Rolls-Royce. "Not over my dead body."

"Haven't we had enough violence for one night, Ada?" replied one of the guys from 3D. "We need an electronic system, even if it means a special assessment. Dick Tracy said you could open the front door with a credit card."

"It wouldn't have made a bit of difference, Frank," his partner retorted. "He came in through the French doors…"

As they began debating the pros and cons of hiring a doorman, Sari tuned her neighbors out. Thank God she'd purchased a unit on the second floor. That poor girl should have been so lucky. The officers were particularly critical of the balconies on the units facing the three-sided courtyard on Bancroft Street. There were no lights and, lovely as it was in bloom, the crabapple effectively screened her side of the—

"—not a burglar," the man who lived in the unit next to Dan's was saying. "If someone wants to get you, he will."

"How do they know it wasn't a burglar?" Sari asked.

"After he came in through the window, he went straight to the front door and chained it so she couldn't get out. And he brought the knife and cord with him."

"She was *strangled*?" Ada said.

"And stabbed. In the face." In response to their shocked stares, he added, "I saw her myself. She must've put up a fight because her hands were cut pretty bad. He slashed her across the eyes, and if she lives she'll lose at least one of them. That's what the paramedics said."

Sari set down her coffee mug and rose. "Count me in on any assessments."

They were still arguing about security measures when she went upstairs to dress for work.

———

A t her desk later that morning, Sari stared at her mail. Although she was supposed to be drafting a commitment letter on a line of credit for a cable franchise, she hadn't been able to focus on anything but the assault. More frightening than the savagery of the attack were its randomness and anonymity. According to Les, the unit was owned by a couple who paid the monthly maintenance fee through a bank in Cleveland, but no one seemed curious about the victim, who might have come from anywhere to die in the apparent safety of her home in Widmark. Because the girl *was* dead; Sari had heard it on the radio just as she was leaving for work. The police thought the intruder was a stranger.

She made it through the rest of the day on automatic pilot. Twice she reached for the phone to call Kevin, but she knew it would only fuel his insistence that she move in with him until the case was wrapped up. And she didn't want to alarm Ray either. There'd been a cryptic message from him the day before, something about staying with friends, but her secretary had left right after the closing for a much-needed two-week vacation so Sari couldn't ask her what it meant, and there was no answer when she called Ray's house. After she'd told Ray what happened to Dan's dog he had stepped up his campaign to convince her to leave the Belvedere, with the unstated assumption that she would move closer to him and Marion in Gillman. But Dan was right; she would leave her home only for a place where she wanted to live, not to run from truths she couldn't face. Confronting Tim was just the beginning.

As Sari laced her sneakers for the run she hadn't taken that morning, she felt more tired than she could remember, but her head was clear and she set off through the park hugging her elbows to ward off the unexpected chill. The afternoon had been unseasonably warm, the culmination of a week of Indian summer that could be cut short by a snowstorm at any moment. With the end of daylight savings time there was more light in the morning but the price on the other end was dear. She smiled as she remembered how she used to work late to shorten the evenings, inducing exhaustion so the nights would be over before they began, and waking only to start the entire process again. Now she wanted to enjoy her days. Kevin Day was aptly named, she suddenly realized.

As she rounded the park a final time, the sky was pressing down on the trees and Sari knew winter would arrive long before the shortest day of the year. In her mind's eye Kevin came to meet her. He moved with an odd grace, so different from Tim's. Not like a cat, but titanic and surefooted like a bear. Now he was lifting her chin. She'd never cared for aftershave, but his was sharp and clean and kissing him was like biting into a pine needle and tasting an entire forest... With a smile she tucked the image away. Kevin would like the idea of her breaking her routine to jog in the evening because her predictability made him nervous, but could he appreciate what it meant to abandon the familiar even to that small degree?

Letting herself in the front entrance of the Belvedere, she wondered how long it would take her neighbors to agree to retool the locks. Because condominium associations were the last true democracy and the battle lines already drawn, any changes to the building's security would require exhaustive debate. One faction would advocate an electronic system, another razing the landscaping, a third armed guards. It would be springtime before they reached a compromise that would satisfy no one but produce rumblings for decades about a special assessment as ruinous as the cost of restoring the roof three winters before.

As she stood at the French windows brushing her teeth, Sari wondered if the crabapple would survive the condo board. Her eyes wandered to the dark windows of the unit directly below and she repressed a shudder. What if she'd called 911 when she first heard the thump instead of wasting time trying to remember if her neighbor owned a dog? Or a moment later, before that horrible scream?

She moved the phone to her nightstand before climbing into bed. Reaching for the receiver, she hesitated. Why bother Kevin now? He was probably exhausted from last night, and random acts of violence were a fact of urban life. She dialed another number.

"Mom? It's me."

"Is everything all right?"

"I'm fine." A match struck as Helen fired up a Kent, and this time the sound was comforting.

"I was just thinking about you, it's been a while since we talked."

"I never know whether to believe you when you say you're fine." Could her mother read her mind? Or was there something in Sari's voice that signaled deception? "You didn't cry when you were a baby either…"

Perhaps it was their lifelong dance of disbelief, each circling the other only to arrive at a marshy middle ground that supported neither. "Mom, I'm *fine.*"

"Sam was the one with the wry neck. It hurt, and he needed to be held." Helen swallowed another lungful of smoke. "You always said I loved him more, but that wasn't it at all."

Couldn't they talk without throwing the past in each other's faces?

"How is Sam, is he still working on his master's?"

"He's subbing at a high school in the Bronx. The schedule gives him more flexibility." Helen exhaled slowly, as if reluctant to part with that last molecule of smoke. "You were right, Sari, I did treat the two of you differently. But it was because you had different needs, not because I— Can't you let that damned chart go?"

"What chart?" she pretended.

"You know what I mean."

"I'm not the one who brought it up."

"I didn't do it to hurt you. I just wanted to make you strong."

Here it was at last, the admission she'd waited twenty years to hear even if it didn't go quite far enough. Lying back on the pillow, Sari remembered all the times she'd searched the baby pictures for clues to what went wrong, why her mother didn't love her. How many times had she compared her face to Sam's in that photo where they squirmed like puppies in a nylon-webbed beach chair, identical pairs of eyes squinting in the sun, Sam's skin more golden, her chin firmer and round? But so what if Helen loved him more, wry neck or not…. That was behind them now. And maybe she was better off.

"Mom, do you remember when you ran out in the middle of the night to save that woman who was being attacked?"

"Your father was away on a trip."

"Weren't you afraid?"

"Sometimes you do what your heart tells you, Sari." Another match was struck. "Later I thought it was pretty dumb, leaving you and Sam alone, but at the time it felt right."

"I always wanted to be as brave as you."

"Courage and stupidity are judged by hindsight, darling. It all depends on how it turns out. But you can't be afraid to live. That's true courage."

"I saw Tim the other day. It's really over."

"You don't know how glad I am to hear that."

She would tell her mother the rest later, no sense making her worry.

"There was something about him…" Helen's voice was soft, confiding. So unguarded, Sari thought maybe now she could ask.

"What was he like?"

"Who?"

"Your first husband."

Long silence.

"Sweet-tempered. Gentle. He made everyone laugh."

"Not like Dad."

Helen gave a little sigh.

"It wouldn't have worked anyway. I would have eaten him alive. Believe it or not, I'm much more suited to your father. He keeps me on my toes." They both laughed, and Sari heard her mother's breath catch, as if she dreaded the reaction to her next words. "Do you think you'll come home for the holidays? It's been so long."

"Yes."

Just before she fell asleep that night, Sari thought she heard a sound in the air shaft. That poor girl... She remembered a ghost story about spirits and unfinished business, and how the walls seemed to throb with Peggy's presence the night after her murder. Could she have saved them? Her last thought as she pulled the pillow over her head was to wonder whether either of them knew what was coming.

Chapter Forty-Four

Ray bought a cup of coffee at the service station before hitting the road, but the liquid stung the inside of his cheek and he tossed the container in the trash after paying for his gas. Too early to call Sari; the switchboard wouldn't be open at her office and she was probably out jogging. He considered having breakfast, but it was four hours to Hatch and five more to Tucson and he'd never make it by nightfall if he kept stopping to eat. The thought of adding another day to his trip, one more night in a motel room away from Marion, was unbearable. He had to wrap this up and head back home no later than tomorrow afternoon. Rubbing his eyes to rid them of the fitful night on rough sheets, he climbed back in the New Yorker and took off.

At Hatch he turned onto Route 26, bypassing Las Cruces and rejoining the Interstate at Deming an hour later. Speeding past a billboard that read "Enjoy Beef—Real Food for Real People," he soon found himself on a road that was desert on one side and an irrigated field dense with chile plants on the other. The day was hot and bright, 87 degrees if you believed the sign outside the bank in Deming, and his air-conditioning was on the fritz. He still couldn't work up an appetite and decided to push on the hundred miles to Lordsburg.

As he approached the town two hours later, the Chrysler was beginning to seriously overheat and it was time to stretch his legs. Coasting past the asphalt-shingled houses with corrugated steel siding that marked the city limits, he searched for a place to eat. Then he saw the sign: SHAKESPEARE GHOST TOWN. Wasn't that where they hanged Russian Bill?

Ray pulled to the side of the road, chest thumping with excitement. To fortify himself for what lay ahead, he needed more than a stroll to the can. In Shakespeare he could kill three birds with one stone, pick up a bite to eat along with a second wind and a real souvenir for Marion, something better than a tourist brochure. And he wanted to see where they did justice to Russian Bill back in the days when there was no Senator Taylor Philips to screw up the works. He would stand at the very spot where Bill was lynched, right beneath the rafters. He was making good time, seven hours of driving already today, and he was almost at the Arizona border. He'd find a phone there and call Marion, she'd probably stayed up all night worrying. And if he still couldn't reach Sari, he'd have his wife track her down.

Exiting the Interstate, he turned south onto a paved road, which he followed for a mile and a half before making a right turn just before a cemetery. A stand of sunflowers eight feet tall appeared so suddenly he thought he imagined them. As the New Yorker lurched past, their golden heads nodded, reminding him of Leeper. The road was asphalt on top of gravel, bumpy as hell and filled with chuck holes, and he began to regret what seemed such a good idea moments before.

Now the surface was scaly, the asphalt vanishing and returning without warning as it wound its way up a hillside. How'd they expect to get tourists? Must be nuts doing this to his car just to get Marion a present when he should be pushing on to Tucson! As the Chrysler bumped and lurched past mounds of cactus and brush, the air-conditioning finally gave out. This place was as godforsaken as Leeper...

The road was nothing more than scraped dirt in both directions now, packed clay and sharp rocks, and the route forked at a small wooden sign. Ray got out to read it, but it was shot through with bullets, leaving a jagged pattern of holes where the writing should have been. An arid wind from the south pricked his nostrils. With it came the scent of olives, so strong he could taste them.

He thought of turning around, but he'd come too far for that. The left fork led up an incline. Mines were supposed to be in hills, weren't they? A mile later he glanced to his right and spotted a cluster of buildings in a valley far below, stone sheds with weathered roofs surrounded by a wire fence with a camper and a pickup truck parked in front of the largest building. Strange place for a farm…He continued up the road, searching for Shakespeare.

At the top of the rise, a padlocked gate barred his path and he stared at the sign in disgust. PRIVATE PROPERTY OF LORDSBURG MINING COMPANY—WATCH FOR BLASTING & MINING ACTIVITIES. Must've taken the wrong fork. Souvenirs or not, he had no right to drag the New Yorker up there. No way to treat a lady, much less a friend. He reversed down the hill, backing up to a point where the path was a little wider and he could turn around, but tire tracks had worn deep ruts on either side of the road and the Chrysler's belly began to scrape against rock. Suddenly Ray was stuck.

The late afternoon sun beat mercilessly on the back of his neck as he bent to examine his undercarriage and he found he was short of breath. Reminding himself another five minutes would make no difference, he climbed in the front seat to rest a moment. He was exhausted and his shirt soaked with sweat. He'd forgotten to fill his thermos in Albuquerque, he still hadn't called Marion, and this was going to set him back at least an hour. Might as well stop feeling sorry for himself and try to extricate his car.

Ray exited the Chrysler and leaned against the left rear fender. Back and forth he rocked, and as steel ground against stone he began to fear for his oil pan. If this didn't work he'd have to pull out his jack and try to use it as a lever…. Kneeling by a clump of golden flowers and prickly cactus that was flat like a beaver's tail, he tried to catch his breath. The olive scent was stronger here and he traced it to an evergreen bush with woody stems and cotton pods as soft as pussy willows. Breaking off a stem, he inhaled the sharp odor of its resinous leaves. A minor mystery solved.

Ray mopped his brow. The race was off, his schedule would be set back a day and there was nothing he could do about it. Accepting he would have to spend the night there, he climbed back in the New Yorker to watch the sun descend over the hills. It was finally cooling off. The sky was peaceful and the stars were winking on, and he remembered all the evenings he'd spent with Marion on their patio in Gillman, hashing over the minutiae of the day. There were certainly worse places to bunk down. And wouldn't she get a kick out of a mining town called Shakespeare, way out here in the middle of nowhere?

Closing his eyes, Ray let his mind wander. It was the Depression and he was sixteen again, enlisting in the army. Yes, there certainly were worse places to spend a night than alone in the desert in his New Yorker. He ran his fingers over the steering wheel, settling more comfortably in his seat. Outside the wind whistled and rocked his car like a cradle. As the Milky Way shimmered behind his lids, the image of an animal on the side of a road slowly took form. It was a dog, lying with its neck twisted to one side. Something to do with Sari...

His eyes jerked open. He had to get out of there, how could he have forgotten to warn her? But his feet were too heavy, and when he took another breath there was Russian Bill dangling from the rafters of the Butterfield Stage Station, with his matted hair falling forward and the stench from his yellowed teeth eclipsing the astringency of the sprig of creosote Ray clutched as he stood in the corner and watched his old man swing.

Awakening with a start, he peered at his watch. It was nine o'clock: he had to get back on the road to Tucson. He had to find a phone. He couldn't afford to wait until morning because he needed to tell Sari about Tim. She had no idea who he really was. Stomach churning with acid from the jerky and lousy coffee, he reached for his thermos, only to remember it was empty. He thought of the ham and eggs Marion fixed the morning he left Gillman, could almost taste them, and was consumed with remorse. God, he still hadn't called his wife. He should've hiked back to the main road before it turned dark. He was doing everything *wrong...*

Clambering onto the hood, Ray knelt and rocked back on his heels. The shock registered from his knees to the base of his skull, but the New Yorker stood its ground and he leaned back to still the pounding in his ears. Marion was right. He had no business going off in the middle of nowhere at his age and worrying her.

All of a sudden the wind was knocked out of him and he saw Peggy's face, her right eye staring at him. *Did she see it coming?* As he struggled to catch his breath, he saw Sari, facedown on a cold cement floor. He was leaning his head back for a gulp of air when it hit again, this time like a punch in the gut but higher, and he tried to take another breath and there was none.

—

On his way to work shortly before eight the next morning Ernie Villa, a supervisor for the Lordsburg Mining Company, came upon a man lying in the road beside his car. He checked for signs of life and radioed the Hidalgo County Sheriff's Department. When Deputy Sheriff Joe Trujillo arrived a short while later, he whistled as he stepped down from his Blazer.

"Always loved them old Chryslers, what is it, 'sixty-eight New Yorker?" He walked around the car, admiring its sleek lines. "Real cruiser, that baby was." Noting the out-of-state tags he phoned Dispatch for a meat wagon and a tow truck, then reached into the backseat of the Blazer for his camera and snapped a couple of shots to pinpoint the location of the body. "Sure was a beaut. Kept her in great condition too."

"What do you think happened?" Villa asked.

"Looks like a heart attack. Poor old guy, probably a tourist."

"What's he doing out here?"

"Damned if I know, Ernie." The deputy bent to look at the undercarriage. "He high-centered. Must've been trying to push her free when his ticker gave out."

"Poor old fart." Walking to the cab of his pickup, Villa poured a cup of coffee from his thermos. The steam rose in the crisp morning air. "These tourists, they come out here and forget whatever sense God gave 'em. See it all the time, don't know where they're goin' or how they're gonna get there." He poured a second cup and handed it to Trujillo. "Must've missed the turn to Shakespeare, but why go there this time of year?"

"Maybe he didn't know it's closed."

"Pity, ain't it?" Villa laughed. "And just a mile from the cemetery. Too bad we can't bury him local."

"Yeah, I'll have to notify his next of kin. If he's got any."

"Everybody's got kin, Joe."

Trujillo shook his head. "You'd be surprised, Ernie, you really would."

Chapter Forty-Five

Kevin Day watched Sari leave the Belvedere at five for her Friday morning jog. Right on schedule. From his parking place near the Bancroft Street entrance behind a battered hatchback Accord with primer paint, he saw the light go on and off through the barred windows in the laundry room. Like clockwork she'd deposited her clothes in the washing machine, and when she left he resisted the temptation to follow. Just like her mother, he thought, independent as a hog on ice…He settled back in the darkness to wait for her return. Not so different from the stakeouts in the old days, right down to the bottle he'd brought to piss in.

His willingness to defer to Sari's need to call the shots had evaporated the moment he learned the girl one floor below her had been murdered. Despite what the Widmark cops said, Kevin knew from the nature of the assault that it was neither random nor impersonal. The victim had no known enemies, but her injuries spoke of rage. He'd been patrolling Sari's street since she returned from work the day before, finally settling in for the night on the curb by the side entrance as he waited for the killer's next move.

—

Enjoying the fat flakes of the first snowfall, Sari cut through the park on her normal route. Running still made her feel invincible, in command of her fears. Her need was rooted in the moment she'd stopped protesting what she knew to be the truth because it displeased another, had blossomed when she pretended to believe in something she knew was false, and scattered its seeds to the corners of her soul the day she decided to cover for Tim's father. But no matter what happened to Warren or Tim, that part of her life was over. She would never be her own victim again.

—

Restless, Kevin circled the Belvedere. When a woman walking a miniature schnauzer stuck out her chin and glared to conceal her anxiety, he nodded as if he belonged there. Relieved at the eye contact she smiled back, and he marveled at how easy it was to win the trust of strangers. Emboldened, he climbed the front steps of the Belvedere and jiggled the brass knob. Locked, but how many people had the key? He eased back into the shadows and, rounding the corner on Bancroft Street, hunkered down in the lee of a Douglas fir. There was no traffic at this hour but a car halfway up the block was emitting an audible purr as the driver drank his coffee. Feeling his way past the junipers, Kevin crept to the entrance to the recessed courtyard. All the windows were dark. As he stared up at Sari's flimsy French doors, he wondered why women always thought they were safe so long as they lived above the ground floor.

—

As she passed the Botanic Garden Sari remembered the time she'd thought she saw Warren crouching by the trees. At the darkest part of the path, when she was farthest from home, and how her imagination had tricked her! She'd cut straight across the bowl to escape and been afraid to run for a week. But that was two years ago, and her fears seemed ridiculous now.

—

Kevin knew that when Sari returned it would be by the door at the foot of the Bancroft Street ramp. On laundry days she finished her run just as the washing machine completed the final rinse cycle so she could transfer her load to the dryer. Then she would shower and retrieve her clothes before leaving for work. Efficient but foolhardy. He returned to his hiding place, knowing that when puffs of fragrant steam began venting from the north side of the basement she would be safe in her laundry room.

—

With the front entrance of the Bancroft in sight, Sari slowed. Now the flakes were falling faster and the snow she kicked up landed in soft footfalls behind her. A shape shifted by the door and for a moment she thought it was Dan, then remembered he and John had moved to South Carolina. Loneliness pierced her. To combat it, she allowed her feet to carry her past the building to an extra lap around the park. Focus on the times to come, she told herself. Maybe she'd give a dinner party for Kevin and invite Ada and a couple of the others. There was protection in friendship, and wouldn't it be nice to know the people who lived on the other side of her walls?

And what about that girl in the apartment below? She still heard that whimper, the begging sound as she pleaded with her attacker. *Please...*Did she know him, did she think she could talk her way out of it? When she'd seen her at the mailboxes Sari had thought about saying hello, but in the end settled for a smile and a duck of the head. She's like me, Sari thought at the time, and now she wondered whether the loneliness the girl projected had made her a target. *Stop it right now,* she warned herself... But Peggy had felt safe too.

As she passed the Botanic Gardens the second time, she glanced over her shoulder. The shadows seemed different, but soon it would be dawn. *You're psyching yourself out,* she thought. Warren was in Tucson and had no way of knowing she'd found the hammer. Not even Tim knew that. She pictured the walls at Tim's shabby apartment, the wrathful faces staring from the portraits, the pastel of the girl with the scarf over her eyes, running barefoot through a field…

She listened for footsteps but heard only the sound of her own feet, kicking tufts of powder as she accelerated her pace. She was cold now, she never should have taken the extra lap, her clothes were waiting in the washer, and…Without another thought Sari abandoned the path and fled through the trees to the protection of the central bowl.

—

As Kevin transferred his weight from one foot to the other to ward off a cramp, he glanced at his watch. Where the hell was she? This was taking far too long. His left knee popped and he rose unsteadily from his crouch. Time to take another walk around the building.

At the corner he peered up Ninth to the entrance to the park. Even if Sari had taken an extra lap, she should be back by now. Then it occurred to him she could have taken a side street. The snow was beginning to blow in drifts and the sidewalks were icing in the predawn darkness. The path around the park would be treacherous.… Crossing Ninth, he walked halfway up the 800 block of Bancroft. There was no sign of her.

—

Sari let herself in the Belvedere by the front door, wet and numb with cold. As she fumbled with the key to her dead bolt, the familiar hum of the ceiling fixtures in the dim hall soothed her. She just needed to catch her breath; the crackling cold that was so invigorating had disoriented her. When would she learn to resist the temptation to push herself on these icy mornings?

Tossing her keys on her coffee table, Sari flicked on a lamp and made her way to the kitchen. She kept her change in a dish on the counter, but her numbed fingers found only nickels and dimes. Scrambling through the utility drawer, she located quarters for the dryer. She hesitated.

Once again she remembered that whimper, so much worse than the scream. Why that girl? Suddenly she didn't want to leave her apartment.

She tried to think of an excuse. Her socks were soaked through, she should shower first and change. By then the newspapers would be delivered, her neighbors would be stirring...She looked at the clock and saw it was already later than she'd thought. The dryers in the basement were slow to heat, and if she wanted to get to work on time...

You're being ridiculous. If she didn't go down and switch her clothes now, someone else would come and take them out. They would be left in a soggy mess on top of a machine, and she would have to face her foolishness when she got home from work. As Sari reached into the drawer again, her fingers touched something solid. Thinking Kevin would laugh at her choice, she slipped it in her pocket and left before she could change her mind.

—

Returning from his trek around the Belvedere, Kevin told himself he was more annoyed than concerned. He'd gone down Bancroft all the way to the corner, then walked up Eighth to the park. Hoping he'd meet Sari on her way back, he no longer gave a damn what she thought when she saw him. But there was still no sign of her. Now back at the entrance on the Bancroft side, he saw a light in her apartment. Must have entered by the front and gone up to her unit while he was making an ass of himself tramping the streets...

As he stared down the ramp, he saw a crack of light so faint he'd missed it from the Douglas fir twenty-five feet away. He moved closer. The basement door was propped open.

—

Sari hurried down the back stairs to the basement, avoiding the elevator as she usually did. Death traps, her father once said, and it was strange to think of that now. You're going to walk to the end of the corridor and turn left to the laundry room, plunk two quarters in a dryer, transfer your clothes and leave. You've done it hundreds of times before, once a week for the five years you've lived at the Belvedere. This will be no different...

As she reached the laundry room she saw the lights were out. Not the first time that had happened, and easy to fix. When she threw the switch she saw Tim.

—

Kevin ran up the stairs to the second floor and banged on Sari's door. She'd left it unlocked, another habit he couldn't wait to break her of.

"Sari?"

When there was no answer he let himself in. To hell with worrying about whether she'd think he was invading her space. He searched the unit quickly, saw no signs of struggle and noted drawers open in the kitchen. Cursing his stupidity for wasting the past two hours outside when he could have been here, protecting her, he took the steps to the basement three at a time.

When he reached the final corridor, he drew his 9mm Glock and ducked into the darkened chamber adjacent to the laundry room. Crouching to the right of the doorway, he peered in, eyes adjusting slowly to the fluorescent light.

"—found the hammer, Tim." Sari was standing in the middle of the floor between the washers and dryers, facing Tim and with her back to Kevin. As it spun, one of the dryers made a metallic sound, *clackety-clack,* from a button or a coin.

"I figured that when the Mustang disappeared. You really suckered me about selling it."

Although Tim was dressed in a sweat suit his hair was dry, and Kerin wondered how long he'd been in the building. But his attention was immediately drawn to the six-inch carbon double-edged blade in Tim's left hand. He held it loosely, brushing the tip against the soft weave of his pants.

"You should have told me what was in the trunk." Sari's voice was calm, and her hands were thrust in the pockets of her down vest as if her only concern was keeping her fingers warm. "When did your father tell you?"

Clackety-clack.

"The next day. When he needed my help."

Didn't she see the damn knife? Just like her to think she could talk her way out...

"When did Laura know?" she asked.

"Not till later. After the funeral."

"What happened that morning?"

"The argument started upstairs, in the bathroom. Dad was cleaning the mirrors, and the nozzle on the Windex bottle broke. He said he'd go to the store and get another, but Mom said, 'Why bother? Maybe Laura's friend can show you how to do the job. I'll bet *he* knows how to work the problem....' She grabbed the bottle and threw it, and it hit him on the forehead."

"Laura's boyfriend? Is that what they were fighting about?"

"Mom saw his pickup truck, that's how it began. She realized Laura had been planning to meet him that morning, and that Dad warned Laura to keep him away. She started taunting him about it." Kevin slipped the Glock off safety, but the room was narrow and Sari was standing between him and Tim. "It was her fault in the first place, but she could never resist throwing it in Dad's face." What was her fault, *what* did Peggy thr"—never would have happened if she'd been there for us like she was supposed to," he was saying. "She blamed him for Allison's death, too."

"Why?"

"The heart defect ran in Dad's family. It was just another thing she kept throwing at him. He went to the Safeway to cool off. Mom taunting him about the pickup truck was too much."

"What was the big deal? I know the driver was the guy Laura was seeing in high school, that's why your mother didn't like him, but—"

"Is that what you thought?" Tim laughed, a grating sound that drowned out the noise from the dryer. "Hell, Mom would've been thrilled if that guy took Laura away with him. It was Dad who couldn't—"

"But he was married. Wasn't that why your father moved you to Indiana, so she would stop seeing him?"

"He moved us away because he wanted her for himself. He was jealous and Mom couldn't let it go." As he waited for a clear shot, Kevin kept his eyes on the knife. That's all he cared about; as soon as Tim's hand tightened on that laminated leather grip he'd fire.

"What happened when he got back from the store?" She kept ragging him. 'What are you going to do?' she said. 'Can't even keep your own daughter in line.' She went in the garage and he followed. She thought it was over, but he'd had enough."

Sari stepped back and Kevin took a deep breath.

"—her fault in the first place," Tim was saying. "Never would have happened if she'd been there for us like she was supposed to. That damned quiet time..."

"And you lied for him?"

Tim's face contorted and suddenly he looked like a boy. "He was all we had left!" As he gripped the knife Kevin raised the Clock. "I want that hammer..."

"I don't have it," Sari said. Her legs tensed and Kevin wondered if she was going to make her break. But the outer door was sixty feet away, and she'd never—"I've already given it to—"

Without finishing the sentence, she pulled her fists from her pockets and dove straight at Tim. Kevin rose and stepped through the door, his heart pounding, his weapon raised.

"Stop!" he cried, but she'd driven Tim back to the clothesline and Kevin saw a flash of metal in her hand. It was a six-ounce hammer, good for driving tacks into soft wood and too light to pack a real punch, but it must have been all she could arm herself with to face her monster in the basement.

Tim saw it coming and turned so the hammer glanced off his cheek. As Sari raised the hammer high over her head for a second blow, it snagged in the clothesline. Tim lunged then, dragging her to the cement.

When he raised his blade, Kevin fired.

Chapter Forty-Six

It was the day before Thanksgiving and Sari was at Marion's house, helping her pack Ray's things. The past weeks had been dreadful but the worst moment had come three days earlier, when Kevin pulled into the Burts' driveway in the New Yorker he'd retrieved from New Mexico. Ray's death hadn't seemed real until they saw someone else behind the wheel of his beloved car. And now it was time to start letting him go.

As Marion reached for the nylon shaving kit, her lower lip trembled and Sari hugged her. Marion held her for a moment, then went to the kitchen to fix them a pot of tea. Sari finished folding a plaid hunting shirt, gently placing it in the Goodwill box. But a moment later Marion returned.

"Look what's in the paper!"

She was pointing at a photograph of a figure being led in handcuffs from a whitewashed bungalow with a flat tiled roof. A saguaro cactus twice as tall as a man was anchored in a bed of gravel to the left of the door, its arms raised in defiance. The caption read, *Former Hallett County resident arrested at home near Tucson for 1980 murder of wife.* Sari stared at Warren's face. He looked tired and much older than she remembered, but was there a trace of scorn beneath his bewilderment? The photo was too grainy to tell…. She looked up to see Kevin in the doorway.

"You got your man," Sari said. "Ray would be proud. How long will it take to extradite him?"

"Depends on how good a lawyer he can afford. The better they are, the worse they make it." Kevin paused. "You know what I mean. But the D.A. is convinced we can nail him. With what Tim told you in the laundry room there's more than enough to convict Warren."

"Quiet time…The shame was that strong." First Nettie's family, then Peggy and Warren, and finally her and Tim. Incest had poisoned three generations.

"How will you feel about testifying against Tim?"

The boy in the glass sphere, still trying to climb out. Not even their dream could save him.

"That ball peen hammer of mine did more damage than your Glock," she replied. "But last I heard, Tim was in his own world at the state mental hospital."

"His lawyers are laying the groundwork for an insanity plea. I guess even they realize killing the wrong girl by mistake is no defense. Think he's faking?"

"I'm the last who could tell…" Marion was gesturing at her behind Kevin's back. "And I'm tired of guessing." Kevin's grin was all the encouragement Sari needed. "I've decided to take some time off," she continued. Flashing her the thumb's up, Marion disappeared into the kitchen.

"Oh?" Kevin replied. "I was thinking of doing that too."

"Have you ever driven across the country? There's a route through Pennsylvania that passes by a gap in the Poconos…"

About the Author

Stephanie Kane is a lawyer and award-winning crime novelist. She lives in Denver with her husband and two black cats. For more information, please visit: www.writerkane.com

CPSIA information can be obtained
at www.ICGtesting.com
Printed in the USA
LVHW041156141120
671373LV00002B/71